The Pontius Pilate Papers

WARREN KIEFER

SPHERE BOOKS LIMITED
30/32 Gray's Inn Road, London WC1X 8JL

First published in Great Britain by
Hamish Hamilton Ltd. 1976
Copyright © Warren Kiefer 1976
First Sphere Books edition 1978
Reprinted 1979

For Mariana and Alden

Filmset in Photon Plantin

Printed in Great Britain by
C. Nicholls & Company Ltd
The Philips Park Press, Manchester

ON THE TRAIL OF A THIEF . .

"Lock the door," Goff said to me, and I dumbly complied. Willi still struggled weakly as Goff punched him low in the stomach, and he would have collapsed if Goff had not bent him around the bedpost and held him by his belt. Willi vomited over the bedclothes, barely missing Goff's extended sleeve, and Goff hit him savagely across the kidneys with the side of his hand. I had never seen anyone act with such swift violence, such sudden economical movement. Willi's eyes streamed tears. He lay panting and coughing as Goff held his right wrist high up against the small of his back. There had not been a sound.

Goff began to speak to him in a low, almost gentle tone, in clear German, most of which I understood. "Willi," he said, "you are going to suffer until you tell me exactly what I came to find out. Do you understand . . . ?"

ONE

Dr. Nathan Marcus, my grandfather, made a fortune and died when I was sixteen, leaving most of it to me. My father, Max, got only 10 per cent of the Marcus Instrument stock because, according to the Jewish side of the family, he had opposed the old man's wishes when he married my mother, Dolly, an Irish-Catholic *shiksa*. Her family insisted the real reason for my grandfather's generosity to me was my promise during his final illness that I too would become a doctor.

Both factions had a point. Old Nate did not much care for his son, he was fond of me, and I did make him such a promise. I was always promising someone something in those days.

No one in the family ever understood why I did not practise medicine or at least put my education to some practical use at Marcus Instrument. Dolly, of course, wanted me to join the Harvard faculty and settle down near her with a nice Boston girl. And Max thought I should at least work with the Marcus Foundation. Only Aaron, my grandfather's younger brother, reacted sensibly. When I told him I was thinking of knocking around Europe for a year or so after I finished my internship, Aaron only said, 'Why a year? Take a lifetime.' And that, in a sense, is what I have done.

By 1965, I had discovered archaeology and was nearly thirty years old. Lacking the patience to chase more degrees, I became an archaeological bum, offering my medical credentials in return for unpaid inclusion in any expedition that caught my fancy.

Since then, I have become an offbeat specialist of sorts. I can still tie a fair suture and distinguish an extrinsic asthma from a mitral stenosis, but the medical problems of the ancients intrigue me more than modern clinical practice. My books tell the story: *Surgical Practice in the Augustan Age*, *Epidemiological Aspects of Rome's Decline*, and my two-volume history of Alexandrian medicine. I own the *Kalina*, a beamy, comfortable ketch of eighty feet, equipped as an archaeological diving platform, laboratory and floating home for me and the friends who join me on summer excavations, mostly around Greece. The rest of the time I live in Paris, a stone's throw from the Sorbonne and the École de Médecin, where I lecture. I have done postmortems on bog bodies in Denmark and x-rayed mummies in the Cairo museum. That's me - Jay Brian Marcus, surgeon *manqué*, dilettante digger, wandering Irish-American Jew.

At least that *was* me until world Zionism and the ghost of my grandfather arrived in Athens one September morning as part of my great-uncle Aaron's rhetorical baggage. Aaron knew me better than to think I would fall for a cornball act. But it was the only one he had, and it served him well. Aaron: retired attorney of Hollywood, California; septuagenarian gadfly and Marcus Foundation head, the Sunset Boulevardier of the family.

'Glad I caught you,' he said, as if hours rather than months had passed since our last encounter. He looked ten years younger than he is - tanned, sporty, trim, with his hair a little long as a slight concession to the fashion. We drove back to Piraeus for lunch and he seemed to know the way as well as I. Forty years as counsel to some of Hollywood's major motion picture figures gave him a certain breezy familiarity with the world.

A great eater and drinker in his younger days, Aaron had been married and divorced two or three times. He had children and grandchildren around the Los Angeles area, but none of them were terribly important in his life.

We sat at an umbrella-shaded table and I pointed out *Kalina* sitting like a majestic sea bird in the centre of the Tourkolimano yacht basin. Aaron studied the menu gravely while the waiter brought a bottle of chilled white wine. 'What the hell - they got lobster and fifteen kinds of fish I never heard of. You like lobster?'

I nodded. 'Have you seen Max or Dolly?'

'I had lunch with your mother, who came to New York for the occasion, and drinks with your father, which is my good deed for the year. I was tied up with museum people the rest of the time. That's why I wanted to see you.'

'I knew it couldn't be personal.'

Among Aaron's 'retirement' activities, he heads the board of trustees of the Nathan Marcus Archaeological Museum in

Jerusalem. Both the museum and his trusteeship were my idea, but all my own studies are carried out independently or with other institutions.

The museum was established ten years ago, when I found it convenient to place three million Eurodollars in a philanthropic enterprise outside the United States. My own bias determined the nature of the gift, but I chose to put it in Israel because I thought Nate would have liked it there.

The waiter arrived with the Greek salad.

'Greece is kind to old men,' Aaron said as he dug into the black olives and goat cheese. Then he remembered his manners and passed me the bowl. 'So what have you been up to, Jay?'

'Down to. Some wrecks off Zante.'

'Anything interesting?'

'There was a French girl with us for a month.'

Aaron chuckled. 'Underwater? My, my.'

'We located some first-century Roman galleys.'

'What was the girl doing?'

'Sketching the sea bed.'

'Sketching?'

'One of the ships was freighting statuary.'

'You lead an interesting life.' He sighed. 'In and out of sea beds with French chicks.'

Aaron is still handsome, with the clear eyes, thick white hair and long lashes of my grandfather, and the same nonstop way of talking. 'Let me tell you what I've been doing,' he said, recounting a dizzying two-week schedule of meetings with people at the Oriental Institute, the Brooklyn Museum, the Fogg, the Louvre, the British Museum and the Vatican. 'Picking brains wherever I find them.' Without pause, he fired off whole salvos of facts and statistics on public attendance at all these institutions, broken down into age groups, economic status, blood type and whatever other divisions are possible among museumgoers, correlating all of it to specific exhibits. Aaron is a man who always does his homework and I was impressed even though I had no idea what he was leading to. I also had the feeling I was not his first audience for this particular speech, and I was right. He admitted having used substantial portions of it on my unsuspecting father. He finished by telling me the Marcus Museum had to promote more.

7

'I'm not sure promotion enters into it much,' I said. 'Like church. Those who care go.'

He looked pained and his confidence in me seemed to drain away momentarily. 'A smart boy, my nephew's son. Always ready with the facile judgment.'

'It's true.'

'The National Gallery's got the best permanent collection in America but who goes? Nobody over sixteen unless they're teachers.' He emptied the last of the salad on his plate, chomping happily as he talked. 'They don't promote.'

'It takes money.'

'Imagination is all it takes,' Aaron said, aiming his fork at me like a javelin. 'I'll give you a for instance. Pre-Columbian Indian ceramics exhibition. Got it?'

'Got it.'

'Gangbangs and cocksucking is what *that's* all about. Dirtiest show in town. So they take a two-inch ad in the Washington *Post* that says: "Come and see the Art of the Incas." Know what I mean?'

'I suppose they have to be a little discreet.'

'Cultural elitism died when I was a boy. Otherwise there never would have been a movie industry.'

'You're a dirty old man, Aaron.'

'Who wants to see thousand-year-old pots? Nobody. But perversion pulls a crowd.' The lobster arrived and Aaron asked me, 'How do you say drawn butter in Greek?'

'Melted butter?' I said.

'I bring you melted butter,' the waiter said, and Aaron smiled, pleased with himself.

'Well, I'm happy to tell you at last we got a crowd-puller for the Marcus Museum. You know how I always liked the Shrine of the Book.' He worked the lobster thorax loose from the tail and proceeded to suck each one of the narrow legs. 'Outside it looks like a tiled mushroom, but inside' – his eyes rolled upward, seeing some private vision – 'an experience of the spirit like Chartres or Grauman's Chinese.'

The Shrine of the Book in Jerusalem was designed to house some of the Dead Sea Scrolls and other ancient documents. It is simple and austere. A dimly lighted tunnel leads to a darkened rotunda, within which the scrolls themselves are displayed behind glass under conditions that duplicate as closely as possible those of the Qumran caves where they were found. The place is impressive, even awesome. The Marcus Museum was never intended to compete with this, or with the Rockefeller Museum, which is larger, or with any of the other private or state archaeological institutions in Israel. My idea had been to supplement their work by funding investigations that others, for reasons of time, money or priority, could not undertake.

'Have a look at this.' Aaron handed me a fat letter from the inside pocket of his seersucker jacket. Then his strong fingers pressed the lobster tail open with a snap. He dug out the morsels of white meat with the deftness of a marmoset, dipping each one in the bath of hot butter the waiter had brought.

The letter was from Lev Vagan, director of the Marcus Museum, and it dealt with some two-year-old discoveries of Victor Lanholtz, renowned paleographer and the most distinguished member of the museum staff. According to Vagan, the elderly Lanholtz had been in charge of a dig north of Caesarea, the old Roman seaport capital, where he and his assistants had excavated the remains of a palatial seaside villa. The dig yielded a small quantity of artifacts, mostly of first-century Roman manufacture, as well as some splendid mosaic floors and a small hoard of Roman and Herodian coins bearing dates from the early years of the first century A.D.

But on the eve of winding things up, when the Lanholtz group had been working the last square metre of a cellar used to store wine and oil, they came upon a strange fissure in the floor. Enlarging the opening to pass a light inside, they found another room, its sandstone walls partly caved in on a stack of enormous amphoras. Lanholtz extended his season a few weeks to investigate the place, which appeared to have been used as a secret storage deposit by the villa's occupants. It was rich in Roman artifacts: furniture, bronzeware, gold jewellery, glass bowls, kitchen utensils and even a pair of woman's sandals decorated with inlaid silver and lapis lazuli. But the most stunning find of all was the last: in fourteen of the largest amphoras, Lanholtz found dozens of papyrus scrolls and codices, untouched for nearly two thousand years.

Lev Vagan's letter reviewed this background and

9

mentioned that Lanholtz had been continuously at work on them since their discovery, studying and translating their contents. He was now preparing to deliver the paper summarizing his preliminary results before the International Congress of Middle Eastern Archaeology at Oxford in a month. Yet it was clear from both tone and substance of Vagan's words that he was dead set against Lanholtz giving any paper anywhere for the time being.

'Why should it take him two years to translate those things?' Aaron asked. 'Latin isn't that hard a language.'

'There may have been problems opening them. Then too, ancient calligraphy isn't always legible.'

Aaron swept the table with his gourmand's eye, helping himself to the last of the French fries. 'You know more about those things than I do,' he said, unconvinced.

I read on. Lanholtz had worked behind a strict, self-imposed cloak of secrecy which apparently excluded even Lev Vagan. Beneath the measured tones of Vagan's desiccated prose I sensed an angry museum director.

In spite of the secrecy, rumours had leaked. There were already inquiries from scholars in France and the Netherlands; and Ramsay O'Hare, a Miami millionaire and archaeological buff, was in Israel that week in hopes of seeing Lanholtz and the scrolls. Vagan felt that things were growing awkward for all concerned. 'Out of hand' would have described it better.

'I don't understand the thing between Vagan and Lanholtz,' I told Aaron, but he waved the trouble away.

'You know what goes on with guys like that. Worse than children. That is not the main reason I came to see you.'

'What, in fact, does bring you here?'

'We need a decent building for these things. There's no room in the present museum even if it was properly designed, which it wasn't.'

Aaron was right. Only a few years after its construction, the Marcus Museum could barely hold its present collections. And there was the further problem with exhibits like scrolls that they must be preserved with great care, in cool, dehumidified semidarkness, and under security conditions tight enough to discourage any random antiquities thief. When I handed the letter back to Aaron, he said, 'I'll be asking the trustees for a million. The question is will they vote it?' The trustees, in addition to Aaron and myself, were a New York banker, a London industrialist, three professors, an attorney in Tel Aviv and my father.

'Why shouldn't they? The museum is well endowed.'

'We can't build what I want out of the budget. We'll have to sell off some bonds to finance it, and for that I need trustee approval.'

'Have you spoken with any of the others?'

'They'll follow whatever you do.'

'A million dollars would pay for a lot of research, Aaron. You think it's wise to put so much into a building?'

'When it's going to house the most important Roman collection outside the Naples Museum, it is.'

'Vagan doesn't say that.'

'I say it.'

'You're promoting.'

'Why do you think I spent the last couple of weeks scouting the big leagues? Look, I can guarantee maybe half the money from the Marcus Foundation. I just want you to approve the rest when the time comes.'

'You don't have to ask me. I know you won't bankrupt the museum. Whatever you need I'll approve.'

'I appreciate that, Jay,' he said, obviously relieved. 'Now how about coming with me to Israel tomorrow?'

'Not a chance.'

'To see the scrolls?'

'Don't try to con me, Aaron. What makes you think Lanholtz would show them to me when he's kept them from Vagan?'

'You've never met Lanholtz.'

'I'll probably have that pleasure in England when he reads his paper.'

'The truth is I'd like you to arbitrate.'

'I knew we'd get to the truth eventually. But no go. I've kept out of things there since the museum was built.'

'I spoke to Lev on the telephone from Rome. He asked me to bring you.'

'No.'

'Only a couple of days. The man needs a little moral support. Life with that meshugana Lanholtz is no rose bed.'

'Sorry.'

'You're a trustee.'

11

'All the more reason I'm reluctant to butt in.'

'I wish you'd change your mind. This is probably the best thing we've ever done, maybe the best we're ever likely to do. In my time anyway. I don't want to see it loused up by a petty fight between a couple of prima donnas. If I had more expertise about these things, I'd handle it alone. But I'd rather have you with me.'

I asked Aaron what he knew about the contents of the papyri and he shrugged. All Lev had told him on the telephone was that samples sent for carbon-14 dating confirmed them as first-century documents. Beyond that Vagan had said little, having seen only a couple of them himself because of Lanholtz's stubborn insistence on so much secrecy.

'The ones he saw were household accounts. Wine bills and inventories written on both sides.'

'Papyrus was expensive.'

'As I was saying –' Aaron began and then interrupted himself. 'Your grandfather would be on that plane with me. I guess you know that.'

'You don't have to invoke him.' Aaron fell silent until I added, 'As you were saying . . .'

'I didn't lose the thread. I was thinking about Nate. You and he are the only two people I ever trusted in our goddamn family. What can a couple of days cost you anyway? It would be a great favour to me.'

'I don't even know if I can get a reservation.'

His old eyes gleamed with mischief. 'You're already confirmed. I booked us both.'

Conned. I would go to Israel with Aaron, whom I love but tend to avoid. The crew could look after *Kalina*. As Aaron said, what could a couple of days cost me?

Lev Vagan, with his twelve-year-old daughter, met our flight at Lod, drove us to Tel Aviv in his crumbling station wagon and checked us into the Dan Hotel. He talked mainly about the museum's current work at a site called Gesher Tel, which bored Aaron so much he ignored Vagan to flirt with the child. A pretty blonde with a shy, quick smile and the lively blue eyes of her father, she had that pensive expression of serious purpose which makes some youngsters older than their years. I guess if you grow up surrounded by

12

people who want to kill you, a certain seriousness comes naturally. I was thinking of something Aaron had said once about Israel being just a bigger ghetto than Jews were used to. The remark was sarcastic, but there is a grain of truth in it, at least in terms of conditioning. When an Israeli politician speaks of national survival, it isn't rhetoric. I have worked in Arab countries as much as in Israel and I have mixed feelings about them all. I never saw a just solution to the plight of the Palestinian Arab that would not penalize the Israeli Jew. And vice versa. Which makes the circle particularly vicious.

'Anything Lanholtz says at the congress is premature,' Lev was telling Aaron. 'He'll leave himself and the museum wide open to criticism.'

'But you haven't even read his paper,' Aaron said. We had finished our meal and the hotel waiter was bringing coffee. Lev's daughter was watching her father intently, silently.

Lev turned to the child and said, 'If you want to look at television, go.'

The girl excused herself, nearly breaking into a run as she headed for the lounge.

'Was Lanholtz always like that?' I asked.

'He's never been exactly a team player,' Vagan said, 'but you get used to eccentrics in our profession.'

Aaron asked why he thought Lanholtz had denied him access to what was going on. When Lev said he did not know, I explained that there is something of a tradition among archaeologists in Israel regarding secrecy. Some even have their digs shut down when they go off to Europe or the States for a sabbatical.

Lev sighed. 'It goes back to the beginning. I wanted to include some of the Hebrew University people, who certainly have more experience than we in this kind of thing.'

'But Lanholtz said no.'

'That was only one of the times. He preferred to work with an untrained assistant rather than accept help from some of the best people in the country.'

'Maybe it was the size of the find,' Aaraon said. 'If a man's sitting on a major discovery all by himself, a certain amount of paranoia is understandable.'

Lev nodded. 'Sure, if that's all it was.'

'Aaron tells me you've seen some of the scrolls.'

13

'Finally. After a lot of unnecessary combat.'

'And what do you think?'

'I can't judge from the few scraps he showed me, but I was impressed. If the rest are comparable, we could have one of the more important collections of classical documents found in this century.'

'And in good shape, I gather.'

'So Lanholtz says. The ones I saw looked as if they'd been written yesterday.'

'They weren't, were they?' Aaron said impishly.

Lev looked at him in horror. 'Whatever else is wrong at the moment, you don't have to worry about that.'

Aaron shrugged. 'Jay was telling me about the Shapira scrolls in the 1880s, when that dealer faked the Ten Commandments and tried peddling them as originals.'

'A thing like that couldn't happen today,' Lev said. 'Our technology is too advanced for fraud. No, it's not the papyri that worry me; it's Dr. Lanholtz.'

'What does he say when you talk?' Aaron asked.

'That's it. We don't. I know it sounds ridiculous, but we haven't exchanged a hundred words in six months, except in anger. I told you about the inquiries we've had at the museum, stemming from the rumours.'

'That's to be expected, isn't it?' I said.

'Except Lanholtz is the leak. He wouldn't tell me a damned thing, but I discovered he had been writing privately to other scholars, making some alarming claims.'

'Such as?'

'The scrolls include private papers from the household of the Roman governor at the time of the crucifixion.'

'Ross at Oxford mentioned that,' Aaron said. 'I think it's terrific.'

Lev shifted uncomfortably in his chair and toyed with a paper-wrapped sugar cube, pulverizing it. 'If it is, don't you agree I should have been the first to know?'

'Absolutely,' Aaron said.

'Well, so far, all I've heard is the rumour,' Lev said.

'How did the trouble start?' I asked him.

'When Lanholtz began excavating that Roman villa, the museum's main effort was the Gesher Tel and frankly we had no extra money to spend on something only he was interested in. When I told Victor that, he said he'd find the money elsewhere and he did. He got the dig permits from the government and went to work on his own.'

'Why didn't you stop him?' I asked.

'Remember he *is* Victor Lanholtz,' Lev replied. 'Corresponding fellow of the French Academy and visiting professor at Princeton and Oxford. Not to mention some other credentials which distinguish him here. He survived Hitler and fought the Nazis.'

'You could have fired him,' Aaron said, 'Nazis or no Nazis.'

Lev shook his head. 'I respect him as a Jew even if he does drive me up the wall as a scientist.'

'Where do you stand now?'

'I'm not even sure I know,' Lev said.

'Tell me how he financed himself,' I asked. 'Does he have money of his own?'

Vagan shook his head. 'He got it privately from an American named O'Hare.'

'It doesn't matter who financed the dig,' Aaron insisted. 'Lanholtz was still on the museum payroll.'

'I wish it were that simple,' Lev said. 'You see, Lanholtz got the permits in O'Hare's name, not ours.'

Aaron went a little white under his California tan. 'Are you saying there's a possibility Lanholtz could leave the Marcus Museum out of the picture?'

'Under Israeli law, there is such a possibility,' Lev said dejectedly.

Aaron was apoplectic. 'How in Christ's name could you have overlooked a thing like that? If it's the law, then it's fundamental.'

'To a lawyer it might be. But I never thought to check until after I spoke with you on the phone.'

Aaron pushed his empty coffee cup aside and demanded, 'Aren't there any goddamn ethics among archaeologists?'

'Lanholtz doesn't feel his action was unethical,' Lev replied. 'When I turned down his request for funds, he moved on his own.'

'Conveniently continuing on his museum salary,' Aaron said acidly, 'and using our facilities for his work.'

Lev acknowledged this to be correct.

'Then it's a museum discovery,' Aaron insisted. 'I could win that case in any court. Even here.'

'I'd hate to see it get to court,' I told him. 'The last thing we want is a litigation with Victor Lanholtz.'

'Absolutely,' Lev said. 'We've got to work this out ourselves.'

'I don't see why you're against his giving his paper,' Aaron said. 'What harm can it do the museum?'

'We'd be criticized by the archaeological community because the work has been hurried –'

'Hurried!' Aaron exploded. 'You call two years hurried?'

'– and because Lanholtz has not invited a single colleague to take a serious look before publishing.'

'Why should that matter?' Aaron wanted to know.

'It's customary,' Lev said primly. 'At least inside one's institutional family.'

'Which puts us back on square one,' Aaron said. 'Pardon me if I sound blunt, but the heart of the matter seems to be that you don't want him announcing anything until you've had a chance to see it all yourself.'

'Do you find that unreasonable?' Lev said.

'No, but goddamn it, I'm not sure it's necessary either. Do you always see everything your people do before they publish?'

'Always,' Lev said evenly. 'It's one of the things I'm paid for.'

I tried to recall what I knew about Lev Vagan before his appointment as museum director. 'A bit of a pedant and an autocrat,' Aaron had said, 'but look at the man's history.' Palmach guerrilla at seventeen, tank commander in the Sinai in '67, reserve colonel during the Yom Kippur War. In between, all the sunbaked digs, the university degrees, the patient work to turn the Marcus Museum into something solid and permanent, like his country. A frail-looking man, and pale in spite of his years in the sun. Thinning blond hair and tweedy, donnish clothes. Only his hands gave him away: they were as hard and strong as a farmer's, and seemed designed for a larger body.

'This time let's make an exception,' Aaron said, 'just to keep peace. I understand what you're trying to do, but in view of the background, it isn't as if we can afford more trouble for the sake of protocol. If you're out on a limb now with Lanholtz, you've got yourself to blame. I don't say you were wrong, understand, but if leaving him alone just means

16

we get a little flak from the profession . . . well, I guess we can stand that.'

'Aren't you forgetting O'Hare?' I said.

'So let him look,' Aaron said. 'He paid his nickel.'

'That's what I mean. Does he have a legal claim on the scrolls, Lev?'

'It's possible. But they could never be removed from the museum without government permission, and I doubt very much he would ever get that.'

'Why did Lanholtz go to O'Hare,' I asked Lev, 'instead of some foundation? Who is he anyway?'

'He supported other projects of Victor's before.'

Aaron smirked. 'Professional Catholic. Flaunts it like some professional Jews. Big contributor to every anti-abortion group in the country, bring back the Latin mass, ban divorce – all that crap.'

'You know him?'

'We've met,' Aaron said. 'He's a crackpot.'

'Lanholtz did indicate O'Hare might make a sizable contribution toward permanent housing of the exhibit at the museum,' Lev said.

'As I was saying,' Aaron amended, 'O'Hare's a wonderful man, and his money's as good as anybody's.'

'I'd like to make a suggestion,' Lev told me. 'When I sent word to Lanholtz that you were coming to Jerusalem, he was very pleased. He's a great admirer of your work, Jay, as you may be aware. I think he'd lay everything out for you, where he won't give me the time of day. Then we'd know where we were.'

'I'm not qualified to evaluate his studies.'

'I'd be satisfied with your impression,' Vagan replied. 'It would be more objective than mine at this point.'

'If I can help, I will,' I told him, 'but I won't intrude if Lanholtz wants to keep things to himself until the congress.'

'I wonder if old Victor doesn't have more promotional sense than you two put together,' Aaron mused. 'Suppose he's deliberately stirring up all this speculation to get maximum exposure when the time comes?'

'Whatever the reason, he's determined to do things his own way,' Lev said. 'Although I haven't read his paper, I've heard all the rumours and I *have* read the official précis he submitted to the congress. My chief concern is that it will cause controversy outside archaeological circles.'

'Why?' Aaron inquired.

'The Pontius Pilate business. We moved beyond archaeology to the slippery ground of Biblical interpretation.'

'I don't follow you,' Aaron said. 'What's slippery about it?'

'Apart from Josephus* and the Gospels,' Lev explained, 'his name has only been found on a few Judean coins of the period and on a carved cornerstone turned up in Caesarea.'

'That's enough, isn't it?' Aaron said.

'You can imagine the effect of any documents that shed new light,' Lev said.

'I can imagine the effect on the museum,' Aaron replied, 'and I love it.'

'The trouble is the kind of people who will get into the act,' Lev said.

'The exploitation possibilities boggle the mind,' Aaron cried delightedly.

'Better than Inca porno?'

Aaron laughed, while Lev looked on in bewilderment.

'It could put Israel on the map,' Aaron said.

'We did that a long time ago,' Lev replied humourlessly.

Not everyone understood Aaron's approach to archaeology, and certainly not Lev Vagan. 'If you recall,' he was saying, 'this kind of controversy went on for years over the Dead Sea Scrolls. And in some of the dustier recesses of Protestant theology it goes on still.'

'Mostly among scholars who can't read a kosher meat label,' I said, and Aaron laughed.

'Go get 'em, Jay.'

'He's quite right,' Lev told Aaron, 'and what's more, we can expect every cheap magazine and sensational newspaper to have a go at the Pilate story. That's why it's important the facts be presented carefully from the start.'

'Do you have anything I can read before seeing Lanholtz?' I asked Lev.

'I'll give you the précis tonight, but it won't tell you much. The photocopies of some of the scrolls and part of Victor's translations into English I have in my office safe. You can see them tomorrow when we go to Jerusalem.'

* Josephus Flavius, first-century Jewish general and historian.

18

'Things will work out all right with Lanholtz,' Aaron said, 'if no one loses sight of the promotional potential.'

'If they don't,' I said, 'it won't be because you haven't willed it.'

Lev's daughter had approached the table so quietly it was a minute before anyone took notice of her. Then Lev and I both saw the small, pretty face at the same time, a caricature of adult shock.

'What is it, darling?' Vagan asked his daughter.

Aaron was saying, 'I've got a hunch everything's going to be okay.'

'Daddy, the television news says Dr. Lanholtz is dead.'

So much for Aaron's hunches.

TWO

The King David Hotel in Jerusalem is bigger than the Intercontinental, better known than the National Palace and more expensive than the Jewish-Muslim YMCA across the street. But by my standards – admittedly spoiled – it's a far cry from what I'm used to when off the boat. I indulge in hotels. Not Aaron. Give him a Hilton mattress or a Sheraton shower and he is a happy man – a conditioned reflex imposed by forty years of California living. But I like the heated towel racks and Olympic bathtubs in London's Savoy, the cheese breakfasts at the Wittebrug in Holland, and the downstairs bar at the Athénée Palace. I am a patsy for the gilded Venetian comfort of the Danieli and the room service at the Ritz. But when I have to, I can make do at the King David.

Jerusalem is the most beguiling archaeological dig outside of Rome, and the Marcus Archaeological Museum, set smack in its centre, was its most confused locus the day after Lanholtz's death. Old Nate would have done a turn or two in his own mouldering Queens necropolis if he could have seen what some people were doing in his name. Moral: if you invent a surgical saw or a self-clamping hemostat, keep it to yourself to avoid posthumous embarrassment. Aaron was in his element, if one assumes that element to be the kind of administrative chaos where his lawyer's calm and playboy charm work miracles. He was superb, picking his way through a lot of academic confusion and bureaucratic pettifogging, and enduring the polite but tiring attentions of the police.

Yes, the police. We saw a lot of them during our stay in Jerusalem because Victor Lanholtz had been found on the floor of the museum laboratory with his skull bashed in and his brilliant brains spattered over the dusty artifacts he had spent his life defining. The scrolls, of course, were gone.

The murder was on the front page of the Jerusalem *Post*, but with few facts Aaron and I were not already familiar with. Although mention of the theft occurred near the top of the story, the papyri were lumped together with other 'archaeological treasures' stolen from the museum. Lev was quoted at length, and there were references to recent archaeological thefts in Italy, followed by a sketchy biography of Lanholtz. Detective Inspector Shmuel Berman was not exactly a mine of information either, but he had a few interesting theories. He also had a way of not answering my questions that was as irritating as it was effective.

Inspector Berman had gone to school in Milwaukee, as Golda Meir had. Soft as a slab of marble and just as hard to move, he seemed dedicated to his work. He had started his career in the U.S. Army MPs in Vienna, riding around in a jeep with a Russian, a Frenchman and an Englishman during the joint occupation there after the war. Later he made sergeant on the Milwaukee PD before he decided to throw it in and come to Israel. Now he was in his late fifties, with a round red face, a paunch, shrewd pale eyes, red hair going grey, and freckles everywhere, even on the backs of his broad, powerful hands. 'Just call me Sam,' he said to me as we were having a cup of tea in our suite at the King David that first afternoon. Looking at his professional expression of patient noninvolvement, I was impressed; the smile was ingenuous, but the eyes were suspicious of everything. Yet a moment later the eyes seemed kind and reassuring, while the mouth was as solemn and immutable as death. Inspector Berman was clearly a man who did not like people to break the law. Strength was in the slightly awkward way he accepted the teacup, like a boxer shaking hands; shrewdness in the roving quick appraisal of the room, of me; it was hard to imagine anyone calling him Sam, even his wife.

He did not have a lot of homicide experience, as he was the first to acknowledge. Twenty years in the country, and except for terrorist killings, only seven murder investigations, two of which turned out to be accidental death and one a suicide.

'But we try to keep up,' he said, smiling gently and slurping at the steaming tea.

Aaron arrived then and wanted to know immediately if Inspector Berman had a clue.

The detective said succinctly, 'We don't know who killed the professor, if that's what you mean. No suspects and no hard evidence.'

'No fingerprints? No struggle? Nothing broken?' Aaron was insistent.

Berman's smile broadened. 'In a museum like yours everything's broken. We got our choice of fingerprints, dust and cat hair. But not enough to hang a calendar on.' He put down his empty cup with great care and fished a little note pad from his jacket pocket. Aaron was obviously disappointed. I wondered too about the difference between Sergeant Sam Berman of the Milwaukee police department and the aging, diffident Israeli investigator who sat facing us in that Jerusalem hotel room. Was he up to the job? The vision of Israel had dimmed, I suppose, but the work habits remained the same. He said he had a few questions to ask, perfunctory and general, about the relations between Lanholtz and other members of the museum staff. I told him neither Aaron nor I had any firsthand information, but he said he would like to talk about it just the same.

'What about the fight between Vagan and Lanholtz yesterday?'

'Dr. Vagan was with us in Tel Aviv last night.'

Berman nodded. 'But what about the fight?'

'If there was one, it's news to me,' I said, looking at Aaron, who nodded his head emphatically.

Berman flipped through his notes and read something to himself. Then he looked up and said, 'One of the staff reports they hadn't spoken to each other in months. Except for shouting matches.'

'You know more than we do,' Aaron said.

'Right. Let me ask you another question, sir. Would you have any idea who'd want to steal those scrolls?'

21

'None at all,' I said.

'Would you say they're priceless, Doctor?'

'In the sense that they're ancient, I suppose, yes.'

Berman looked from me to Aaron.

'I can't add anything to that,' Aaron said.

'Would you pay to get them back?' Berman asked. Aaron and I both looked at him, slowly absorbing the implications of what might have happened. 'I was just wondering,' Berman said simply. 'Sometimes a priceless thing's got a price.'

'A ransom?'

'Let's call it extortion,' Berman corrected me. 'I'd say there was a good chance you'll be hearing from the people who took those documents.'

'It would be a relief.'

Aaron started a fresh cigar and offered one to the inspector. 'Is this a bribe?' he said, smiling, and lit up with grave appreciation.

'They could ask anything,' Aaron said.

'Would you pay anything?'

'Behind the museum is a foundation,' I told him, 'and behind the foundation is a board of trustees.'

'So it's out of your hands?'

'Not at all,' Aaron replied, 'but how can we know what we may pay?'

'What about the jewellery?' He turned a page in his notebook and glanced at it to refresh his memory. 'Dr. Vagan says there were some necklaces, rings, bracelets and a' – he hesitated over the word –'diadem. All gold. Would they be worth more than the other things? Could they be sold?'

'Again, I think you're asking the wrong people,' I said. 'We haven't seen any of the artifacts. But they were photographed, so I would doubt they could be sold publicly.'

'Is it the kind of stuff could find its way into a private collection?' Berman asked.

'Some pot-hunters buy antiquities without asking too many questions,' I said.

'Suppose the people who stole all these things asked a lot of money to get them back. How do you think you'd handle it?'

'I don't know,' Aaron said. 'I guess we'd try to negotiate

something. And if we couldn't, maybe the Israeli government would. I don't know.'

'Right,' Berman said. 'Anyway, the government would act like it was going to pay and that's what you should do.'

'How?'

'If I'm wrong about them getting in touch, I guess there are ways you can spread the word you're willing, aren't there? Through dealers?'

I told him there were.

'Dr. Vagan said very few people even knew this stuff existed,' Berman said. 'Is that true?'

'You can rely on anything he told you.' I sensed a certain antagonism in Berman toward Lev Vagan, but was unable to account for it.

'That may narrow the field,' he said. His cigar had gone out and he scowled at it, groping in his pockets for a match. 'Do you know anything about the dead man's correspondence with other professors regarding the scrolls?'

'There were some inquiries, I believe. Friends Lanholtz told about the discovery.'

'But no one knows very much,' Aaron said.

'Somebody knew enough to kill an old man,' Berman replied flatly.

'Not a colleague, certainly,' I said.

'Let me give you a scenario,' Berman countered. 'Somebody hates the professor enough to beat in his head. Then they take the things from the museum to make it look like that was the reason.'

'I can't believe that,' I said. 'People may have envied a famous man like Lanholtz. Jealousy and backbiting are as common among archaeologists as elsewhere. But murder is a good deal rarer.'

'Understand we got a special situation in this country,' Berman said. 'Not counting guerrilla violence, things are pretty quiet. When I was a cop in Milwaukee we had more rapes and assaults in any ordinary month than I've seen here since I immigrated. Burglary's not a big thing either. Your typical felon in Israel is a scam artist or maybe an accountant who cooks his company's books. Or a tax dodger or a customs cheat. We don't get too many guys with hammers.'

Aaron was thoughtful. 'So you lean toward the theory the murder was personally motivated?'

'That's just an idea,' Berman said. 'Let me give you another scenario. Word leaks out about all this stuff in your museum. Some crooked dealer's willing to spend some money to rip off the collection. The people he hires to do it kill the old man for a simple professional reason – to prevent identification.'

'That seems more likely,' I said.

'Except they could have waited till he left the premises and then taken the stuff. It was locked up, but it wasn't guarded, and the old man never worked much past eleven.'

'So you think the killing was deliberate.'

'It sure wasn't an accident,' Berman replied stiffly.

'I meant premeditated,' I said.

'I'm just trying to put it together. We got to have a point of departure to make up for the lack of evidence.'

'Let me give *you* a scenario, then,' I said. Berman frowned at his newly lit cigar, rolled it over his lips and looked at me coldly. 'Somebody just wanted the scrolls or the jewellery or both. Lanholtz returned to the museum by chance, discovered the robbery in progress and was killed. And that's the last anybody ever hears about it.'

Berman flipped through his notebook again, found the page he wanted, and read: ' ". . . Real estate leases, bills of conveyance, some blank pages, cargo receipts, a household inventory, certificates of manumission and a bunch of old letters." Fact: they're worth a fortune to your museum. Fact: the jewellery is too. Fact: somebody's probably going to try to sell them back to you and that's how you can help us find a murderer.'

'How?'

'Give me your word you won't deal with the thieves without bringing us into the act.'

I bristled. 'There's no need to ask. Neither of us would consider such a thing.'

'Don't misunderstand me,' Berman said. 'But if you hear from them, and their demands are what you can meet money-wise, you might decide to go it alone. We understand that. You want your property back.'

'They aren't precisely our property, Inspector,' I reminded him. 'All of it belongs to the Israeli state. The Marcus Museum only serves as custodian.'

'I wasn't talking about the law. I was talking about how you gentlemen would react.'

I started to repeat assurances of our cooperation, but Aaron cut me off. 'He's right, Jay. Lanholtz is dead, yet I'd probably deal with the devil himself and say to hell with the police if we could recover the loot.'

Berman smiled. 'I appreciate your frankness. Let me give you an idea how it might go. They'll send a sample to prove they're on the level, probably from someplace in Europe or the States. They'll make the exchange fairly complicated – different banks, different countries, different intermediaries and a lot of chasing around before you see any results. They might even threaten destruction of the goods if you quibble, if you're late or if you contact the police.'

'It sounds as if you've handled this kind of thing before,' I told the inspector.

'Patterns are patterns,' he replied, 'and I don't get to see too many new ones.'

Aaron was as fascinated as I. 'Exactly what do you want us to do?' he said.

'Cable me or telephone the minute anybody contacts you about the stuff.'

'Suppose it's outside your jurisdiction?'

'We get first-class cooperation almost everywhere, including some places might surprise you. If it turns out to be a terrorist money grab . . . well, we have ways of dealing with that too.'

Aaron poured himself a cup of tea, found it tepid and made a face. 'Suppose they've been taken to Europe or America?'

'Our outbound baggage checks are the best in the world,' Berman said. 'They won't leave Israel except for the sample, which is probably gone already, wrapped around somebody's middle. Too much chance of getting caught.'

'How can you be sure there's more than one person involved?'

'The bulk. A thing this big has to be a joint effort.'

I asked him what he thought the odds were of recovering the collection.

'Let me put it this way: we got a reputation to protect.' On his note pad he wrote his name, some telephone numbers and a cable address. He ripped out the page and handed it to me. 'Anytime, night or day, you can always reach me.'

I folded the paper into my wallet and thanked him.

'Keep us in the picture,' he advised. 'We aren't as casual as we come on.'

Nicoletta Calvi, Victor Lanholtz's assistant, was that rarest of all endangered species, the natural beauty with brains. Long black hair, the face a little angular in a patrician way, with dark, intelligent gypsy eyes that seemed to find a kind of sad humour in all the world about her. Voice pitched like a boy's but soft as Tuscan velvet. It was the day after Lanholtz's funeral and I had gone to the museum with Aaron, who fell in love with her at first sight. She was dressed in faded blue jeans and a sleeveless khaki shirt and was carrying an armload of books stacked to her chin. When I offered to give her a hand, she smiled and said, 'I know who you are.' While Aaron went on to his appointment with Lev, I relieved the girl of the larger volumes and followed her through the great stone exhibition rooms to the shadowy, book-lined retreat that was the museum library. Had it not been for the brilliantly flowered garden glimpsed through casemented windows, the place might have been in Cambridge or Morningside Heights. Except for Nicoletta Calvi. 'You were a long time getting here, Dr. Marcus,' she said with the lightest Italian accent.

'I didn't know I was expected.'

She looked at me to see if I was serious, and then asked, 'You didn't get Dr. Lanholtz's letter?'

'I'm afraid not.'

'He wrote you – it must have been two months ago – at your Paris address. He was surprised you never answered.'

'I was in Greece all summer.'

'We should have known, I guess, but in view of what happened it probably does not matter.'

'Why did he write to me?'

'He wanted your advice on one of the papyri having to do with Roman medicine. You are the acknowledged expert.'

'That's an exaggeration, but thanks.'

'If he said you are, then you are,' the girl said with finality. 'Dr. Lanholtz was never mistaken in a scholarly judgment and he read all your published work.'

'Will you continue now without him?'

'At the moment, I'm not even sure I want to. But I guess the feeling will pass.' Her voice caught and she turned away.

'How long had you worked together?'

'Ages, on and off. I was a student volunteer in Florence following the 1966 floods. Victor went there to help salvage the worst-damaged manuscripts and I dropped out of the university to work under him, resuscitating books and documents.' For a moment she was extraordinarily immobile, her exquisite profile like a Pompeian cameo held to the light. 'There were some married years,' she said at last. 'When my husband and I broke up, I began appraising Italian collections for a London auction house. Victor asked me to come here after he found the scrolls.'

'You're more of an expert than I realized.'

'I'd think you were being facetious, Doctor, if I wasn't aware of that "untrained assistant" story Lev Vagan puts out about me. Now I've embarrassed you and I did not mean to do that.'

'It's true Vagan said that. Why?'

Nicoletta raised small hands in an Italianate gesture of incomprehension. 'Perhaps by his rigid academic standards I am,' she said. 'Degrees count a lot with him. Also, he had no control over my work because I was on an outside grant.'

'From Mr. O'Hare?'

'You know him?' From time to time she pushed her hair back from her temple with a swift, graceful movement of her expressive hands. I told her I had heard about O'Hare's generosity. 'Without his help there would have been no dig,' she said. 'Now I find his attitude puzzling.'

'In what way?'

'I don't know whose side you're on yet, Doctor.'

'Yours.'

'That could be costly.'

'I can afford it.'

'In other ways than money?'

'I'm not easily discouraged.'

She regarded me for a moment as if trying to make up her mind where I fit into her own mysterious equation. Then she said gravely, 'Dr. Lanholtz let Mr. O'Hare read the paper shortly after he arrived. Then O'Hare summoned him to his hotel and asked him to withdraw it from the congress.'

27

'Did he give a reason?'

'He objected to what he called "speculation." '

'Is there?'

'Certainly not. Victor returned very upset. He did not like to disappoint Mr. O'Hare, but he had enough bullying from Vagan.'

'Have you read the paper?'

'I helped write it.'

'Maybe O'Hare was opposed for the same reasons Vagan was,' I suggested. 'To avoid controversy.'

'That would be too remarkable a coincidence,' Nicoletta said frostily, 'for anyone to credit.'

'Vagan said something of the sort to me when we spoke in Tel Aviv before the . . . tragedy.'

'Who accepts Vagan's reasons?'

'Don't you?'

'He was against everything Victor did. I find it hard to believe a man so full of envy and malice.'

'That's a bit rough, isn't it?'

'I saw how Victor had to work. A less dedicated scholar would not have put up with Vagan's harassment.'

'How did he harass him?'

'You think I'm overstating it, don't you?'

'I'd like to know why you feel so strongly about it. Vagan told me he asked Dr. Lanholtz to show his work to some other scholars and he refused.'

'That would be the way he'd tell it.' She gave a small sniff of contempt. 'The truth is that Victor didn't want a regiment of graduate students tripping through the laboratory just so Lev Vagan could show off.'

'But I understand he also refused to show Vagan the completed paper.'

'Because it wasn't completed when Lev asked to read it. Vagan didn't believe Victor and accused him of holding back. They had a terrible quarrel and Victor said he'd be damned if anyone would call him a liar. That's when he told Vagan he'd know the contents of the paper at the congress and not a day sooner.'

'Rashomon.'

'What?'

'The different versions, the different textures of the truth.'

'You don't believe me?'

'I most certainly do. It comes to the same story in the end, except that Lev Vagan's version differs significantly.'

'That may surprise you, Doctor, but if you knew Vagan better, you'd realize all his interpretations differ significantly when his cancerous ego is involved.'

'Anyway, I'm anxious to read Lanholtz's paper.'

'It's a fine piece of work. If he had lived to present it . . .' Her voice caught and her eyes slowly filled with tears. 'I still can't believe it.' She withdrew a man's handkerchief from her jeans and dabbed at her eyes. 'Excuse me.'

'Did the police talk to you?'

She nodded. 'The thieves didn't break in. Either he let them in or they let themselves in with a key. And only he and I had keys.'

'You told Inspector Berman that?'

'I also told him I thought Dr. Lanholtz would still be alive if his desire for secrecy had been respected.'

'But Lanholtz himself told other people.'

'Three,' Nicoletta said. 'Father Damien from the Vatican, Professor Ross at Oxford and Professor Merle in Paris.'

'That's a fairly long list for a secret.'

'He trusted his friends. Ross was a former student and Professor Merle helped him escape from the Germans during the war.'

'And the man from the Vatican?'

'A Frenchman. He came with Mr. O'Hare.'

'But you don't think they respected his trust?'

'I'm sure they did. I was talking about Lev Vagan. *He* was spreading the word, not the others. Every scholar in Israel knew what we were working on.'

'You don't like him much, do you?'

'I can't stand the man,' Nicoletta said, 'and I can't forgive him. Always preening himself, always playing to the crowd. He's taken you in too, hasn't he? I can tell. He can say what he wants now about why he wanted to delay the presentation. The real reason is he wanted to share the credit. You know, work by Vagan and Lanholtz.'

'That's not a very attractive picture.'

'He's not a very attractive man. Look, Dr. Marcus, in my narrow little world one meets one's share of fakes. But the worst kind are the hypocrites who build their reputations on

29

the backs of honest scholars. Lev Vagan is a prize specimen and if I didn't know better, I'd almost think he did it.'

'I hope you didn't say so to Inspector Berman.'

'I don't even know why I'm saying it to you. After all, he's your creature and you didn't know Victor.' She was right in estimating my reaction, but she did not realize how her reckless style affected me in spite of her dislike of Vagan. I had the feeling she was saying nothing she had not said to Lev in person.

'If you had to guess who killed Lanholtz, could you?'

'Someone who had access to him, someone he would admit to the laboratory late at night.'

'How long is that list?'

'Not very. I suppose I'm at the head of it.'

'You evidently satisfied Berman.'

'If I had to guess, I'd say everyone satisfied him, probably including the murderer.'

'What did you tell him?'

'That I was having dinner with Ramsay O'Hare. You might say he is suspect number two.'

'And the others on the list?'

'Vagan, perhaps. And two or three members of the museum staff.'

'Didn't Lev Vagan have his own keys to the laboratory?'

'Victor had all the locks changed months ago. He would have moved everything out of the museum if another facility had been available.'

'I'm surprised he didn't resign.'

'Oh, he thought about it. After every fight with Vagan. Then he'd calm down and return to work again. All he wanted was to be left alone.'

'What will you do now?'

'Until today I was determined to deliver Victor's paper in England. I thought it was the least I could do, to read it into the record.'

'What happened to change your mind?'

'I told you about Mr. O'Hare's opposition. He feels even more strongly now that things should be left alone until the papyri are recovered. He seems confident they will be, although I'm not. I'm not even sure the congress will allow the paper now that the originals are missing.'

'But you have photocopies.'

'You know how it is. Vagan is the only established professional archaeologist who saw any of the originals. His opposition would probably be enough to keep me out.'

'I'd like to read it.'

'And show it to Vagan?'

'How could that matter now?'

The girl sighed. 'Probably it doesn't, but it would seem like a terribly disloyal act if I let it happen. Would you promise not to let him read it?'

'If you insisted, I would.'

'There were only two copies,' Nicoletta said. 'One was taken by the thieves and I have the other in my apartment. Let me think about it.'

'If the congress is still willing to accept the paper, I think you should deliver it,' I said.

'Maybe you'll change your mind after you've read it.'

'Not if the scholarship is sound.'

'Are you such an advocate of academic freedom?'

'Something like that. But I have another reason.'

'Tell me, please.'

'The publicity might be helpful in getting back the collection. I have a hunch if anyone is going to contact us, as the police think they will, the logical place would be that meeting.'

'Suppose they don't.'

'Then you've still put Lanholtz's work on the record. I'm inclined to support a full disclosure.'

'I like you, Dr. Marcus.'

'Then call me Jay.'

'You're on a collision course with Lev Vagan, Jay.'

'Not if he changes direction.'

She was sprawled in one of the library chairs, hands jammed in her blue-jeans pockets and a frown of worried concentration on her face. 'I'm a little afraid.'

'Of what?'

'It's one thing to sit in the crowd and worship a genius like Victor Lanholtz. It's another to stand up on a platform and shock them all out of their seats.'

'Why should you shock anyone?'

'You'll see when you read the paper. There's one group of papyri that could change some thinking about the synoptic Gospels.'

31

'Vagan mentioned that.'

There was anger as well as incredulity in her stare. 'But Victor never showed them to him.'

'He knew about them. It's the one part of the collection he thinks will bring the vultures.'

'The only ones who knew beside ourselves were Professor Merle in Paris and Sir William Ross.'

'Ross discussed them with my uncle when he visited the British Museum last week. He calls them the "Pontius Pilate Papers." '

'Ross calls them that?'

'My uncle. It's his promotional sense.'

'Oh, my God! So Ross told Vagan.'

'No. Someone else told him first. Even Inspector Berman knows they exist.'

'I don't understand it,' Nicoletta said.

'Lanholtz gave Vagan the précis of the paper.'

'But the letters aren't described that fully. Oh, the hell with it. Who cares? I talk as if Victor were alive.'

Lev Vagan's secretary came looking for me, but before I left Nicoletta Calvi I asked her if she would have dinner that evening. 'I think not, but thank you. Here.' She scrawled her address and telephone number on a slip of paper. 'I'm usually home by seven, if you want to drop by for the paper.' I thanked her and when I turned to go, she said, 'Maybe tomorrow, if your invitation still holds. After you've read a little.' I felt the warmth of her smile as I followed Lev's secretary through the echoing halls to join Aaron.

Around the conference table in Lev Vagan's office were gathered five people who had known Victor Lanholtz.

Vagan's secretary, a dowdy, heavy-breasted woman in her fifties, adjusted thick glasses and opened her shorthand note pad. On her left, my old friend Ari Ascher, the tanned, sinewy expert in Byzantine art, flipped lazily through a German professional journal as he waited for the meeting to begin. Next to him a staff photographer was holding up slide transparencies of the Gesher Tel and gossiping with Menahem Sherif, the balding, gnomelike little archaeologist in charge of the Gesher excavations. Watching them with sullen interest was the youngest member of the museum staff, Avraham Beni, Vagan's protégé and, according to

Nicoletta, the museum fink. She was not present, having no official connection with the museum itself. It was a mixed bag, each with his speciality, his politics and his dreams.

While I was acquainted only with Ascher, Aaron seemed to know them all. He might have been running for office, the way he charmed and flattered everyone and made corny remarks that put the whole table in good humour.

Lev Vagan opened the meeting on a more solemn note by making a little speech about the Lanholtz tragedy, at the end of which he irrelevantly asked them all to carry on. Young Avraham Beni hung on every word, nodding, and I decided Nicoletta had been right about him. His sycophancy seemed all too transparent. Ascher sat through it impassively, his bronzed brow wrinkled in a scholarly frown. We had worked together under Professor Yadin at Masada. He was a good man, a serious archaeologist and a loner.

The secretary pursed her lips and dutifully jotted down every one of Vagan's words, a faint smile of maternal tolerance lighting her expression whenever anyone else spoke. Although Dr. Sherif looked up when Vagan was talking, his mind seemed far away. He peered through thick glasses as if not quite able to make the rest of us out.

Vagan passed from one to the other, asking for reports and observations. No one had much to say until it was Sherif's turn. He beamed at us all, his small dome reflecting the overhead light and his pipestem arms extending from his short-sleeved shirt in a kind of caricature of the public speaker. 'I wish to protest in the strongest terms the behaviour of the police.' His smile never dimmed and he had a nervous tic, which did not help his presentation; his jaw strained and jerked as if his shirt collar was choking him.

Lev Vagan was not pleased. 'Under the circumstances,' he told Sherif placatingly, 'we have to be a little patient.' His gaze moved to Avraham Beni, but before that young man could speak, Sherif said, 'I was kept a prisoner in my office for three hours this morning and they would not permit me to discuss anything with other members of the staff! They threatened to take me to headquarters if I did not cooperate. Is this a free country or is it not?' he demanded.

'We can talk about that some other time,' Vagan said blandly. 'It doesn't really concern us today.'

Dr. Sherif gazed at him, still smiling and twitching. 'Oh,

33

but it does,' he said in his mild voice, folding his skinny hands like an acolyte. 'Justice is everyone's business.'

Vagan looked pained and I could not blame him. A museum staff meeting is no place to debate the concept of absolute justice, least of all in embarrassing clichés. But Aaron showed the kind of stuff that had made him one of the best contract lawyers in Hollywood. 'Dr. Sherif is absolutely right,' he said with judicial emphasis. 'What he has just said is worth thinking about.' He leaned across to Sherif and touched his arm. 'I'd like to hear your views on it *over lunch*, Doctor.'

'Well, yes,' Sherif said, pleased, and unaware of his defeat. 'I have written a letter to the Ministry of Justice I thought we might all sign.' He extended a piece of paper toward Aaron, who took it immediately, folded it and put it in his pocket.

'We'll kick it around,' he said, returning Sherif's smile full force.

Vagan moved on to Ari Ascher and asked him for a status report on his own projects. Ari was dry, succinct and fast. In a few words, he covered what he and his assistants had been up to during the previous month and pushed a site report across the table toward Vagan. 'There's another copy,' he said to the group in general, 'if anyone cares to read it.'

After some housekeeping details and instructions from Vagan to various members of the staff, the meeting was adjourned.

Sherif fluttered at my arm. 'Dr. Marcus, I do hope you'll be in Jerusalem for the opening of the Gesher Tel exhibit next week.'

'I'm not sure. . . . You know. . . .' Smiling.

Avraham Beni appeared at my other elbow, bouncing. 'I reserved the luncheon table. We are expected in fifteen minutes.'

I ignored him and went to seek out Ari Ascher. A warm handshake. 'Been a long time, Jay.'

'Are you coming to lunch?'

He shook his head.

'So when can we talk?'

He gave me a telephone number. Ari is one of the hardest-working men I have ever known, most at home when he is scratching away the centuries under the broiling

34

sun. Cheeks and chin like crabapples stud his good-humoured face. I remember times with him atop Masada drinking warm beer by starlight, talking ourselves hoarse beneath the ancient sky. And on a day off, bobbing like two puppets in the tepid saline of the Dead Sea, unable to swim for the buoyancy and laughing at our helplessness.

'I don't go out much,' Ari said.

'Not married yet?'

He grinned. 'Thinking about doing it soon. You?'

'Not thinking about it.'

'I'll call you, if you have time.'

'Call me. What's her name?'

His ears glowed. 'Would you believe Sarah?'

'Can she join us?'

Ari's grin split his scholarly reserve in two. 'Jay, she'd love it.'

'Tomorrow night?'

'You're on.'

I asked him, off to one side, how he got along with Nicoletta Calvi. He smiled again. 'Let me put it this way,' he said. 'She's the only one around here we ever see socially. Bring her with you.'

'If she'll come.'

I felt a small wave of gratitude toward Ari Ascher. What greater pleasure is there in life than the rediscovery of a friend unchanged by years?

'We'll be late for lunch, Doctor,' Avraham Beni was saying in my ear.

I gave him my best smile and said, 'Not very good planning on your part, was it?'

His bright toady face fell as if he'd been struck. He started to stammer some explanation, but Aaron said, 'C'mon, or the pasta gets cold.'

Outside, the sun was a furnace and Aaron looked a hundred years old. 'Are you all right?' I asked him.

'Just get me to the air conditioning in time,' he gasped, bearing up.

Once, my father made me attend a Christmas party at the Marcus Instrument offices in New York. Except for the nonalcoholic drinking habits of the Israelis, Lev Vagan's luncheon was equally unfortunate. Everyone tried too hard. Dr. Sherif shrilly insisted on bringing up his crusade for justice again. Vagan's secretary praised the glutinous mess the waiter called spaghetti. The photographer chattered ceaselessly; an incipient hysteric. And Avraham Beni did a whole circus act between Vagan and Aaron and me, like a performing lamprey. Lev made a show of good fellowship. 'The food is usually better,' he said unconvincingly.

If there was a killer in this crowd, he or she was giving away nothing. None of them seemed to mourn the passing of Victor Lanholtz. Aaron, catching my glance at one point, said under his breath, 'You'd never know, would you?'

THREE

Back in the seventeenth century, Christian Huygens proposed a mathematical problem he called The Duration of Play, the idea being that the probability of winning a game determines how long the game will last. For Victor Lanholtz, who died in his seventy-third year, the duration of play was not long enough. So, I asked myself, if Huygens was right and the end of the game was predetermined, what kind of chance did Lanholtz have in the first place? To answer my own question with any authority I would have to know more about Lanholtz and the game. The overriding fact was that it did not matter except to an insurance actuary. Except . . .

The theft of the papyri and the death of their discoverer seemed to be the classic illustration of how things get balled up when too many chance processes are at work. One of them was Ramsay O'Hare, the Florida entrepreneur, who called me at the hotel that afternoon with a dinner invitation.

I hesitated, thinking something more interesting might still develop with Nicoletta Calvi.

'Perhaps a drink, then?' O'Hare suggested. He agreed to come by our suite at six. When Aaron telephoned shortly after that to tell me he was still trapped with Vagan at the museum, I told him about O'Hare.

'Better you than me,' he said.

As it turned out, Ramsay O'Hare was not at all the man Aaron had led me to expect: he was, in fact, quite a bit more.

Big with the beefy build of an ex-athlete, grey-haired, fiftyish, urbane, articulate, he made a commanding first impression.

He had gone into hotel construction after World War II and made money speculating in Florida and Nevada resort properties. Ex-officer in naval intelligence and loser in a Dade County congressional race. 'An empty drum,' Aaron had characterized him somewhat redundantly, but I was not at all sure. Aaron had a flip Hollywood way of disparaging people he did not like, and my first impression was that he had once again made a mistake in judgment.

After some preliminary words eulogizing Lanholtz and lamenting his violent death, O'Hare asked me about my own degree of involvement in what he called 'this whole sorry business.'

I explained I had only come to Israel to meet Lanholtz and see what he had turned up.

'After hearing the rumours, I daresay,' O'Hare said.

I looked blank.

'Don't tell me you picked this time just by chance,' he said. 'Come now, Doctor, I've been too close to this thing.'

'Well, I have not.'

'You? An archaeologist?' For an instant I thought he might burst out laughing.

'I'm not an archaeologist,' I told him. 'I'm a physician who writes about archaeology.'

'Well, it's your museum,' he said blandly. 'I would have thought you'd be on top of things.'

'Obviously I wasn't, or your money would not have been needed.'

Then he did laugh, with forced heartiness, I thought; his baritone filled the room as he clapped one heavy hand on my arm and said, 'Right on, Doctor! I see you tell it like it is.' His use of language, I soon realized, was probably one of the qualities that annoyed Aaron. By trying to sound like an enthusiastic twenty-year-old, O'Hare only reinforced the impression of a man of fifty at odds with himself. Like so many who succeed in a hurry, he carried a rather heavy load of guilt into middle life, and he was now embarked upon a quixotic search for something he called 'spiritual equilibrium,' but which others might see only as simple expiation. He was an absolutist and, as Nicoletta Calvi had

37

implied, a bully. In the course of his search he had re-discovered 'Holy Mother Church' and now seemed bent on doing whatever he could to help bolster the crumbling bastions of medieval Catholic dogma.

'I'm not a rich man,' he said to me. 'Not the way I'm pictured by the press. But helping a deserving scholar here and there brings me more kicks than writing cheques for the Internal Revenue.' He smiled confidently, one dissembling millionaire to another, but his patronizing air effectively suffocated any impulse of mine to give him sympathetic attention.

'Had you known Dr. Lanholtz a long time?' I asked.

'I helped him out once or twice in the past. We shared a mutual interest in Christian material from the first century after Our Blessed Lord was crucified.' The last phrase rolled out with the practised smoothness of long use. He let out a long breath and shook his head. 'Now that we've turned up the biggest, most exciting, incredible papyrus trove of all time –'

'Aren't you overstating the case? There have been larger finds.'

'You mean Herculaneum?' O'Hare said in a bored tone. 'Worthless. The Naples Museum has eight hundred nobody's even bothered to read yet.'

He was partly right. In the so-called Villa of the Papyri, which had been buried by the eruption of Vesuvius in 79 A.D., nearly two thousand scrolls were discovered in the late eighteenth century. To date, almost half remain unopened because our technology cannot yet cope without destroying them. Most were carbonized by the lava heat and resemble the pages of a burnt newspaper where the ink impression may only be read in a certain light, and the material crumbles at the touch.

'Have you seen what Victor found?'

'Unfortunately no.'

'That's right; how could you have?' O'Hare nodded to himself. 'You arrived a little late. Well, I read his paper. And we were in continuous correspondence before that. I'm no scientist, but I like to play at it.' The smile was meant to be disarming. 'The papyrus collection is fantastic and the other things he found were first-rate. But . . . he should have been more careful.' O'Hare twirled the ice in his glass. His expression was pensive. 'I blame Vagan. Lanholtz couldn't trust him. He told me a lot I would not repeat.'

'I'm glad,' I said, 'because I shouldn't care to hear it. Since Lanholtz's death it seems to be open season around here on the museum administration.'

O'Hare's eyebrows shot up. 'It's about time. Too much pussyfooting. Vagan's a lousy administrator and everybody knows it.'

'Caesarea wasn't the museum's only interest,' I told him. I had heard enough criticism of Lev Vagan to last me awhile.

'Two sides to every story,' O'Hare said, 'when there aren't three or four.' He laughed, enjoying his own wit. I wondered at the contradiction in a man whose inner needs failed so completely to coincide with his obvious outward self-satisfaction. He moved out of his chair and paced the room for a moment, a restless giant. He was in his shirt-sleeves now, with his tie loosened, although the room was overcooled by the air conditioning. 'The police don't have the least idea what happened. When I think of it . . .' He paused in his passage and shook his head angrily. 'You're tempted to give them a lot of credit here. Too much, if you ask me. We start to think of this country like England or the States, but it's still the Middle East. They may grow a couple more oranges than the Arabs, but it's the same defective mentality. Look at those police! Did you talk to them?'

I nodded.

'That chief detective is a beaut. I don't know how he came on with you, but I found him pushy and obnoxious. I've had experience with that type in Miami, and they don't reach me. Not at all.'

'I hear Miami's full of them,' I said, unable to ignore the whiff of anti-Semitism I was sure I smelled.

O'Hare seemed neither embarrassed nor surprised. He looked at me in a kindly, baffled way and said, 'I'm sorry if you choose to misunderstand me, Doctor, but you don't know how far off base you are. My personal relationship with Dr. Lanholtz speaks for itself.'

'Good Jews and bad Jews?' I said.

'That's precisely it,' Ramsay O'Hare said as he put down his glass. 'The Sadducees and the Pharisees. The renegades and the keepers of the Temple. Foolish bureaucrats like your man Vagan and visionary geniuses like Victor Lanholtz.'

As he talked I was thinking of Nate when I last saw him in the hospital before he died. I don't know why. Maybe part of my genetic legacy or possibly a remnant of childhood confusion about where I fit into this world of ethnic partisans. I had been summoned from lacrosse practice by a telephone call. I took the B & M to Boston and without supper caught the Merchants Limited to New York, descending at midnight into the hostile iron-girdered world of 125th Street, where a kindly black taxi driver picked me up and delivered me to the door of Columbia Presbyterian. My Jewish grandfather was dying in a goy hospital. And my goy mother waited in the lounge, her mascara unmarred and her voice coolly telling me Nate was not expected to make it through the night. For weeks we knew he was not going to live; he had a thing eating out his insides. Yet I felt hot tears come when Dolly confirmed it all so matter-of-factly. I went outside on the steps of the hospital, where a young nurse in a blue cape offered me a cigarette. She was plain, ginger-haired and rosy-cheeked, with a Bronx accent and buckteeth. She was off duty and her boyfriend had failed to show. We talked over a cup of coffee in the cafeteria, and she said she would wait for me while I went up to see my grandfather. My father was in the hospital corridor and did not notice me. Dolly was arguing with the private nurse in the lounge. Nate was a skeleton in an oxygen tent, the sheet clinging to his emaciated body like puppet clothes. Aaron was there, a tragic ghost in the shadows, saying, 'He asked for you, Jay.'

'I couldn't get here any faster, Uncle Aaron.'

'Go by his feet, where he can see you.'

I remember trying to talk. Nate opened his eyes once or twice, but I don't think he recognized me. Aaron put his arm around my shoulder and wept. The nurse led us out of the room. My father and mother had disappeared. Aaron gave me fifty dollars and told me to go home and get some sleep. Home then was Dolly's apartment, where I took the Bronx nurse, who was popeyed at the luxury. Around five in the morning my mother called from the hospital to say Nate had died. He was fifty-six, had made his fortune and been very good to all of us. I remember trying to explain some of that

40

to the girl who relieved me of my virginity. And I remember her saying, 'But what does that make you?' It is a question I am not sure I can answer yet.

'What I have to say,' O'Hare was saying, 'may be irrelevant now that the papyri are gone. But because Vagan formally refused museum support to Lanholtz, everything was carried out under my name. Legally, what was stolen belonged to me.' Before I could speak, he raised one hand imperiously and said, 'Please, let me finish.'

I thought of Aaron's confidence that he could win a dispute in an Israeli courtroom and I wondered. Ramsay O'Hare seemed to have all the resources of a tough adversary.

'The point,' O'Hare continued, 'is not the ownership of these treasures. Frankly, it never would have come up if Vagan had not been such a horse's ass. I wasn't asking for anything in return for the financial help I gave Victor. And as I told him, I was prepared to put up more to see the exhibit properly displayed. What I wanted to tell you is I'll still do that if the collection is recovered. In fact, as a memorial to him I might even consider setting up a trust that would take care of the major financial responsibility.'

'That's a very generous gesture,' I said.

'There's one condition,' O'Hare said. 'I won't do it as long as Vagan is in charge.'

'You're not serious.'

'Think about it. I'll put the offer in writing for your board, minus the condition.'

'You don't have to. We would not fire anyone under that kind of pressure.'

'Even after the mess he's made?'

'You must realize that by making it a condition, you make it impossible for us to accept. Which doesn't strike me as a legitimate offer.'

O'Hare patrolled the room like a Doberman. He was used to having his own way and having it quickly. 'Let me put it differently, then,' he said gently. 'Why throw it in the street for the sake of a single employee?'

'However you put it, we'd have to reject it.'

'In that case, the question of ownership could raise its ugly head again,' O'Hare said coolly. 'If the scrolls are recovered, I might be persuaded to offer both the collection and the money elsewhere. I don't say that as a threat, just a possibility.'

'I'm inclined to take it as a threat.'

'Suppose you investigate things a little more carefully before you decide.'

'Why the overkill on Lev Vagan?'

'In all conscience, I could not consign Victor Lanholtz's best work to the hands of a man he despised,' O'Hare said solemnly. 'It's that simple.'

'Is that why you asked Nicoletta Calvi to withdraw Lanholtz's paper from the congress?'

'She told you, did she?' O'Hare rubbed his jaw thoughtfully and shook his head. 'I was trying to keep her from embarrassing Victor. There's some stuff in that paper that frankly seemed half-baked to me. I told him so. Even suggested he might cut one or two sections before he presented it. He was going to think about it, but he never had the chance.'

'What sort of stuff?'

'Frankly, I thought he was trying too hard to read into the material things that weren't there.'

'Such as?'

He shrugged. 'Victor was a great paleographer, maybe the greatest of all time. Let's just say his imagination seemed to be getting the better of him toward the end.'

'Not having read the paper, I have no idea what you are talking about.'

'It's all academic anyway. No pun intended.' O'Hare laughed. 'I think it's wise for that girl to stay away from high-powered conferences where she'll only make a fool of herself.'

'She didn't strike me as the kind of woman who ever makes a fool of herself.'

O'Hare's glance was elaborately expressionless. 'Maybe not. The old man had good taste. She's decorative. But if she wants her grant continued, she'll stay put. If you recover the papyri we can always find someone to review Lanholtz's work and present the whole thing in the right light at a later date.' I started to smile and O'Hare looked puzzled.

'You may not like Vagan, but for a moment you sounded just like him.'

'I never said he was dumb,' O'Hare observed, 'only that he's a damned nuisance.'

At seven I called Nicoletta's apartment, but there was no answer. I waited half an hour, and on the second call the line was busy. At the hotel desk the concierge told me the address was no more than a ten-minute walk. It took me twenty minutes because I made a wrong turn off the Kikar Plumer, but I finally found the place, one of those modern eight-storey apartment buildings in white stone that have become a feature of the Jerusalem skyline since the Six-Day War. I rang and her voice told me to come to the top floor.

The door was open when I arrived; it was, in fact, nearly ofs its hinges and Nicoletta was studying its splintered frame with a bearded man in Jordanian headdress. 'Come on in, Doctor,' she said cheerfully. 'As you can see, I've been ripped off.'

Books were everywhere, but most of them had been thrown there by whoever had done the job on her apartment. The Arab building manager was in a state of shock. He could only look at the shattered door and shake his head until Nicoletta finally pointed him toward the elevator and suggested he wait downstairs for the carpenter he had called.

'Would you like a drink,' she said, 'if they didn't steal that too?'

'Scotch, thanks.' I followed her to the kitchen and got the ice tray out while she brought the bottle.

After we sat down, she said calmly, 'The Lanholtz paper is missing. Tells us something, doesn't it?'

'It tells us we should call Inspector Berman.'

'I did that. He asked me not to touch anything, but I doubt the thieves were considerate enough to leave a forwarding address. Sometime today, perhaps while you and I were talking, Dr. Lanholtz's killers were having a field day in my house.'

'Why do you say that?'

'Put it together. They did.'

'Was it a clean sweep?'

'Not quite. They must have left in a hurry.'

'Can you reconstruct the paper from notes?'

'Not in time for the congress, if that's what you're thinking.'

If someone was determined to steal the scrolls and the gold artifacts and sell them back, I could understand how Victor Lanholtz came to be murdered. But if the murderer was also trying to prevent the publication of Lanholtz's data, we were in worse shape than even Inspector Berman guessed.

He arrived smoking a pipe, his short hair still damp from combing. His face, sad as an old clown's, reminded me more of a cartoon character than any real-life policeman, adding a faintly comic dimension to that early-evening moment high above Jerusalem. Nicoletta sat cross-legged on the raffia rug as Berman circled the room. Nothing surprised him, certainly not my presence in the apartment and apparently not the theft of Nicoletta's papers either. I expected him to offer some Milwaukee platitudes, but he said nothing for a while. No questions, no observations – nothing.

Two uniformed policemen entered a few minutes later, followed by a wizened man in a rumpled linen suit who carried a doctor's bag. Berman introduced them all formally. The last man was Berman's technician in residence, who took pictures with a battered Contax, dusted for prints and hummed mindless snatches of old musical-comedy songs as he worked.

Nicoletta's spidery sofa bowed noticeably under Berman's weight. He declined the drink she offered before the questions began. When had she arrived? Had she moved anything? And so on. The building manager soon returned with another Arab, who carried carpenter's tools. There was a lot of conversation in Hebrew and Arabic before Berman's investigator finally said they could begin to patch up the door. Then the carpenter seemed upset because he could not do a proper job without taking the door to his shop, while the manager seemed to be insisting the work be done on the spot. Berman did not comprehend much more of it than I, but Nicoletta entered finally as arbiter and I was surprised at her skill. In a minute the Arab carpenter was at work and the Israeli detective was shaking hands with the building manager. When she returned to her place on the rug facing Berman, he said, 'You ever want to change jobs, Miss Calvi, we got a place for you in the Foreign Ministry.'

'After what happened today, I'll take it,' Nicoletta said.

'Let me ask you something,' Berman said. 'What's in that

research paper that would make somebody commit two robberies and a murder?'

'I can't possibly imagine,' Nicoletta said.

'Describe it,' Berman said.

'The first part is general information on the dig. The section on the papyri is longer. Thirty pages of commentary and analysis, in addition to the translated texts of several scrolls and codices.'

'Is that the part Dr. Vagan doesn't like?'

'He has not read any of it, so I don't see how he could have an opinion.'

'What kind of analysis?'

'Well, there's the physical chemistry, which includes a summary of the Oxford University report on the carbon-14 dating.'

'A chemical analysis of the paper?'

'Of the papyri; at least of some fragments and the ink and also one container, a kind of linen sleeve.'

'What else?'

'Commentary on the exhibits included in the body of the paper.'

'What sort of commentary?'

'Dr. Lanholtz's observations.'

'All the scrolls were written in Latin, weren't they?'

'Most were. A few of the papyri were blank, with no writing at all. Others were in Greek.'

'You read those languages?'

'Yes.'

'And Hebrew and Arabic too?' Berman asked.

Nicoletta nodded. 'I speak Arabic,' she said. 'I don't read it very well. Hebrew I can read, but I'm afraid I don't speak it correctly.'

'Neither do I,' Berman said, 'and I been here twenty years. How many other languages you know, Miss Calvi?'

'Ancient or modern?'

'Sorry I asked,' Berman said, and Nicoletta smiled. 'Look, I'm going to leave a man here in the building for a few days. I doubt they'll come back, but let's not take any chances.'

'That's considerate of you, Inspector, but I think they got what they were after.'

Berman turned to me. 'How about you, Doctor? You haven't said a word since I came in the door.'

45

'You said it all,' I told Berman.

'This changes things, but maybe you'll still hear from the ones who got the originals.'

'I wish I had your optimism.'

'It makes up for my lack of information,' Berman said, rising to leave.

When the police were gone, I stood on Nicoletta's small balcony looking out at the Jerusalem night. The carpenter still pounded and scraped on the apartment door. Nicoletta brought him a cup of tea when he finally had the door back in place and I heard them behind me, chatting in Arabic. But the night held my interest. The theatrical quality of the view compelled attention. Off to the left, floodlights played on the Zion Gate of the old walled city behind David's tomb, and the stones glowed warm and golden against the purple evening shadows. The windows of the Intercontinental Hotel across the shallow Kidron Valley were alive with light, and beyond them I could see the Mount of Olives, not a mount at all but a rock-strewn hillside slashed by occasional swaths of moving headlights on the road to Hebrew University. How many Jerusalems lay below that balcony; the litter of millennia strewn like so much cast-off stage scenery after the show has changed. Judeans, Romans, Franks, Turks; all of them and more had had their season. David, Solomon, Christ, Herod and Ben-Gurion played their roles here. Sacred to three religions and profaned by all, this complex jumble of stone was mute witness to centuries of suffering and survival. If sanctity can be conferred by sword and fire and artillery shell, surely there is no holier city. And if the real measure of man's relation with his gods is felt in the siege engine or the spear's thrust, if it is written in the ashes of martyrs and the blood of innocents, then here is where that measure might be found. In the ritual sobbing of old Jews at the wall one hears it still, current and contemporary, a lament for the picked-over bones of the world. Despair, where death has been the norm, and peace the great exception.

I was aware of the faint scent of perfume. When I turned, Nicoletta stood beside me with a fresh drink. I saw she had made up her eyes and put on a long skirt. The carpenter was gone, the door repaired.

'Aceldama,' Nicoletta said, pointing to a stretch of rubble-covered ground not far from the building. 'The Field of Blood. They say the Temple priests bought it with the thirty pieces of silver Judas returned after the betrayal. I suppose that makes it the most tragic piece of ground in the Christian world, and one of the cheapest.'

'After Gethsemane.'

'I can't tell you anything, can I, Doctor?'

'You can tell me you've changed your mind about having dinner this evening.'

'Is that why you're sad?'

She had a way of cutting to the quick, which now brought an embarrassed laugh from me. 'It shows?'

'It's the place, isn't it? They say a little hope was born here too, occasionally, if you believe in hope.'

'I believe.'

'I'm not keen on being alone tonight, Jay.' Her eyes narrowed as she smiled. 'But you know that.' She put her hand through my arm, gripping it lightly. 'I can't pretend I'm not frightened by what happened. Will this afternoon be the end of it?'

I looked down at her. She was silent for a long time before she said, 'Remember I told you about Professor Merle in Paris? Victor sent him an early draft of the paper several months ago for his remarks. It was substantially the same as the final one.'

'He still has it?'

'He never returned it.'

'Does anyone else know?'

'I don't think so. Why?'

'Whoever's been tearing up the pea patch here might find it worth a trip to Paris.'

She looked at me in alarm. 'You don't think he's in any danger?'

'We've had enough surprises. Do you have his address?'

'Jay, if I could get the copy back, I think I could revise it in time for the congress. Once the paper is entered into the proceedings, the whole thing is out in the open.'

'What makes you think that's a good idea?'

'I thought we agreed it was. No one would have to know what I'm doing.'

'So far, their sources seem to be pretty good.'

Nicoletta sipped at her drink and looked downcast. 'Then

it means giving in. Letting his life and his work go for nothing. Because some vicious bastard has frightened us all.'

'Vicious is the key word. There are a couple of things we should do, however. Tell Berman. Then contact Merle.'

We looked out over the city for a while in silence and I was thinking that of all the puzzling discoveries I had made since coming to Jerusalem, Nicoletta Calvi was the best of them. I am not a wise man and I have spent my life in search of my own philosopher's stone. Usually I have been a coastal explorer, content to know the outline of my spirit without too many trips to the interior. As I felt the velvet presence of this remarkable girl beside me, I wondered if, after all, Aristotle had not been right when he claimed the heart was the seat of intelligence.

Late the following afternoon, Berman and I were in his dingy office, a concrete cubicle inside a large, dusty building off the Bethlehem Road. The place reeked of industrial disinfectant, which Berman did not seem to mind. He was in shirtsleeves, sitting on the edge of a battered desk, while I faced him in an uncomfortable metal chair. Two uniformed policemen worked at typewriters nearby.

Berman was in one of his moods of pensive preoccupation, with which I was becoming familiar. He was, among other things, something of a brooder. 'This won't take long, Doctor,' he said, opening the desk drawer and withdrawing a packet of letters tied by a piece of string. He narrowed his eyes and looked at me with his tough cop expression, his wide, flat features as barren of feeling as a Dead Sea shore. 'You trust this Calvi girl?'

The expression – or lack of it – intimidated me enough to cause my hesitation. 'Certainly,' I said. He continued to stare a few seconds after I spoke and I felt myself fidgeting. Then he turned his attention to the packet of letters.

'We collected these from Lanholtz's desk and from his apartment. Frankly, I don't know what the hell they're all about because they're mostly in Latin. It seems to be his private mail because his name's on the envelopes. The thing is who can we trust to translate them? You understand?'

'I'm sure you can trust Miss Calvi, Inspector.'

'You read Latin?'

I nodded. He glanced at me suspiciously and extracted

one of the letters from the packet. The envelope bore a Paris postmark. 'Can you read that?'

I opened the letter. The writing was heavy and bold, with square, jerky letters. It was written in what appeared to be a lucid mediaeval Latin, but was not easy to read. I told him so.

'Read me a little.'

I did.

'You know what it means?'

'Of course.'

'Tell me. I mean word for word.'

'Look, Inspector –'

'What's it say in English?'

' "Dear Vic: You cannot know what pleasure your ... letters bring an old friend who is these days ... laid up with the gout among his books ... suffering the pains of the damned instead of the insolent stares of his students. ..." '

'That's fantastic,' Berman said. 'That's a gift, Doctor. A gift! We don't need the Calvi girl. You can translate these letters for us.'

'What for?'

'It's all we got,' Berman said. 'Would you do that? There is nobody at the museum I can ask. And if we go to the university, that's an official pain in the ass. You understand?'

I looked at the letters doubtfully.

'It's in your interest, Doctor. If I had your gift, I'd do it myself, but I can't even read Hebrew good.'

'I'm leaving Israel in a day or two, Inspector.'

He was smiling now, almost wheedling. 'The way you rattled that off, you could do them all in an hour. If I get you somebody can you dictate the translations? First thing in the morning.'

'Why do you think they're so important?'

'Like I said –'

'I know, it's all you have.'

'Nine okay?'

The telephone rang shrilly. He ignored it. One of the officers took the call and waited for Berman to finish. He gave the letters to the other officer with instructions to photocopy everything.

He took the call – 'Berman!' – as if there were no line connecting him with the voice on the other end. A long pause. His eyes roamed the cracks in the leprous ceiling as he listened and grunted. Then finally he spoke in atrocious Hebrew, punctuated by an occasional English word. At last he dropped the telephone into its cradle. 'We been doing some checking on the people who work in your museum,' he said to me.

'Something's turned up?'

'From under a rock.' He pulled on his baggy jacket, covering the pistol he wore strapped tight under his left arm, and held the door of his office open for me. 'But we do business with anybody right now.'

'Where are we going?'

'How much time you say you got?'

'Less than an hour.'

'No sweat, Doctor.' He was steering me through a long, dismal corridor to the main stairwell. 'You ever specialize in anything like psychiatry or forensic medicine or any of those things?'

'No.' He was only making conversation to keep me from questioning him. Inspector Berman's cuteness could grate on my nerves.

'This is a funny country, Doctor. We probably got a higher level of college graduates here than in the States. Talk about Jewish achievement!' He chuckled to himself, guiding me down four flights of concrete stairs to a sub-basement. 'But we get our share of candy-asses too. Otherwise I'd be running a traffic detail – which, believe me, is dangerous work for a cop in Israel.' Our way was blocked by a steel door. Berman pressed a buzzer and an officer passed us through. We walked by a number of cells where dim, shadowy figures lurked beyond steel-wire grating. The place had more the appearance of a kennel than a jail. When we reached the end of the cells, Berman said, 'You aware of any homosexuals at the museum, Doctor?'

'That's a leading question, Inspector. Why?'

He looked at me shrewdly, appraisingly, the way a dentist looks at teeth. 'Well, you got one,' he said brusquely, 'who can't or won't pay for his fun.'

I stopped in the jail corridor, puzzled and a little annoyed. 'Inspector, you have my cooperation all the way. But I'm not interested in exploring the private lives of people who work for the Marcus Museum.'

Berman smiled reassuringly and put a hand on my shoulder. 'This freak we're going to see doesn't work there,' he said in a low voice. 'A patrol picked him up last night in a respectable neighbourhood, a little off his turf.'

Berman steered me into an office at the end of the cell row, where there was a desk and several chairs under bluish fluorescent lighting. Two more uniformed policemen occupied it. They rose when Berman entered and told one of them to bring the prisoner into the office.

He motioned me to take a chair and said, 'Don't say a thing, Doctor. He'll think you're another officer. Play along.'

The man the policeman ushered in was fat. But for Berman to call him a freak was an understatement. He was heavily made up. He wore platform shoes, tight-fitting sky-blue slacks and a matching shirt open to the waist. His mannerisms were exaggeratedly feminine and he pouted with distaste at Berman and me.

'Sit down, Charlotte,' Berman said in a friendly tone. 'Cigarette?' He held out a pack, but the fat man shook his head and looked at me. His expression was part curiosity and part flirtation.

'Who's the new boy, Berman?' Charlotte said with a lilt in his baritone.

'I'll ask the questions, Charlotte,' Berman said soothingly. 'Tell me why they ran you in last night.'

'It was a private matter,' Charlotte said. He had an accent in English that was pure East London.

'So private all the neighbours were complaining.' Berman picked up a charge sheet from the desktop and pretended to read it. 'Now, the gentleman you were beating up when the officers arrived has refused to make a complaint. But I want to know what you were doing there and why the fight.'

'If there's no complaint, why did they keep me here all day?' the fat man demanded. 'I'm supposed to be at work in two hours and I have to change.'

'Charlotte's an entertainer,' Berman said to me. The prisoner flashed a self-satisfied smile, which was even less attractive than his Kewpie doll pout. 'I didn't say there was no complaint,' Berman said in a harder tone. 'I only said the man you worked over refused to make one. I can fix that. So cut the shit.'

'You have to let me go.'

Berman just looked at the man as if he were a small dirty spot on the floor and Charlotte glanced down nervously at his red-lacquered nails. 'I was a little high,' he said finally, 'and I lost my temper.'

'Why?'

'He owed me money.'

'He claimed he never laid eyes on you before.'

Charlotte laughed. 'Don't they all?'

'Money for what?'

'Really, Berman, I don't give it away, you know.'

'That's not what I hear,' Berman said. 'I hear you're the one that pays.'

'You don't have to embarrass me in front of people,' Charlotte said, glancing at me. 'He owed me a hundred pounds.'

'How long did you know him?'

'Six months, on and off. He used to come to my place sometimes. Then, about two weeks ago, he stopped coming.'

'So you went to collect.'

Charlotte nodded.

'How'd you know where he lived?'

'He's in the phone book, baby.'

'Was that the first time?'

Charlotte hesitated, then shrugged. 'No. I was there before.'

'When?'

'Two or three times. I don't remember.'

'At his invitation or to shake him down?'

'I never go where I'm not wanted,' Charlotte said archly.

'You did last night.'

'That was different.'

I failed to see the purpose of Berman's questioning. If anyone on the museum staff was involved with the man, I would just as soon not know about it. Yet Berman was no fool, and even if he sometimes appeared a bit heavy-handed, he was as anxious as I to explore the slimmest lead to Lanholtz's killer.

'Were you there Sunday night?'

Again a hesitation. 'No.'

'Two residents in the building saw you.'

A pause. 'They're mistaken about the night.'

Berman was standing with his back turned toward Charlotte's chair. Suddenly he whirled, lithe as a cat for all his paunchy bulk, and caught the fat man's chin in his powerful grip, tilting it up and squeezing the cheeks so Charlotte's painted lips formed a frightened O of surprise. 'Listen, asshole!' Berman rasped. 'If you want to work tonight or any other night, you tell me the *truth!*' Only then did he release his grip, leaving red finger marks on the prisoner's pale face.

The policeman sitting across the room never looked up from the file he was reading.

'Maybe I went there Sunday night,' Charlotte said in a subdued voice.

'And?'

'He wasn't there.'

'What time?'

'About eight.'

'Then what?'

'Then nothing.'

'Bullshit nothing! You were seen entering his apartment.'

'I didn't take anything,' the fat man whined. 'If he says I took anything he's lying, the bitch!'

'Where'd you get the key?'

'He gave it to me.'

'I thought you said he went to your place.'

'Sometimes I went to his apartment late. Not often, because he was afraid of people finding out.'

'Some romance,' Berman said. 'What time did he come in Sunday?'

'I don't know.'

Berman turned toward Charlotte menacingly.

'I don't!' the man cried shrilly. 'I hung around until after twelve and played some records. Then I went home.'

'Without your money?'

He nodded. 'Why do you think I went back last night? The damn cheapskate.'

'You got to be more careful of your friends.'

'Can I go now?' The lilt came back into the voice.

'He didn't call you while you were there?'

'No.'

'So you had no idea where he went?'

'No.'

Berman told the police officer to bring Charlotte's things.

'My advice is forget about the money,' Berman said. 'Every business has its ups and downs. Next time hire a good collection agency.'

'You know one, Inspector?'

'Get out of here.'

The policeman returned, carrying a woman's handbag. He passed it to the fat man, who returned a receipt for it. Charlotte went through his purse to check its contents, held up a pocket mirror and gasped at his appearance.

Berman herded him out the door and closed it after him. He laughed as he came back to where I sat. 'I had to come all the way to Israel to find Charlotte, and suddenly it pays off.'

'I don't understand.'

'Lanholtz was killed Sunday night. And our boy wasn't home, where he said he was. So where was he and why did he lie?'

'I don't even know who "our boy" is, Inspector.'

He frowned. 'Sorry. It's Dr. Sherif.'

'*Sherif?* With that . . .?'

'The odd couple, aren't they? Doesn't pay to have secret vices unless you can afford them. Now, why would Sherif lie? Because he hit his colleague over the head and took the scrolls?'

I was too bewildered to reply. While I had been witnessing Berman's professional performance, Menahem Sherif's name was probably furthest from my mind. He seemed such a timid little fellow it was difficult to link him in my imagination with the man who had just flounced out the door. I asked Berman how he could be sure Charlotte wasn't lying.

'You saw him. What do you think?'

'It hurts to say it, but I think he was telling the truth.'

While Aaron was off politicking that evening with some Israeli government friends, I went to collect Nicoletta at her apartment. She was wearing a very sensuous long skirt made up of strips of different-coloured cloth, a gauzy low-cut blouse that matched part of the skirt, and a heavy gold choker formed like a serpent about her throat.

'I like it.'

A small frown of doubt lined her face. 'Is it too much? I like to dress up and hardly ever do.'

I singled out the gold choker for a compliment.

'It's a copy, but the design is four thousand years old.' She made us each a drink and said, 'I phoned Professor Merle this afternoon. He still has the paper.'

'What did you tell him?'

'That it was the only one. He offered to return it immediately, but I asked him to put it in a safe place. He said he had not spoken to anyone because Victor explained he wanted it kept quiet until the conference.'

'Good girl.'

'I'm a little afraid to trust it to the mail.'

'There are better ways. The important thing is we have a copy.'

'For the moment. Jay, suppose someone else knows?'

'Can you call him again now?'

'I can try. At this hour it should go through.'

In fifteen minutes Professor Merle was on the line. Nicoletta introduced me.

It was important to guarantee the safety of the paper without alarming the professor. I explained that I was sending someone by his home to pick it up, and that I looked forward to meeting him when I returned to Paris. He was very cordial and agreed to do whatever we thought best. I wrote down the address he gave me; it was only a few blocks from my own apartment.

After I rang off, I asked Nicoletta if she had Vagan's home number. She found it in the book and watched me suspiciously as I called him.

'Lev, the museum does business with the local branch of the Federal City of New York, does't it?'

'We have a trust account there, Jay. Why?'

'Do you know the manager's name?'

'Nelson Levy, but I'm afraid they're closed now. Is it anything I can help you with?'

'No, nothing, thanks. I may have to use their facilities while I'm here and I like to know who I'm dealing with.'

Nelson Levy was a little gruff at first, until I gave my name. Then he came across like a soap salesman. I asked him for the telephone of the bank's Paris branch. In two minutes he called me back with the private office line of the

Paris manager. So much for the power of Marcus money. As the banks in Paris were still open, I placed the call and then rang Ari Ascher and asked him to meet us at Nicoletta's apartment. I barely had the telephone in place again when Paris came through.

Ken Rolfe knew me well because I had accounts running to six figures in his branch. Although less unctuous than Nelson Levy, he was every bit as eager to please. I apologized for disturbing him, but made it clear I wished a very particular favour. I gave him Merle's address and said I wished the paper collected today, if possible by him personally. It was to be kept in the bank vault until he heard from me.

'That's all, Doctor?'

'Not quite.' I gave him my King David Hotel number and asked him to call me back as soon as he had the paper. 'If I'm not there, leave a message.'

Nicoletta freshened my drink and sat beside me. 'That was terribly efficient.'

'They're well paid for their efficiency.'

'I was talking about you and the exercise of power. Do you always get everything you want so easily?'

'No. Not always. What about you?' I put one arm around her and kissed her. Then again. Our movements were as easy and natural as if we were long accustomed to each other. I got rid of the drink and held her in both arms, feeling her cool fingers behind my neck. The downstairs buzzer sounded and she rose from the sofa with a smile to answer Ari Ascher.

On the way down in the elevator we stood apart silently. Nicoletta seeemed deep in her own thoughts. A second before the elevator stopped, she said, 'When are you leaving, Jay?'

'In a day or two.'

'I don't know why I asked.'

Ari's fiancée turned out to be as bony and sun-browned as he, with short flaxen hair and thick glasses which magnified her round grey eyes. Ari said Sarah worked as a cryptographer for the Ministry of Agriculture.

'There's no such thing.'

'Don't tell her.' He insisted on a roundabout tour on the way to a Yemeni restaurant in the old city, pointing out places of interest for my benefit. We passed through the Geula Quarter, where most of the Hasidic Jews live, and I saw banners spread across the streets between telephone poles.

'Do they say what I think they say?' I asked Ari, and both girls burst into laughter.

'Death to the pathologists,' Ari said.

'It's not quite that bad,' Nicoletta said. 'I would translate it *"Down with* the pathologists".'

'Down with pathologists, Zionists and Communists,' Sarah added.

Along the sides of the street were groups of solemn, bearded Hasidic men, and pale, pink-lipped boys in their beaver hats and black silk caftans. Ari explained that there was a world medical conference scheduled for the city that week and the Hasidic Jews wanted the doctors barred from Israel. 'Thanks to them,' he said heatedly, 'a Jew can't marry a Christian or an Arab or even a divorced Jew in this country. A widow can't remarry unless she has her brother-in-law's permission. Her *brother-in-law*, for God's sake!'

'As you gather,' Sarah said sarcastically, 'all scholarly detachment is suspended when Professor Ascher lectures on the Hasidim.'

Later, when we all went to the bar of the King David for a nightcap, I asked Ari about Victor Lanholtz. He was thoughtful and seemed to fix his gaze on some invisible point halfway across the bar. 'In a word, crazy,' he said.

'Be serious.'

'I mean it, Jay. Although he shared my views about the Hasidim.'

'Are you on that again?' Sarah said. She was sketching the floor plan of their new apartment on the back of a paper napkin for Nicoletta.

Ari smiled and lowered his voice.

'I don't know how to describe the craziness in a believable way,' he said. 'He was competent, but he carried a lot of hatred in him. One day I found some notes he left in the library. A whole list of German-Jewish names, the kind you used to have to buy in medieval days. You know, if you were rich the local baron would sell you "Goldfarb" or "Stein" or "Morgenthau." '

Sarah looked up and said, 'What does that mean?'

'What?' Ari said, surprised she was listening.

'Morgenthau. What does that mean in German?'

He sighed. 'Morning dew,' he said, 'as in the Morning Dew Plan for Germany.' Sarah resumed her conversation with Nicoletta and he continued. 'Victor's list was filled with the cheap names, the baddies. And many of them had exclamation marks at the end.'

'Such as?'

'Schweinfuss, Hass – names like that.'

'What do they mean?' Sarah asked him, not looking up from the napkin on which she was sketching.

'Schweinfuss means pig's foot and Hass means hate,' Ari said patiently. 'Anything else you want to know?'

Sarah shook her head.

'And Schleim. I remember that one. Imagine the poor sonofabitch who wound up with Schleim? Must have cost all of half a pfennig.'

Sarah was looking at him again, deadpan.

'Mucus,' Ari explained. 'Slime. That was on his list. Doodling, I suppose. I understand it. But with him that kind of thing was a lifetime obsession. What the hell. Who am I to criticize?' He took a long sip at his beer. 'It will always puzzle me, Jay, how so many people could take so much shit for so long.' Suddenly he smiled. 'Who but a Jew could have come up with that "turn the other cheek" idea?'

Ari listened to the two women for a few moments and then turned back to me. 'Israel is full of people like Lanholtz, but most, after a while, recover. I don't think Victor's scars ever healed. Whatever they were, from the war, from Germany when he was young, they were still suppurating until he died, and that's a kind of madness.'

'What made him any different from any other survivor?'

'He was born different, as I have been saying. And he seldom hesitated to talk about it.'

'You must have heard from other sources too.'

Ari nodded slowly. 'What I heard was that he escaped Hitler in the thirties and went to Switzerland. He already had an international reputation' – Ari laughed – 'as a Carolingian scholar. Did you know he wrote the definitive book on Charlemagne's relations with the papacy? Look it up. It's a masterpiece. Came out in the fifties. He returned to Germany during the war as an intelligence agent and was caught. He was a key witness at the Nuremberg trials. By that time he held a major's rank in the American army.'

'I didn't know he was American.'

'I think he was naturalized,' Ari said. 'Yeah, he was an American citizen when he came here.'

The conversation between Nicoletta and Sarah had faded again and both women were listening to us. I said, 'So far, you haven't told me anything to support the idea Lanholtz was crackers.'

'I think I know what Ari means,' Nicoletta said.

'It's damned near impossible to convey,' Ari said, 'but if you had heard him run on, you'd wonder if a few hinges weren't loose somewhere.'

'Yet he was not a fanatic,' Nicoletta said.

'I didn't mean that,' Ari agreed.

'Once at a party in Florence someone brought up the pope's decree absolving the Jews from killing Christ,' Nicoletta said. 'He grew very excited and I suppose you could say he over-reacted. I mean it was all in fun but Victor was serious. He used to insist anti-Semitism was born in the Roman Empire.'

'The thing is,' Ari said, 'when you peeled his brilliance away, he was a hard case. He regarded practically every non-Jew in the world as a kinetic anti-Semite.'

'He accepted me,' Nicoletta said.

'Inconsistency is the first mark of a madman,' Ari argued. 'Ask your medical friend.'

'It's usually the other way around,' I said, 'but I wouldn't care to list the clinical exceptions.'

'It's still a kind of paranoia.'

'You only say that because you were born here,' Sarah told him. 'My parents felt differently.'

'It's another way of thinking,' Ari said. 'I'm an Israeli and an atheist. So was my father. My grandfather was probably the last practising Jew in our family.'

'Now you're splitting hairs,' Sarah said.

'Just telling the truth,' Ari said. 'Victor was born in Germany and weaned on other people's spit and insult. I understand that. But I don't feel it.'

'Victor was an atheist too,' Nicoletta reminded him.

'Sure, but he was Super-Jew when it came to his

emotions. Otherwise he never would have come here. He had it made in America after the war.'

'Maybe he didn't think so. Would a man like that be comfortable in America, Jay?' Sarah asked.

'Let's not get into that,' I told her. 'I'm still waiting for someone to define Lanholtz's psychopathology.'

'Maybe it's like this,' Nicoletta said. 'If one accepts anti-Semitism as an irrational state of mind that sometimes becomes a mass psychosis, as in Nazi Germany, then Victor's response was sane in proportion to what provoked it.' We all waited in silent agreement. 'But when the provocation disappears and his reaction remains the same, then Ari's right. It gets a little crazy.' She felt my approval and smiled.

'All this has been on my mind since his death,' Ari said, 'because I cannot help wondering if the two were related.'

'In what way?' I asked him.

'Victor lived with the incandescent dead of all the centuries of Jewish persecution. Maybe whoever killed him was somehow involved in that too.'

There was a long silence until Nicoletta said, 'During the translation of the papyri, he kept entirely to himself. There was one period when he did not see me or talk to me for weeks. Before that we usually met daily. But he always initiated the meetings. If he didn't, I was under strict instructions to leave him alone.'

'Did the police go through his personal papers?' Ari asked.

'They have them,' Nicoletta said.

The bar was closing then and we returned to Nicoletta's. After Ari and Sarah said good night, I took her to her door. 'Will we see each other again before you leave, Jay, or do we carry on from here by telekinesis?'

'That wouldn't be very satisfactory, Nicky.'

'No,' she said, 'it wouldn't.'

She was in my arms again and after a long time she whispered, 'We can't stand here all night, Doctor.'

'No.'

'But you're not helping.'

'I thought I was.'

'Yes, you are.'

We made love in her apartment until the first pink trace of dawn appeared in the Jerusalem sky. Then we stood for a while on her balcony, looking over the old city, where the Dome of the Rock glistened bright gold in the sharp morning air. The loudspeaker voice of a muezzin called the Moslem faithful to prayer.

'Such short acquaintance,' she said huskily.

'What are you doing for breakfast?'

Nicoletta laughed. 'Careful, Marcus. Don't lose that extraordinary detachment I so like about you.'

'I think I lost it several hours ago.'

'But we don't really know when we'll see each other again, do we?'

'On the plane?'

We went back inside and it was after eight when I finally returned to the King David, where the Paris bank manager's message awaited me. The paper had been collected from Professor Merle and placed in the vault.

FOUR

When I entered the suite, Aaron was having breakfast, his face buried behind the pages of the Jerusalem *Post*. 'It's a good time for a war,' he said after I had ordered some coffee from room service and joined him. He lowered the newspaper and lit one of his cannon-size cigars. He was wearing a voluminous burgundy-coloured dressing gown and could have been cast for a role in one of the old Hollywood romantic comedies his clients used to produce. When I told him this he only grunted.

'Why so gloomy?'

'As Mr. Pickwick said, "I am ruminating on the strange mutability of human affairs." Last night my hosts were about evenly divided. One man, high up in the Labour Ministry, claims there's no chance of anything but stepped-up guerrilla attacks before the end of the year. His opposite, high up in the Defence Ministry, seems to think the Egyptians are getting ready again to swallow Israel now that the Russians have replaced the weapons they lost in the Yom Kippur War.'

I sat across from him as the waiter arrived with more coffee and some soggy croissants. 'What do you think?'

'What do I know?' Aaron said. 'Can you imagine two Israeli officials arguing like that on the eve of the Six-Day War?'

'Are you implying we're on the eve of another one?'

'Aren't we always? There was even talk the Americans might start it to get back the Persian Gulf oil. But I go along with the Labour Ministry guy. The Arabs won't try anything until they think they've got Israel whipped before they start.'

I discovered I was ravenously hungry and began gobbling the croissants. Aaron told me the King David served a good English breakfast if I wanted one. The skeletal remains of two kippers glistened on his plate as testimony.

'Can't be more than a thirty-day war,' he said.

'Which Israel wins?'

'If you call it winning.'

'With American help.'

'How else?'

'Then why worry?'

'I only worry about the Marcus Museum, and why you had to put it in the middle of a battlefield.'

'I take back what I said about Hollywood. You're sounding more like Aaron Marcus every minute.'

'Very funny,' Aaron said. 'You should appreciate how much it means to me to have a witty relative so far from home.'

'I was minding my own business in Athens when you pulled every sentimental stop to bring me to this battlefield. Remember?'

He raised his cigar admonishingly. 'A great-nephew should show respect for his elders,' he said. 'It is written. Tell me what you know this morning you didn't know last night?'

'You're prying.'

'I'm family,' Aaron said, 'so how can I pry?'

'You want to know where I was all night.'

'I'll admit I'm curious. For a man who was happy in his Greek sea bed a few days ago, you made the transition okay.'

'I was with Inspector Berman.'

'You can do better than that.'

'Right. I was walking down the street when this

62

stupendous, sexy Arab girl came up and asked me if I knew her cousin who lives in Syracuse.'

Aaron chuckled. 'You sound like Nate. Boy, I'm getting senile. Sometimes there's a way you talk, or some gesture or something. Like your grandfather when he was your age.' His smile faded and he said, 'That's it. Take me out and shoot me. If that's not senility, I don't know what is.'

'You're going to give me a complex.'

'They say genes skip a generation. God knows, your father never reminded me of anybody.'

'You once told me he reminded you of Warren Harding.'

'You remember that?'

'I remember everything.'

He nodded thoughtfully. 'That's one of my problems too. I could write you a season-by-season report of what's happened to me since 1910. The trouble is your body gets old, but not your brain. But how would a forty-year-old kid understand that?'

The telephone interrupted us and the hotel operator said there was a police officer on the way up. For a moment or two I wondered why until I recalled Berman's promise to send someone over for my dictated translation of Lanholtz's correspondence.

While I waited for the officer to arrive, I told Aaron about my meeting with Berman. His only comment was that Dr. Sherif naturally lied to cover his bizarre personal life. I was inclined to agree.

'Is Berman going to have another talk with him?'

'He may have arrested him by now.'

Aaron grunted. 'We come here to see some scrolls. Instead we get robbery, murder and gay lib.'

'Two robberies,' I said.

'How is the young lady holding up, by the way? This must be as tough on her as anybody.'

'Between Ramsay O'Hare and Lev Vagan, she has her problems. But I don't think they're anything we can't resolve.'

'Do I infer a personal reference?'

'You do insofar as paying her expenses to the Oxford conference, where she will present Victor Lanholtz's paper.'

'Vagan told me there was no paper.'

'I'll tell you all about that later.'

63

The buzzer was ringing and I went to let in a boyish-looking officer whose identification said he was a detective second grade named Suriel. He was carrying the packet of Lanholtz letters. I invited him to sit down and told him we could begin in a minute. Aaron was on his feet, and after greeting the young man gruffly, said to me, 'You better tell me now. I got to see Vagan in half an hour and don't want to put my foot in it.'

'You won't put your foot in it because you won't tell him anything. The girl doesn't have the paper; it's in Paris. She'll be going there to get it and then to England.'

'I love it!' Aaron said. 'What does Berman say?'

'He's enchanted. He even promised to give me the names of some reliable private detectives before I leave.'

Aaron went off to his own end of the suite in a much better humour. Only once did he return to interrupt my dictation to Detective Suriel. He put his head in the doorway and said, 'Was it her idea or yours?' When I only smiled, he said, 'You can't fool me. It was probably Berman's.'

The translation went quickly. Few of the letters were long. Most were from Professor Merle, with two or three from other colleagues; mainly shoptalk between scholars. Merle had a habit of switching from Latin to Greek and sometimes to French. His Greek often baffled me. When it did, Suriel simply left a blank space or used the original words in brackets.

In less than two hours we had nearly reached the end of it. After struggling through a particularly long letter from Professor Kittering of Oxford, detailing the process of thermoluminescence,* I was ready to quit. Then I came to the one interesting piece in the entire collection. Apparently Berman had not noticed it, because it was tucked between two others. It was an unmailed letter from Victor Lanholtz to Merle.

The officer sat with his pen poised, ready to jot down my words, but I became too absorbed in the letter to continue dictating. This was my first personal acquaintance with the dead man. Here, in this one letter, Lanholtz at last was speaking for himself, and on a subject very close to his heart.

*A method developed at Oxford for precise dating of ancient pottery, based upon the principle that reheated clay releases a measurable flow of electrons from radioactive trace elements.

His calligraphy intrigued me, the letters rounded with an almost feminine quality in the full loops and long curving sweeps. It was an egotist's writing, to be sure, with a feeling for form and a sense of its owner's confident superiority expressed in every graceful, swiftly written phrase. His Latin had an elegance of style which that of his correspondents never approached. My own knowledge of the language is academic and workaday; in Victor Lanholtz's case, Latin was a formidable instrument of precise communication. Reading the dead man's unposted mail came as both a pleasure and a shock.

'I won't try for a translation of this one,' I said to Suriel. 'Just a synopsis of its contents.'

'Whatever you say, sir.' He was poised, alert and seriously professional. When I asked him if this was his regular police function, he smiled politely. 'I'm with the Tel Aviv fraud division.'

'They loan you to Inspector Berman?'

'We like a change of pace once in a while.' There was a note of enthusiasm in his voice.

'Do you think we'll recover anything?'

'I certainly hope so, sir.'

'But you're not optimistic.'

Detective Suriel smiled apologetically.

'I'm not planning to quote you to Inspector Berman,' I told him.

He reddened a little and looked down at his notebook.

'Were you present when most of the people from the museum were questioned?'

He nodded.

'Did you get the impression any of them were lying?'

His blush seemed to deepen.

'I know about Dr. Sherif,' I said.

'Yes, sir.'

'Do you think he was the only one?'

'People try to protect their reputations. They don't always realize it would be better to tell the truth from the start.'

'What people?'

'We have no proof anyone was lying except Sherif.'

'Do you think Dr. Vagan was telling the truth?'

The question obviously embarrassed him. It would have embarrassed me too, before I read Victor Lanholtz's letter.

But I was wrong about Suriel. The answer embarrassed him more than the question. 'I had the impression,' he said cautiously, 'that he wasn't telling it all, or that he was telling it in a slightly distorted way.'

'Anybody else give you that impression?'

He was reluctant to commit himself.

'I'm only trying to clarify some of my own impressions,' I assured him.

'Dr. Lanholtz's assistant.'

That rattled me, but I skidded around it quickly with another question. 'Did you discuss this with Inspector Berman?'

'No, sir. The inspector doesn't solicit opinion, as you may have noticed.' He laughed. 'He says there's already more than enough of that in Israel.'

'Why do you doubt Miss Calvi's story?'

'I think she left some things out and neglected to give the correct importance to others,' Suriel said. 'Her loyalty to Dr. Lanholtz, probably, but that's an impression I got.'

'Can you give me an example?'

He shifted awkwardly in his chair. 'Well, during our first chat, I asked her if she had any copies of the material that was stolen from the museum and she said no. Then two days later somebody breaks into her place to steal something she claimed she didn't have. Maybe she forgot or maybe it was just a misunderstanding, but it shakes your faith in people.'

It was my turn to smile. 'Is that all?'

'I've been on this case from the beginning,' Suriel said. 'I never saw so much jockeying for position among people we've questioned. Most of your employees only seem to care about protecting their own shirttails.'

'You find that unusual?'

'I find it faintly disturbing in the face of what happened,' Suriel said. 'But I'm new at this kind of investigation.'

'Inspector Berman tells me you don't have a lead yet.'

'If the murderer had ascended a golden ladder and disappeared into the clouds with the loot, he could not have left a colder trail,' Suriel said flatly.

'But he didn't. He hit Miss Calvi's apartment two days after he killed Lanholtz.'

'Maybe.'

'What?'

'We don't know who hit her apartment. There seems to be a link, but I wouldn't jump to any conclusions.'

'You don't believe the two are related?'

'They could be related and still have been carried out by different people.'

'I don't follow you.'

When Suriel smiled, he looked about sixteen years old. 'I don't always follow myself,' he said, 'but I learned early that every case has its own special character, its own special smell. At least that's the way they appear when you spend all your working time with them. This one is no exception.'

'What's the smell?'

'Faintly rancid. If we put all the pieces together and caught the murderer tomorrow, I'd probably still have questions. Some of them only Professor Lanholtz could have answered. What's murder anyway? A mad minute or two often preceded by months or years of unconscious preparation. Dr. Lanholtz's life was a controversy for forty years. Probably lots of people hated him. Yet maybe the guy who killed him didn't even know his name. So looking for a motive isn't necessarily productive.'

'Go on.'

'This kind of talk doesn't sit well with Inspector Berman,' Suriel said. 'He wouldn't agree with any of it.'

'I'm not so sure.'

'He likes facts.'

'That's an American weakness. You have to make allowances for his background.'

Suriel laughed. 'He's the best cop in Israel, you know. With the best intuition.'

'What would you look for, if you lack facts?'

'I'm not sure we lack them, sir. But it takes concentration to organize them into an intelligible pattern. The same for archaeologists, I suppose. You find the unrelated pieces scattered all over the place. Then the puzzle begins. Sometimes intuition is a shortcut, but sometimes it can get you in a hell of a lot of trouble. I mean in police work. I don't know the first thing about archaeology.'

'Do you see an intelligible pattern yet?'

'I have some intelligible suspicions.'

'Any you can discuss?'

'No, sir. They're fragmentary, like the facts.'

'I understand. Inspector Berman seemed satisfied it would be very difficult to take the scrolls out of Israel. Do you agree?'

'He knows more about that than I do, Doctor.'

'But if you were a thief and wanted to get them out, how would you do it?'

'It's nearly impossible by ship or air, as he probably told you. But it might be done into Jordan.'

'How?'

'There's regular traffic back and forth over the Allenby Bridge. Fruit and vegetable sellers ... Arab workers and civil servants visiting relatives. The searches are thorough on incoming vehicles because of the terrorists, but a smart thief might manage to smuggle those scrolls out without too much trouble. Assuming he'd be willing to take the risk.'

'You think he'd be more apt to hide them here?'

'That would depend on what he wanted in the first place. And we don't know, do we?'

'No intelligible suspicion?'

'I'm afraid not, sir,' Suriel said. 'But if it was worth a murder, then we might assume they'll be careful as hell with the loot. If I were the thief, as you say, and I'd killed somebody, I wouldn't take a chance on the Allenby Bridge; I'd tuck everything away in a safe cellar in Jerusalem.'

'And that would be easy?'

'It would be a piece of cake,' Suriel said, 'in a city of cellars. Would you like to give me the synopsis of that letter now?'

I held up the letter: four pages written on both sides. 'The first part is just talk about Lanholtz's paper, which he sent to Professor Merle. The only significant fact is that Dr. Lanholtz tells Merle he also gave a duplicate to Dr. Vagan.'

Suriel stopped writing and looked up sharply. 'Vagan denies he's ever seen that paper. Why would he have lied about it?'

'Aren't you jumping to a conclusion now? Lanholtz may have failed to give the copy to Vagan. Or changed his mind.'

Suriel's rosy blush crept back again. 'You're right. But I'd like to ask him the question anyway.'

'I'd be interested in his answer myself.'

'Is that all, Doctor?'

'There's an odd quote at the end of the letter. Completely out of context. "*Qualis artifex pereo.*" '

68

'Which means?'

'Nero's last words. Roughly, "What an artist dies with me." Maybe a premonition?'

Suriel jotted it all down and I handed the letter back to him as he closed his notebook. 'That's the kind of thing gives Inspector Berman an acid stomach,' he said, shaking his head. 'Nero's last words.'

Berman was, in fact, drinking something that looked like Alka-Seltzer when I met him in the hotel bar late that afternoon. His normally dour expression had eroded since our previous encounter, and his ruddy, freckled face appeared creased with fresh disappointment. He thanked me for translating the correspondence and I complimented him on the services of Detective Suriel.

'He's a bright kid,' Berman said. 'Like all bright kids, he likes to show off, but hard work don't shake him.'

We talked about the Lanholtz paper and Berman asked me to mail him a photocopy of the one in the Paris vault.

'Did you ask Vagan again about it?'

'Same story. Claims he never laid eyes on it. I even showed him that letter. But I got another piece of news might interest you. Two of your scrolls turned up this morning.'

'My God! And you wait until now to tell me. Did you catch the murderer too, or are you saving that for later?'

'Take it easy,' Berman said. 'I been through that already with your uncle. The traffic division brought them in. They were found in a stolen car abandoned on the road to Jericho. We got Miss Calvi to take a look at them.'

'Why would the thieves leave the papyri like that?'

'Let's call it careless,' Berman said. 'They also left a tire iron that could have been the murder weapon. And cotton gloves like they wear in your museum when they're handling things they can't touch with bare fingers. The car belongs to a Tel Aviv rental agency and was stolen from the Sheraton parking lot the day of the murder.'

'You work fast, Inspector.'

'There's more. The same day as the car theft, a Volkswagen van was reported missing from a bakery here. The scrolls were found in a tray the bakery people identified as coming from their van.'

'Two scrolls, you said?'

'Undamaged, according to Miss Calvi.'

'What luck.'

'Let me give you a scenario,' Berman said. 'They were driving to Jericho from Jerusalem on the night of the murder, with the stuff loaded in the two vehicles. When the car quit, they shoved it into a wadi and transferred everything to the van. Because it was dark, they missed two of the scrolls. Even left a brand-new flashlight. But they wiped the car clean, probably with the cotton gloves. Not a print on anything.'

'And no trace of the van?'

'Not yet, but we got everybody looking. It'll turn up.'

'If they didn't drive it into the Dead Sea.'

'Then it would float,' Berman said, and something approximating a smile touched the heavy lines around his mouth. 'At least we got a clearer idea of what we're up against.'

'In what way?'

'They ran out of gas, which shows they're sloppy. So what else did they overlook? That's what we got to think about. The flashlight, for example. It's one of those heavy-duty ones not sold in too many places. I got an idea it was bought for the job. No prints, but maybe some clerk in Tel Aviv or Jerusalem remembers who bought it.'

'What about Dr. Sherif?'

'We had another talk. When I told him about Charlotte, I thought the old guy would have a stroke. He was at the museum the night of the murder, maybe even the moment it happened. But he says he didn't see or hear anything. He's scared shitless Vagan will find out he's a fairy and fire him, but for us he's a false alarm.'

'I thought so last night.'

Berman shrugged. 'We got to check 'em all, Doctor.'

'I realize that, Inspector.'

'Who understands how much time you waste in an investigation? Not even the minister. I got ten open cases besides this one. You know what people like Sherif cost us in man-hours?' He glanced at his watch. 'I didn't drop by to bellyache. If I don't see you again before you leave, you need to know who you can depend on in Europe.' He fished in his pocket for his notebook and thumbed the dog-eared pages.

You understand these are only recommendations, but if you don't mind spending a little money, these people might help us.'

'I understand.'

'The best is a guy named Goff in Vienna.' He read the address, which I copied. 'Franz Goff,' he said. 'He operates out of his hat, like a magician. Tell him everything. He's straight and he gets good people. Mostly professional officers who moonlight for him, but all top-level.'

'Franz Goff.'

'Take another name. George Panagoulos, a Greek-American who lives in England. You'll find him' – again he went through his book – 'near Abingdon, which isn't far from London. It's a health farm owned by his wife. If he's not there call his London flat.'

'He hardly sounds like a detective.'

'We work with people we can trust.'

'But you recommend Goff over Panagoulos.'

Berman looked around the bar expressionlessly, almost as if he had not heard me. 'Either one can handle it, but Panagoulos is a bit of a thief.'

'What about Goff?'

'Goff's not a thief,' Berman replied solemnly.

'Tell me about Panagoulos.'

'Talented. Grew up in the States and went back to Greece after the war to help fight the commies. Worked for the CIA until they caught up with him. The CIA, I mean, not the reds. He was supposed to have a whole stable of left-wing informants. Panagoulos's little spy ring cost the Americans a fortune until some bright guy at the American embassy found out they were all related to George. He'd been pocketing sixty thousand a year on top of his salary so . . .' Berman drew a finger across his throat.

'How do you know him?'

'We use him when we can't put an Israeli on a job. He's a guerrilla expert, among other things.'

'But if you can't trust him . . . ?'

'You can. You just have to watch him or he'll screw you on expenses.'

'I see.'

'Like all Greeks, he's got relatives everyplace. Istanbul, Las Vegas – you name it. He can pass himself off as French,

71

Arab or what have you, and he's afraid of nothing except maybe one or two other Greeks.'

'But you prefer Goff.'

Berman shrugged. 'Go with Goff if he'll take the job. He may seem high, but he'll turn out cheaper.'

'And better.'

'No. Just different. Panagoulos will bleed you for every cab fare.' His face was dark with the recollection of Panagoulos's past deceptions. 'He has no shame.'

'Goff sounds dull by comparison.'

'Maybe, but Panagoulos only kills in self-defence.'

Every family has its folkways and mine is no exception. Max and Dolly, during the eighteen-year battle they called a marriage, wrote their own separate mythologies. Dolly was sustained by her four brothers and their wives and children in the paths of her self-righteousness. Max found refuge after a couple of martinis by telling other people he could not be sure I was his son. Whatever victories they won over each other cost them the skirmish with me. Dolly retired to a Beacon Hill town house, where she plays the Boston grande dame, lording it over her relatives and running with a small retinue of burly masseurs and fey hairdressers. She is a snob and something of a fake, and what Max ever saw in her is difficult to understand. At the same time, Aaron, the most charitable member of the Jewish side of the family, acknowledges that beyond Max's money there was not much for Dolly to see in him either. My father's life revolves around the Dow-Jones averages and conservative Republican politics. And Marcus Instrument, of course. It was he who directed the company's expansion during the fifties and sixties, acquiring pharmaceutical laboratories, a perfume and cosmetics house, and a web of factories in foreign countries. The stock Nate left me is worth fifteen times what it was at the time of his death twenty-four years ago, thanks largely to Max's single-minded concentration on corporate growth.

Dolly still pretends regret that I was an only child. She can even get a little choked up on the subject of unborn grandchildren. Max never mentions such things in my presence.

Neither of them knows that Nate had a mistress during

his last years, Mae Broman, who was once a fairly well-known actress. She came to Nate's funeral on Aaron's arm, but attracted no particular attention because the service was jammed with other celebrities – senators, scientists, generals, even a few show-business personalities who had been friends of Nates.

On one of his periodic visits to New York, when I was eighteen or so, Aaron invited Mae Broman to have lunch with us. She was about my mother's age and still glamorous. She had been in semiretirement for several years (probably the years with Nate), but people still recognized her and came by our table for autographs. Aaron was trying to persuade her to do a Hollywood film at the time: Catherine of Russia or something like that. I recall Mae claiming she was too old.

'You're a natural,' Aaron insisted. 'The role covers the empress's whole life.'

'And I dislike Hollywood hours,' Mae said. 'Who wants to be up every morning at six?'

'It's a lot of money.'

Mae Broman smiled. 'You know I don't need money.' Years later I discovered Mae was a substantial stockholder in Marcus Instrument. My grandfather was nothing if not generous with those he loved. He had made Mae a million-airess.

After that memorable luncheon she invited me to walk in Central Park. Mae walked or cycled five miles a day wherever she was. She also worked out in a dance studio, saw every play in New York and London, took annual holidays in out-of-the-way places like Sarawak or Bolivia, and read a dozen books a week. I became her friend and her Sutton Place house became my New York base when I went east on holidays from college and medical school. She had been married and divorced before she met my grandfather. When I asked her why she had not married him, a widower, she said, 'We talked about it, Jay, but it was more fun the way it was.' She had several gentlemen escorts, but I think Nate was her only big love affair, and the Karsh portrait of him was the first thing that caught your eye when you entered her library. Mae was a lively storyteller and she enjoyed reminiscing about Nate. It was through her that I learned something of his early years in Denver.

The first **Marcus** surgical instrument was a bronchoscope, pirated by a manufacturer Nate had shown it to. Poorer and wiser, he worked through a Washington patent attorney after that, and the years between the two world wars saw a dazzling array of surgical gadgets that became the basis of his fortune. According to Mae, he was working on a kidney prosthesis until shortly before he died. My father cancelled the research the year he acquired the perfume company.

Mae was the one who revealed that Nate had played the violin. 'Medicine's gain was not exactly music's loss,' she said, 'but he wasn't bad for someone who took his first lesson at forty-five. He used to practise here.'

'While you listened.'

'After he improved. Not even a lover's love is strong enough to embrace a student violinist before he's learned the vibrato.'

Mae is the only one in my 'family' who reads my books. She is medically sophisticated after all those years with Nate and quite a sharp critic of literary style. She even joins me aboard *Kalina* for a few weeks each summer, an activity that seems to suit her inquiring mind and eternally restless spirit. In her sixties now, she is thinking about making a comeback next year in a Broadway musical.

Mae and Aaron and the ghost of Nate Marcus formed a kind of Greek chorus for much of what happened on the small stage of my adult life. When I took the plane from Lod, Aaron, as chief chorister, was talking all the way to the passenger embarkation gate.

'I'm sorry the trip turned out so bad for you, Jay. But nobody could have predicted a mess like this.'

'How long will you stay on?'

'Until Vagan opens his Gesher Tel exhibit after Yom Kippur. I'll see you in England then?'

'Don't forget to take care of the travel expenses and all that for Nicoletta. She has to leave in a day or two.'

'Stop worrying.'

'First-class ticket and a thousand for expenses. I'll pick up the slack in Paris when she arrives.'

'I'll bet you will. Will I see any more of you in Oxford than I did in Jerusalem? Nights, I mean?'

We had arrived at the luggage examination area. A pretty girl in uniform directed us to another equally pretty girl, who worked at one of a series of low counters like the check-out stand of a supermarket. Flight information was being announced on the airport loudspeaker. I slid my single suitcase across the counter, open.

'Passport and ticket, please?'

I gave them to her. She glanced at the ticket and flipped through the passport quickly, never losing her smile, but never appearing to force it either. Behind her a few feet, an armed security guard lounged with his Uzi slung from one shoulder. This was the same room in which a group of Japanese terrorists had gunned down a score of innocent Puerto Rican pilgrims three years earlier. One is never very far from violence in Israel, and yet the atmosphere belies it. These people have learned to live with terror, I suppose, because they never really had an alternative: the weekly casualties from settlements along the Lebanese and Syrian frontiers, the grim sharpshooting at the canal, the steady, slow drain of a nation's blood, like American highway accidents . . .

The girl was expertly rifling everything I owned, weighing the shaving cream, palpating the toothpaste tube. And just as expertly she left everything in order, even a little neater than she found it. The bag was sealed and checked aboard my Olympic flight for Athens. We had nearly an hour before the flight would be called and I asked Aaron if he wanted a drink.

'You got to be joking. What makes you think there's a decent bar here?'

'American-operated,' I told him. 'Follow me.' I led him through four doors, the last one marked EMPLOYEES ONLY, up a flight of stairs and down a short corridor. I rang a bell and the door was opened by an Israeli girl in uniform, freckled and as pretty as the one who'd checked my suitcase. Beyond her was a small, comfortably furnished lounge. 'Yes, sir?'

'I'm Dr. Marcus.'

'Oh, *yes*, sir.' We had the place to ourselves. The windows on the far side overlooked the apron where the jets were parked. Aaron was open-mouthed.

'All right,' he said, sinking into a huge sofa. 'I give up.'

'You like it?' Before he could answer, the girl came with drinks, a small tray of beluga grey and Melba toast.

75

'I don't believe it.'

'We're Berman's guests.'

'*Berman?*'

'It's the government VIP lounge. He called and laid it on.'

'He's got heavy influence for a police inspector,' Aaron said.

'Where it counts. The girl who brought the drinks is his daughter.'

Aaron started to laugh.

'He has five. One in the army, one in the London embassy, one a chemist, this one, and another still in school.'

Aaron was watching the girl as she talked on the telephone. 'If they're all that terrific-looking, Berman's got the most important national resource in the country.'

'But no sons, and that makes him very sad,' I said.

'He's lucky,' Aaron said. 'The man with five boys is the man I pity.'

'Or the man with none, like me,' I said.

'So get married. You're the perfect age to be a father.'

'Look at you.'

'I've been there,' Aaron said stoutly, 'three times. The first marriage didn't count. She ran off with a trumpet player in Bunny Berigan's band.'

'So you divorced her.'

'She divorced me, but the feeling was mutual. The second lasted a year. I left her. The third, Sheila, you know, or at least you know about. That lasted sixteen years and we had three kids I hardly ever saw. Now *they* have kids I see even less.'

'So get married and have another family.'

'Everything in its season,' Aaron said.

'Why didn't you marry Mae Broman after Nate died?'

'I was still married to Sheila.'

'And?'

'Mae wouldn't even marry Nate. She was the original independent woman. Not a ball-breaker like these liberation freaks today. Mae was all female.' Aaron chuckled. 'The only man ever could have handled her was Nate.'

'You're copping out, Aaron.'

'Okay. Mae and I had a little go once. I was the one introduced her to Nate. She fascinated me, that girl. Still does, even though she must be a little long in the tooth by

76

now. But I was out of my depth. I couldn't even get her to do a picture I was going to produce.'

'I remember that.'

'She and Kate Hepburn are probably the only two women I was ever in love with,' Aaron said pensively.

'Forget the three wives?'

'Passing fancies. Mae still turns me on. So does Katharine. They smile and I melt. That's why I never made it.'

'You lost me.'

'Women like that recognize the reaction and lose interest. That's what it means, boy, when they're absolutely female. They don't want marmalade. They want macho.'

'You telling me you're not?'

'Don't be a smart-ass, nephew. I'm telling you I melt. And if you melt you can't dominate because you're lying if you tell them anything is more important than they are.'

'How do you think Nate managed it?'

'Nate loved her. That was a great love affair, if there ever was one. A great love affair. Make a helluva film, their story. She never went near his bed when he was dying. But she sent him a letter every day. I read them all to him. She didn't want to embarrass the family. It was me talked her into coming to the funeral.'

'She told me they talked about marriage.'

'Nate wanted to marry her. He must have proposed on a monthly basis for years. Mae was the one always held off.'

'What did Nate do that was different from you?'

'It's not what he did,' Aaron said. 'It's what he was. Nate loved her, really loved her. But he didn't melt. She didn't make him forget everything else in the world. Only his work did that.'

'Marcus Instrument?'

'I said his work. He never gave a shit about Marcus Instrument or any other business. He hired people to look after that, and he had your father, who did a better job, some say, than all the hired men. All Nate cared about was inventing. You know how many patents he had? Over a thousand. Legitimate, certified U.S. patents for ideas he had that nobody else ever did. Nate couldn't look at a cloud without thinking how he could make it better than the Almighty. Jesus, when I think of what that man would have

77

done if he'd lived. You think of him as old because he was your grandfather and you were only a kid. But he wasn't even sixty when he died and his mind running like a motor until the end. Just the other day I saw an article about the new Carnegie Hall electronic organ, which duplicates all the sounds of a symphony orchestra. Well, Nate was even into that kind of thing. "Aaron," he used to say to me, "we're getting better. People are getting better. This is the first time we got a chance to solve everything." He really believed that. After fifty thousand years of fucking around, the human race at last had a chance of making it, as far as Nate was concerned. I am a cynic about such things and I never tired of telling him so, but Nate always brushed that kind of talk aside. He used to say if he could live a hundred years, he could live a thousand, because he'd sure find out in the first hundred how to survive nine hundred more.'

'They've announced your flight, Dr. Marcus.' Berman's charming daughter smiled down at us. Aaron drained his glass and smiled back.

'Why don't you have another one,' I suggested. 'I hate long goodbyes.'

He looked from me to the retreating figure of Berman's daughter. 'Maybe you're right,' he said. 'I didn't even ask her name.'

'I'll see you in England.'

'Stay out of Arab air space, Jay.'

'Her name, by the way, is –'

'I'll find out her name as soon as you beat it.' I was closing the door behind me when I heard Aaron say, 'Miss Berman, do you suppose you could find another dollop in that bottle for a thirsty traveller?'

FIVE

There is a Paris for almost every taste, and perhaps that is the city's real claim to survival. Hitler, they say, wept with joy at the news his armies were entering Paris. Napoleon, walking the barren moors of St. Helena, is said to have remarked, 'It is not France I miss, but Paris.'

My Paris is a cluttered universe of noisy traffic and musty

bookshops, crowded cafés and draughty lecture halls. I have never passed a summer in the city. I know the winter town, where it rains a lot, where the smell of wet wool rises from the seats in the amphitheatre as I lecture on Galen, on surgery in the Roman legions, on the medical school at sunny Epidaurus. Paris is a thimble cup of bitter black coffee at a stand-up bar on a cold day where the red-knuckled barman rubs his chilblains, sips his *vin rouge* and gives me tips on the day's races. Paris is where I crouch in winter. Odéon, a block from my apartment, is a metro stop on the Boulevard St. Germain. Carrefour de l'Odéon, which arrives at Place Danton after running down a short hill from the National Theatre, also ends fifty yards from my apartment, off the Cour de Rohan, in one of the last quiet corners of seventeenth-century Paris.

It is a conceit, but I see myself there sometimes living in the age of Pascal, playing my insulated role as Renaissance man. For someone whose tastes are simple (and mine lamentably are), Paris is still the sweetest place on earth to spend a winter. The bread is rich; the girls are pretty; the wine, if one buys carefully and early, is good still. My Spanish housekeeper pampers me. As do the butcher and the grocer. Breton oysters arrive by plane. The artichokes are tender as violets. Chicken and cheese and eels and beefsteak take on an aesthetic importance they have nowhere else in the world. The maître at the Méditerranée, a serious fellow doing a serious job, telephones when he has sole from Lesconil or trout from the Pyrenees.

There have been love affairs along the way. One, with the wife of a television producer, endured a memorable three years, and ended as abruptly as it had begun, by mutual consent. The others were mostly liaisons of convenience: warm, comfortable, short and often sweet. Friendships: a couple of faculty colleagues and their wives, an American painter, an Italian architect, a French film producer. Archaeology buffs all. Sailors or divers who sometimes join me in the work aboard *Kalina* each summer.

I arrived at Orly after two days in Athens attending to some details on the boat, and our descent through the smoggy overcast made me nervous as usual. Zero visibility down to a few feet above the runway. A light drizzle as I left the plane and moved inside the terminal with the other passengers. Fast French service through to the taxi stand and then a typical Parisian charmer behind the wheel who grouched all the way to the Carrefour de l'Odéon.

The ancient wooden floors of the apartment gleamed with the pleasant-smelling lemon wax Nelida uses on just about everything. Fresh flowers were on my desk, the coffee table and the old carved marble mantel. Fat Nelida was there to welcome me home, gold teeth flashing in a broad smile as she chattered in her best Barcelona French about everything that had happened in the neighbourhood since May. She had cold jellied tongue for me to eat in the library while I went through the stacks of mail that had accumulated over the summer. I telephoned the bank and left a message for the manager to call me.

In the heap of magazines, newspapers, book catalogues and junk that littered the study, I found Victor Lanholtz's letter. It was direct, polite, hopeful and short. He asked for an opinion on one of the papyri found at the Caesarea dig, a copy of which he enclosed. He detailed the now familiar circumstances of the find, the cellar, the amphoras, the surrounding objects, and briefly summarized some of the other scrolls found in the same packet. I began to read the papyrus copy with interest, charmed by the clear Latin script and style of the writer. Lanholtz wanted to know if I had ever come across anything like it before.

The first few pages formed part of a treatise on medicaments which recommended the use of hellebore and aloe purgatives – familiar stuff from the Encyclopaedist school of early Roman medicine. Abruptly this terminated, and the following section dealt with the antisepsis of wounds with thyme, pitch, turpentine and arsenic. Again there was a familiar ring to the prose and the contents, but I could not have identified it until I was near the end. There, in a description of fevers, appeared the sentence: '*Notae vero inflammationis sunt quatuor, rubor & tumor, cum calore & dolore.*' Beautifully written, beautifully copied. Words that ring down through two thousand years of medical practise, still repeated by the medical student today when he learns: 'The signs of fever are four, redness and swelling, with heat and pain.' I went to the bookshelf and brought down my edition of Celsus, printed by Pope Nicholas V in the fifteenth century. I found the page and the passage. Celsus, the first-century Roman Encyclopaedist, had written one of the great books on medicine, which was rediscovered in the Renaissance and published by the good Pope Nicholas. And Victor Lanholtz had found what looked like part of another Roman copy in his dig at Caesarea. I was poring over the different pages, forgetting Nelida's lunch, when the telephone rang.

'Dr. Marcus?' A pretty-girl voice.

'Speaking.'

'Mr. Rolfe on the line.'

'Dr. Marcus? Ken Rolfe speaking. Sorry I wasn't in when you called earlier.'

'It was about the manuscript you collected from Professor Merle.'

'It's on ice, as ordered,' Rolfe said.

'Could you have two photocopies made? Send one to Inspector Shmuel Berman by registered mail.' I gave him Berman's address. 'And the other to me at home.'

'We'll have them for you in an hour. Anything else?'

'I need a couple thousand francs.'

'I'll send it with the messenger. Shall I make out a bank cheque for you to sign or would you prefer to write your own?'

'I'll do it. Otherwise I lose track.'

I went back to Celsus, wondering where the original Roman manuscript was, from which Pope Nicholas got his edition. Early afternoon in Paris is not the best time to start asking. Those who know are eating leisurely Parisian lunches and seldom return to their libraries and bookshops before four. Except Hippolyte Mansour, who eats his own gargantuan Arab meals in the back room of his shop on the Rue Racine. I rang Mansour and was about to hang up, when his gruff basso came on the line. When I told him it was I, returned in the flesh from my Grecian summer, his voice ran up the scale to Arab falsetto. 'I have a book for you, a beautiful book for you. I was thinking of you this morning and saying to Coco, "Wait until Marcus sees what we have for him." Are you well, my dear?'

'What is it?'

'Let it be a surprise. Can you come now? We have halvah and coffee. Have you eaten?'

I told Mansour that I had, in order to avoid his overwhelming hospitality. 'I'll pass by around four. I have something to show you too.'

'Something you bought in Greece? And paid too much for? Why do you deal with thieves and charlatans when you have Mansour?'

'Remember the Celsus you sold me several years ago?'

'One does not forget the milestones of one's life,' Mansour said. 'Why?'

'I've come across another.'

'You did not buy it, I hope,' Mansour cried. 'It's probably a forgery. There are only seven copies in the world and I know where each one is.'

'I didn't buy anything, Hippolyte. I'll tell you about it when I see you.'

During the next hour, I answered a few minor questions about the Celsus Papyrus from other references in my own library, already crowding me out of what used to be a rather spacious bachelor apartment. The doorbell rang at one point and Nelida entered, carrying a fat manila envelope and a receipt book. 'A messenger says he has two thousand francs for you.'

I signed the receipt, wrote the cheque and told her to give the messenger a five-franc tip. She went out grumbling about my extravagance while I ripped open the envelope to find the stack of photocopies. They were a little blurry in spots, but readable. What I had was at least a third generation of Lanholtz's first draft. Not including the ten papyrus scrolls, the whole thing ran nearly a hundred pages. I settled into one of the overstuffed chairs near the window that looks out on my courtyard, and began to read. I was still reading, quite a time later, when Nelida reappeared to say Mansour was on the telephone and wanted to know if I was coming or not.

When I left the apartment, the weather was still grey and raw, the pavements slick from the drizzly haze. I turned up the Rue de l'École de Médecine to where it intercepts the Boulevard St. Michel, then doubled back on the Rue Racine to Mansour's shop, a long block of stores actually, all barred like a jail front, with the enormous gilt signboard that reads: M. MANSOUR & FILS – LIVRES – ENCHÈRES. The business had been founded in Damascus by Hippolyte's great-grandfather, moved to Paris after the Franco-Prussian War by his grandfather, nearly bankrupted by his playboy father, and run by Hippolyte and his daughter, Coco, for the last twenty years.

I rang and Coco let me in. She is a gaunt, cheerful spinster of forty-odd, with mouse-brown hair and a clear, pale complexion; a sharp contrast to her obese father with his hypertensive skin and popping coal-black eyes. From behind her I could feel the musty breath of the place: old glue and yellowed paper, faded ink and dried-out leather. Books everywhere: on the floor, stacked literally out of sight above the last shelves where the dim yellow light reached. A great heap of books to step over and around, no order anywhere apparent. Yet to open the door Coco disengaged an elaborate series of burglar alarms which protected this chaos. For the treasure of Hippolyte Mansour is great, and it was not unusual for the old man to have a fortune in rare volumes scattered about among the lesser books he also buys and sells.

Coco preceded me, threading her way among the stacks, through two huge shadowy rooms to the office-flat Hippolyte maintains at the rear. They do not live there He owns, in fact, a stunning nineteenth-century mansion in Neuilly, which once belonged to a famous courtesan. But his business, and his heart, is in the book-jammed apartment behind the shop, where he studies his beloved volumes, reads catalogues, works out mathematical puzzles, smokes Gauloises in an endless chain (if his weight does not kill him, chronic bronchitis will) and does his deals. He seldom goes to sales anymore: Coco handles that part of the business. I believe she is the only licensed woman auctioneer in the trade, as well as an exceptionally sharp-eyed buyer.

Mansour rose with effort to greet me, wheezing, enveloping me in his great round arms and then standing back to study me with shrewd eyes. He told me I looked magnificent after my summer of so-called hard work and said he would really try to get away next year to join me, if it could do that much for a fellow. Coco made a face when I asked how his behaviour had been in my absence. The standing joke between us was that Hippolyte constantly asked for medical advice, which I gave and he never followed. 'He won't get on a scale, but I am sure he's gained ten kilos since you went away,' Coco said.

'What is ten kilos at my stage in life, I ask you?' Mansour said. 'Sit down and tell me what you found in Greece.'

'Do you know where the original of the Celsus manuscript is?'

'I know where they all are,' Mansour said.

'I mean the *original* original. The Roman scroll or codex from which my edition was copied.'

'The Vatican Library,' Mansour said. Both he and his daughter had that indispensable tool of the antiquarian book dealer, the perfectly indexed encyclopaedic mind. Between them they carried in their heads a wealth of information on editions, libraries, collections, buyers, sellers, prices and all the other pertinent arcana dealing with thousands of rare volumes and manuscripts in virtually every printed language. Mansour's own specialized knowledge of the works of the great Arab physicians and all the early translations is probably unsurpassed by any scholar anywhere, while Coco remembers virtually every price paid for important volumes at *every* sale since the turn of the century. 'The Roman original was in the Duke of Urbino's library until around fifteen hundred,' Mansour said, 'but he donated it to the church, together with two of his daughters.' He smiled at Coco and passed me a silver plate filled with soft, sugared squares of halvah. 'Probably to save his soul,' he said. I accepted one for civility's sake, although they make my teeth ache. Hippolyte popped two into his mouth and lit a cigarette. I handed him the copy of the Caesarea papyrus, telling him something of the circumstances surrounding Lanholtz's discoveries. He was immediately intrigued.

'I should like to read what he has done. Can you leave it with me?'

'Tomorrow?'

'Splendid, my dear. Now, you have not asked what I have for *you*.'

'Something very beautiful, you said, very rare, I suspect, and very expensive, I am sure.'

Coco giggled and Mansour went into his rug-dealer act, which consists of (1) the wringing of hands, (2) expressions of pained suffering, which only a dedicated aesthete such as himself could manifest at the reactions of a philistine such as myself, and (3) the final renunciation of the whole affair (a little like an actor in a silent film), which is to show me that after all his trouble and expense, I cannot question something that is practically an outright gift! According to Mansour, no illustrious forebears, not his father nor himself nor his poor unmarried daughter ever made a centime on a book transaction. They are a family of victims stranded in their Neuilly mansion since the *Belle Époque.*

'What is it?' I asked him. He raised both hands, palms upward, in a plea for mercy.

'My dear, it is better you do not know.'

'Suppose I say I am interested.'

'No. You always want to joke about my discoveries. I bought this ... I don't know why. Because I am a fool, because I am a trusting, gullible scholar who leaps before he looks. The Evel Knievel of the book business.'

'What is it?'

'You have heard of Albucasis?'

'Don't play games, Hippolyte.'

'You know then that he wrote the first independent work on surgery, the first illustrated treatise a thousand years ago –'

'*What*, goddamn it!'

'The Venetian edition I suppose you have seen?'

'You found it!'

Coco was laughing. For years, almost since I had known the Mansours, I had been after a copy of the Albucasis work. It is one of the seminal texts among early Arab medical writing and I long ago asked Hippolyte to hunt one down. I think there are supposed to be still half a dozen or so of the Latin edition around, but few in private hands. Published in Venice in 1500, a companion piece for my Celsus.

He brought it out from a pile of other volumes with the same delicacy, care and pride with which one would present a new-born child. As wily as I know him to be, and as wily as he is, he could not suppress the smile of pleasure, of triumph.

'He bought it in July,' Coco said. 'He was going to write you, but I told him to save it as a surprise.'

'You're incredible,' I said, taking the volume. It was a jewel. Leather-bound, in mint condition after nearly five hundred years – almost as old as printing itself – with brass bosses in the leather and heavy engraved hinges holding the boards.

I held it like a chalice. 'How could I quibble?'

Mansour shrugged as if the whole matter was insignificant. In a sense it was. I knew as well as he that I would pay whatever the volume was worth because I had wanted it for so long. It is part of the madness of collecting: the expensive part.

While I fondled the volume and we talked, Coco brought tiny cups of sweet black Turkish coffee. Mansour finished the plate of halvah with no help. After a while, he asked me about the Lanholtz murder. There had been an article in one of the Paris Sunday papers highlighting the theft of the gold jewellery. The papyri were not mentioned. When I told him what I knew, including the story of the second robbery to get the Lanholtz paper, Mansour suggested the museum might advertise to get back the artifacts.

'In the trade publications?'

'Among others. But I was thinking of the newspapers.'

'Where?'

'Here, London, Germany, the States.'

'Saying what?'

'That the Marcus Museum is prepared to pay a large sum for information leading to the recovery of the papyri, a sum negotiable with those who provide such information.'

'Meaning the thieves.'

'Or someone they might approach to handle the transaction. Someone like me.'

'Not someone like you, Hippolyte. There was a murder involved too.'

'Still . . . it is the sort of thing that would attract certain dealers. A clever man could collect from both parties.'

'But only an unprincipled man would get involved.'

Mansour sighed. 'I love you, Jay,' he said. 'You are the one person I know besides myself who still speaks of principles. I am having other thoughts as we speak. Suppose I took out the advertisements? It might be more attractive to the thieves. Yes, your prospects would be much improved, although the recovery might be more costly.'

'You're forgetting one thing.'

'It wouldn't be the first time, at my age.'

'The second robbery all but ruled out hope of recovering

86

much. Whoever took the scrolls went to the extra trouble of stealing the only other known copy of this research paper. They also knew who had it.'

'His assistant, you said?'

'Yes.'

'To have been Lanholtz's assistant, he must be quite a brilliant chap.'

'She. Not only brilliant, but beautiful.'

'Indeed?' Mansour was the original male chauvinist, in spite of his talented daughter.

'The police are keeping a guard on her home,' I said.

'That would seem wise.'

'She's coming here tomorrow.'

I told him of the early draft in the bank vault and our intention to have Nicoletta read it into the proceedings of the archaeological congress.

Mansour reached across a stack of volumes on the ancient table he used as a desk – the effort made him puff – and extracted a newspaper. 'Yesterday in this great city,' he said, 'there were eleven crimes of violence which the press has recorded for history.' He tapped the paper.

I asked him what he was talking about and he folded his clasped fingers over his large, round belly. A freshly lit Gauloise dangled from his lips, and smoke hung in stratified levels of blueness, filtering the yellow light that bathed the books and papers, the green felt cover on the table, and his impish, choleric face. 'My dear, the times they are a-changin', as Dylan says. We must recognize there are different kinds of criminals at work these days: the result of rising expectations, upward mobility and unlimited educational opportunity.'

'Oh, for God's sake, Hippolyte.'

'Fortunately, they are a negligible minority, or I would long since have been mugged for my books. The *common* thief would find only cold mutton in the fridge' – he raised his hand, indicating the entire establishment with a small motion – 'and a hundred francs in my pocket. The sophisticated thief would find some obviously valuable books which could be disposed of for small sums. The *bibliophile* thief could make himself rich in half an hour.'

'You're getting paranoid.'

'The volume you hold in your lap is insured for a hundred

thousand dollars. Underinsured, I should say. I advise you to correct that when you take it home. I have a copy of the policy somewhere.'

'So who do you think stole the papyri? Some frustrated antiquarian with an unlimited educational opportunity?'

'I have no idea who stole them or who killed Dr. Lanholtz,' Mansour said, 'but from what I know of the world, and what you have told me of the criminal particulars, I would bet the same people did not steal the Lanholtz paper from his assistant.'

'Why do you say that?'

He shrugged. 'Think about it.'

'I've done little else for days.'

'One is a serious archaeological disaster – a wipe-out, as the surfers say – while the theft of the scientific paper is nothing, the mischief of some embittered colleague who had nothing to do with the original crime.'

'As far as I'm concerned, all of them at the museum are suspect.'

'Including the great man's assistant?'

'No. She's the only one I would exempt.'

Mansour sat like a Buddha, half obscured by his Gauloise incense. 'I'd ask why, but I have an idea I know.'

The papyri that Victor Lanholtz reproduced and translated at the end of his paper were representative of separate groups found in the Caesarea cistern, known as Exhibits 9 through 18 of NE Sector 247, the archaeologist's designation for that part of the site. Exhibit 9 was, as Nicoletta had told me, a collection of commercial records including a household grain inventory, several wine and oil bills, and a quitclaim deed to a local orchard owned by one Gaius Longinus Procula, military tribune. Exhibit 10 turned out to be part of the same medical papyrus from Celsus that Lanholtz had sent for my comments. The surprises were tucked away in Exhibits 11 through 18. Even Nicoletta's description had not prepared me for the contents. I suppose when one is working as closely as she was with such a wealth of material, one's perspective shifts: what may seem sensational at first pales after intensive study.

The papyri were preceded by some paragraphs of Lanholtz's which described Exhibits 11 through 18 as a group of letters from the same Longinus Procula. Nine of them, including the ones he had selected as his examples, were special in that they were in codex form – paginated and arranged like a modern book – rather than rolled, as were the scrolls. Lanholtz pointed out that this was of particular interest in helping to date the find, inasmuch as the Romans were gradually changing from scrolls to the codex in the first century A.D. He also suggested that the codices were, in effect, file copies retained by Longinus for future reference. The wrapping in which Exhibit 11 had been found was carbon-14 dated by the Oxford laboratory at 50 B.C. with a possible error of 110 years. A thermoluminescence test supervised by Professor Kittering at Oxford dated the amphora at A.D. 20 with an error margin of fifty years. But the papyrus itself could be pinpointed even more precisely by its contents, very likely to A.D. 36 or 37.

This was because the writer had been so helpful. The first part of Exhibit 11 was missing and one had to read awhile to make sense of the remainder. There seemed to be pages missing as well, which sometimes left puzzling gaps in the narrative. But all in all, it was an absorbing document. It began:

. . . preoccupied with his own reputation to listen to anything I try to tell him. He is increasingly harsh towards my poor sister these past months and yesterday ordered two of her slaves flogged for loitering along the garden paths when he was returning from his swim. He often seems to lose sight of what he was before he married into our illustrious family or where he would be without the preferment bestowed upon him because of that marriage. Claudia never speaks of divorce, but I know it has been on her mind.

I have seen most of his dispatches to you, and believe me, they give little idea of the real situation here. Since the Passover disturbances, our military patrols have been ambushed in outlying villages. According to army intelligence, the Zealots still command large followings in the north. Casualties for August were two dead and four wounded, all Parthian or Greek mercenaries in our service. Luckily, no Roman life lost as yet. But weapons were stolen again and our authority challenged.

He does not see these outrages in their true social context. The Judean religion encompasses more prohibitions than you can imagine, and that is where the trouble starts. While proclaiming the divinity of their own god, they refuse our Emperor the same courtesy. This feeds the Governor's rage, of course, and he persists in seeing all their overt acts as challenges to his personal authority. Since the spring disturbances, he has ordered more than a score of executions on some of the flimsiest pretexts. Any ambitious scoundrel, if he knows my brother-in-law's temper, can eliminate a competitor by denouncing him. It is useless to protest and futile to argue, as my sister has been doing these many months. He never seems to realize that the harsher his methods, the more they grow to hate us. I have urged him to follow Cicero's advice: 'Kill them with love, strangle them with mercy, besiege them with smiles and starve them out with honeyed words and fond embraces.' In short, assimilate them as we have done with Italians, Egyptians, Greeks and Illyrians.

Here, a large part of several pages seemed to have been lost. The document continued:

. . . am a soldier, not a butcher. If we must execute a man according to the laws of Rome and his whim, then I am obliged to carry out orders. But I am not obliged to impose undueg on the victims, nor am I under orders to refrain from helping them across the bitter and painful chasm we all must cross at death. In Lusitania, as you recall, we used to garrote them after the crosses were set in place. This he now forbids, and I can tell you, if the effect on the troops is not good, which it is not, the effect on the populace is worse. Cruelty is the last resort of the bankrupt conqueror. My brother-in-law calls me . . .

The telephone was ringing. I picked it up to hear a Paris overseas operator ask for me. There was a lot of buzzing and switching before a brisk, familiar voice came on the line. 'Dr. Marcus? Berman. How are things?'

'Fine, fine, Inspector. Where are you?'

'Tel Aviv.'

'The line's so clear.'

'From Jerusalem you never know. Did you see . . .?'

'Who?'

'The professor with the paper.'

'No. Not exactly. But I have the paper. I am reading it now, as a matter of fact. I had a copy sent to you today.'

'We got something for you, Doctor. Got a pencil?'

I found a felt pen and a pad. 'Okay?'

'. . . found on the bakery tray in the van.'

'What?'

'I thought you said the line was clear.'

'What was found on the bakery tray in the van?'

'A fingerprint. You read me?'

'Yes. A fingerprint.'

'We have a report on it. Identified as one Willi Gansfeld, Dutch passport number C-1348562-A. Got that?'

'Got it, Inspector.' I read the passport number back.

'Believed to have left the country for Vienna, so I suggest you contact Goff.'

'And do what?'

'The man's fingerprint was in that van, Doctor.'

'I understand, Inspector, but I can't arrest Willi what's-his-name.'

'Gansfeld.' He spelled it. 'Don't worry. Suriel should be there in time for that. I already sent a telex to Goff. But we can't afford to pay for his services. You understand?'

'I understand.'

'He can deliver. Then the Austrian police take over from there. We want this creep and the print is enough to get him back on a murder warrant.'

'You think he did it?'

'I only know he's not in the bakery business. We had him booked two months ago on suspicion of smuggling diamonds. Had to let him go, but at least we got his autograph.'

'Is Goff expecting my call?'

'By now he's expecting your cheque. Otherwise he won't move. That's why I called you. This is a live one, Doctor.'

'I'll telephone him immediately.'

'Doctor?'

'Yes, Inspector.'

'Can you go to Vienna yourself?'

'Is that necessary? I don't see what I can do there.'

There was a silence on the other end.

'Inspector?'

'Just a minute.' The low, unintelligible sound of a conference came through.

'Jay?'

'Aaron?'

'Jay, I think you should go to Vienna and see Mr. Goff personally.'

'Aaron, I have a lot to do here. If I call him and guarantee the money, there shouldn't be any problem.'

'Jay?'

'I heard you, Aaron.'

'Jay, Nate would go.'

'Don't pull that crap long-distance, Aaron. Just tell me why it's so damned important I hire Mr. Goff personally. I can telephone him and have a cheque in his hands first thing tomorrow.'

'Berman says Goff likes to work that way and I agree it would be better to have someone from the museum see the man. I'd go myself, but it would hold things up a couple of days.'

'Nicoletta's arriving tomorrow.'

'This man might be the murderer, Jay.'

'Have you already booked my reservation or am I supposed to do that?'

'I couldn't from here, but you shouldn't have any trouble. . . .'

'Never mind. I can probably be back the same day.'

'Thanks, Jay.'

'Tell Nicoletta.'

'Yes, of course.'

'She should come directly to the apartment. I'll leave the paper with the housekeeper.'

I had scarcely put the telephone down when it rang again. The caller was Jeanette Mowbray, my secretary, who has an uncanny way of always turning up when needed. I put her to work on my plane reservations for Vienna, *aller-retour*, explaining meanwhile about Nicoletta's arrival.

When I hung up, Nelida was standing in the doorway.

'You barely touched the tongue for lunch. I wasn't going to say anything, but you look terrible.'

Her sense of proportion in these matters has always been

at odds with my own. To be lean and bronzed like a fisherman is, in her view, an unfortunate physical handicap for a serious scholar.

I returned to the Lanholtz paper, but it took me a while to find my place. I was still thinking of Berman's news. In a vehicle abandoned by those who robbed and murdered Victor Lanholtz, one single fingerprint had been found. *Believed* to be in Vienna. Suppose the man was in Salzburg or Stuttgart? Suppose he was in Tokyo? That would be Goff's job, presumably, to track him down. A fingerprint might be enough for a warrant, enough to move the Israeli Foreign Ministry and the Austrian police, but it did not guarantee a conviction without a host of other evidence or an admission from Willi what's-his-name that he had stolen the scrolls and beat in Victor Lanholtz's brains. Berman had implied an odd thing about Goff – that he too was a killer. This was on my mind when the operator quickly put me through to Vienna.

SIX

'Five thousand dollars?'

'In advance and nonrefundable,' Goff replied with scarcely a trace of accent. 'I work seven days a week. My people are charged off at between fifty and one hundred dollars daily. Travel expenses extra. Any laboratory work, ballistic analysis or other technical service extra. I retain full control.'

'It's expensive, but –'

'One other thing,' Goff said.

'Yes?'

'No results guaranteed.'

'I'm surprised you stay in business on those terms, Herr Goff. But Berman recommends you, so I accept.'

'No,' Goff said, 'you misunderstand me. I was not offering anything. You must come to Vienna and explain first what it is you want for your money.'

'Has Berman talked with you?'

'This morning.'

'Then you know.'

93

'Only the outlines. I prefer to get the details from you in person.'

'Tomorrow, then?'

'As you like,' Goff said. 'Anytime before seven.'

I slammed down the receiver after Goff rang off. Whatever else Herr Goff might be, he took a prize for abrasive manners. If the circumstances had been one whit different, I would have told him where he could put his five-thousand-dollar minimum with my compliments. Yet Berman had said he was good – the best, in fact, and scrupulously honest in all his dealings. Where had I ever got the idea Austrians were charming?

A plate of Breton oysters took the edge off my anger. The FM was broadcasting the Fauré requiem. I sat listening to the clear sweetness of the children's voices, wondering at myself, at the eccentric life I had chosen, pondering, as Aaron would say, the eternal things. At forty, more was behind me than ahead, yet the years had been little more than preparation. For what? I thought of Nate learning the violin; his time of happiness with Mae Broman. And I reflected a long time about Nicoletta before I picked up the Lanholtz paper again and began to read the ancient Latin script. Longinus's two-thousand-year-old complaints stirred a certain sympathy. He had an engaging way of distracting my mind from things that might require decision.

My brother-in-law calls me imperial agent and family lackey when he is angry, which is most of the time now. His fits are more frequent, and one last week left him frothing and thrashing on the guardroom floor until the Greek surgeon came, held him down and kept him from swallowing his tongue. In my last letter I gave you the particulars of the events in Jerusalem during the Passover holiday, but the priests did not like my idea of fixing the blame on them. Once the pilgrims dispersed, I worked through much of the summer to bolster our reputation for fair dealing and tolerance, a task never made easy by a governor who persists in seeing this country as a slave-labour camp.

In the late summer, many of the Bedouin came to trade, and with them another wave of prophets, mountebanks, diviners and charlatans, who breed like lice in these parts. Although the threat of a Zealot revolt seems diminished, the climate of religious extremism is still as dangerous as dry leaves in a drought. For three months the traffic has been constant, and nowhere, not even in Rome, was there ever such manoeuvring around the seat of power, encouraged by him because his stunted vanity requires it. Mostly, it is the priests trying to enlist official support against the popular street-corner preachers. There has been no more talk of messiahs and no new claimants to imaginary kingdoms. But that is not to say we haven't had our share of near disasters.

The worst occurred when a mob of Samaritans went looking for some sacred vessels believed buried on Mount Gerizim by their prophet Moses. The Governor ordered one of our Greek units to stop them. Don't ask me why. They were peaceful enough until opposed by the Greeks. The slaughter that followed was shameful. Over a thousand bodies were counted before the mob dispersed. All for what?

Do what you can to have him recalled, Lucius, or Rome will certainly pay a heavy price in the future for his mistakes. I sometimes think he waited all his life to find a people he could hate, despise and humiliate, and the Jews, because of their natural arrogance and exclusive religious customs, have provided him with . . .'

Part of one page was again missing here. The next continued:

. . . obstinate, merciless and inflexible in his prejudice against these people, an attitude which cannot but negatively influence those around him and give un-scrupulous persons all manner of license to subvert Rome's and the Emperor's good justice.

Nelida had brought a tray with the rest of my supper and was now standing in the doorway to make sure I began eating. 'Your flight leaves at eight-fifteen in the morning,' she said as I turned to the crispy brochette and creamed broccoli.

When she had left the room, I gulped the food and laid the Lanholtz paper aside to search my bookshelves for a

New Testament encyclopaedia I rarely use. Pontius Pilate was worth three fine-print pages with ample citations from Mark, Matthew and Luke. The crux of the article was that Mark probably authored the earliest version of the Crucifixion story, most likely about thirty years after the fact, relying on the memory of the ageing apostle Peter. Mark is the only one to lay the responsibility for Jesus's death on the heads of the Romans, although he implies that the priest Caiaphas and the Jewish Sanhedrin were morally guilty for demanding the execution.

For nearly two thousand years, Mark's interpretation has embarrassed Christian propagandists, not a few of whom resorted to the most blatant anti-Semitism to counteract it and make the Jews alone accountable for killing Jesus.

Matthew's account followed Mark's, but Luke, that patron saint of doctors and artists, whose gospel had been called the most beautiful book ever written, took a different tack. Writing to the Roman nobleman Flavius Clemens, a cousin of the Emperor Domitian, from whom he expected some favours, he lets the Romans off the hook completely. His version of the trial of Jesus places the entire blame on the Jews, a premise used to justify official church anti-Semitic persecution until its formal codification in Catholic dogma was repealed by Paul VI after the last Vatican Ecumenical Council.

I replaced the heavy volume on the shelf and saw by the ormolu clock on the mantel that it was nearly midnight. Gaius Longinus was keeping me up. I dug out other volumes, rubbed my eyes and kept reading. In one I read the legend of the Roman centurion Longinus, who had been in charge of the death squad on Gethsemane and was converted to the new religion when he saw Christ die. Could this have been the brother of Claudia, wife of Pilate?

And what of Claudia? I went back to the shelves again and spent a couple of hours checking other volumes on the early Roman Empire. Claudia, wife of Pilatus Pontius, née Claudia Procula, princess of the royal blood, granddaughter of Caesar Augustus and illegitimate daughter of the third wife of the Emperor Tiberius. With a pedigree like that, it was no wonder her brother was furious at her for staying with an obscure professional soldier who suffered from epilepsy. About Longinus, nothing, no hint that the man in command at Gethsemane might have been the governor's brother-in-law. Yet the name was not common.

Process of elimination. It was unlikely there were two men named Longinus in positions of high command under Pilate. Ergo, let us assume there was only one. Yet the writer of Victor Lanholtz's Caesarea scroll was no convert, which seemed to make the legend propaganda. He was also a tribune and not a centurion – the difference between a brigadier and a lieutenant – which further muddied the comparison.

Lanholtz himself did not speculate. Where was the earlier letter to which Longinus referred, which apparently described the trial and crucifixion of Jesus in detail? A tantalizing prospect for any scholar to ponder: the first and only eyewitness report on what really happened that week in Jerusalem, recounted by an articulate Roman aristocrat who may actually have given the orders that nailed Christ to the cross. Was that account, too, found in Caesarea and stolen by Willi what's-his-name the night Lanholtz was murdered? Sitting in the library of my Paris apartment at three o'clock that morning, I experienced a sense of awe thinking about what Lanholtz had found in the sands of Israel.

Lev Vagan had called them potentially controversial. Aaron had characterized them in his inimitable promoter's fashion as fantastic. Ramsay O'Hare said they were incredible. But only Nicoletta had come close to my own reaction when she acknowledged they could change our thinking about the synoptic Gospels.

On the strength of what I had already read, it was clear that the Lanholtz discoveries were among the most valuable in the history of Middle Eastern archaeology. Small comfort when all we had to show for them was a handful of fuzzy photocopies.

In the morning I staggered out with Nelida's help, dozed in the limousine to Orly, sleepwalked aboard the Austrian Airlines DC-9 and slept like a marmot until the wheels touched the tarmac at Vienna. As a result, Jay Brian Marcus was as fresh as a Danube daisy when he descended from the taxi on the Mahlerstrasse behind the Staatsoper and rode to the top floor of a grey stone building in a clanking birdcage elevator. The brass plaque on the heavily varnished door said simply: GOFF.

A rosy-cheeked woman with sharp, ice-blue eyes and an unconvincing smile let me in after I identified myself and stated my business. From the way she walked, she was more likely Goff's bodyguard than his office receptionist. She kept me waiting ten minutes in an impersonal kind of parlour that reminded me of a dentist's waiting room in Pelham when I was a child. There was even a rubber plant and a few back issues of a golfing magazine on a glass end table next to the leather sofa. I was unprepared for Goff's private office. Cold yet prepossessing; Spartan luxury rather than kitsch. A vast room covered with green broadloom carpeting; the walls in green and gold, severely modern; his desk and all the office furniture chrome and glass. No prints or paintings on the walls. The only suggestion of warmth in the place was a long box of flowering indoor plants under the window behind Goff's desk. He was watering them when I entered.

Goff himself went with the room. Thin and sharp-featured, pale hair, eyes and skin. He might have been a Swede. He was conservatively dressed in a light-grey suit. His manner as cold as his furniture. He motioned me to a chair, handed me a file folder and went back to his plant-watering. He had not shaken hands or said hello. I was already angry.

'Look that over first,' he said without glancing up from the watering can. 'It's the print-out on Willi Gansfeld.'

'Have you located him?'

'We know where he was at nine last night.'

'In Vienna?'

Goff nodded. 'Read that before you ask me any questions,' he said curtly. Then he suddenly looked up. 'You do read German, don't you?'

'No,' I lied, 'so it might be wise if you tell me what all this says.'

He sprinkled the last of the water on a flourishing out-of-season azalea and put the can aside. 'Willi Gansfeld is a thirty-three-year-old Dutchman,' he began, unspooling the file from his memory, 'first arrested Stuttgart 1959 for car theft. He is clean here but has a sheet in France, in Switzerland and elsewhere. Several aliases, but never changes his first name. Did time in Holland for armed robbery, three years in Württemberg for drug dealing, and six months in Switzerland for possession of a forged passport. Twice arrested on suspicion of murder – once in Hamburg and once in Brussels. No proof. Berman is convinced he was mixed up in a diamond-smuggling operation between Tel Aviv and Rotterdam, but again no proof.'

'Can he be arrested now?'

'They can pick him up. But then you only have seventy-two hours to put it through diplomatic channels for the Viennese police. You don't need me.'

'Berman seemed to think we did.'

'If Berman gets the necessary papers and sends an officer from Israel, that's it. In a week you have him in jail in Tel Aviv. Murder, Berman said it was.'

'That's right.'

'So why throw your money away? Up to now, this is a favour to Berman. If I have to get involved in the arrest and all that, you're out a lot.'

'Did Berman tell you about the theft from our museum?'

'He mentioned it. What did they take?'

As I recounted the story, Goff lost a little of his aloof manner and appeared genuinely interested. More so when I told him of the robbery of Nicoletta's apartment, the Lanholtz paper, and our decision to read it into the record of the archaeological congress. I also gave him my own reaction to what I had been reading the night before in Paris. He interrupted occasionally with questions, one of which gave me a particularly sharp insight into the way his mind worked.

'How badly do you want Willi Gansfeld?'

'As Berman told you, there's the murder –'

'Leave Berman out of it. I mean you. Suppose Gansfeld told you where you could find the missing things in return for money and a ticket to Brazil. Would you go along?'

'Do you think that's realistic?'

'If you are more interested in your property than in convicting this hood, I might take on the case.'

'Does it make a difference?'

'Catching Willi is a police affair. If I work for you, it will only be to get your property back.'

'I see.'

'No guarantees, as I told you yesterday.'

'But you wouldn't take it on if you didn't think there was a good chance.'

Goff's face was as devoid of expression as a store dummy. 'I don't cheat people,' he said.

I was thinking of my conversation with Berman when he had put a hard question to Aaron and me. We had both given our word we would not deal independently with the thieves to recover the scrolls. Yet Goff was suggesting what amounted to that. There seemed nothing to lose by telling him so. He made the slightest movement of his shoulders and turned his attention from me to his flower box. It was not a shrug, but he could not have made his indifference to my scruples plainer. 'Gansfeld will be taken care of,' he said finally. 'If Berman doesn't get him, someone will.'

'I'd like to think about it.'

'We have no assurance that he will be in Austria tomorrow,' Goff said.

'I think I should talk to Berman.'

'You don't have time. Bear in mind we may not be able to negotiate with this man. I am only guessing. But if we can, then we must do it immediately. Let Berman have him after we get what we want. Agreed?'

'Now?'

'Certainly.'

'All right.'

'Come on, then. We don't want to miss Willi.'

'We?'

'Why not? Your Paris flight doesn't leave until five.'

Waiting at the kerb was a Mercedes sedan with a long-haired, acne-scarred youth at the wheel. We climbed into the rear and Goff gave him an address in Grinzing.

'Do you know Vienna?' Goff asked me as we rolled smoothly along the Burgring. I glimpsed the grey stone façades of the last home of the Hapsburgs and remembered, for what reason I do not now recall, that Austria has one of the highest suicide rates in the world. Mayerling and all that.

'I gave a series of lectures at the university here a couple of years ago,' I said.

His eyebrows rose, the first indication I had that he was capable of registering surprise. 'On what subject?'

I told him.

Suburban Grinzing is only about five miles from the centre of the city as one heads away from the Danube toward the Vienna woods. From what I knew of Willi, I would have been far less surprised to find him in a cheap hotel near the West-bahnhof. I asked Goff what Willi was doing in Grinzing.

'Ladies' man,' Goff said. 'He has a widow friend who owns a restaurant there.'

The driver found it easily, a prosperous-looking place with a large parking lot and gaily painted designs on the stucco walls. Goff told him to drive on and park along the street a hundred yards beyond. We got out and walked back.

The tables were crowded with tourists. Middle-aged waitresses in taffeta dirndls and flowered aprons bustled back and forth with heavy trays of steaming sausage and pitchers of cold wine. The succulent odours suddenly gave me an appetite. Goff went straight to the nearest waitress, who directed us to an alcove off the kitchen. There, a stout woman in her forties stood controlling the food on its way to the customers. At sight of her, Goff transformed himself into a cheerful, joking, irresistible old pal of Willi's from Stuttgart. Although the woman's eyes darted suspiciously from Goff to me and back in the first seconds, she quickly became his prize as he giggled and flattered his way into his confidence, even repeating what he claimed was Willi's description of her magnificent kitchen.

She explained that Willi was not yet down, having retired late the night before. His room was on the second floor. Waitresses with heavy trays were beginning to queue impatiently and Goff suggested it would be fun if we went up to see our old friend. He winked mischievously at the smiling owner before we mounted the stairs.

Outside the room, his expression reverted to ice again. There was no trace of the laughing, hearty fellow I had been watching a moment earlier.

He listened at the door, tried it with deft fingers and found it unlocked. He swung it open and stepped into the room. Sitting on the edge of a large bed was a round-faced man with thinning brown hair and pink-white skin, in the act of putting on his shoes. Goff was across the room in an instant. The man on the bed was too startled by our entrance to do more than open his mouth. Goff struck him without warning, a vicious open-handed blow on one ear. Willi's hands went up to ward off another, but too late as Goff hit him with a left across the other side of his head, straightening him upright. I had never seen a man act with such swift violence, such sudden economical movement. We had not been in Willi's room half a minute before Goff had snapped him off the bed and reduced him to a moaning, gasping, frightened hulk.

'Lock the door,' Goff said to me, and I dumbly complied.

The man still struggled weakly as Goff punched him low in the stomach, and he would have collapsed if Goff had not bent him around the bedpost and held him by his belt. Willi vomited over the bedclothes, barely missing Goff's extended sleeve, and Goff hit him savagely across the kidneys with the side of his hand. The man's eyes streamed tears. He lay panting and coughing as Goff held his right wrist high up against the small of his back. There had not been a sound.

Goff began to speak to him in a low, almost gentle tone, in clear German, most of which I understood. 'Willi,' he said, 'you are going to suffer until you tell me exactly what I came to find out. Do you understand?'

Willi's bulging eyes did not seem to be focusing on much beyond his pain.

'Do you understand me?' Goff repeated, raising the wrist so that the man whimpered. 'Answer quickly or I will break it.'

'I understand,' Willi gasped.

'Where are the things you stole from the museum?'

There was no answer until Goff jerked the wrist again, then only a falsetto whinny. With his free hand Goff delivered another slap on the side of the head. 'You don't understand, Willi. Once more. Answer me properly.'

'I don't know,' Willi said.

I heard the arm snap out of its socket as Goff shoved Willi's face down into the bedclothes to stifle his cry.

'Stop it!' I said. 'We didn't come here to kill the man!' But Goff ignored me. He let go of Willi's dislocated arm and bounced him upright on the bed, grasping the other arm behind his back the same as before. His speed was a blur. How Willi retained consciousness I will never know. Fear, probably, pumping enough adrenaline to overcome the blinding pain.

Goff began again in the low, toneless voice. 'Do you understand me?'

Ropy strings of saliva mixed with the flecks of vomit on Willi's sagging jaw. His lip bled a little where it had struck the bedpost. 'Don't . . . please. I understand.'

'We know you robbed the museum, Willi, and we know you killed a man. But we want to hear it from you.'

'Are you police? You can't be the police,' Willi gasped.

Goff put pressure on the good arm so that Willi's face contorted.

'I don't have the things.'

'We know that.'

'God! . . . I need a doctor. I . . . we got a thousand dollars each. I didn't know he was dead until . . . I saw the papers. The . . . look . . .' Willi was whimpering softly, weeping. 'I can't stand this. . . .'

Goff relaxed his grip and Willi rocked to and fro on the edge of the bed, holding the broken arm, staring at the grotesque angle of the elbow.

'We delivered all those things . . . to a house in Nablus,' he said slowly. 'They were supposed to be dropped in Jericho . . . but we had to leave one of the cars . . .'

'Whose house?'

'I don't know.'

'Who was on the job with you?'

'Sussman . . . and the Frenchman.'

'Willi, I am only going to ask each question once and I want a complete answer.'

'Shaul Sussman . . . an Israeli . . . Used to work at the museum.'

'Doing what?'

'Cleaning.'

'Where does he live?'

'Tel Aviv.'

'Complete, I said.'

'He lives with, you know, his sister. Same name. She has an apartment on Rehov Tarsat. I don't know the number.'

'Who's the Frenchman?'.

'They call him that. Frenchy. His name is Roche. La Roche. I never knew his first name. He had a room in the Intercontinental.'

'Where'd he get the money to stay there?'

'He had money. A lot of money.'

'He paid you the thousand?'

Willi nodded.

'Why?'

Goff watched Willi silently. The man shrank back against the bedclothes. 'Where'd he get the money?' Goff asked.

'I don't know,' Willi said. 'I never dared ask.'

'Yes, you did,' Goff said.

'But he didn't tell me. I swear,' Willi said quickly. 'They talked English on the telephone. He was at the Intercontinental, I think. I heard Frenchy call him there once.'

'You never saw him?'

'Not that I know.'

'Where's the Frenchman now?'

'Paris.'

'Address?'

'I only know a bar where he hangs out.' He gave Goff the name. 'It's in Montmartre.'

'I hope so,' Goff said, 'Where is Sussman now?'

'In the army. God, it hurts. Please . . .'

'Since when?'

'I don't know. He was in the army when I met him.'

'Stationed where?'

'Near Mount Hermon . . . I can't stand this.'

'We'll take you to a doctor.'

More terrified now than ever, Willi watched Goff. I could not imagine what the detective was up to as he turned toward a nearby chair where Willi's coat lay and briskly checked the pockets. He found a silver money clip with some dollars, Willi's passport and a small automatic. To my astonishment, he handed the gun to Willi with the money while he flipped through the man's passport. 'Hurry up,' Goff said.

Still suspicious, but less frightened now that he was armed, Willi managed to slip his jacket over his shoulders. There was a small sink in the bedroom, where Goff soaked a towel and passed it to Willi, who wiped the mess from his unhappy face. Goff propelled him out of the room and locked the door behind us. The general commotion in the restaurant had heightened since our arrival, and the lady owner was too busy with her waitresses to notice our passage. As we arrived on the street, the Mercedes purred up and Goff motioned us in the back – me first, then Willi, which placed the fractured right arm conveniently next to Goff.

He gave the long-haired driver no instructions, yet the man seemed to know precisely where to go. I was still in a state of stunned bewilderment, angry and not just a little ashamed of myself. Goff himself had warned me in his way, but I had chosen to misunderstand the warning. I wondered how much of his sadism had been for my benefit. Surely he could have got the same result without actually twisting a man's limb out of its socket. Berman said he was the best. Did Berman really know what he was best at?

Swiftly behind such thoughts came others even less comfortable. Why did I not interfere? Or walk out? Because my revulsion had given way to fascination, and then to curiosity at the results Goff was getting from his brutal inquisition. In less than twenty minutes he had turned up more information than everyone else since Lanholtz was killed.

'I feel terrible,' Willi said. 'Where are we going?'

'Tell me more about Frenchy,' Goff said. 'Describe him.'

'Forty. Educated.'

'Did he speak Hebrew?'

'Hebrew no. Only Sussman speaks Hebrew.'

'Why did you kill the old man?'

'I didn't kill him.'

'Tell me about the people in Nablus.'

'I don't remem – aaaaah!'

'Sorry,' Goff said casually. 'What do you remember?'

'Frenchy knew them. They run a garage there.'

'Describe it.'

'It was the middle of the night and we only stayed long enough to dump the stuff.'

'Then what?'

'Sussman got rid of the van.'

'Where?'

'Nathanya, I think. On the coast.'

Goff looked at me.

'One of the cars was found in Nathanya,' I said.

'And then you did what?' Goff said.

'Took a bus back to Jerusalem.'

'In the middle of the night?'

'Early in the morning.'

'Where'd you spend the night?'

'On the road.'

'Where did Sussman live when he worked at the museum?'

'I don't know.'

'How did he know Frenchy?'

'Through me.'

'How did you know Sussman?'

'Through his sister.'

'Why did you go to Israel?'

'I'm a Jew,' Willi said.

'Is Frenchy a Jew too?'

'No.'

'Why did he go to Israel?'

'To work.'

'Doing what?'

'We had a couple of things going.'

'Diamonds.'

'That didn't come off. The dealer got scared.'

'So you hit the museum.'

'Ya.'

'Willi, we're interested in finding the things from the museum. You hold back anything?'

'No.'

'What!'

'Only some earrings and a bracelet.'

'Where are they?'

'I gave them to Liselotte at the restaurant.'

'You might as well know there's a murder warrant out on you.'

'I told you I didn't –'

'Tell them, not me. Tomorrow there will be an Israeli officer to take you back.'

'They can't –'

'They can,' Goff said sharply, 'and they will because you were stupid and left fingerprints.'

The driver had rolled to a stop and was waiting for a traffic light. We had been circling Grinzing for some time and were headed back toward the centre of Vienna along the west bank of the canal. As the light went to green again, before the car could move, Willi lunged across me against the left-hand door. He must have planned the moment well because his good hand went straight for the handle, the door flew open and he was out before I knew it. The driver hit the brakes, throwing us nearly on the floor. Horns hooted behind us. I expected Goff to leap after the man and chase him along the busy Sittelauer Lande, but he only sighed and shut the door. The last I saw of Willi, he was running toward the Franz-Josefs Bahnhof as fast as he could go.

'A hysteric,' Goff observed calmly.

'What are you going to do?'

'He has nothing else to tell us.'

'You believed him?'

'Most of the time,' Goff said. He asked the driver to take us to the *Polizei Hauptquartier*. 'Will you call Berman or shall I?' Goff gazed out at some passing barges on the canal. 'He should receive that information about Nablus immediately. Maybe your stuff is still there.'

'Or one of the others knows where it is.'

'The soldier might.'

'Or the Frenchman with the English-speaking boss.'

'Will you be coming to Paris?'

'That won't be necessary. I have someone there.'

A chill wind was blowing as we reached police headquarters. The sky had turned to slate, matching the Danube, and the first dead leaves of autumn scudded over the grey cobbled courtyard where the driver let us out. I followed Goff up a wide stairway to the main entrance of the forbidding stone palace. A hundred years earlier, this grim compound on the Rossauer Lande had housed the upper hierarchy of the Austro-Hungarian police apparatus, one of the most efficient in nineteenth-century Europe. Behind it loomed the walls of the prison where the enemies of the last of the Hapsburgs had languished. During the Second World War the Gestapo had occupied the same premises until their lease was terminated by the Allied armies. Then came the military police during the four-power occupation that followed. As we walked along the dimly lighted, high-ceilinged corridors past dark portraits of long-dead police presidents, I asked Goff if he had known Berman during his army days in Vienna.

'He didn't tell you?'

'No.'

'When the war ended I was sixteen, a Gestapo prisoner here. The American MPs assigned me to work for Berman, who was a sergeant.'

'Why didn't they turn you loose?'

'Only political prisoners were released.'

'I don't understand.'

'I had been convicted of murder,' Goff said, 'and the Allies kept the wheels of Nazi justice turning, even after Götterdämmerung.' The corners of his thin mouth turned down slightly as if he savoured the irony.

I thought perhaps he was going to tell me of his days as a boyhood resistance hero. I have heard a good many such tales from middle-aged Europeans, and most of them I discount. But Goff surprised me.

'The man I killed,' he said, 'was my boss in the black market. There were about a hundred of us awaiting execution here for criminal offences when the Germans ran. Most were dragged out and shot on the last day. I hid in the latrine and they missed me. Later, the Allies were reviewing our cases one by one with the Austrian police. Berman liked me and I tried to please him. When my turn came for review, my file had disappeared.'

'That's one of the favours you owe Berman?'

'He never said so, but I knew. They let me go then. Berman found me a job and gave me a reference when I applied for the police academy. In those days American references were gold.'

We had passed through several cluttered offices where secretaries and police clerks worked busily among ringing telephones. Most of the people acknowledged Goff with a smile or a gesture. Some of the uniformed older men saluted smartly.

'I gather you worked here,' I said.

'Fifteen years. I was head of the criminal investigation division when I quit to make some money. I'm probably the only convicted felon ever to hold the post.' Goff smiled for the first time in our short acquaintance. He had paused to hold open a door which led to a large, richly furnished private office.

'Please,' he said. I entered and saw a balding older man at the far end of the room, working behind a handsome

108

Biedermeier table. He rose and greeted Goff warmly. 'Chief Inspector Kalb,' Goff said. 'My successor.'

'Did you find your man?' Kalb asked.

'He ran away,' Goff said, 'but he can't go far.' He removed Willi's passport from his pocket and tossed it on Kalb's splendid table-desk.

'The formal request from the Foreign Ministry just arrived,' the chief inspector said, 'so we can have him picked up.'

'I got all I needed,' Goff replied carelessly, 'but he's armed and dangerous, *Schatzerl*, so don't expect an easy bust.'

Kalb already had the telephone in his hand, and was giving orders to a subordinate. It began to dawn on me that Goff, for whatever perverse personal reasons, had stage-managed more than the questioning of the fugitive Willi. He had wanted him to escape when he was finished, armed and running with all the odds against him. Was it a game he liked to play? Or was it some vengeful compulsion he could not resist?

SEVEN

I believe every love affair has its own life independent of the people involved. There must be a natural reason for this, as little understood as instinct or the need for mystery.

With Nicoletta and me, I think this really began the night I returned from Vienna, wet and cold after a long wait for a taxi at the airport. I let myself in and hung my dripping jacket in the hallway. Nelida was bustling about the kitchen, but I did not pause to tell her I was home. I snatched a towel from the little lavatory and went into the library, rubbing my hair vigorously, hoping she had laid a fire in the hearth. She had, and before it, cross-legged on the floor, silver-rimmed granny glasses balanced on her small nose, Nicoletta sat reading the Lanholtz paper. I stopped to watch unobserved. She was wearing a long velvet dress of emerald green and her hair was done in a chignon, lending her something of the haughty, severely sophisticated allure of a high-fashion mannequin. Only the glasses and a frown of intense concentration gave her away. She sat very straight, her back arched naturally like a Degas figure, her luxuriant dark hair glinting in the firelight.

She sensed my presence and looked up, turning her head to peer over the glasses. Her smile was all the warmth I needed. 'How long have you been standing there?' she asked me.

'Long enough.'

'How was Vienna?'

'Cold. How was Jerusalem?'

'Lonely.' She rose with a slow, graceful movement, letting the paper fall as I kissed her. Later, she said, 'Your shirt is damp, you know. Have you eaten?'

'No, but Nelida always provides. Are you hungry?'

'Yes. If you tell me where the booze is, I'll make you a drink while you change.'

I retrieved the Lanholtz pages from the carpet. 'Think you can revise it in time for the congress?'

'I don't see why not. Did you read it?'

'Most of it.'

'And?'

'Make the drink and I'll tell you. You are very beautiful tonight, by the way.'

'Gets you does it?'

'It does.'

'That was the idea. Go change before you catch cold. Hurry. I want to hear everything.'

My Paris apartment occupies the second floor of a seventeenth-century building overlooking its own private courtyard. The layout is like an elongated C, with my bedroom, library, study, living and dining rooms taking up the centre part. One wing is devoted to the kitchen, laundry and Nelida's quarters, while the other forms a small suite which can be separated entirely from the rest of the place. Nelida had installed Nicoletta in there according to my instructions, but from the start she spent most of the time with me.

Over a Scotch, and Nelida's roast lamb, I gave Nicoletta my impressions of the day in Vienna, which by then had begun to seem more like a week.

'Goff sounds awful,' she said after I had described his treatment of Willi Gansteld.

110

'I'd call him that. But maybe it's an occupational neurosis among policemen.'

'Berman doesn't strike me as a man who breaks bones,' Nicoletta replied loyally. 'And he was investigating a murder too.'

'When Goff took me to the airport, I asked him, thinking the arm fracture might have been partly accidental after all. You know, maybe I was imagining too much because of all the other things that had happened.'

'What did he say?'

'His answer had the kind of hard-edged logic I find hard to refute.'

'Because he justified it?'

'He said the Willis of the world have to experience violence. Threats are a waste of time. The Gestapo used a similar system, I suppose with the same success.'

'That's probably where he learned it.'

'He was first a victim, remember.'

'Did you talk to Berman from Vienna?'

'Goff did. They're looking for that soldier. And combing Nablus for the scrolls.'

'Was Berman hopeful?'

'When is Berman ever hopeful?'

Over a brandy in the library, our talk wandered to Longinus and I found my eyelids growing heavy.

Nicoletta's cool fingers brushed my cheek. 'To bed, my love.'

'You too, Nicky.'

'Is that a proposition, Doctor?'

I drew her to me. 'Think of it as a standing offer.'

'But you're exhausted and I'm falling asleep.'

'Then why not do it together?'

'Fall asleep?'

'And whatever else comes to mind.'

She laughed softly and kissed me on the cheek.

All the next day there was no word from Jerusalem or Vienna. Nicoletta spent her time on the Lanholtz paper in the library while I dictated to Jeanette Mowbray in my study-office, working through the mountain of correspondence that had accumulated during my four-month absence. The amazing thing each year was that so much was left after she forwarded the really important mail to me in Greece.

Catalogues and book-sale lists she put aside; a third of the letters she was able to answer in my absence, and did. But there was always that same small mountain, mainly inquiries from students, comments on my books or requests for articles on other people's work, which had to be dealt with on my return. By five that afternoon I was fed up and Jeanette was half cross-eyed from deciphering her own shorthand. We had disposed of only a tenth of the pile, yet she had a week's work, most of which I knew she would have ready for signature the following day.

I was about to go in and see if Nicoletta felt like joining me for a drink, when the telephone rang. It was Ramsay O'Hare for Nicoletta. 'That was a mistake,' she said as she went to take it.

She dodged a supper invitation from O'Hare, but could not gracefully avoid luncheon the following day. When she asked me if I cared to join them I shook my head. She replaced the receiver. 'I'm sorry about that, Jay. Before I left Israel, he said he might be stopping off here on his return to the States and I had to tell him where I could be reached.'

'I didn't tell you he offered the museum a handout if we would fire Vagan, did I?'

'That sounds like him. But he's not a bad man, even if he sometimes approaches people the wrong way.'

'I'll have to take your word for it. He wasn't exactly my type, I'm afraid.'

'Nor mine, darling,' she said. 'But his money made things happen when Vagan was dragging his feet. We all owe him that.'

'I can't understand why he wanted Victor to hold off the paper in Oxford. You must have some clue.'

'I think I do,' she said thoughtfully. 'But I'm afraid it will sound terribly silly.'

'Try me.'

Nicoletta tapped the end of a pencil against her teeth, frowning before she spoke. 'Ramsay's a very devout Catholic, Jay. Communion every morning, wherever he is. That sort of thing.'

'Aaron told me, and O'Hare added a few colourful details himself the time we talked.'

'When I first met him, I couldn't stand him. He seemed to

112

personify most of the negative qualities of the American businessman abroad: smug, aggressive, patronizing and supremely confident that the world needed him more than he needed the world.'

'That sounds like the man I met.'

'But he isn't like that. Really.'

'It's a façade to cover the sympathetic, warm-hearted, open-minded philanthropist lurking behind those reptilian eyes.'

'You see? I said it would sound frivolous.'

'It does. But go on.'

She eyed me suspiciously.

'Please. I'll withhold the sarcasm.'

'Jay, it isn't easy for me to defend a man like O'Hare. It's only recently I found myself revising my original opinion of him, which was probably lower than yours.'

'I'll shut up. After all, I only saw him once.'

'Religion is the key to the man. At least it explains a few things. What I'm trying to say is he is infinitely more complicated than he appears on the surface.'

'That I suspected. More devious, too.'

'Do you know why he financed Victor?'

'Only what he told me.'

We went into the library, where Nicoletta had spread papers and open volumes over most of the carpet. Her natural working space seemed to be the floor, where she spent hours in her inimitable cross-legged pose, filling pages on a legal pad with notes in her fine, even script. While I made a drink, she explained a few of the unexpected connections between the obsessions of Victor Lanholtz and the gospel according to Ramsay O'Hare.

'I'm no psychiatrist,' Nicoletta said, 'so I don't know where O'Hare fits into the case-history books. But he has an idea that by contributing money to certain kinds of scholarly research in the "holy land," as he calls it, he is fulfilling himself as a good Christian.'

'This is what he says?'

'In his own way. He talks about rediscovering Christ and things like that. He's supported a lot of nonsensical projects too, from what I've heard. Studies of the true cross and other things, which the Vatican did not approve. Why are you smiling?'

113

'They make a curious pair. Lanholtz searching for a brush to whitewash the Jews and O'Hare redefining his religion to suit himself.'

'He told Victor once that the victory over sin and death was what concerned him, rather than the discovery of a few old documents. You can imagine Victor's reaction to that. Furious.'

I informed Nicoletta I thought she had earned a doctorate in human relations, working with those two crazies for so long.

'Victor was easy once you understood him. And I never had much to do with Ramsay except to listen to some of his theories every time he came to Jerusalem.'

'All the same . . .'

'Working like this is more to my taste.' She gestured toward the chaos around us and smiled. 'Do you mind the mess?'

'I like a lived-in library.'

'We haven't really lived in it, though, have we?'

I took her hand and drew her close against me. After a while, she said, 'Maybe we should close the door.'

'Or go to the bedroom.'

'We could do that, Jay.'

We made love and we talked a little and we made love again. After a steaming shower together, we dressed and went to Prunier's, where we laughed a lot and ate like lumberjacks. By two we were home in bed again, nestled in each other's arms. At eight-thirty the next morning the telephone rang and I groped my way back from the sleep of angels. Nicoletta never stirred.

'My dear' – it was Mansour – 'the text for your advertisement must be sent off this morning if we're to make the Sunday editions. Shall I read it to you?'

'If you think it's necessary.'

'The *Times* ad will be two columns, *discret*, but in display type. It reads: "Antiquarian intermediary authorized to recover Roman papyri, ceramics, jewellery and other artifacts from recently dispersed Jerusalem museum collection. Original owners open to negotiation. Payment in dollars, sterling or other currency as desired. Place of delivery immaterial. All communications absolutely confidential." Then I give my Paris telephones as well as the newspaper post box.'

'Sounds fine, Hippolyte, assuming the thief reads the papers.'

'It will appear on the same page as the sales ads of Sotheby's. You did not send me the Lantholtz paper to read, as you promised, by the way. Did you change your mind?'

'Sorry. I forgot.'

'Shall I send someone?'

'You'll have a copy this morning.'

I wrapped myself in a bathrobe and wandered out to the kitchen, where Nelida already had the coffee ready and was withdrawing a tray of hot buttered croissants from the warming oven.

The courtyard below the windows was dry, but the sky was the same milky grey it had been since my return. Did the sun only shine in Greece and the Middle East? Where were the beautiful golden days Air France talked about? Yet I was pleased in spite of the weather. I even complimented Nelida on the coffee, which brought a look of puzzled wonder to her face.

In the dining room, the Paris *Herald Tribune* told me Chris Evert had won another tennis championship. Giscard was in London. Rabin was giving the Arabs hell. A government crisis was shaping up in Italy, floods in Bangladesh and famine in Mauritania. In Rome, Monsignor Giulio Ricci, archivist of the Vatican congregation of bishops, told the press that his twenty-year study of a winding sheet in Turin proved it to be that of Jesus Christ. The ancient shroud, brought by crusaders from the Middle East in 1353, clearly revealed the telltale marks of a scourged and crucified body, pierced in the side by a spear. Bloodstains and the imprint of a crown of thorns also proved its genuineness, Ricci said. I wondered what Ramsay O'Hare would make of that.

I was turning to the inside back of the paper to catch up with the Jets when another small headline caught my eye. GUNMAN KILLED BY AUSTRIAN POLICE AFTER MANHUNT. Before I even began to read, I knew what the article had to be about. 'Police shot and killed a suspected murderer today in the Vienna woods after tracking him with dogs and helicopters. The fugitive, Wilhelm Ernst Gansfeld, a Dutch national, tried to shoot his way out of a police trap yesterday, wounding two officers. Gansfeld was wanted by authorities for questioning in connection with a robbery and murder in Israel earlier this month.'

Berman must be furious. And Suriel? I could picture the young detective's frustration upon arriving in Vienna to be told his prisoner was at the morgue. And the soldier Sussman? He should be behind bars by now. But the other one, Frenchy La Roche in Paris, could be eating breakfast at this moment reading the article I had just finished. I thought of telephoning Goff to ask what was happening. Before I finished my coffee, however, Nelida announced that there was a gentleman who wished to see me.

'At this hour?'

She handed me a business card which read: 'Dreyfus & Sterne, Commercial Credit Investigations.' Scrawled across the back were the words: *'Recommandé par M. Goff.'*

'Show him in, Nelida, thanks.'

The man who entered the dining room could have stepped out of an old French comic film. He was short, thin, probably in his fifties, dressed in black and carrying a battered grey homburg. The suit was shiny from wear, and the hat, close up, was in bad need of a cleaning. He had a long, dough-coloured face of pure tragedy, punctuated by a Chaplin moustache that looked as if it had been stuck on with spirit gum. He extended one thin white hand to shake mine.

'Sterne,' he said, and then in French went on to excuse himself for disturbing my breakfast. I invited him to sit down and Nelida served him a cup of coffee. It was hard to believe such a slight, diffident fellow could possibly be Goff's representative in Paris.

When I asked him if Herr Goff had given him the facts of the case, he nodded vigorously.

'Oui, Monsieur le Docteur, by telex.' Somehow, the idea of this odd little fellow working with modern tools of communication seemed the ultimate anachronism. If he was an ex-cop like Goff, he certainly disguised the fact. As he talked, I found it difficult to give him serious attention. His voice was high-pitched, his eyes moist and creased like stewed fruit. Most of the time he gazed dejectedly at his folded hands with a fixed expression around the down-turned mouth, shaped, it seemed, by

decades of anticipated disaster. He was telling me that he had located La Roche, but had not yet questioned him. 'Monsieur Goff did not know whether we would be able to arrest him now or not.'

'Did you read this?' I pushed the *Tribune* across the table and pointed to the article on Willi.

'Yes, this morning.'

'I'm no better informed than you, Monsieur Sterne, but I assume if the Israelis had a warrant for Willi Gansfeld, by now there must be one for La Roche as well.'

'Our Interior Ministry knows nothing and the Israeli embassy had not opened when I left to come here. Perhaps we could call them?' He made the call without looking up the number.

After being shunted through two or three desks, he found someone he knew. Yes, the request for La Roche's extradition had arrived that morning, but it would take a day to process through the Interior Ministry. Sterne hung up and smiled weakly.

'Goff told me how you are mainly interested in recovering your museum exhibits,' he said, as if it was the most tragic news he had ever heard. 'You are prepared to cooperate with us in interrogating this man?'

'If I can be of any help, yes.' By no stretch of the imagination could I see Sterne dislocating a suspect's arm to get a question answered.

'Very well,' he said, rising from the table and retrieving his absurd hat. 'I will pick up La Roche today and call you when he is ready to answer questions.'

'Will the French police be called in?'

'Not by us,' Sterne said. 'La Roche is wanted for questioning here on other matters and we would not like a routine arrest to hold up our business. Herr Goff gave me strict orders.'

'How did you locate him, by the way?'

'He doesn't pay his bills. Our main business is collecting bad debts. Only last month we repossessed his wife's car because he was three months behind in his payments.'

'Let's hope getting our property back is as simple.'

Sterne said he thought La Roche would be helpful once he realized the seriousness of his situation.

I walked him to the door and told him it had been a

117

pleasure. His pale smile of appreciation was heartbreaking, and he shook my hand limply as if he had just lost his last appeal for clemency.

When he was gone I telephoned Goff.

'Sterne is very efficient,' he said.

'I can't say he filled me with confidence.'

Goff seemed surprised. 'You mean his appearance? Yes, he could clean himself up a bit. But he gets results.'

'When are you coming?'

'That shouldn't be necessary. Detective Suriel is arriving in Paris today. He has a warrant for La Roche.'

'Sterne doesn't want the French police involved.'

'Follow his judgment. And avoid the Israeli until Sterne has had a chance to get your information.'

'He wants me to question La Roche.'

'That was my suggestion,' Goff said.

'Except I am paying *you* to do it.'

'If you'd rather not, you need only tell Sterne,' Goff replied evenly. 'As I said –'

'He gets results.'

'Exactly.'

'I read about Willi.'

'I wish they were all that neat,' Goff said.

'I think it stinks, Goff. I want you to know.'

'Yes, of course.'

'It doesn't bother you at all, does it?'

'I'm not sentimental, Doctor.'

'What about the two officers he shot?'

'I warned Kalb to be careful.'

'Jesus!'

'Well, is there anything else, Doctor?'

'Not if I can help it.' I slammed down the receiver, hoping one day Herr Franz Goff would meet someone tough enough to twist *his* arm until it snapped. By the time Nicoletta appeared for breakfast, her eyes still sleepy and her voice huskier than usual, my black mood had deepened. She kissed me softly and asked why I looked so murderous.

'Because I'm an ass.' I showed her the newspaper story. 'I lose track of reality. Why should I be furious with Goff for engineering the official police shooting of one of the men who robbed us and killed Victor Lanholtz?'

'Oh,' was all she said.

'Why didn't I feel such righteous anger over the Lanholtz murder? My values are as warped as O'Hare's.'

'Perhaps because you didn't know Victor,' Nicoletta said.

'Not good enough. I felt sorry for Willi Gansfeld and I didn't know him either.'

'Maybe you should get someone besides this Goff.'

'The problem is who? Berman recommended him. And I can't say he isn't earning his fee, outrageous as it is.' I poured us both some coffee. 'You should have seen the creep he sent around here earlier today. His man in Paris. A skip-tracer who claims he's located the Frenchman.'

'Have they arrested him?'

'No. That doesn't seem to be the way Goff operates. I'm really over my head in this business, Nicky. Sterne wants *me* to question him before they call in the police.'

'Are you going to, Jay?'

'I don't know. No. Of course not. They can do it themselves with or without police assistance.'

'You told me Berman recommended some other detective too, didn't you?'

'A Greek-American who cheats on his expense account. But he's not here; he's in England.'

The telephone was ringing and I answered it.

'Dr. Marcus, this is Suriel. How are you, sir?'

Fine and dandy, ginger peachy, on top of the world! 'Not bad, Suriel. How was your trip?'

He was calling from the Israeli embassy to say he had already talked with the Sûreté and was on his way to a meeting with them concerning La Roche. 'I'd like to drop by afterward, if it's no trouble,' he said.

'My pleasure.'

'Around noon all right?'

'Well . . .'

'I can make it later if you prefer.'

'Why don't we have a drink around seven?'

'That would be fine, Doctor. See you then.'

'Will you arrest La Roche today?'

'We have to find him first, sir.'

'I thought by now . . .'

'Only the address of a bar in Montmartre. But the Sûreté is pulling all stops to help.'

'Well . . . ah . . . good luck.'

I replaced the telephone slowly. Why had I not told him the truth? I had given my word to Berman to keep them posted and at the first chance I had broken it. I knew what Goff was and I was privately appalled at the impression Sterne had made with his brief visit. Yet that ridiculous man in his shiny black suit had found La Roche in a day while the Paris police were still searching. Goff had better be right about Sterne's capacity for results. Otherwise I was making something more than a hash of things; I was obstructing the very officers assigned to bring the man in. There could be no excuse for that if things went badly.

'Would you like another cup?' Nicoletta asked.

I shook my head and smiled uneasily.

'Now tell me,' she said, 'how you plan to spend your day.'

EIGHT

Victor Lanholtz was a Berliner. He had grown up in a massive turn-of-the-century house near the Wannsee, with a park, a small pond and a croquet court under stately trees. His father had been a prosperous patent attorney, adviser to two generations of Bayers and Farbens. Childhood was a succession of tutors, English nannies and French governesses for him, his older brother, Franz, and two sisters. His mother gave lavish dinner parties in their oaken hall for the Kaiser's cabinet ministers. The place was a warren of maids, footmen, cooks and grooms in those days. Although Franz was clearly bright and athletic, and the girls were lively and pretty like their mother, Victor was the prodigy. His gift for languages, his photo-retentive memory and his consuming curiosity were apparent from an early age and he became the centre of a doting family. The First World War changed all that. Franz was killed serving as a medical officer in the Second Battle of the Marne. Victor's father died in the influenza epidemic of 1918. His sisters married and the last of his mother's property was 'purchased' by a Nazi party official in 1935, the year Lanholtz was dismissed from his post at Marburg University for being a Jew. The home near the Wannsee was bombed out of existence by B-17s in March of 1945, when Major Victor Lanholtz was reentering

Germany as an American intelligence officer. Most of the others in the family – the mother, the two sisters with their husbands and children, the uncles and aunts and a score of cousins – perished in the ovens of Auschwitz.

'That's him, on the left,' Professor Merle said, indicating a blond, tousle-haired officer in American fatigues who smiled and made the victory 'V' for the unknown photographer. There were four of them in the snapshot, taken in the formal garden of an English estate on Boxing Day 1942. He passed me the photograph with a trembling, liver-spotted hand. 'It was a long time ago,' he said.

I sipped at the sherry Merle had asked me to pour because of the Parkinsonism from which he suffered. Outside the windows of the small apartment, the metallic sky descended again and the cobbled pavement grew slippery from the drizzle. We sat at his desk, pictures spread about under the soft yellow light of a bronze reading lamp. The enamelled Empire clock on the wall behind him pinged four times in muted tones.

When Merle rested his hands on the desk, the fingers trembled against the thumbs as if he were rolling imaginary cigarettes. 'Vic and I were sent to Strasbourg that fall. Or rather we were dropped into a field near Saverne. That's where I got this.' He indicated the pink line of an old scar which ran across his forehead above thick white eyebrows. 'It's hilly around there. We went in at night, jumping from four hundred feet. Hit my head on a rock and thought I'd bleed to death.' His English was crisp and cultivated. Occasionally he switched to French for a sentence or two and then back again.

'Was that when you were captured?'

'Much later. We had a good winter. Vic's cover as an inspector for the French railways held up well. I posed as a French fascist. We lived it up, gorging ourselves on *coq au Riesling* and *choucroute garnie* at Le Crocodile with our German officer friends. I was helping to organize a local resistance network during those months, while he scouted intelligence, which he radioed back to England. Troop movements, bomber targets – that sort of thing. Until one night what every agent dreads happened. A Nazi walked into Le Crocodile who had once been a student of Vic's. Vic disappeared like smoke but I stayed on after this officer

121

joined the group. He had seen Vic get his coat, however, and stared at him as he left the restaurant. When one of the other officers asked what he was gawking at, he said, "That chap who just left. I could swear he is a Jew from Marburg." I was gnawing on a chicken leg at that moment and had all I could do to keep from throwing up, I was so frightened.'

'Did they go after him?'

'They thought it was a marvellous joke. Imagine a district inspector for the French railways who looks like a German Jew! That night I radioed London to get us out, but the plane they sent was shot down. We decided to leg it to Paris and were arrested by French police who questioned my documents.' Merle laughed mirthlessly. 'Mine had been provided by our intelligence staff in London. Vic had forged his own and they passed perfectly. He was very clever at things like that. But he couldn't help me. From there it was only a short drop to the Gestapo net. Luckily we had our act well rehearsed.'

'What did you tell them?'

'We admitted to being escaped prisoners of war.'

'But couldn't they check?'

'In my case it was true. I had been captured once in Africa. In Vic's it wasn't, but they believed him. He was a gifted liar and lucky. They never discovered he was a Jew.'

'Not even suspicious?'

'Remember he was blond and very fit, and their propaganda described a Jew as being the opposite of that. Although he was in his forties then, he looked ten years younger. He also wore his American dog tags.'

'What about the man who recognized him?'

'We never saw him again after that night in Strasbourg, but for thirty years I have been unable to smell chicken or sauerkraut without feeling a slight wave of nausea.'

'I was told you were the one who got Lanholtz out.'

Merle selected another snapshot from the stack he had been sorting and passed it to me. 'He was ill. There were ten in the breakout. I lagged behind to help him and let the others go on. They were all killed or recaptured. So you could say he saved my life as much as I saved his.'

The photograph showed Lanholtz, grinning again, in Eisenhower jacket and ribbons, with his arm around a smiling, rather plump young woman in Wren uniform. 'Battersea Park,' Merle said, 'the day they were married.'

'Did he have any other family?'

'Hitler got the rest.'

'Where is she now?' I said, passing the picture back to him.

'England. They were divorced years ago.' He slid the bottle across the desk. 'Please help yourself.'

My visit had been on impulse earlier that afternoon when I found myself close by his house. Although I dropped in only to thank him for his cooperation on the Lanholtz paper, we had become deeply involved in discussing the man Merle had known for more than thirty years.

'He had enemies.' Merle tilted back in his chair and folded his hands to stop the tremor.

'Because of his brilliance?'

'Because of his arrogance. His behaviour sometimes verged on the unethical.'

'In what way?'

'The usual. Stealing the work of talented graduate students. Mind you, it is an accepted practice in some academic circles, a quid pro quo where the professor approves the student's doctorate and gives him a glowing recommendation for a faculty appointment at another university. In return the professor absorbs the student's work into his own when he publishes, and questions are rarely ever asked. Certainly not by the ex-student, who can and often does get revenge in the future by stealing from his own crop of protégés.'

'Surely Lanholtz never had to stoop to that.'

'Not consciously, perhaps. He considered anyone who worked under him a mere extension of himself. Do you know Ross at Oxford?'

'I know of him.'

'He was a student of Vic's after the war. Together they picked through half the ruins of Aachen and turned up some remarkable Carolingian stuff. Vic used him like a machine, but in five years never allowed him to publish a word on his own. It all came out in Vic's Charlemagne book, which some of us consider Ross's finest work.' The old man chuckled and leaned across the desk again, shuffling the pictures about. 'There's one of him here somewhere.'

'But they remained friends.'

'The best of enemies, you might say,' Merle replied. 'They had other differences too, of a more personal nature. But

Ross got his chair at Oxford through Vic's influence when he was still quite young, so I suppose he considered it a fair exchange.'

'Do you believe Lanholtz looked at it that way?'

Merle smiled woodenly, and the rhythmic shake of his head became more pronounced. 'You can be sure he didn't. Vic never felt he owed anybody anything. Except me, and that was an endless source of embarrassment to us both. He could never understand anyone doing him a favour.'

'Let alone saving his life.'

A dry, empty laugh came from Merle.

'I've been told he was obsessed by anti-Semitism.'

Merle turned his gaze toward the grey afternoon beyond the window. After a while he said, 'No one could know Vic long without discovering that side of him. Mind you, he had his reasons. He spent a year after the war supervising the most gruesome digs in history, sifting through ashes at the extermination camps for trial evidence. Vic was a key witness at Nuremberg and remained very bitter because so many convicted Nazis served such light sentences.'

I told Merle what Ari Ascher had said about Victor Lanholtz's commitment, and how Ascher even suggested it might have related in some way to his death. If his testimony had been vital in convicting people after the war, could one of them have hated him enough to kill him nearly thirty years later?

The professor was thoughtful before saying, 'You would agree it is far-fetched?'

'To me, yes. Anyone with such a motive could have killed him ages ago. It isn't credible that some paroled ex-Nazi saved his Deutsche marks all these years for a trip to Israel in order to do in his old nemesis.'

'So many aspects of the Nazi experience defy credibility,' Merle said.

'Did he ever return to Berlin?'

'Once. When we were in Strasbourg. He had faked a great many papers with the hope of getting the rest of his family out. Strictly against regulations.'

'Did you help him?'

'I was young then, and not exactly reconciled to the idea of the whole mission being compromised for the sake of Vic's relatives.'

'That was when?'

'The winter of '43, '44. The peak year of the "final solution." His mother and sisters were already dead, although no one knew it then. The reaction finally sent him to Israel. He was an arrogant bastard even *in extremis*. Ah, well. I hope he found whatever he was looking for before he died, poor Vic.'

When I was leaving, Professor Merle accompanied me to the door and said, 'Does Israel have the death penalty or is it like our enlightened France, where killers are pensioned off in prison?'

I told him I did not know.

'I hope they do,' the old man said. 'I believe a punishment should fit the crime.'

In one of those surprisingly abrupt changes familiar to Parisians, the drizzle ceased, the overcast shredded into scattered dirty clouds and the lowering sun suddenly broke through the nacre sky. Pavement glistened silver, and the old grey trees in the Luxembourg Gardens rustled with chill gusts, their brittle foliage flashing like minnows. I turned up my collar against the wind and hurried along the Rue des Médicis toward home, the taste of sherry lingering like the old man's words, dry and a little rough, but appropriate.

Nicoletta had not returned when I arrived. Jeanette was at the insurance company arranging for the policy on my unpaid-for volume of the Albucasis work, and Nelida had gone to do the marketing. The telephone began to ring almost immediately.

It was Sterne, who sounded even more abandoned than when I had met him that morning. He gave me the address of a private clinic in Neuilly near the Ancien Cimetière. Convenient for a clinic.

'We have him here, Doctor. Could you drop by in about an hour?'

'Is he sick?'

Sterne made a clucking noise on the telephone. 'He's quite well, monsieur. Tired, but looking forward to meeting you.'

'I can imagine. All right, Sterne. I'll get there as soon as I can.' I hung up. Then, in a sudden spasm of conscience, I looked up another number and dialled it. After a short wait, the switchboard operator put me through. 'Look, Suriel,' I said, 'are you free right now?'

If I were ill in Paris, I would go to the American Hospital because fear brings out my patriotism and causes me to forget my French. But if I simply wanted a few days' rest in luxurious surroundings without leaving the city, the Clinique Mornet would be as good a choice as any. A limestone mansion set back from the Boulevard Jean Mermoz and half hidden by a dozen ancient oak trees and trimmed barriers of laurel, the clinic looks like any private home or embassy residence in Neuilly. There is no sign or number, nothing to give it away.

Sterne waited shivering by the gate when Suriel and I arrived in a black CD Citroën he had borrowed from the Israeli embassy. A uniformed security guard clicked a remote lock and the gate swung open. Sterne got in the back seat and we drove up the circular drive beyond the laurel and the oaks, to park under a formidable porte-cochere at the side of the building. I introduced the Israeli detective to the French bill collector.

Sterne led us inside, along a silent, freshly painted corridor past an abandoned wheelchair and a pair of chintz sofas. There was not a soul anywhere. He stopped at a door and knocked. A voice answered from the other side and Sterne announced himself. The door opened to reveal a man of massive proportions, with close-cropped hair and tiny button eyes which darted from Sterne to me to Suriel. The man was dressed in a hospital attendant's high-collared white jacket which was much too tight.

'This is Edgardo,' Sterne said, walking past him to stand beside a figure in a cranked-up hospital bed, 'and *this* is La Roche.' The full-bearded man in the bed might have been an ordinary hospital patient except for the handcuffs that locked his wrists to the bed frame and the tight gag that cut across his mouth like a badly tied surgical mask. I had explained about Sterne and Company to Suriel on the way to the clinic and he had agreed to defer calling in the Sûreté until after he had seen and questioned La Roche. Sterne was not at all happy about my bringing the Israeli.

La Roche's eyes followed us as we gathered around the

126

bed. There were some straight-backed metal chairs against the wall and Sterne invited us to sit.

'If necessary, we have a little Sodium Pentothal to help him.' Sterne cleared his throat nervously. 'One cc. as needed in an intravenous drip, Doctor. Correct?'

'I wouldn't know,' I said.

Suriel moved close to the bed. Edgardo brought him a chair, but he ignored it. 'Can you take off that gag?' Suriel asked. Edgardo obeyed. La Roche worked his lips but remained silent, his body motionless beneath the light cotton sheets pulled up under his chin.

The Israeli sat on the edge of the bed and smiled reassuringly at La Roche. Then he said, 'I've been told you understand English. I have a warrant for your arrest on a charge of first-degree murder, Mr. La Roche. Your extradition has already been arranged with the French government. Would you like to see the papers before we begin?'

La Roche's stare was pure hostility. He said nothing. I had an idea the session was not going to be as easy as Sterne had indicated. The man in the bed was big, not along the gargantuan lines of Edgardo, but tall and broad-shouldered and powerful-looking, even in repose. He had a sharp-featured, sullen face, a vain little sliver of a mouth beneath the beard, and pomade on his thick, greying hair. A lady-killer; something in the smirk that indicated a man who shoots his cuffs, leers and tugs his crotch around women.

'Shall we begin?' Suriel said.

'*Salaud!*' La Roche hissed.

'You'll sign this as witness, Doctor? Monsieur Sterne?'

I nodded. Sterne shrugged.

'Your name is Arnaud La Roche, is it not?'

La Roche looked at the ceiling, too bored to reply.

'Answer him,' Sterne said unconvincingly.

La Roche ignored him.

'Your name?' Suriel repeated.

Nothing.

'Oh, my God,' Sterne said.

'Maybe the Sûreté should handle this,' Suriel said to me. 'Apparently he doesn't understand.'

'He understands everything,' Sterne cried. 'La Roche, why do you make trouble?'

'It's all right,' Suriel said. 'He doesn't have to talk now. If

127

he'd rather save it for Tel Aviv, that's his privilege. Willi told us all we need to know anyway.' He rose from the bed and put away his notebook.

'*Merde*,' La Roche said.

Suriel responded cheerfully. 'Willy admitted to the thefts with you and Sussman, but they both said you were the murderer. So it's your word against theirs.'

La Roche only glared at the detective. Edgardo was whispering with Sterne in a corner. Sterne came over to me and said, 'If you and the other gentleman don't mind waiting in the hall for a minute, Doctor, maybe I can talk a little to this chap.'

'I don't think so, Sterne. Mr. Suriel has a point. It's time we called the Sûreté.'

'It makes it awkward for me, monsieur, Sterne pleaded in a barely audible voice, moving me toward the door with a soft hand at my elbow. 'If we have the police here, the clinic director will be furious. I had no objection when you showed up with the Israeli detective. That's all right.' He cleared his throat. 'But I believe you have an agreement with Herr Goff, monsieur, to let us manage this case as we see fit.'

'To let *Goff* manage it. Not you, Mr. Sterne.'

'I'm sorry you don't have confidence, monsieur,' Sterne replied in his whining whisper. 'But if you insist on the police, then Edgardo and I must leave.'

'That's up to you.'

'And we would . . . ah . . . have to take the prisoner.'

'Now just a goddamned minute, Sterne!'

He had the door open and was shushing me humbly, all the while propelling us both into the hallway.

'Please . . .' he pleaded.

Suriel came out behind us. 'Is there a telephone?' he asked Sterne.

'I was just explaining to Dr. Marcus how awkward things could be if you called the Sûreté,' Sterne said.

'He's threatening to release La Roche.'

The detective hesitated. 'It would help,' Suriel said, 'to get something definite out of him.'

'You have the statements of Willi and the soldier,' I protested. 'Can't we let La Roche do his talking in Israel?'

'I don't have statements from anybody,' Suriel replied bitterly.

When I stepped back through the door, Edgardo was standing over La Roche's form. He had on heavy rubber gloves of the kind workers wear in chemical factories and was hooking up a step-down transformer which stood on the bedside table. From the transformer ran two long wires with vicious little alligator clamps on the ends.

'What the hell do you think you're doing!' I pulled the transformer plug from the wall socket. Sterne wrung his hands nervously as I pushed Edgardo back out of the way. La Roche lay with his eyes closed, bathed in sweat in the draughty room.

'I was only trying to help,' Edgardo said in French.

'Get the police,' I said to Suriel. 'This has gone as far as it is going.' La Roche opened his eyes, searching the room until they rested on Edgardo.

'Never mind the police,' La Roche said in English. His voice was a deep-throated rasp. 'Get him out of here and I'll tell you what you want to know.'

Sterne, taken by surprise, glanced nervously from La Roche to me. When I nodded, he said curtly, 'Wait outside.' Edgardo, sinister in his indifference, closed the door behind him while Suriel resumed his place on the edge of the bed. La Roche did not look at him as he opened his notebook and checked the time on his watch. 'On the night of September 28, did you rob the Marcus Museum in Jerusalem, Israel?'

'I . . . yes.'

Suriel began to take notes, glancing from time to time at La Roche. 'With who?'

'With . . . others.'

'Name them.'

He did.

'Did you kill Dr. Victor Lanholtz?'

'No.'

'He's lying,' Sterne said. He stepped to the bedside and leaned forward, putting his face close to La Roche's, whispering in French.

'Did you kill Dr. Victor Lanholtz?' Suriel repeated.

'Willi hit him.'

'Willi says it was you.'

'I never killed anybody.'

'So you say it was Willi.'

'Yes.'

'What happened?'

'We were loading the van, Sussman and I. Willi was still inside the building and I saw someone go into the museum. I went to warn Willi. When I reached the room where the things were, I saw the old man between us. He was shouting at Willi. He picked up a hammer and hit him.'

'Willi did?'

'No. The old fellow hit Willi, but he was too strong. He got the hammer away and hit him – I don't know – two or three times on the head until he fell down. We told him to shut up, but he wouldn't. So Willi hit him again.'

'And killed him?'

'He wasn't even out. We hurried to get the rest of the things loaded. I made Sussman stay outside in case anyone had heard. But nobody came near the place.'

'Then?'

'We left.'

'No one gave him a few final licks so he wouldn't be around to identify you?'

'He was sitting up, moaning, when we left. He was tough,' La Roche said.

'No, he wasn't,' Suriel said. 'He was face down on the floor. The top of his skull was crushed so badly, pieces of brain and bone were found a metre away.'

'We didn't do that.'

To my surprise, Suriel did not insist. 'Where did you go from the museum?'

'Sussman knew a place near Jericho. We started out for there.'

'You, Sussman and Willi.'

'Yes.'

'Go on.'

'I drove the van. That stupid Willi had another car, but he ran out of gas.'

'We know all about that,' Suriel said. 'We also know you took the things to Nablus and not to Jericho.'

La Roche said nothing.

'Who did you give them to?'

'A couple of Arabs. They were supposed to get them out of Israel.'

'Names?'

'One was Mahmoud Rassan, who owns a garage there.

The other one worked with him, but I don't know his name.'

'Who introduced you?'

'Willi knew them.'

'He says you did.'

'No.'

'Who hired you?'

'Willi.'

'I don't believe that.'

'He hired me and Sussman.'

'Stop lying.'

'It's true. I don't know who paid Willi. Can I have some water?'

'Be my guest.'

'My hands,' he said, and at my insistence Sterne reluctantly freed him from the bed frame. Suriel put his pad aside and leaned forward to take the glass and water pitcher from the bedside table. In the same half second, La Roche swung the handcuffs like a flail hard at the detective's head, knocking him to the floor. The Frenchman bounced upright, to land on his feet next to Sterne. I heard Sterne cry out as La Roche's knee found his groin and doubled him into me. I lunged clumsily around the bed, expecting La Roche to rush for the door, but the man fooled us all. He grabbed one of the metal chairs near the French window and swung it in a wide arc. Narrowly missing me, it crashed through the glass, and La Roche followed it like an acrobat, his white half-clad body a blur against the outside darkness. He stumbled when he hit the lawn below the window, but he was on his feet and running again in an instant.

Suriel, on his knees, had his revolver out and was aiming at the retreating white figure. Sterne, from his foetal position of agony on the floor, gasped, 'Don't!' and I caught Suriel's arm, pulling him off balance.

La Roche was gone as surely as Willi, but this time no one had planned it that way. Edgardo stood cursing by the smashed window as I helped Suriel to his feet. Sterne lay on his side, hands clutched at his belly and knees drawn up.

An angry white-haired woman in nurse's uniform appeared in the doorway and screamed at Sterne. While Edgardo began to explain, Suriel said, 'He can't get far.'

After a careful search of the grounds with the clinic watchman, we roamed the neighbourhood streets in the

Citroën for two discouraging hours without a sign of the pyjama-clad fugitive. When we returned to the clinic, Sterne was feeling better. At least he was able to speak and move, even if he could not yet stand straight without some pain.

Only then did I realize Suriel was angry at Sterne. 'Why didn't you have his feet tied to the bed?' he demanded of the hapless investigator.

'I couldn't have a ground.'

Suriel tore back the cover from the hospital bed to reveal the rubber sheet. 'Excuse me, Sterne,' he said in a voice heavy with disgust, 'but you're a damn ass.'

'We were only going to tickle him a little,' Sterne replied defensively, cushioning the criticism.

'Next time, tie him down with plastic clothesline. You can buy it in any hardware store.'

'I didn't think of that,' Sterne said meekly.

Suriel dropped me off at a taxi stand on the Boulevard Haussmann before continuing on to the Sûreté headquarters to report the evening's developments. He was confident La Roche would not get far once the Paris police went after him. I was not so sure. The handcuffs still dangled from one wrist, he was penniless, barefoot and dressed only in hospital pyjama bottoms, but a man nimble enough to escape four others and vanish into the well-trimmed hedgerows of Neuilly was not without resources. Whether I liked it or not, I had been getting an education these past days. From Goff's perverted sense of gamesmanship to Sterne's tickling. What bothered me most was the apparent acceptance of it by the parties concerned, particularly young Suriel. I preferred my own quiet world, where the hardest questions are answered by the long-dead. Yet the chase stimulated me; it was only the kill I had to get used to. Suriel was probably right. The police would run La Roche to ground by daybreak. How far could he get? He was lying, surely. And terrified enough of someone to make his desperate rush tonight even though he must have known Suriel was armed. As I was getting out of the Citroën, I asked Suriel what information they had got from Sussman, the soldier.

'Not a damn thing,' he said.

'But he must have corroborated some of Willi's story.'

'How could he?' Suriel replied. 'He was killed by a sniper

132

on Mount Hermon last Tuesday. Buried with honours, the sonofabitch.'

NINE

If the serious student of human behaviour discovers anything special about our species, it is that we are the ones who developed murder as a form of social expression and refined it to its present level of sophistication. Fossilized skulls of our axe-toting ancestors three million years old have been found by Dr. Leakey in Africa, *all* of them bashed in by other axe-toting ancestors for reasons known only to the killers, but easily guessable by modern paleontologists, anthropologists and policemen. Skipping down through the millennia quickly to the period I am most familiar with, when politics, technology and a certain moral laissez faire fused to produce that historical phenomenon known as the Roman Empire, we find murder happily institutionalized as social custom in a closely regulated society. Ritual murder in the temple, political murder in the forum, mass murder on the battlefield, or murder for entertainment in the circus were all acceptable to those who made the rules.

Although mass murder has retained its social standing among nations, random murder seems more in keeping with casual modern life styles. The strangled housewife, the dismembered child and the mugged subway traveller tell us most about ourselves.

Pull a trigger, press a button, throw a stone. It is all of a piece. Violence is the most easily understood of all human actions because it is easily the most commonplace. Only the random victim fills us with occasional dread, and comprehension of a motive becomes more important than apprehension of a killer.

In Jerusalem, Victor Lanholtz dies in a manner that is three and a half million years old, from a depressed compound parietal fracture of the skull. What would Berman say? What scenarios is he sketching for his own guidance? Rule out the long-suffering Nazi bent on revenge. Rule out the disgruntled student and the people on the museum staff. Ari Ascher liked Lanholtz. Nicoletta worshipped him. The others were awed by him except for Lev Vagan. But I discount Vagan because he was with me the night it happened.

Proving what? He could have hired three men to steal the collection from the museum while he was dining with us in Tel Aviv.

Give me a scenario, Berman, or better yet, let me give you one. Lev Vagan hired the soldier Sussman, who used to work in the museum, to steal the collection. Sussman brought in Frenchy La Roche and Willi Gansfeld. When Victor Lanholtz showed up that night unexpectedly, they killed him to shut him up and it matters little which one actually wielded the hammer.

Berman listened politely on a very good connection and heard me out, before he said, 'It don't make a lot of sense.'

'No? Why?'

'That's just it. Why? Lanholtz shuts Vagan out. Vagan don't like it. Lanholtz is going to give his paper at this archaeology meeting no matter what Vagan says. The collection is good for the museum. Vagan may be sore, but he's no dope. So he makes his peace and things work out. Maybe he can't take credit for finding the stuff, but he can take credit for keeping crazy old Lanholtz on the payroll, where another museum would have canned him. No. Vagan wouldn't steal those scrolls, because he already had them.'

'Suppose he was afraid of losing them?'

'How?'

'Legally. To Ramsay O'Hare and another museum.'

'There's easier ways to prevent that.'

'Then who, Inspector?'

'Doctor, if I knew –'

'Suppose it was O'Hare? How does that grab you? The frustrated religious crank pays for the heist and has the collection safely disposed of.'

'Disposed how?'

'There's a flourishing black market in antiquities. He could find buyers for almost everything.'

'Why? To get his money back?'

'Maybe.'

'Give me a better reason.'

'I'm afraid I can't think of one.'

134

'Neither can I, Doctor, which is why O'Hare got crossed off our list early.'

'What about the Nablus garage owner? Don't tell me. He escaped to Damascus.'

'He's a Christian Arab who remembered three guys that serviced a Volkswagen van the morning after the robbery. He had never seen them before and had no reason to be suspicious.'

'Why did both Willi and La Roche tell the same story about Nablus? No, Berman, there's more to that garage owner than you think. He is the only lead we have and you ought to put him through the wringer over there in Jerusalem. Bring Goff to talk to him; he'll find out.'

'We questioned him a whole day, and not gently.'

'And you believe that crap about greasing the van?'

Berman chuckled. 'Unless La Roche incriminates him officially, we have to.'

'Who knows where La Roche is?'

'Well, we can't talk to this guy again without a damn good reason. The archbishop of the Melchite church in Jerusalem was on to the interior minister. Heavy leaning on yours truly. Charge him or let him go. So we let him go.'

'But you believed him.'

'I believe everybody, Doctor.'

'Berman, you're mistaken. The murderers went there. He's part of it. Otherwise why would they have gone to him in Nablus?'

'He lives in Nablus.'

'Very funny.'

'I'll tell you something funnier. I agree with you.'

'Did you search the garage owner's place?'

'Clean as a fresh diaper.'

'I don't believe it.'

'Doctor?'

'Yes, Inspector.'

'Neither do I.'

'Then why don't you . . . ?'

'We can't.'

'But –'

'If he'd been a Jew, you understand, I wouldn't have this kind of problem. But a Christian Arab in occupied territory is something else. We need all the friends we can get these days, as our interior minister explained to me, and the archbishop qualifies.'

'Surely you can do something.'

'Right.'

'What?'

'Wait.'

'Why?'

'Oh, they come and go, these guys, you understand?'

'No, I don't understand.'

'It's bigger than both of us, Doctor.'

'What is that supposed to mean? Are you still being pressured?'

'I should be the exception?'

'What can I do?'

'Hire Panagoulos if you're fed up with Goff. Find La Roche. Suriel's been ordered to stay in Paris until you do. But get him into a cheaper hotel or he'll bankrupt the government. And don't forget one thing.'

'I'm listening.'

'The three assholes who pulled this job did not break into the museum. Either Lanholtz let them in or somebody had a key.'

'Sussman used to work there as a janitor.'

'But Lanholtz had the laboratory locks changed.'

'Vagan . . .'

'. . . didn't have a key. It was one of the things made him angry.'

'Lanholtz knew Sussman. Maybe he let him in.'

'Sure. Ask La Roche about that when you see him.'

A week after the unfortunate session at the Clinique Mornet, there was still no trace of La Roche. Suriel had said he could not get far, but for all we knew he was already sunning himself on the Copacabana or cruising the coast of Borneo. Either the Paris police were making only a small effort to find him (which seemed possible) or they were hopelessly inefficient (which seemed unlikely) or La Roche had got clean out of the country before the manhunt began (which now seemed certain).

Suriel called daily or dropped by the apartment to report. He was as discouraged as I, but satisfied the French authorities were doing everything possible. Sterne surfaced four days after La Roche's disappearance, as shabby and dejected as ever, to complain that *he* was having trouble finding Goff, and to apologize for not contacting me sooner. He had been convalescing at his daughter's house in St. Cloud and was still quite ill, he said. One of his testicles was twice its normal size and he found walking an agony.

'Have you seen a doctor?'

When he shook his head, I called a medical colleague whose consulting office was near the university, and told Sterne to go there. Before he shuffled out the door, he said, 'I hate to bother you with this, Doctor, but we incurred some heavy expenses on La Roche.'

'Just send me the bill,' I told him. 'And tell Goff, if you talk to him, that he should at least return a client's calls.'

Sterne agreed absolutely, but said, 'This is a very personal business, sir. I think that is why Herr Goff is often absent, sometimes out of touch for days, attending to things personally.'

'Attending to other cases, you mean.'

'He is a busy man,' Sterne said helplessly.

'Let me know how things go,' I told him as he backed out the door.

'It's very kind of you,' he said, nodding in agreement with himself, birdlike fingers clutching his ridiculous hat, the tragi-comic face a bas-relief of suffering. When I closed the door I half expected to hear the crash as he did his pratfall off camera.

His visit had been in the early afternoon, while Nicoletta was at work in the library with Jeanette, editing and typing the final draft of Victor Lanholtz's rewritten paper. The Oxford conference was scheduled to start in a week and we had notified the steering committee she would present the paper. An acknowledgment from them confirmed her on the programme for the second morning session. We had seen little of each other during the days since the La Roche incident, but our evening ritual of drinks and quiet suppers made up for that, as did the nights that followed.

By the end of the week I would have been hard pressed to describe what my life had been like before she entered it. Certainly it had not been dull or unfulfilling. If I had never married, I could honestly say I never felt the need, at least not often and not really for more than a few irresponsible hours when I was very young. I did not feel any such impulse now either; no primordial urge to procreate, no wish to bounce a child upon my knee. I only felt drawn, deeply and naturally, to this girl, in some unique way, and I was determined to protect that feeling. If love is a trap, if it is bondage, if it is a necessary self-deception, it is also a good deal more; Nicoletta brought a pervasive joy to my life that was more than sexual mystery.

I was telling her one evening about Mae Broman and my grandfather Nate, a story about them on holiday in the south of France, where Nate spent a whole weekend trying to calculate the energy needed by an atmospheric clock she had given him. Mae did not have the heart to tell him that it had all been worked out by the Swiss and the results had been included with typical Swiss thoroughness in the folder that came with the clock. After Nate spent two days filling pages with figures until he was satisfied, she checked his results against the Swiss folder after he went to bed.

'And he was right,' Nicoletta said.

'There's more to it. You see, his figures disagreed with those in the folder. So Mae sent his to Geneva with a letter suggesting the manufacturers check their math because Nathan Marcus had found an error.'

'And?'

'They wrote her a letter which Mae described as apologetic in substance and abject in tone.'

Nicoletta was laughing.

'She remembered it when he was dying in the hospital a couple of years later, and sent it to him. Aaron said it was the only time he really smiled.'

'Did you love him a lot, Jay?'

'I was a boy. What do you know at that age?'

'You know,' Nicoletta said.

'It's a funny thing,' I told her. 'Nate never awed me until long after he was dead. I mean when I was little, he was a friend. Like Aaron says, he could charm you. He could make anything sound exciting because to him everything was. He'd tell me stories about . . . his heroes. You know?'

She waited silently.

'A collection of oddballs. Pascal, Spinoza, Benjamin Rush. And Cotton Mather. Did you know Cotton Mather championed smallpox vaccination when Ben Franklin opposed it? That's the kind of bedtime story I used to get from Nate. He admired Teddy Roosevelt as a naturalist and David Dubinsky as a politician. Nate hated war but thought General Marshall would have made a wonderful president. He loved Mendelssohn and Fritz Kreisler. He admired Glenn Curtiss, whom he had known, and Lindbergh. He used to insist the great lifesavers were Semmelweis and Westinghouse, but that Stradivarius and Guarneri were the only artists. In short, he was a bit of a nut.'

'And Mae Broman loved him.'

'So it would seem. He had a wife once too.'

'What happened to her?'

'Died young. I gather it was no real marriage. Arranged by a broker. Nate seldom mentioned her to anybody.'

'Not even Mae?'

'Who knows all the things he told Mae? She only touches the highlights.'

'You never talk about your mother's side of the family.'

'They're not very interesting.'

'Sure? Or is it that your grandfather eclipsed the whole crowd?'

'That too. But they're not. Really. Priests and drunks and Boston city pols. What's to say?'

'But you're so Irish.'

'What is that supposed to mean?'

'That story you told me about when you were in school. That other boy might have been persecuting the little Jewish snob, but it could have been the Irish street fighter who nearly killed him.'

'Maybe it was the Jewish street fighter and the little Irish snob.'

'I like that interpretation too,' Nicoletta said.

'I'm glad, because I think it's closer to the truth.'

'No,' she said. 'Both interpretations are probably wrong and you know it.'

I loved her for cutting through my own pretension like that. 'Maybe,' I said, unwilling to give in.

'What did Nate think of the Irish?'

'In his own words, a glorious disaster.'

'Before or after your father married your mother?'

I laughed. 'It's true. He did employ an army of her relatives. But what about you? Born in Piacenza. Rich? Poor? You never told me.'

139

'My mother had to fight for every lira after the war. My father was a communist who placed principle before anything else, including his family. My grandfather, who *was* rich, accommodated Mussolini. They both lost.'

'You don't make that sound too complimentary.'

'It isn't. If it hadn't been for my mother, I would have become a postwar statistic in infant mortality. All my father gave me was a name.'

'And your grandfather?'

'I rather liked him, as I remember, although it was my mother and the nuns who had the most to say.'

'Yet you're not religious.'

'I dislike the Church, if that's what you mean. But I'll tell you a secret. I'm a bit of a closet Christian.'

We were both smiling. Nicoletta pretended not to find it funny when she said, 'You believe me?'

'As Berman would say, I believe everybody.'

'I am,' she said, straight. 'But you're laughing.'

'Not really.'

'I believe,' she said, tapping her heart, 'in here. I used to pray a lot when I was little, according to the rules. And nothing ever happened. Then I went the other way. The hell with the saints if they weren't going to answer my prayers. They almost never did, you know. I read a lot and drifted from the church in a tidal way. Then there was my marriage and the breakup and my work. I got hooked on work, and much of it had to do with putting little pieces of other people's faith back together again, literally. Always in the name of science. But in time, something began to get me. Who was it said anyone who seeks God has found him?'

'Pascal, I think. But Nate Marcus used to talk like that too.'

Mansour's invitation had been extended too many times to ignore, even though my idea of lunch coincided in no way with his. As he had often said to me, 'My dear, you don't eat enough to keep a pig alive.' Thus Nicoletta and I were sitting with him in his book-crowded parlour behind the shop at noon, breathing exotic odours from the nearby kitchen, where Coco was at work. Nicoletta succumbed to the old rascal's Levantine charm as we sipped our apéritifs while he devoured handfuls of pistachio nuts. They had friends in common at Sotheby's and the British Museum, and gossiped about a score of others – restorers, binders and cataloguers whose work was known to the cognoscenti from Bombay to Boston.

Mansour talked to her in Italian. I had no idea he spoke it so well. When I told him so, he fluttered his fingers disparagingly, letting a little blizzard of pistachio shells fall around the ashtray at his side. His charcoal eyes never left Nicoletta until she went to the kitchen to help Coco. Then he said, 'Marry her.'

'What?'

'You heard me.'

'Don't be ridiculous, Hippolyte. We're getting along very well the way things are.'

'Do you realize she is the first intelligent woman I have met in forty years?'

'Nonsense. You live with one.'

'Let us be under no illusions about my clever daughter. Coco is a computer, but she is not truly intelligent.' His face darkened, then brightened, as if a rheostat were working in his jowls. 'What a divine woman. Marry her before she is lost forever to the competition.'

'I'm not in the book business, Hippolyte.'

He called out to the kitchen, 'Coco, the doctor is wasting away before my eyes! We invited him to lunch, not supper!'

Coco ignored her father, but appeared a few minutes later with a restaurant-size tray covered by a dozen different plates containing a marvellous *mehze*. Half an hour later, having cleaned most of the plates with only occasional help from the rest of us, Mansour tucked into a steaming goulash of lamb and spicy dumplings, moving it along with stacks of warm Arab bread and countless glasses of good *Bourgogne*. Computer or not, Coco was a talented cook. Mansour filled his own plate twice more from the stew tureen and then demolished two large portions of baklava.

Between bites, he amused Nicoletta with observations on everything. 'De Gaulle showed us feudalism was dead, didn't he? So what choice does an honest Frenchman have today but to plunge recklessly into the mainstream of seventeenth-century thought and see where it carries him? Americans are a credit to their race ... Doctors? ... Carrion birds who feed off the suffering of the credulous!' When I reminded

141

him I was a physician, he dismissed the fact impatiently. 'You are simply a scholar who lapsed in his youth.'

'Then why are you always asking me for medical advice?'

'I ask *all* my friends for medical advice.'

'Don't believe him,' Coco said.

'You have never followed one suggestion I've given you. You still smoke two packs of Gauloises a day . . .'

'Three,' Mansour corrected me. 'Sometimes four if I read late.'

'. . . in spite of a chronic respiratory condition which will one day give you serious trouble.'

'My dear,' Mansour said, 'only the laws of probability give me trouble.'

'For a man who is otherwise kind to people,' I said to Nicoletta, 'his treatment of himself is unconscionable.'

Mansour chuckled and coughed, nearly choking with pleasure. By the time Coco brought us little cups of steaming sweet black tea, the air was once more blue with Gauloise smoke. 'I smoke forty thousand cigarettes a year,' he said as if he were imparting some precious confidence to Nicoletta, 'and have done so for forty years – no, closer to fifty. That's two million, give or take a few thousand. And more than forty thousand nourishing meals apart from breakfasts. My liver is the size of a sofa cushion, and I am, of course, inclined to put on weight . . .'

Coco laughed, shaking her head at his preposterousness.

'. . . but I have never been ill, never suffered pain or discomfort from bad digestion, nor lost a moment's sleep.'

'That last part is true,' his daughter said, 'though not terribly surprising.'

'But interestingly put,' Nicoletta said, causing a grateful smile to blossom on Hippolyte's round features.

'You *see?* She under*stands* what pleasure vices bring.'

'Did I say that?' Nicoletta asked, bewildered.

'No need, my dear. We understand each other perfectly.'

He took Nicoletta's hand between both of his and pointedly ignored me. A loud bell rang in the front of the shop and Coco went to answer it while Mansour groused about the inconsiderateness of clients who called without warning at four in the afternoon. She returned and handed him a special-delivery letter. Excusing himself, he opened it and turned aside to read through gold-rimmed pince-n

142

which hung from a black ribbon attached to his coat. Finally he passed the letter to me and said, 'First fruits.'

The letter came from the firm of Cunningham and Pine, Antiquities and Objets d'Art, Bond Street, London. It informed Mansour that the writer, Desmond Osbourne Cheney, had been approached regarding the possible private sale of certain scrolls, manuscripts and codices from a recently dispersed Middle Orient collection. Mr. Cheney's delicacy in skirting such harsh realities as robbery was notable. He managed to write three paragraphs of exquisite imprecision ('the artifacts in question,' 'objects under discussion' and 'specimens of which we have been apprised') which compromised no one.

'Do you know him?' I asked Mansour, giving the Cheney letter to Nicoletta.

'I know the firm, but . . .'

'Do you doubt their offer?'

'I must ask them for a detailed description of what they have for sale, which they will probably not provide, _or_ I must give them similar information about what you are expecting to recover.'

'We can do that,' Nicoletta said excitedly, 'at least for most of the things.'

'Should we call this Cheney?'

Mansour shook his head emphatically. 'A telephone call only alarms a man in the book business and has a tendency to push up prices. Get me the information and I shall write him today to arrange a meeting.'

'Here?'

'Certainly. You know I never travel, my dear.'

That evening Suriel joined us for a drink to celebrate Nicoletta's completion of her work on the Lanholtz paper. Come what may, she was now ready to take on the assembled delegates of the International Congress of Middle Eastern Archaeology in Oxford. None of which cheered our guest, who drank two rather rapid Scotches before describing his own troubles.

Nicoletta offered him a cigarette, which he accepted, holding it inexpertly between thumb and forefinger, letting the smoke erupt in little nervous puffs without inhaling. 'I used to be a tax examiner,' he said sadly, half to himself, 'and at times like this I miss the excitement.'

I said, 'We're all impatient.'

His boyish features registered genuine astonishment. 'I don't know, but I guess I never considered myself up to this job. I'm probably suited for dull work.'

Nicoletta was listening to this in her usual cross-legged position on the carpet before the hearth, dressed in a clingy jersey blouse and wearing a green ribbon in her hair. 'I'm sure no one blames you for what happened,' she said. She rose to freshen Suriel's drink, sensibly cutting down the Scotch measure and doubling the soda. He did not notice.

'Oh, no? You should have heard the inspector today. He just received my report in the diplomatic pouch, which is why he didn't call sooner. He can be very expressive when angry. "Incompetent" was the kindest word he used. The others I wouldn't repeat.'

'If anyone was responsible for that clinic debacle,' I said, 'it was I for letting Sterne manage something that was clearly beyond him.'

'I should have shot him,' Suriel replied.

'Sterne or la Roche? You're forgetting I spoiled your aim.'

His grin was sly. 'Only because I wanted it spoiled. Doctor, I failed to take the most elementary precautions. When La Roche went out the window, I compounded my mistake. Any uniformed officer would have brought him down.'

'You're wrong,' I told him.

'Am I?'

'What authority do you have here? None. Remember the El Al security guard who killed the hijack terrorist in Switzerland? The Swiss tried him for murder.'

'Still . . .'

'You're not in Tel Aviv. All you can do here is follow the leader. Or you'd be in trouble with the Sûreté.'

Suriel groaned. 'I'm as welcome as a case of diphtheria with them now. The first day I was *Monsieur* Suriel; then just plain Suriel; now all they say is: "Is he still here?" '

'And still no trace?' Nicoletta asked him.

He shook his head disconsolately. 'The Interpol computer reports La Roche has a record in no less than eleven countries. Not bad for an ageing juvenile of forty-two. Before the Tel Aviv robbery his activities seemed to have centred around our Arab friends. Currency dealing and gun

144

running. They searched his home here and found two passports he recently used, one with Syrian and Lebanese police stamps only a few weeks old.' Suriel snickered and I assumed the Scotch was getting to him. He had tossed off the third one as quickly as the others.

'Did he have any business in England?'

'He went there occasionally. Why?'

I mentioned the response Mansour had received to the *Times* advertisement and Suriel's eyes brightened. He wondered aloud if one of us should go there immediately, but he accepted my suggestion that we would be better advised not to until we were sure Cheney could actually produce.

'I think he will,' Nicoletta said. 'The letter sounded careful. He knows and he wants to do business.'

'He's playing for the commission. Mansour predicted some dealer would.'

'If it is your stuff they're selling, then' – Suriel glanced at Nicoletta – 'it would be the first solid indication we have that there were two sets of thieves.'

'But only one set of murderers,' I reminded him.

'Suppose La Roche has gone to England?' Nicoletta asked him. 'Can't the police there arrest him?'

'Interpol circularized his picture earlier this week,' Suriel said miserably. 'If he's running he'll go farther than England.'

'But the police should know about this book dealer,' I said, 'in case La Roche is in touch.'

Suriel shrugged. 'He's probably only a middleman, so no charge could be brought against him.'

'Jay, what about the other detective Berman recommended?'

'I think it's time he went to work.' While I searched for George Panagoulos's telephone number, Suriel said, 'Funny thing about those two passports they found. One of them identified La Roche as a priest. Not bad cover for a thief in Jerusalem. Not bad here either, when you come to think of it.'

The Rose and Thistle at Abingdon is a little too Dickensian for my taste, done up like a cozy stage set and just as draughty. But Nicoletta and I were lucky to get a suite on such short notice. Panagoulos had invited us to stay at Les Sylphides, the health farm operated by his wife, but the idea did not appeal to me. He had been quite charming when I called from Paris, a refreshing change from the icy Goff. Panagoulos not only agreed to check on the London dealer, but would undertake the responsibility for Nicoletta's 'security' before the Oxford conference and her delivery of the paper. He suggested we spend the five remaining days in Abingdon as an added precaution. 'Catch the first plane and tell no one,' was his advice.

I rented a Rover saloon at the airport and we enjoyed a tourist drive through the postcard villages of Berkshire in the crisp early-autumn morning. There was bright sunshine, the first I had seen since the Mediterranean, and Nicoletta was more carefree and cheerful than I had ever known her to be. The completed paper, ready for delivery in Oxford, lay under several layers of tweed and cashmere at the bottom of her suitcase and she seemed satisfied she had been as faithful as possible to the old man's original. Panagoulos left a message at the hotel inviting us to lunch at the health farm. When I voiced suspicions of celery and hard-boiled eggs, Nicoletta said I was probably being unfair.

She was quiet for a moment, bemused – perhaps thoughts of lunch making her mind wander. 'Sir Thomas More,' she said abruptly. 'I always rather admired him.'

'What made you think of him? But I admire him, too,' I said, laughing. 'A great humanist mind; why not?'

'And willing to die for his principles.'

'Did you ever wonder how willing he might have been if his ideas hadn't included belief in an afterlife?'

We passed a Thames-side village common, fronted by thatched cottages. Some red-kneed schoolchildren in blue blazers chased a large dog, swinging identical book bags and pummelling each other roughly. A police constable bicycled by, ignoring them as they scattered like birds, pretending mortal fear of the law.

'Nonbelievers martyr themselves too,' Nicoletta said. 'My father was one.'

'He was a communist, you told me.'

'Among other things.'

'That qualifies as religion.'

Nicoletta smiled. 'But not as afterlife.'

We were following a lovely narrow road, cut deep between high hedgerows with only an occasional strip of wire fence revealing rolling, neatly-cared-for fields.

'That's it!' she cried, turning around in the seat.

'What?'

'Les Sylphides! You passed the gate.'

I backed down the road. Half hidden in a clump of gorse was a white wooden gate which stood open at the beginning of a gravel drive. A sign not much bigger than a car licence plate bore the words LES SYLPHIDES – PRIVATE.

The drive wound through a small, dense forest of oak, already brown with the advancing season, and came out past some fenced pasture where a dozen fat Guernseys grazed. On a slight rise ahead was a building of immense and ungainly proportions, half Wuthering Heights, half army barracks. The main part was three-storied Victorian brick, gabled, turreted and massively mansarded, while the barracks wing – single-story, asbestos slab siding and glass – thrust itself gleaming across the lawn parallel to a parking area half-filled with cars.

Nicoletta's expression was eloquent as her eyes took in this grotesque architectural mistake. She chewed her lower lip and shook her head with deliberate slowness.

We entered the reception hall of the old part, but saw no one. It was darkly panelled in carved, heavily varnished wood, interrupted occasionally by Tiffany windows which let beams of coloured light through to the new linoleum floor. The place smelled of boiled vegetables, like a baby's nursery.

On a vinyl-topped table near the door Nicoletta found a stack of brochures and passed one to me. 'Les Sylphides, where the slim come to trim,' it said. 'The most completely integrated programme of medically supervised Body Harmonics in the world. The Sylphide Way is the way of ancient Greece where the Body is a Temple, where mind and muscle harmonize to produce that perfect state of being called Radiant Health.' There was more of that kind of thing and at the end, 'Hermione Panagoulos, Directrice.'

Hermione herself was the first person we heard, rather than saw – a disembodied voice chanting, to the accompaniment of a tom-tom, 'Umpty-do, three, four. Keep your tummy off the floor. Umpty-do, three, four.' We walked in the direction of the voice, passing through a panelled corridor to what must once have been the main salon of the mansion. A muscular blonde in ponytail and black leotard patrolled the cracked parquet, tapping her bongo and watching fifteen panting human beings strain to lift their tummies off the floor.

When she saw us in the doorway, she smiled acknowledgement but never missed a beat. 'Umpty-do, seven, eight. Think about the weight you hate.'

'Dr. Marcus?' A stage whisper from behind us. I turned to see a black-maned giant about my own age, in cotton windbreaker and sweat pants, beckoning us back into the corridor. The thing one noticed about George Panagoulos, after his size, was the whitest, brightest smile outside a toothpaste ad. Then the bone-crushing handshake, the dimples and the good-humoured dark eyes, in roughly that order. I am nearly six feet tall and tend to be stringy. Panagoulos topped six-three and had the chest and thighs of a football linesman. He led us into a lounge in the new wing of the building, where he asked about our flight and how we liked the Rose and Thistle. His accent was pure California.

My concern about a diet lunch had been unjustified. Panagoulos hospitably poured us a pair of Scotches and after we had talked awhile, escorted us to a private dining room, where we enjoyed an excellent steak-and-kidney pie. Hermione looked in briefly to introduce herself and explain apologetically that she was obliged to lunch with her 'working' guests.

At first it was hard to reconcile the Panagoulos I saw with the picture Berman had provided me. Could this engaging, all-American superman be the same light-fingered two-timer sacked by the CIA, the guerrilla expert who cheated on taxi fares?

Over lunch, we talked about security. 'While you are in

148

Abingdon there will be two men covering your hotel. Who else knows you're here, by the way?'

'My secretary.'

'Right. That's all?'

'A Paris book dealer named Mansour.'

He asked me for more information on Mansour and I gave it to him, adding that I felt Berman should know too, although I had not notified him before we left.

'I'll handle that,' Panagoulos said. He smiled charmingly at Nicoletta and asked, 'Did you tell anyone you were coming here?'

She shook her head.

'Goff know?' Panagoulos said to me.

'No, why?'

'Just wondered. You mentioned he was working on the case.'

'I haven't heard from Goff in days.'

'Fine. Now tell me about this Cheney.'

Panagoulos could have been a movie actor, with his flashing eyes, pearly teeth and Tyrone Power lashes. I was not surprised when he told me that in a small way he was. When not on duty at the health farm or chasing around the world, he worked as a film stunt director and actor under the name George Pan. After lunch, he showed Nicoletta and me his private office, which turned out to be a kind of trophy room, filled with props and photographs from his cinematic career. Pirate dramas in Yugoslavia, westerns in Spain, spy thrillers in Germany; all were documented with signed location photographs showing George Pan and the stars. Nicoletta was fascinated. He had smashed cars, jumped from burning buildings, parachuted into the sea and taken more horse falls than he could remember.

'Have you been injured often?' Nicoletta asked him, her tone carrying a trace of awe.

'A few times,' Panagoulos said lightly, 'but my only recent brush with death was him.' He pointed to a photograph of a famous British actor standing with one arm around Panagoulos's shoulder. Both men were dressed in seventeenth-century costume, wigs and plumed hats. 'In stunt work you have to be very precise, like a gymnast . . . Good actors often get so deeply into their roles they become a menace, even with prop weapons.' He raised one side of his cotton windbreaker to reveal an ugly red-and-white scar along his rib cage.

'I hope your other work is safer,' I said.

'When I play with real people, Doctor, I allow less margin for error.' The teeth flashed again in his dimpled smile as he showed us out of the office to begin a short tour of the premises. We passed Hermione and her charges, squatting on the floor of another salon, all silent, eyes closed. 'Digestive meditation,' Panagoulos explained, straight-faced.

The old mansion was built upon a slope, and at the back, on what would have been basement level, was a room that opened out to the gardens, its windows shuttered and steel-barred, its massive door a piece of sheet iron on greased hinges. It housed the Panagoulos gun collection: carbines, machine pistols, assault rifles and grenade launchers from everywhere. Panagoulos circled the room slowly, pointing out various treasures he had acquired over the years. He stopped before one display case and removed a steel tube as long as a pencil. 'World's smallest shotgun,' he said. He held the tube between right thumb and forefinger, snapped the fingers on his left hand, and made it vanish. Nicoletta laughed with childish delight and I found myself suddenly quite tired of Panagoulos. He was working for me, but it was a little too obvious who he was trying to impress.

ELEVEN

The bed Nicoletta and I shared that evening was as comfort-able as we could have wished. 'I feel vaguely illicit,' she said to me after we made love between cold sheets and lay wrapped in a thick patterned quilt that gave off a faint odour of camphor.

'I hope not.'

'Do you realize this is the first time we've slept together in a public place?'

'I'd hardly call room 28 of the Rose and Thistle a public place.'

'You know what I mean.' She giggled.

'We could try the lawn at Les Sylphides tomorrow, if you really want a public place.'

'*Fanfarone.*'

'Keep your tummy off the floor?'

'Wasn't that a horror? But I liked George.'

'He liked you too.'

'All right, Doctor. Just because I enjoyed myself.'

'I like George myself, for different reasons.'

'He *is* beautiful,' Nicoletta said wickedly as she trailed her fingers lightly around my neck and kissed me softly on the nose. 'But I question his taste in wives. What do you think holds a couple like that together?'

'Body harmonics. Same as us.'

'Be serious. Don't you think it's a strange marriage? She running a fat farm while he plays James Bond? I would guess he's very good at his job, though.'

'Let's hope so. I'd hate to think we're in the hands of another incompetent.'

'It's not funny. I mean, suppose he really was . . . careless. What could happen?' Her tone was still light, but there was anxiety in her voice.

'I'm joking.'

'But I'm not. Victor was killed for these fripping papyri and I certainly don't have any desire to follow him.'

'What did you call them?'

'I didn't want to use the other word.'

'What other word?'

'I'm not being delicate,' Nicoletta insisted, 'but "fucking," to me, has a very sweet; specific, personal meaning and I refuse to use it as freely as you Americans do.'

'But where did you get "fripping"?'

'It's English. A euphemism.'

We stared at each other in the darkness of the room, seeing with our fingers. 'You mean "flipping"?'

She was silent before she said, 'Now you're making fun of me.'

'Look,' I said. 'Your English is flawless. It really is.'

Nothing.

'Nicky?'

'What?'

'What do you think of my Italian?'

'Flawless, Doctor. Flipping flawless,' she said and gave me a stinging punch on the shoulder with her small fist.

Mr. Desmond Osbourne Cheney kept an office on Old Bond Street that was a model of Edwardian taste and refinement. Cheney himself, barely thirty, wore the dandified clothes of the period, muttonchop whiskers and what could only be described as a serious mien. He rose when Panagoulos and I were ushered in by a middle-aged male secretary. The hand I shook was cool, soft and slightly damp.

Cheney sat behind a heavy oak desk and watched me through watery blue eyes. His ginger beard and hair were trimmed for effect, and obviously a source of some comfort to him. He constantly fingered the moustache or toyed with the locks that curled over his collar. The skin on the backs of his hands was veined marble, the fingers long and delicate. I sensed a softness about him generally, a weakness around the full pink lips that he was at some pains to disguise. The full-muscled vitality of George Panagoulos made an interesting contrast, to say the least, and I felt that Cheney was aware of it.

'Very nice chat with Mr. Mansour this morning,' Cheney said. 'I have his letter as well.' His voice was as thin and insubstantial as the rest of him, and seemed to come from high in the back of his throat. 'How may I be of help, Doctor?'

'Mansour told you we are prepared to pay a reasonable price to recover the papyri?'

'He implied as much.'

'But we have to be satisfied first.'

Cheney nodded and opened a drawer in his desk, withdrawing a large sheaf of photographs. 'These,' he said, pushing them across to me, 'are supposed to be what the seller is offering. I have not seen the originals, so our firm cannot vouch for them.'

I looked over the prints and saw that they showed a duplicate set of the Lanholtz discoveries. Whether they were complete or not I did not know, but there were a lot of them.

Panagoulos studied them too, raising his eyebrows and looking at me for a cue.

'Where do we go from here?' I asked Cheney.

'Do I understand they were stolen?'

I nodded.

'As I explained to Mr. Mansour, we shall be happy to help you recover them, but we cannot be involved in the receipt of something we know to be stolen.'

'I understand.'

'What we can do is put you in touch with the people offering them for sale. But even in this we must be circumspect. Cunningham and Pine has an old reputation in the trade.' He sighed. 'It is a delicate matter, for which we do not feel we could safely ask our usual commission.'

He seemed to be reaching the heart of the matter now, which was how much and in what form the money would pass. I could not resist the temptation to turn the game around a little. 'That's very kind of you,' I said, 'not to accept anything for this. I hope someday I can return the favour.'

After a moment, fiddling nervously with his moustache, he said, 'That is not exactly what I meant. You see, I prepared a little letter of agreement.' He buzzed for the secretary and the man appeared instantly, carrying a paper which he placed on Cheney's desk. 'It covers these special situations and I think protects both parties.'

'Against what?'

He passed me the letter. I scanned it and handed it to Panagoulos. 'You want me to sign this?' I asked Cheney.

'If it meets with your approval,' he said, giving me a weak smile, meant to be reassuring. I did not like him at all, yet I would have been hard pressed to find a reason. The turn-of-the-century affectation, the soft, waxy features, the little leering glances all added up to nothing.

'Would you mind explaining the part about paying you fifty thousand pounds?' I asked him.

The little smile again, the quick look that said, *Come on, you and I understand these things*. We *know*. At that instant I *did* know why I disliked him so intensely. This shifty, foppish joke of a man considered me his equal.

Cheney leaned forward and glanced at his copy of the agreement. 'You'll see that it is explained,' he said, 'as a finder's fee, if you like, for putting you in touch with the sellers. It is payable to me personally to avoid involving the firm.'

'In what could be a doubtful transaction, is that it?'

'Correct, Doctor.' He beamed. 'It is on my responsibility alone.'

I was holding the photographs on my knees when Panagoulos passed back the letter of agreement. 'Suppose I simply went to Scotland Yard with all this and let them handle it?' I said. 'Telling them who to contact, naturally.'

Cheney's smile faltered and then held, stiff and insistent. But his eyes dodged about the room for a second or two. 'As you wish. We would give them whatever help we could.'

'Free.'

'I am a book dealer,' he said primly. 'I don't trade in stolen goods and I cooperate with the authorities. You tell me these things were taken from your museum in Israel. I know they are offered for sale through reputable agents in another country. I am pleased to put you in touch with the agents, if you are serious. But I would not wish to embarrass them with the police.' He raised both hands in a gesture of airy dismissal. 'I expect to be in business a long time and I cannot afford misunderstandings with others in the trade.'

'Who are these agents?'

'That information, sir, cannot be disclosed until the conclusion of our business.'

'Mr. Cheney,' Panagoulos interrupted, 'what would you say the chances are of compete satisfaction if Dr. Marcus plays along?'

'I beg your pardon?'

'If we deal through you quietly,' I said.

'Excellent.'

'And with the police?'

'I have no idea,' Cheney said blandly. 'They might be helpful.'

'But not bloody likely,' Panagoulos said, with some irritation. 'Is that what you're trying to tell him?'

'My dear fellow,' Cheney replied, 'I am not trying to tell you anything. If Dr. Marcus wishes to sign this agreement' – he fluttered his fingers at the paper on his desk – 'we'll be pleased to do what we can. If he chooses not to, that's the end of it.'

No question that Cheney belonged on the list of the bastard elite I had been accumulating lately, right up there with Goff and Ramsay O'Hare. On the other hand, he seemed confident of recovering the Lanholtz papyri intact.

154

In that respect, it did not matter much who he was dealing with: La Roche or someone unknown; not if he could deliver.

Panagoulos was on his feet, pacing nervously at the other end of Cheney's office. 'I think we should take a little walk, Doctor, and talk this over.'

His movie-star smile seemed lost on Cheney, who by this time affected indifference to whatever I wished to do. He kept his eyes averted and did not bother to see us to the door.

Panagoulos and I went to a pub around the corner and stood elbow to elbow with the preluncheon customers who were beginning to flood the place.

Panagoulos took a long swig at his mug of bitter and wiped the foamy moustache from his upper lip. 'We're onto a live one,' he said with the smug delight of someone who has just received a tip on a sure winner.

'The question is what to do.'

'Sign,' Panagoulos said, as if that were the most obvious thing of all. 'Otherwise it's a dead end.'

'For fifty thousand quid?'

'That's bullshit,' Panagoulos said. 'He's got his eyes on bigger stakes. Probably a split from the other end. But he wants this to protect himself from the cops.'

'What makes you so sure he can do business?'

Panagoulos looked at me sharply. 'You don't think he has the stuff?'

'I only know what he told us.'

'I felt it from the minute we walked into the office. He's a class-A fake, but he's ready. I don't know why he's ready. Maybe he's afraid of somebody. Maybe he needs the bread. But the place was full of vibrations, Doc, and I never miss them.' Panagoulos ordered another bitter while I sipped at my first one. 'You know what I mean?' he said.

'You think he'll produce the scrolls.'

'I'd hate to search the premises.'

I looked closely to see if he was serious.

'If he doesn't have them in his desk, he knows goddamn well where he can put his hands on them. Mr. Fussy-Butt Cheney is out for the big hit. That letter is just a bonafeeday to see if you were willing to play. The hard part comes later. I love it. He's so fucking obvious, this twit, he excites my sympathy.' Panagoulos licked his lips.

'I wish I knew what you were talking about.'

'You know, Doc. You know. Why do you think I come on like a high school gym teacher?' He laughed loudly and people turned to look.

'You lost me,' I said.

'They take me in at a glance. A musclehead. If I shut up and nod, I win the game.' When I did not reply, Panagoulos said, 'That's what you thought, wasn't it?'

He watched me, his eyes narrowed. There was the suggestion of a smile, but no pearly-toothed display.

'You're right,' I said.

'I'm an actor, remember? George Pan. I'm always *on*, Doc. But let me tell you something, as long as you're the client.'

'I'm listening.'

'Cheney's an actor too. All that crap about the firm, and doubtful goods. He's a born thief, our Cheney baby, and he's hungry. Salivating. But I have to make him before we know where we're going.'

'Make him what?'

'Check him out. Who is he? How long with that outfit? What do they think of him? Who does he know? Who does he owe? I need a couple of days.'

'You have a couple of days.'

'Cheney's a mother lode. Oh, he's a pregnant lovely.' He laid a hand on my shoulder and I felt the grip of powerful fingers. 'We're going to get your scrolls back, Doctor, if you don't mind doing business with that fey little fellah. And we're going to get them back for a lot less than he thinks they're worth. It's the gut reaction that counts,' he added with a broad grin, 'and Cheney's all gut, believe me. All gut.'

Before we returned to Cheney's office, I talked with Mansour by telephone. When I mentioned my threat to bring Scotland Yard into things, he only sighed.

'My dear, this is no time to stand on principle. The idea is to get back those manuscripts. There are ways of handling this fellow later.'

I asked Mansour if he had any idea who Cheney might be dealing with in Europe, but he didn't.

'Are you having a nice holiday otherwise?'

'Very nice, thanks, Hippolyte.'

'Tell Cheney you insist on seeing a specimen before you do business, and, my dear, don't worry. Virtue and the resources of the Federal City Bank are with you.'

'That's no advice and you know it.'

'Why must you suddenly be so American?'

'Goddamn it, I don't like to be had.'

'Don't tell me,' Mansour said abruptly. 'Tell Cheney. If he wants to deal, he will accommodate even your anger.'

Mansour was right. Cheney poured on the charm the moment I signed the agreement. He promised to do what he could to provide an example from the collection and said he would telephone me at the Rose and Thistle as soon as he had word.

Panagoulos left me right after that to look into the life of Desmond Cheney, bookseller, while I made the long drive back to Abingdon alone, ruminating most of the way on how life had changed since Aaron's arrival in Greece less than a month earlier. And not for the better, I decided, except for Nicoletta Calvi's part in it. I could do without the Willis and the Goffs and the Cheneys of the world. I could even get along quite well without the Vagans and the Bermans and the Suriels. From the whole crowd of new faces, there was probably only one I felt at all comfortable with: the restless garrison soldier and querulous critic of Pontius Pilate, Gaius Longinus Procula.

I had yet to reach the end of his story, if there was one. But each day I managed to read parts from the letters; needling, complaining, pleading with his friend Lucius or other officials in Rome. How old was he? He never says, but my guess is about thirty at the time of the letters. Chafing at bureaucratic indifference, military stupidity and his brother-in-law's maladministration in a province far removed from Rome and misunderstood by most Romans. A thoroughly modern man was old Longinus, tough but sensitive, devoted to his profession, to his sister and to Rome. A believer in the capacity of man to work out his own fate through effort, goodwill and a little influence in high places. Like me.

From Exhibit 12 of the Caesarea dig, a part of one letter, unadorned by any of Lanholtz's commentary, particularly fascinated me. The translation is mine.

L: 'Get me out of here. I don't care where. The farthest reaches of Britain, even a combat command in Libya. Damn them, and damn him. Leave them to this dusty, inhospitable place. Give me a cool grave in the German forest or the Carpathian mountains. I have had enough of their stubborn faith, their indifference to civilization, their refusal to bow to my mad brother-in-law. How many of these people can Rome kill in the name of Rome? Since the riots, vagrants, faith healers, self-confessed prophets – all the commonplace trash we laugh at in Rome – are being trussed up here and crucified for sedition. Different values, thanks to You Know Who. If Jupiter himself appeared on the street tomorrow, he would be scourged, mocked and staked out like a butterfly for the Governor's collection. If you love me, old friend, get me out of here. I have killed my last Jew.'

The exit signs on the motorway flashed past. I left Heathrow Airport behind and then Windsor, with its great Norman tower visible above the scrubby fields and distant trees. It was three in the afternoon. The sun, which had favoured me since my arrival in England, continued to shine through the mustard smog that reached Windsor Great Park. I got off the motorway and passed through Henley-on-Thames, over the bridge, checking my route signs carefully. Professor Merle had said, 'It's beyond Henley in the Chiltern Hills. On the road to Watlington, but don't miss the turn or you wind up in Nettlebed.'

I found the house with no trouble. As Merle had told me, one could see it from the road. Indeed, I almost ran into it. Like so many old cottages in rural England, it was scarcely a yard from the pavement's edge. Two stunted yew trees, clipped like cockades, marked the short drive that led around to the rear. I pulled in, parked and knocked. A plump, rosy-cheeked, aproned woman answered, brushing a stray lock of grey hair from surprisingly young and lively eyes. She wore gardener's gloves and carried a trowel. A pair of yapping Yorkshires leaped past her to sniff around my shoes.

'Lady Ross?'
She had an infectious smile. 'Yes?'
I told her who I was and she immediately said, 'Oh, you

158

will stay for tea, Doctor. Bill should be home by then. Say you will?'

I said I would and she led the way into a cosy parlour cluttered with books and fat feather sofas. She excused herself for a moment and I sank into one of the couches in front of a flower-filled bay window. The house was larger than it appeared from the road, rambling and low-ceilinged, with the patina of three centuries of living. I inspected the nearby shelves of Ross's library and one thing caught my eye immediately: a row of books by Victor Lanholtz. I rose and went to the shelf, taking one down at random: *The Carolingian Awakening*, Oxford University Press, 1954. It was inscribed: 'For Bill Ross, with appreciation, in spite of everything. V. Lanholtz.'

I returned the book to the shelf as Lady Ross arrived in the room followed by her dogs, her smile bright and happy, apron, gloves and trowel gone, smoothing her dress. Change the hair from grey to light brown, take off a few pounds around the middle, and she was still the same smiling girl in the Wren uniform in Battersea Park. Ex-Mrs. Victor Lanholtz . . . 'in spite of everything.'

'You're here for the conference, Doctor. Are you giving a paper?'

'I'm supposed to chair one of the symposia.'

'You can imagine how Bill's been working, being on the organizing committee. What a silly job for a grown man, checking slide projectors and booking hotel reservations.' She laughed gaily. 'Would you like a whisky or something? Tea will be a while.'

'Thanks, no.'

'I'll put it out anyway. Just help yourself.' She went to an antique cupboard and set a bottle and glasses on a tray, which she brought to the coffee table near my knee. 'If you like ice . . . but of course, you're American.' She disappeared again and returned with a small leather bucket and a soda siphon. 'There. Now we can talk a bit. I feel I know you because I've heard your name often enough. You seem to be a staple source for some of my husband's lectures. But you and Bill have never met, have you?'

'I'm afraid not, Lady Ross.'

'How did you ever find our house?'

I told her about my visit with Merle and the reason for it.

159

Some of her good cheer faded and for a moment she let her fingers play with a seam in her dress.

'It was shocking about Victor,' she said. 'Just God-awful. We were stunned. I mean if he'd been shot by a Palestinian or something, I don't believe it would have been so terrible. But this.' She made a little gesture of horror.

They had read of Lanholtz's death in the *Times*, and according to her, there had been quite a stir among her husband's colleagues at Oxford. 'Everyone knew Victor,' she said.

'Did you see much of him during these last years?'

She hesitated before she answered. 'I have not seen him since Bill and I were married, and that was twenty years ago. In the beginning, it was awkward. Later there seemed no point. But I followed his career through Bill, of course.' She laughed again, in a gay, girlish way. 'They maintained a relationship, as only two intellectuals could, through everything. Victor stole Bill's book and Bill stole Victor's wife, so I expect they considered it a fair trade.'

Natalie Ross had a way of making the world laugh with her, I decided. I could easily understand what a vivacious young charmer she must have been in London during the war for Major Victor Lanholtz, at least twenty years her senior. I told her Merle had shown me a picture of them taken then, and to my surprise her eyes misted.

'You can't imagine those days,' she said softly. 'I was trapped in a clerical job at SHAEF. I dreamt of princes and all I got were sex-crazed bores until Victor appeared. I was twenty-one, he was forty-three. The most urbane man I had ever met, and in those days very handsome and very busy as well. We spent our honeymoon at the Dorchester, listening to the V-bombs and ordering sandwiches at midnight. When the war ended, we should have ended the marriage with it. But I went to America and tried to be a faculty wife to the distinguished Professor Lanholtz. It was a series of small disasters, I'm afraid. We were going our separate ways long before we actually went our separate ways. Victor had his own interests and I mine. When Bill came to study under Victor, I fell in love. Eventually . . . but it is an unimportant story.'

'Not to me, Lady Ross. Quite frankly, anything connected with Victor Lanholtz's past is of interest.'

'Why is that, Doctor?'

I tried to explain how, almost by accident, I had become involved through my interest in recovering the papyri.

'I should have thought by now they'd have found him. Is it really possible for a murderer to escape in a tiny country like Israel? They're frightfully efficient, aren't they? But I suppose they have their hands full with other problems.'

I thought of Berman, overworked and probably underpaid. And Suriel, convinced he had muffed the opportunity of his career in Paris when La Roche escaped. Was I beginning to sound like them? Maybe. Man was a hunter until ten thousand years ago, too recent to lose the instinct completely. Why should I be any different?

Lady Ross was saying, 'The past never really fades, Doctor. It just drifts out of reach somehow.' She gazed critically at her fingernails. One of the Yorkshires snuggled against her on the sofa. 'The war was yesterday afternoon to me. I don't really believe thirty years have intervened. I was stunned when I read Victor was seventy-two. But I have trouble believing I'm fifty.'

Lady Ross had an unaffected dignity and naturalness of manner that lent a special charm to everything she said. She did indeed look every day of her fifty years, but there was a youthful quality of frankness, of direct coming to terms with life, which appealed to me in quite a surprising way. It was an older, English version of what I saw and enjoyed in Nicoletta, a combination of honesty and sex appeal that transcended age and beauty.

'How can I describe it?' she was saying. 'He was an encyclopaedia of enchantment at times, but he could also be a terrible bastard.' She sighed. 'Very challenging to a young woman. But not the stuff for marriages. Are you married, Doctor?'

'No.'

'Bill and I have a marriage now into its twenty-first year. And it's been a good show, I suppose . . . most of the time. Anyway . . . Victor and I had an affair we tried to convert into a postwar living arrangement and it didn't work.' She smiled. 'I don't know which of us was the more deluded. Victor believed in an orderly, systematic universe, and if World War Two taught me anything, it was that there is no such thing.'

161

When I mentioned to her that more than one person had commented about Lanholtz's preoccupation with anti-Semitism, she only shook her head.

'I used to think his whole career was only a kind of long footnote to that,' she said. 'I suppose we all have our little idiosyncrasies. Mine happen to be dogs and flowers, especially the varieties – flowers, I mean – unsuited to the English climate. Give me a geranium cutting from Cairo or Tripoli and I'm off and away. With Victor it was . . .' She paused reflectively. 'Perhaps it was the same kind of thing. Give him the Jews, who might grow anywhere and flower only in Israel, and he was absorbed all his life.'

I suggested that the fate of his family might have had something to do with it.

'With his conscience, perhaps,' Lady Ross agreed, 'but not with the real Victor. When they were killed, I think it only confirmed his views. It was by no means a cause.'

'Could I ask you a question? A rather intimate question?'

She picked up the Yorkshire and scratched its belly. 'I don't see how it could be intimate, Doctor. We've only met.'

'You were married nine years to Victor Lanholtz. Was there any reason why you had no children?'

She continued to play with the dog, considering the matter. Finally she said, 'Bill and I have a lovely daughter studying in Florence, and a rather brutish son who just got his blue at Oxford. Does that answer your question, or do you really want to know?'

'If it tells me one new fact about Victor Lanholtz, I really want to know.'

She reached for the Scotch and the ice bucket. 'You're sure you wouldn't like a drink? I'm having one.'

I nodded and held up the soda siphon.

'No, thanks. Neat for me.' She poured the Scotches and sat back against the sofa. 'I was all for it from the start,' she said. 'I rather fancied myself something of a broodmare. Good genetic pool in my family. But Victor believed in minus zero population growth. It was one of the causes, to tell the truth, of things turning bad. *If* I tell the truth, it makes him sound the terrible bigot, and he wasn't generally, not Victor, except perhaps in this one thing.' She sipped at her warm Scotch, her other hand caressing the dog idly. 'You see, he wanted me to convert. We had terrible fights

162

about it. He was the rational elitist, the pragmatic atheist. Yet he wanted *me* to become a practising Jewess before he would even consider the idea of our having a child.' Again, her laughter punctuated the conversation. 'God, it's so long ago and so absurd. I haven't thought of it in years. The quarrelling and the tenuous reconciliations. I accused him of being an intellectual bankrupt. I mean why make me join a religious organization that treats women as chattel, while he, the great liberal Jewish scholar, the famous paleographer who'd written bloody books about the Torah, did not believe in any of it? He was a persuasive talker, but I did not care a tinker's dam about the study of Jews, which to him was an all-consuming passion.'

'Yet he didn't believe in God.'

'Is that so unusual? Didn't Shaw say the church was a magnificent edifice founded on nonsense? Well, that was Victor, a Jewish Shaw in terms of his thinking about Judaism and Jewishness, which he was always at great pains to separate. I longed for a man with a simple view of life' Again the infectious laugh. 'I never found him, by the way. I decided, after I met Bill, the best I could hope for was a man with a *consistent* view. May I freshen your drink?'

Natalie and I – for by the time an hour and a half had passed we had dispensed with the Lady Ross – Dr. Marcus ritual – managed to go through a fair part of the bottle before sunset, and a fair part of her life with Victor Lanholtz. Professor Ross – Sir William – the missing link in our relationship, telephoned at six-thirty to say he would be late. The effect on Natalie was abrupt and negative. Whatever excuse he had given she did not believe. Her smile came harder and she poured herself an unusually large drink. I had the impression he often left her alone with her dogs and the bottle, and that her marriage was not such a good show as she had pretended. There was no tea, only some soggy potato chips she resurrected from the kitchen, which mostly went to the two Yorkshires. It was dark and the air was chill and damp when she walked me to the car. 'Do be careful,' she said. 'The roads between here and Abingdon were built for carts.'

I said I looked forward to seeing her and her husband soon, if possible before the conference. She smiled, leaned in the car window and bussed me on the cheek. She said,

'Thank you for this afternoon, Jay,' When I started to speak, she shook a finger at me. 'Before you came, I was very down.' Her laugh again, but forced. 'My mind was on those years, on Victor and the war. Odd, isn't it? All day I was sad because he was dead and because I am growing old and because ... Then you appeared and asked all the right questions.' She grew quite solemn and seemed to hesitate over the words. 'Can you understand the importance of that? Of course you can't. Wait till I put the dogs in the house before you back out. And, Jay ... I hope they find the people who killed him. He wasn't cut out to be a victim.'

TWELVE

Nicoletta was in the public bar of the Rose and Thistle when I arrived. A fire blazed in the hearth at the end of the low-ceilinged, timbered room, cosy and welcoming, and the smell of beer and wood smoke cheered me. The only other customers in the place, were a fat young man in a wool cap and an elderly gentleman in tweeds. The fat man glanced at me while the old fellow stared off into space, his pint of bitter before him on the table, a springer spaniel curled at his feet.

'He's blind,' Nicoletta whispered. 'He does rubbings.'

'Rubbings?'

'You know, when you put a sheet of paper over an old tombstone and then scribble on the paper with crayon or soft graphite? You get an impression of the inscription. He sells them all over the world, mostly to collectors in America.' She looked toward the two men, keeping her voice low. 'He was blinded at Dunkirk. The other man is his son. The dog's name is Ralph the Fifth. He's not a real Seeing Eye dog, but Mr. Emmons' – her voice dropped even lower – 'says he's got more brains than Heath or Wilson.'

'You should change jobs with Panagoulos.'

'Would you like to know how many drinks I've had?'

'By no means.'

'Two.'

'Good grief.'

'And a dozen Colchester oysters. Interested?' Without

waiting for an answer, she called the bartender and ordered the oysters. The man grinned and vanished through a door behind the bar.

'Now, Mr. Close-Mouthed Marcus, suppose you tell me what happened in London today.'

I told her about Cheney and my visit to Natalie Ross. Then it occurred to me to ask if anyone had called.

'No one,' she said pointedly, 'except Berman at three, Suriel at three-thirty, your secretary at four, and Mr. Cheney at four-thirty.'

'And you let me sit here and order oysters?'

'Cheney said he would call again. Ditto Suriel, who is in London, by the way. Your secretary asked that you call her back at home after eight. Berman left a message. Would you like to hear it?'

The oysters came with lemon, horseradish and a bottle of Tabasco sauce.

'Only if it's good news.'

Nicoletta robbed my plate and, chewing greedily, said, 'Well, he was trying to reach Suriel, who, it appears, has not exactly been keeping our favourite inspector informed. You seem to be the main communications link for the Israeli police department abroad. He also wanted to know about Panagoulos.'

'Only questions? No answers?'

'He was paying for the call, and he was very concerned about the three minutes. But he did mention they had arrested the Melchite archbishop.'

'What for? Did he say?'

'No, but he was obviously very pleased.'

'That's all?'

'Sorry, my love. That's all. Who on earth is the Melchite archbishop?'

'Head of one of the Christian Orthodox sects there. Syrian, I think, or Lebanese.' I looked at my watch. 'It's after seven. Is there a telephone here in the bar?'

'Finish your oysters first.'

The operator gave me half an hour wait on the Paris circuit and an indefinite on the line to Jerusalem.

Nicoletta said, 'Are you optimistic about Cheney?'

'Yes.'

'How does George feel?'

165

'He seems to think we'll get the papyri back this week if we handle Cheney with the right combination of money and muscle. You know who is expected to provide which.'

'You're not so confident?'

'Cheney's cunning. I must say Mansour was no help. When I called him, all he said was "Deal." '

'Well, he's right, isn't he?'

'If Cheney is linked to the people who robbed the museum and killed Victor, then he ought to be sweating it in a lockup. What did Suriel have to say? Have they caught La Roche?'

'He wanted to talk with you tonight. My impression was he was very excited, but he didn't mention catching anyone.'

I had a second drink. A few minutes later, the bartender called me to the telephone.

Jeanette Mowbray, that wonderfully efficient woman who brought order to my chaotic life, got right to the point. 'The telephone hasn't stopped since you left, Jay. Do you have pen and paper?'

'Go ahead. In order of importance, if possible.'

'I'll do my best. One, Inspector Berman. He finally talked to me and I gave him your London number.'

'Next.'

'Mr. O'Hare. He wanted you or Nicoletta, and I don't think he believed me when I said I did not know where you were. He left a number.' She read it off, including the Miami area code. 'Then there was Professor Merle, who said it was not important, but to ring him when you returned to Paris. He sent over a sheaf of notes you had asked for.'

'Victor Lanholtz's notes. Do you have them in front of you?'

'Yes.'

'Can you read them?'

'Now? On the telephone?'

'If it's not too much trouble.'

'There's quite a bit.'

'I'll tell you when to stop.'

There was a pause before Jeanette said, 'The first few pages are labelled in Latin, which I can't read. Then some Hebrew, which I can't read either. Then it says, "The Talmud on Trial. Disputation at Paris in the year 1240,

166

including the charges of Christian churchmen against Jews, particularly against the teachings of the Talmud or Jewish oral law as opposed to the teachings of the Torah or written law. Defence of the Rabbis. Talmud more important than Bible study." Does that make sense, Jay?'

'Fine. Go on.'

'A lot more seem to be Hebrew.'

'Read the English.

' "Any man who does not observe the counsel of the Rabbi deserves death." Wow!'

'It's a tough religion,' I said.

'I guess *so*,' Jeanette replied. 'I'm still reading. "Among the unworkable Talmudic laws is that which says it is permissible to deceive a Christian by a ruse or any ingenuity without committing a sin." ' Suddenly Jeanette giggled. ' "Jews cannot suffer in hell longer than twelve months, but Christians stay in hell forever. Talmud states that the filth which the serpent injected into Eve during intercourse has clung to the Gentiles since that time, but the Jews were cleansed on Mount Sinai." Are you writing all this down, Jay? Do you want me to go slower?'

'No. That's fine. I'm just listening.'

' "God weeps three times a day," ' Jeanette said. 'I should have thought more often. That's me talking.'

'Just the notes, please.'

' "God studies Talmud. God also confesses he was defeated once in an argument by the Rabbis." And the last one reads simply, "God sins too." ' '

'Beautiful. What else is there?'

'A reprint of an article from the *Jewish Quarterly Review* of October 1956 entitled "The Shapira Mystery," another one from the June 1970 *International Journal of Archaeology* . . . a book review, it appears to be. Wait a minute . . . *The Life of Charles Clermont-Ganneau*, by Sir William Ross. Reviewed by Dr. Lev Vagan of your own museum.'

'What else?'

'Just a covering note from Professor Merle.'

I asked her to send everything to me special air mail and I returned to join Nicoletta.

'Hungry?' she asked. 'Or would you rather wait a bit?'

'Peckish, but I have the call to Berman.'

'They can pass it to the dining room.'

'Was Lanholtz working on anything to do with the Talmud when he died?'

'Not that I know of. Why?'

'Some notes he left with Merle. Full of bizarre Talmudic lore.'

Nicoletta smiled thoughtfully. 'Victor was a compulsive jotter. Biblical references, observations on articles he read: Goethe, Ralph Nader, the Essenes. Things he wanted to check, things he just wanted to think about.'

'Are you familiar with a biography Professor Ross wrote about Charles Clermont-Ganneau? It was reviewed by Lev Vagan in one of the journals.'

'I never understood what fascinated Ross about him. Except maybe Clermont's part in the Shapira forgery case.'

'He exposed him, didn't he?'

'That's a matter of opinion. In the 1880s, when Shapira offered his scrolls to the British Museum for a million pounds – imagine! – they asked Clermont-Ganneau to authenticate them. He studied them for five minutes and said they were fakes. Poor Shapira committed suicide and the scrolls disappeared. Victor had studied the case closely at one time and felt, as others do, that they may well have been part of the Dead Sea Scrolls. But unless they turn up again, who can say? There was no way to date them positively in those days.'

'Why did Clermont-Ganneau call them fakes?'

'He claimed the size was wrong and that they had been aged with tar and turpentine. A few were coated with a kind of asphalt. Victor's guess was that Clermont-Ganneau was an anti-Semite, who made his decision on the basis of Shapira's Jewishness rather than scholarly evidence.'

'Did Lanholtz ever comment on the Ross book?'

Nicoletta doodled in the damp rings made on the polished table surface by her glass. 'He respected Ross as a careful scientist, but he considered him a pedant. I think the knighthood burned him up a little too, just between us. Victor could be terribly jealous of other people's honours.'

'You don't think his wife's leaving him for Ross had a bearing on his attitude?'

'Not really. It was aeons ago, and if it had really mattered to Victor, he would have broken with Ross then, but he never did.'

The barman was at my elbow. 'Telephone, Doctor.'

The gravel voice on the other end of the fuzzy connection was familiar.

'Hello, Inspector. How are you?'

'If I told you, you couldn't afford to listen. Is Suriel with you?'

I hesitated. 'Well, not exactly . . .'

'Don't cover for him. Just tell him, that *momzer*, that people higher up take a dim view of the way he's carrying on. And in case he wonders who they are, they are me! Remind him, please, that he works for a police department, not the United Nations.'

'Honestly, Inspector, I have not seen him here, but I believe he's got a lead.'

'Illusions of grandeur is what he's got. I should know better than to send a *putz* like him out of the country for the first time. Let me give you a scenario, Doctor. He was supposed to collect a felon in Vienna and hike his ass back here direct. On his own cognizance he's now in London. If he's still employed when he gets back, we got jobs for him – just pass it on, please – and they involve a substantial reduction in rank, you understand?'

'Inspector, he's doing the best he can.'

'We can't afford him,' Berman said.

'I know he's sweating this assignment . . .'

'He ought to be.'

'. . . but he's doing a job.'

'The job's done.'

'What did you say?'

'We recovered sixteen of your parchments late yesterday, right here in Jerusalem.'

I was speechless for a few seconds, but finally managed to ask, 'How?'

'That make you happy? Your uncle is happy and Professor Vagan is happy. I'm not so happy.'

'How did you do it?'

'We made four arrests,' Berman said, 'and they'll all stick. The archbishop, where we found the stuff, his driver and the two smart-asses that run the garage in Nablus. Trouble is we got an international incident on our hands. The archbishop wasn't just into stealing scrolls; he was running guns and information to the PLO too. So army intelligence is in up to its elbows.'

'What about the rest of the things?'

'Never satisfied, are you, Doctor?'

'Certainly I am. I'm delighted.'

'Since Suriel blew the La Roche interrogation in Paris, we are, as the saying goes, in the dark. La Roche is the murderer and we are still looking for him.'

I told Berman we might be getting a little closer. I also mentioned I had hired Panagoulos.

'Suriel should work with Panagoulos,' Berman said. 'He might learn something. On second thought, it would be better if he worked with Panagoulos and didn't learn anything. How is he working out? Panagoulos, I mean.'

'So far, I'm very pleased, Inspector. He's a lot easier to take than your friend Goff.'

'Are you crazy? How can you knock a man like Goff? He's the best in the business.'

'I wouldn't know; I haven't heard from him in a week.'

'Jesus, Doctor, I don't know what you expect. Who do you think recovered your stuff? Goff, that's who. He's been on top of things here while Suriel's lolly-gagging around the fleshpots of Paris. You want to talk to him? I'll put him on.'

'No, that's not necessary, Inspector,' I said meekly. 'I had no idea he was with you. Just thank him for the fine work. Sorry I was too quick off the mark.'

Mollified, Berman said, 'Tell Suriel he'll get his authorization tomorrow through the embassy, but remind him he's eating up our foreign exchange. If he comes home without results I'll send him to the Negev. Goodbye, Doctor.'

'Goodbye, Inspector. We miss you.'

'What?'

'Goodbye, Inspector.'

To avoid the telephone for a while, we drove the five miles to the White Hart in Fyfield, where we ate as good a dinner as I have ever had in England. The softly lighted fifteenth-century dining room with its beamed ceiling and redolent smells gave us what the guidebooks called 'a festive medieval glow.' Talk, a little hand-holding, laughter, a saddle of mutton with mint sauce and a bottle of expensive claret took up the next two hours. Over coffee I even smoked a cigar.

On our way out to the car, I noticed a battered Austin parked a few feet away. There was nothing surprising about that, except that behind the wheel sat the fat man I had seen in the public bar at the Rose and Thistle, and next to him was the blind Mr. Emmons. As I pulled out of the parking lot, the Austin started up and followed us on the short drive back. I decided against saying anything to Nicoletta.

Instead, while she went up to our room, I waited downstairs in the smoking lounge, watching through the window. In a moment the old Austin drew up and parked. The two men got out, followed by the dog, and entered the bar. At that moment, the night manager, a cheerful undergraduate type strangling in tie and collar, hair over his shoulders, found me. 'Your messages, sir,' he said with a smile, handing me a sheaf of slips.

'Just a moment.' I caught the young man's arm before he escaped. 'Do you know the blind man who was in the pub with us earlier this evening?'

He looked puzzled. 'Afraid I don't, sir.'

'Or the fat man with him?'

He shook his head apologetically and hurried off toward the dining room, just as the fat man poked his head into the smoking lounge, glanced around, saw me and looked away, backing out of the room.

'Mr. Emmons?' I said.

'Eh?'

'You are Mr. Emmons?'

He twisted his cap in sausage fingers and looked behind him as if expecting help. A kind of strangled 'Aarrr ...' caught in his throat before he said, 'Mr. Emmons, that's me dad. I'm Ted.'

'Why did you follow me to the White Hart tonight?'

'Arrr ...' The look behind again.

'Who do you work for?'

His tongue moved over the edges of his teeth and his eyes were desperate as they rolled wildly right and left.

A voice called from the hallway between the entrance to the smoking lounge and the bar. 'Ted?'

'I'm here, Dad.'

The old man came out, moving with that tentative majesty the blind have. The dog trotted behind him.

'Have they gone up to bed yet?' the old man inquired.

'Not yet,' I said. 'What the hell business is it of yours?'

'Er. Marcus?'

171

'That's right.'

The old man touched his son's arm and said, 'Wait for me in the pub.' Ted backed away, still terrified. He didn't take his eyes from me until he reached the doorway and disappeared. 'Don't mind the boy, sir. He's a mental, but harmless. My name is Emmons. Harry Emmons.' He put out his hand.

I shook it, but said, 'I don't know whether I'm happy to meet you or not, Mr. Emmons. Why did you and your son follow us to the White Hart this evening?'

He felt for the dog, who had squatted obediently at his feet.

'I wasn't supposed to let you and the lady out of sight. A figure of speech.' He forced a smile. 'But Mr. Panagoulos didn't think you should know it was us looking out for you. Me blind and the boy a bit backward, you know.'

'You live around here, Mr. Emmons?'

'Abingdon.'

'Come to the Rose and Thistle often?'

'Every night for the last thirty-five years, barring a few.'

'The night manager says he doesn't know you.'

'The new lad?' He shook his head sadly. 'Why should he know me?'

'Do you know why Mr. Panagoulos wants us watched?'

'All he said was to call him if anyone suspicious showed up while you were here.'

'Has anyone suspicious shown up?'

'Not that I'm aware,' Emmons said. 'And we've been following the lady since you left with Mr. Panagoulos early this morning.'

'Where?'

'To the abbey, sir. And then to that restaurant where she ate lunch, and then here again. A nice missus, sir, very kind she is, and Ted tells me pretty as a postcard.'

'What are you being paid for this job?'

'Fifty pounds, but we could get the sack, now you caught on to us.'

'Don't worry about that. I won't mention we talked.'

'Very kind of you, gov'nor. You're a Yank like Mr. Panagoulos; I can tell by your speech.'

'Yes.'

'But the missus, she's foreign, am I right?'

172

'Italian.'

'She was interested in my rubbings.'

'So she told me.'

After shaking hands again, he went off to the bar, followed by the spaniel. 'Two men watching your hotel around the clock,' Panagoulos had said. Just an oversight if he failed to mention their qualifications.

Before I settled down at the telephone in our bedroom, Nicoletta said, 'I wondered what had become of you.'

'Chatting with Mr. Emmons.'

'Isn't he sweet?'

'In fact, he is.'

'Did he tell you about his work?'

'Yes, he did. All about it.'

THIRTEEN

Once at Monte Carlo, not too many years ago, one of the roulette wheels turned up an even number twenty-eight times in a row. The probability of this, according to Mansour, is something like once every 270 million spins of the wheel. But it happened, he says, and I believe him the same way I believe Anwar Sadat or Moshe Dayan. Which is to say that anything can happen if people persist. Suriel's success in locating La Roche was a case in point.

'He's in a Soho hotel, half a block from where I am now,' he said when he came on the line.

'Have you told Berman?'

'There hasn't been time.'

'How in hell did you find him?'

'Patience and luck. Mostly luck. I checked train and channel-boat personnel until I found someone who remembered a bearded priest.'

'Eastern Orthodox?'

'As a matter of fact . . .' Suriel was surprised.

'You should keep in closer touch with the home office. Berman arrested an archbishop this morning with sixteen of our papyri.'

He whistled, then cursed. 'Is it in the newspapers?'

'It will be in the morning.'

173

'Jesus. He'll bolt.'

He gave me the number of a phone booth and I told him to hang up while I rang him back. When I had him on the line again he said, 'That's better. I was running out of change.'

'Who is your contact with the police here?'

He gave me the name of an Inspector Rowan in CID, saying, 'He may be able to act on the Interpol circular they have for La Roche. I'm not sure.'

'I'll do what I can. You're certain it's him?'

'The hotel porter identified him from his picture. The place is on Lexington Street, right off Brewer.'

'How long can you manage alone?'

'As long as necessary. I *want* this one.'

'Suriel, who is the Israeli ambassador here?' He told me; fortunately the man was a friend of Aaron's, so I would be able to trade on that a little.

'I'll get back to you, probably indirectly through the police. Will that do it?'

'Doctor, it's a pleasure knowing you.' He gave me the name of the hotel he had booked a few blocks from where he was keeping his vigil. 'When will I see you?'

'As soon as I can catch up.'

When I replaced the telephone, Nicoletta looked up from the book she was reading. She had changed into a nightgown and an emerald velour robe, and was quite fetching, perched on the edge of the bed. 'Do you expect to get any sleep tonight?' she asked me.

'What did you have in mind?'

She laughed and said she was talking business, not recreation. 'You may be winning this little game after all. Thanks to Goff and Suriel.'

'And Marcus,' I said. 'Don't forget him.'

She put the book aside and leaned across the bed to kiss me. Her soft, familiar form arched beneath the robe and came into my arms. After a long time, we both had to breathe.

She asked where Suriel was.

'Stamping his feet on a Soho sidewalk, watching La Roche's hotel.'

She pushed me away. 'How can you lie there? Why aren't you calling the police or whoever you're supposed to call? I

174

really believe you would let him wait.' The robe had fallen open as she jumped up from the bed, and all of her was enticingly, beautifully exposed under the sheer nightgown.

She hugged the robe around her and tied off the view securely. 'He may be risking his neck while you gawk. Come on, Marcus, that boy needs help.'

I raised one hand in a weak gesture of protest. 'What I have in mind won't take a minute.'

Withdrawing to a safe distance, she said, 'Think of me as a sister.'

I heaved myself off the bed and reached for her, but she side-stepped nimbly. Very fast on her feet, my Nicoletta. As she began to curse me in Italian, the telephone rang again. It was Cheney.

'I have located one of your pieces.'

'Good work, Mr. Cheney,' I replied in my smoothest bedside manner.

'Could we meet in my office tomorrow morning? Say about tennish?'

'If you like. Will you have it with you?'

'Yes. I look forward to seeing you, Doctor.'

When I put down the telephone, Nicoletta said, 'He has one of the scrolls.'

'So it would seem.'

'What do you want me to do?'

'Find the Israeli ambassador while I use the downstairs telephone to call the cops.'

'What do I tell him?'

'To please stand by for a call from me. Just mention Marcus of the Marcus Museum and hope he thinks it's Aaron. Tell him it has to do with the robbery and Lanholtz's murder if necessary, but make sure he's available to talk in ten minutes.'

'Yes, sir. Anything else?'

'A kiss.'

'Absolutely not. What about George? Can't he help?'

'Maybe. But I don't know where to reach him. If he calls while I'm in the lobby, shout.'

With pen and paper, I hurried down to the desk. The scrawny night manager was watching television, but he tore himself away long enough to give me a London line. 'How long have you worked here?'

175

He blushed. 'This is my second night, sir.'

No wonder he didn't know the Emmons family. Bravo, Panagoulos, hiring a blind man and the village idiot to look after us!

'Sergeant Battle speaking.'

'Is Inspector Rowan in, please?'

'Not at the moment, sir. May I take a message?'

'When do you expect him?'

'Who is speaking, sir?'

'Dr. Marcus.'

'Any moment, Doctor, if you'd care to leave your number.'

'It's urgent, Sergeant. Do you know where I can reach him?'

'Sorry, sir. I don't.'

'I'll call back in ten minutes.'

'Very good, sir.'

The next call was to Panagoulos at the health farm. 'You may find him at Churchill's after midnight,' his wife suggested. 'He sometimes drops in for a fast pass at the tables.'

I returned to the room, where Nicoletta handed me a slip of paper. 'The Israeli ambassador is attending a fund-raising dinner at the Savoy,' she said. 'That's the number and the suite of Sir Giles Morris, the host. The ambassador didn't sound at all friendly.'

There was some background noise when I had him on the line, which only increased his irritation. For a diplomat, I thought, he might be a little more ingratiating. 'Exactly what is it you want of me, Doctor?'

'Simple enough, Mr. Ambassador. A telephone call to the Foreign Office requesting immediate police assistance for Detective Suriel.'

'Can't it wait till morning?'

I wanted to shake the complacent bastard. 'The man Suriel is watching a murderer. Israeli police have just arrested his accomplices in Jerusalem. Suriel has no authority to make an arrest in London and if the fugitive is not brought in before morning, there's a good chance he may get away.'

'It's a very dicky business,' the ambassador said.

'Will you make the call?'

'I'll do what I can.'

'Thank you. Is Giles Morris there with you, by any chance?'

There was a shocked pause. 'Sir Giles? Yes, he is.'

'Could you get him to the telephone before you hang up?'

'Well, he's in a conversation right now . . .'

'Please interrupt.'

'You *know* Sir Giles?'

'Tell him Jay Marcus would like a word with him.'

There was a thud on the line as the ambassador rested the receiver, then the hum of background voices again. Nicoletta was watching me, shaking her head. She snapped her fingers and said, imitating me, 'And be quick about it, Mr. Ambassador, or we'll have your portfolio, Giles and I. Who is Giles, by the way?'

The deep, familiar board-room voice was on the line, mellifluous as ever. 'That you, Jay?'

'*Wie geht's*, Giles? What are you doing in such doubtful company?'

'Giving away money like a mad fool. When did you arrive and when shall I see you?'

We agreed on lunch together before I explained what I wanted him to do. He would be delighted, he said, to lean on the ambassador and see that he called the Foreign Office immediately. He also volunteered to ring up the Home Secretary and provoke a little faster action with the police. 'I appreciate that, Giles, and I apologize for interrupting your party.'

'Nonsense, old boy. You probably saved me money. I heard that bloody rogue Mansour bought up your Albucasis for you.'

I laughed. 'Were you there?'

'Naturally. I wanted it myself, but when the bidding reached outer space, I dropped out.'

A question crossed my mind. 'Giles, while I have you on the phone, do you happen to know a bookseller named Cheney?'

'Should I? Who's he with?'

'Cunningham and Pine.'

'Young fellow? Heir to the firm?'

'He could be. Muttonchops, old-fashioned clothes, bit of a fag.'

'Knew his father and I've seen the son at auctions once or twice. The firm's been in some trouble lately. Trying to be trendy, like so many. Are you buying through them?'

'In a small way.'

'Right. I'll get onto the coppers for you, don't worry.'

When I was off the telephone, Nicoletta said, 'I never realized power was such a casual tool.'

'Is that power? I guess it is.'

'You're shameless, putting the ambassador on the spot like that.'

'It's Suriel who's on the spot.' It was ten forty-five. 'If and when Panagoulos calls, tell him what's going on. I'll be in touch.'

'From where?'

'The nearest London telephone booth.'

The drive from Abingdon is a little over sixty-five miles. If one obeys the speed signs, it takes an hour and a half. By ignoring them I condensed the trip and swung the rented Rover into Brewer Street at five minutes past midnight, parking under a no-parking notice.

No sign of Suriel. I passed an empty telephone booth. Nearby, a long-haired man in a loden coat was feeling up a girl in the shadows of a stone porch. At the end of the block, at Broadwick and Lexington, a woman with electric-red hair and a powdered face lined by the years grinned profession-ally. Her smile faded to a grimace as I passed her by. No Liza Doolittle she.

I crossed over and retraced my steps down Lexington Street, past unlighted shopwindows and shadowy entrances. It had been an hour and a half since my talk with Giles and the ambassador. Had the police come and arrested La Roche? I was returning to the telephone booth to call Nicoletta when a figure stepped out of a darkened doorway in front of me. 'I thought it was you,' Suriel said, 'but I didn't want to shout. Did you reach Inspector Rowan?'

I told him what I had done.

He shrugged with the resignation of the professional policeman, giving everyone the benefit of the doubt. 'He's still in there.' He nodded in the direction of a narrow row house opposite us. The peeling sign in front read: LEXINGTON PALACE HOTEL.

'He had a visitor, right after I talked with you,' Suriel

178

said. 'A guy in an Aston Martin, for about fifteen minutes. I got the licence number.'

'How do you know he was seeing La Roche?'

'I've already contributed ten pounds to the night porter's pension fund. So he's been informative. La Roche has shucked his monk's garb, by the way. He's registered as a commercial traveller.'

I was about to start for the telephone booth when a black Vauxhall pulled up at the kerb. A uniformed constable got out and flicked a light over us as he came forward. 'Mr. Sorrel?'

'Suriel; that's right.' He smiled with relief.

'Could I see your identification, please, sir?' He glanced at me suspiciously as Suriel handed him his open wallet. The flashlight played briefly on the police card and then went out. The constable touched his helmet. He was a young man with walrus moustaches and a heavy, florid face. The driver of the Vauxhall got out then, a rumpled plainclothes policeman who introduced himself as Sergeant Battle of the Criminal Investigation Division of Scotland Yard. He might have been forty, but had the melancholy, ageless features of a man who has spent his life sorting out the seamy side of London. He immediately took charge in a gruff, bored way, questioning Suriel about La Roche.

'No point in all of us trooping up there,' he said as we entered the building. 'Constable, you go with Detective Suriel and the night porter. The other gentleman and I will wait here in the lobby.'

The 'lobby' was little more than a scabrous alcove off the bottom of the stairs, dimly lighted by a fly-specked chandelier and furnished with a pair of green plastic-covered divans from which the kapok seeped.

The night porter, an ancient man in a grey cambric shirt with rheumy eyes and the reddened, knobby nose of rhinophyma, regarded us all with deep suspicion. The constable asked him to bring his keys and lead the way to room 11 on the second floor.

'Is there a fire escape there?' Suriel asked, no doubt recalling the debacle in the Paris clinic. The old man shrugged and started up the stairs, taking them slowly, pausing often. I could hear his wheeze at the top of the first flight.

'Understand this bloke got away once before,' Sergeant Battle said, 'after the French police caught him.'

I nodded. No need to explain the rest.

'Every muckety-muck and his brother was ringing up the Yard earlier on. You'd think we didn't know our bloody business.' The sergeant yawned and I found myself yawning as well. He crossed the small room to the porter's desk, turned the register around and began flipping idly through the pages. 'You're American, are you, Doctor?'

'That's right.'

'My sister married a Yank. Air Force chap from Florida. Love to visit them someday, but with one thing and another, the inflation –' He closed the register just as we heard the first shot. For an instant, he seemed suspended. A second shot reverberated in the hallway above.

Sergeant Battle was out of the room, taking the stairs three at a time, and I followed without thinking. He reached the top of the first long flight of stairs, turned and pounded down the dim, narrow hallway to the open door where the old porter stood gasping against the wall. I thought it was he who had been shot. He was trembling, his eyes rolled upward and his mouth agape. Nearby on the floor, the constable sat like a stunned doll, one hand clutched to the side of his neck, from which the blood streamed brightly through his fingers, soaking the front of his dark uniform.

There was no sign of Suriel. We heard a door slam and running footsteps from the stairwell above. Battle was off again, revolver in hand, disappearing up the stairs toward the top of the building. I bent to do what I could for the constable, pulling his hand away to look at the wound, a quarter-inch furrow through the skin and muscle tissue, just above his collar on the right side. The slightest change in angle could have cut the spinal cord or a carotid artery. I took his hand and pressed it against the artery, telling him to keep the pressure. Farther down the hall, doors were opening and closing, people were coming out to see what was happening. Then, muffled, more shots from above.

The wounded man drew me closer with his free hand and whispered hoarsely. 'Your mate . . . he's in there.' He motioned toward the open door of the room, from which a brighter yellow light spilled. I entered and saw Suriel sprawled on the rug, the centre of a widening red circle, his breath coming in short, shallow gasps, eyes half open. I knelt to get a pulse and rolled him gently on his side so he would not asphyxiate on his own blood. Then I returned to the constable in the hallway.

'How close is the nearest hospital?'

'Royal National,' he managed to say. 'Around the corner. Beak Street.'

'Can you walk?'

'I think so, sir.' He gamely struggled to his feet with my help and swayed against the wall. Several people were staring at us. The nearest of them, a middle-aged fellow in undershirt and carpet slippers, looked on dumbly, rolling a cigar over heavy, sensuous lips. 'You!' I barked. 'Help this officer down the stairs!' He shuffled forward sheepishly and thrust a beefy hand under the constable's elbow. As they started down, I motioned a bearded young man in blue jeans to give me a hand. We got a blanket carry under Suriel and cautiously made our way down the narrow stairway to the frtnt entrance. A woman went ahead and opened the door. Then to the Vauxhall, and gingerly on the back seat. The constable was already in front. As I pulled away from the kerb, he reached forward with his free hand and turned on the siren.

Inspector Rowan of the Yard was probably not an even-tempered man on the best of nights, but the lugubrious events of Lexington Street turned him into an absolute volcano of wrath as the facts were revealed in the visitors' lounge at the Royal National Hospital an hour later. Half a dozen police officers, including the unfortunate Sergeant Battle, stood around shamefacedly, uneasily, like school-boys, as the inspector poured abuse on them without pause. A communications sergeant was upbraided for failing to communicate to his chief the moment he received the request to pick up the fugitive murderer. An administrative deputy was excoriated for failing to conceal the true facts of what had happened from some curious newspaperman, and another for failing to insist on certain safeguards when the man they were after was known to be armed and dangerous.

'Armed and dangerous,' he said with quiet intensity, fixing his gaze first on one, then on the next and the next, accusing them all. 'Armed and dangerous.' He held the Interpol circular in his hand, shaking it at them from time to time as he spoke. 'In five languages, so if you don't understand the Queen's English, which none of you seem to have grasped yet, you can read it in frog, kraut, spic or wop.' One of the men made the near-fatal error of allowing a faint smile at this obvious barbarism on the part of his chief, and Rowan turned on him. 'Two seriously wounded officers in surgery upstairs' – he waved the circular at the ceiling – 'and you find it amusing? God help your children, with an imbecile for a father.' This without raising his voice. 'Please excuse me, Doctor,' he said to me, taking notice for the first time. 'Now, Battle.' He turned away from me immediately and faced the unhappy sergeant. 'You say this armed and dangerous fugitive got away, did he?'

'Over the roof, sir. I fired four times, sir, but I don't think I hit him.'

Rowan was pacing the room, pausing to peer at the circular from time to time as if it held new surprises, or notes for a speech he was preparing. He was a short, compact bulldog of a man, neatly and conservatively dressed – more like a lawyer than a cop – with longish greying hair and heavy dark eyebrows that gave his expression a satanic cast. His soft, darting hands were as expressive as a woman's. 'No, I don't think you did,' he said with a sigh.

The door popped open and a house resident looked in. 'Your man's been moved to a private room, Inspector, if you wish to talk with him.'

'No sedatives?'

'We're holding off, as you requested.'

'I'll be quick,' Rowan said, pushing past him.

The resident smiled. I asked him if there was any further word on Suriel and he shook his head.

Battle and I followed Inspector Rowan down the corridor to the room where the police constable had been placed. Along the way, Rowan beckoned to one of the uniformed officers in the corridor and told him to take down everything that was said.

'I'll only bother you for a minute or two, lad,' he said to the constable, who lay in his bandage collar, chalky-faced and still. 'Can you tell me what happened while it's still fresh?'

'Yes, sir.'

Rowan turned brusquely to the policeman taking notes. 'Can't you see it's hard for him to speak? Lean closer.'

'Wull ...' the constable began, 'I went up the stairs behind the porter, with Mr. Sorrel, the Israeli detective, and when we got to the suspect's room – room 11, that was – we ... knocked, sir.' The constable's speech was an effort and it was apparent that the neck wound was now giving him a great deal of pain.

'You were not armed,' Rowan said.

'Oh, no, sir. I'm only the regular constable, sir.' He smiled weakly.

'Yet Sergeant Battle ordered you to arrest this man alone?'

The constable's eyes shifted to Battle. He didn't want to make trouble, but he sensed it clearly in the air. 'Wull ... not exactly ordered, sir. He said I could make the pinch with the Israeli gentleman.'

'Knowing you were the regular constable and knowing you were unarmed.'

'Mr. Sorrel had a gun, sir.'

'Who knew that when you went up to the suspect's room?'

'I didn't, sir. No. Fat lot of good it did him, poor bloke. Is he dead?'

'Not yet,' Rowan said. 'What happened after you knocked, Constable?'

'At first there was no answer. I tried the door, but it was locked. I knocked a second time ... Finally, he answered. He said, "Who is it?" I said, "Open up, please, sir. I'm a police officer and I must have a word with you." '

The constable was exhausted and for a few seconds squinted against the pain. I glanced at Rowan, but his eyes were riveted on the man's face. The constable focused finally, and continued. 'He said, "Wot about?" And I said, "Please open up, sir. It will only take a minute." I had the feeling then he wouldn't open up, and he didn't ... There was some noise from inside the room, like he was trying for the window ... Mr. Sorrel snatched the keys from the porter and ... as luck would have it, the suspect had not left his key in the door ... so Mr. Sorrel opened it easily with the passkey. He swung the door open and stepped into the room. The man was by the bed. I caught a glimpse of the gun an instant before he fired ... Point-blank it was, sir, at Mr. Sorrel's chest. When he fell, I grappled with the man through the hall ... He pointed the pistol at my face, but it jammed.' He paused, turning this over in his mind. 'I'll not forget that soon ... I caught his hand the second time he fired. That's when this happened. He ran out then and to the roof ... Sergeant Battle went after him and this gentleman' – his eyes moved to me – 'helped stop the bleeding.'

Rowan stepped next to the bed and took the man's hand. 'I'll send the doctor in now, lad, so he can give you something to make you sleep.' He squeezed the hand in both of his and added, 'We're proud of you, you know.'

In the hospitable corridor, the disconsolate Sergeant Battle still tagged behind. 'Oh, Battle,' Rowan said casually before we reached the lounge again. 'You are suspended. You know the form. Turn your work over to the deputy inspector for reassignment and drop around in a day or two for a copy of the charges.'

'Sir, I've nineteen years' service,' Battle said, stunned.

'I'm aware of that,' Rowan replied coldly. 'You'll have an impartial hearing.'

'Impartial?' Sergeant Battle's voice rose. 'How can it be impartial when you're the one brings charges?'

Rowan paused, and for a moment I thought he was going to reconsider. He took the sergeant gently by the elbow and led him off to one side. 'There are two kinds of mistakes in police work. One can cost you your life. The other can cost someone else's. Tonight you committed the second kind.'

'No one died,' Battle said weakly.

'Pray no one does,' Rowan said and turned his back on the other man.

I sat alone in the lounge to await the results of Suriel's surgery. It was after three when Rowan swept out of the hospital, followed by a phalanx of grim-lipped detectives. He had been on the telephone in the hallway almost continuously since his words with Sergeant Battle, and I had the impression that the entire London Metropolitan Police had been mobilized to find Arnaud La Roche. I hoped they would have better luck than the French. I called Nicoletta, but a sustained conversation was impossible at that moment. She suggested we talk later when I knew more.

People came and went: the orderlies at the emergency entrance had no peace as Soho's wounded arrived like

184

casualties at a field hospital. Fractures, scalp lacerations and punched-up faces, a coronary victim, a stabbing and a spangled dancer with a wrenched ankle, all passed inside before the figure of George Panagoulos loomed in the doorway, sleek in black tie and red velvet dinner jacket. He sank into the seat beside me and clapped me heavily on the knee. 'Doc,' he said, 'you look as if you had a night.'

'Nice of you to drop by, Panagoulos.'

'You're not sore at *me*, are you?' His smile faded into a frown of genuine astonishment.

'That was last night. This morning I have more important things on my mind.'

'I heard the Israeli took a bullet.'

'In the chest.'

'They're good here.' He gestured toward the hospital at large. 'The best.'

'Your endorsement should encourage them.'

Panagoulos studied his fingernails before he said, 'Okay, Doc, what's the beef? You sore because I wasn't on the job all night?'

'If you really want to know, it all began with a nice old gentleman named Emmons.'

FOURTEEN

'So you think I was putting one over on you.'

'Not at all. You're simply a good soul who believes in hiring the handicapped.'

'Actually,' Panagoulos said, 'there *is* truth in that. I felt sorry for old Emmons and –'

'Spare me the details, Panagoulos. My emotions aren't up to it. As a security guard you're a humbug. Tell me something to restore your credibility.'

He sat back in the lounge chair, crossed his long legs and undid the black string tie he wore. From an inside pocket he withdrew a handsome alligator wallet, fat with crisp ten-pound notes, so fat indeed that he glanced self-consciously at me to see if I had noticed. Smiling guiltily, he said, 'Little run of luck tonight.'

He extracted a slip of paper, which he unfolded carefully.

185

'Cheney's an ex-con. I smelled that, but I wasn't sure. Served two years on a narcotics rap in France. That's almost a guarantee he can't get himself a bond, which is a big handicap in the rarefied book business. People have to trust you and apparently Lloyd's of London doesn't trust Mr. Cheney.'

'Someone did. Otherwise he wouldn't be director of the firm.'

'Wrong. He inherited the directorship. Cheney is the black sheep who counted on grandpa's will to set him up when he came out of jail, but the company had lousy prospects. Assets of two hundred ninety thousand pounds and debts of three hundred thousand when he took over.'

Panagoulos yawned and begged my pardon. It was nearly four and I too was running down. 'Cheney isn't clever,' he said, 'and when people don't trust you, creditors push. He laid off most of his old-time employees. Two months ago it looked like the hammer for dear old Cunningham and Pine.'

'But he found an angel.'

'Are you guessing or do you know?'

'You tell me.'

He stroked his chin thoughtfully.

'It's obvious without someone to buy up his debts, he wouldn't still be in business.'

'Who?'

'Lawyers acting for a Bahamian investment company.' He glanced at his notes. 'An outfit diversifying into the gold market and *objets d'art*. A letter box in Nassau and offices in Miami. Before they bought Cunningham and Pine their main interest was resort property.'

'Name?'

'Hi-Rise Investment, Ltd. Ever heard of them?'

I shook my head. 'Did you find out who they are?'

'It occurred to me your bankers might get that information faster than I can.'

To my surprise, he allowed himself a long, satisfying belch. 'Champagne,' he explained. 'It's good for the gambling image.'

'Is that all you have on Cheney?'

'Drives a new Aston Martin registered in the company name, has a thousand-quid overdraft at the Midland Bank and shares a mews flat off the King's Road with a boyfriend he seems to be supporting. He likes expensive French restaurants and has recently applied for membership in the Diner's Club –'

'Slow down. The Aston Martin.'

'He owes money on it.'

'Suriel said somebody in an Aston Martin was at La Roche's hotel earlier tonight. He wrote the licence tag down. Do you have Cheney's registration?'

'I can get it with a telephone call.'

'Can you check it against the number Suriel has?'

'If it's still in his pocket. The hospital staff must have his clothes. But what does it do beside tie Cheney to our fugitive?'

'Isn't that enough?'

'I've got something better.'

'What?'

He took his time answering. 'When Nicoletta pointed me as far as that fleabag hotel, after the shooting, I decided to take advantage of the fact that the other police had not yet arrived. Would you believe three of your papyri were in a suitcase under his bed?'

'Are you serious?'

'I'm no expert, but they look old enough. And the suitcase is initialled "D.O.C.," which has to stand for Desmond Oddball Cheney.'

'Did you turn them over to the police?'

'The hotel people were under the impression I *was* the police.'

'How convenient.'

'The Yard isn't worried about your scrolls. They just want La Roche for shooting a constable.'

An exceptionally pretty nurse entered and looked from me to Panagoulos. 'Dr. Marcus? Telephone.'

Before I left to take the call, I heard Panagoulos say, 'Yes, I'm an actor. Films, television, the stage.'

'Marcus speaking.'

It was Nicoletta. 'Oh, God, Jay. He'll live, won't he?'

'No one's betting on it.'

There was silence on the line. 'Are the police with you?'

'All over the place.'

'Jay?'

'Yes.'

187

'I've changed my mind about reading the paper at the conference. Vagan can handle it any way he wants.'

'Let's talk about it when I get back.'

'I just wanted you to know.'

A house doctor was beckoning me from the hallway. 'They're calling, Nicky. I'll phone you back.'

The emergency intern said Suriel was out of surgery. The bullet had skidded off his sternum and ploughed through a lung and some ribs, breaking into pieces on the journey. He had received five pints of blood and seemed to be holding on, but the prognosis was not good. Heartbeat erratic and blood pressure dangerously low. 'If he lives through the day,' the intern said, 'senior resident thinks he has a chance.'

'If the lungs don't fill up.'

He shrugged. 'He's young. There's that in his favour.'

Panagoulos directed me as I sleepily guided the Rover around Hyde Park to a block of nineteenth-century flats on the Bayswater Road. I had suggested a hotel, but he felt it would be better if we simply flopped a few hours at his place. There, he said, I could see the things he had rescued from La Roche's hotel, shower and be ready for our meeting with Cheney at ten.

'Why not simply tell the police about Cheney and let them handle things from here on?' I said, more to myself than to him. The muscles in the back of my neck were as taut as guitar strings, and what seemed like London fog turned out to be nothing more than a grey scrim of fatigue over my eyes.

'The question is not should you see him,' Panagoulos said patiently, 'but whether he is still greedy enough to take a chance on seeing you.'

'He'll know about La Roche.'

Panagoulos flicked the front page of a tabloid he had bought near the Marble Arch. There was no picture of La Roche yet, nor was he named, but the circumstances of the shooting were detailed under a two-inch-high headline that read: OFFICERS SHOT, and there was a photograph of a brace of constables at the entrance to the Lexington Palace Hotel. The article referred to an Inspector Sorrel, who was in critical condition, but made no mention of the Israeli government.

'What do you suggest?' I asked Panagoulos.

'The suitcase will worry him. He may even try to negotiate something fast with you this morning.'

'An on-the-spot sale?'

'Something like that.' I parked the car and wearily followed Panagoulos up two flights of stairs. He had a key and went in ahead of me. 'Everybody seems to be asleep,' he said.

The suitcase rested in the middle of the carpet, waiting to be tripped over. Panagoulos set it on a nearby couch and flipped it open. Buried inside, in a messy wad of clothing and crumpled newsprint, were the papyri: two scrolls and a linen-covered codex. Panagoulos picked up the small volume and slipped off the ancient, brown-stained fabric, which resembled a mummy wrapping. The pages of papyrus were neatly held between what seemed to be backs of horn or tortoise shell.

'Careful,' I said, beginning to wake up.

He laid it gently on a tabletop, then opened the cover, turning the pages slowly, touching only the edges. All were blank. He turned to me, expecting an explanation. 'Weren't these supposed to be full of hieroglyphics or something.'

'There were several like this. They were found with ink pots, styli and a kind of Roman abacus. Apparently from the scribe's supply closet.'

'When I first saw it, I thought somebody was playing a joke.'

'No joke. That has to be part of the collection. Nicoletta should be able to identify them easily.'

I slipped the codex back into its wrapping. Panagoulos suggested we keep everything together in the suitcase for the time being. As we were closing it, a sleepy blonde with ironed hair and a thin, androgynous body appeared in a doorway. Panagoulos nodded, but neither he nor the girl seemed the least concerned that she was naked. 'This is Amalia,' Panagoulos said as the girl rested one sleek buttock on the arm of the couch, yawned and brushed the hair from her sleep-furred eyes. 'She stays here sometimes.'

'Did you win?' Amalia asked him.

'Naturally.'

'Oh, my.' She smiled at me, acknowledging my presence. '*Naturally*. I'll make tea if you like.'

I smiled back and tried to be as nonchalant as they. But it

was hard to keep my tired eyes from wandering conspicuously over those tanned flanks to the upright cinnamon nipples of her small breasts. Her luxuriant hair, which ended just above the breasts, was counterpointed by the sparsest muff of gold between long legs. Her manner was natural rather than bold, as if clothing was something she had not yet experimented with. Yet there was, I thought, the smallest glint of impishness in those languid eyes.

'Take the bed,' Panagoulos said to me, showing me through the doorway from which the girl had entered, into a room lit only by a bedside lamp and littered with some bits of ruffled lingerie. It was nearly five when I sprawled across the messy bed, minus tie and jacket, not the least sorry George Panagoulos and his enticing girlfriend would just have to make do on the couch.

I remember Panagoulos saying he would wake me. I remember the click of the door as he closed it behind him. Then from somewhere, half dream, half reality, I remember nimble fingers unbuttoning my shirt, soft hair brushing my face. I was more asleep than awake, but groggily co-operative. My clothes were kicked off the bed as she pulled a silky quilt around us. I remember saying, 'I thought you were George's girl,' and the whispered reply, 'No . . . I just stay here sometimes.'

At nine, I felt Panagoulos's strong hand pat my shoulder none too gently. 'It's time,' he said. 'I talked with Cheney. He doesn't want to meet at the office.' My eyes were gluey with unsatisfied sleep. The girl Amalia, warm as a puppy, was curled against me under the quilt. I swung my naked torso out of the bed and sat upright, trying to focus on Panagoulos.

'Where, then?'

'A Lyons tea shop off Piccadilly.'

'Is that all right?'

'I told him you would prefer it.'

'Why would he believe that?'

'He's satisfied it's only the scrolls you want. He has one with him and wants five five-thousand-pound cashier's cheques to cover his finder's fee. I said ten thousand quid was all you could manage. You can manage ten, can't you?'

'I can, but why should I? If we just collect the sample and blow the whistle, that puts us ahead.'

'You're a devious man, Doc,' Panagoulos said. 'But you run the risk of losing the rest that way.'

'You really think he has them?'

'He knows where they are.'

'Then maybe he'd bargain them for his freedom.'

'Not with Scotland Yard he wouldn't.'

I let the warm shower run over my body for a long time, kneading muscles in my arms and shoulders to work the stiffness out. Then I turned off the hot tap and let the cold water run on my head until my teeth chattered. My eyes still burned as I shaved, but I was making a comeback. There were faint red teeth marks on one side of my neck and some scratches on my back. Except for those and the sleeping presence of soft Amalia in the big bed, I would have sworn I had dreamed the whole crazy encounter.

The cashier's cheques were a matter of a telephone call and a ten-minute stop by the bank's Oxford Street branch. They were made out to the bearer, and the clerk who handed them to me frowned in disapproval.

Cheney was waiting for us at the Lyons, dressed in another outlandish Edwardian suit, looking like Renniel's Mad Hatter: less the evil genius than the corrupt fumbler. He had taken a booth at the back and was morosely nursing a cup of milky tea as we sat down. He pretended to go on with the act he had begun at the first meeting in his office. He had been in touch with the people who had the artifacts on the Continent, he said, and they had set forth the terms of the sale. The items numbered twenty-eight, one of which he had with him. The rest were in a vault in Europe – he could not say where because he did not know – but as soon as five hundred thousand dollars was deposited to a blind account in a Cayman Islands bank, I would be informed through Cheney where the first fifteen articles could be recovered. Then, once I had examined them and was satisfied, a further half-million dollars would have to be divided between accounts in Beirut and Basel, before the remaining pieces would be turned over.

'They'd be escrow deposits,' I said, 'to be released only after the artifacts are received.'

'That won't do. They want the money direct.'

'What protection do I have from your plan? If the papyri

turn up damaged, or if they don't turn up at all, the museum is out a fortune.'

'It isn't my plan,' Cheney insisted. 'I'm only trying to bring you all together.'

'Then I suggest you get back to them with a counter-proposal. I won't risk a million dollars when I don't even know yet if what they're offering is genuine.'

'Did you bring the one we asked for?' Panagoulos said.

Cheney nodded and tapped an attaché case on the seat next to him. A waitress was waiting for our order.

When the girl had gone, Cheney nervously laid the attaché case on his lap and opened it. He withdrew a near duplicate of the codex Panagoulos and I had examined in his apartment at five that morning. There was a significant difference between the two, however: these pages were covered with a neat Latin script I recognized immediately.

'Well?' Cheney said.

I withdrew the cashier's cheques and passed them to him without a word. He seemed relieved.

'Jolly good,' Cheney said. 'But you'll have to agree to the straight deposits, Doctor. Otherwise these people won't do business.'

'Tell them they will have to accept the escrow deposits because it is the only way I can do business.'

'It's nothing to you, that much money,' Cheney hissed.

'But that's the way it's going to be,' Panagoulos said, patting Cheney on one arm. Panagoulos had a locker-room jock's repertory of pats, punches and reassuring grips, but the one he used on Cheney now was clearly threatening in spite of the smile that accompanied it. 'We want to do business,' he added. 'We really do. Don't make it any more difficult than it has to be.'

'I looked you up, Marcus,' Cheney said. 'You're one of the richest men in America.'

'Did you look me up too?' Panagoulos said sweetly. 'I'm one of the meanest.'

Cheney smiled uncertainly. 'You know what I mean.'

I did indeed. One of the unfortunate consequences of wealth is the frequency with which I run into this kind of attitude. Rarely in as bald-faced a presentation as Cheney had just made, but it exists nevertheless – in the eyes of waiters when they arrive with padded cheques, in the smiles of salesmen in expensive shops, in the reluctance of contractors and agents to give advance estimates or discuss professional charges before I am billed. There seems to be common agreement among the hustlers of the world that the rich man is fair game. I understand it, but I don't like it. In fact, I resist it angrily. 'We'll work on an escrow basis,' I said, 'or not at all. Tell your principals that. Do you have the numbers of the accounts?'

Cheney gave them to me.

'Can you have an answer by tomorrow?'

'They won't like it.'

'Tell them I don't like it either.'

Between bites of toast dipped in runny egg, Panagoulos nodded agreement. 'Another thing not to lose sight of,' he told Cheney when I stopped talking, 'is the time element. You saw the papers today, so I'd get this thing moving real fast if I were you. I sure would.'

We left Cheney and I locked the codex in the glove compartment of the Rover as we drove along Piccadilly. 'Do you think he'll run?' I asked Panagoulos.

He said he thought Cheney was already running without admitting it to himself. 'He's afraid to go near his office. He's afraid the police will trace his suitcase and question him. He is probably withdrawing his ten thousand quid from the bank now as he cashes your cheques. By noon he'll have his ticket.'

'And by evening he's out of the country. Is that it?'

'He won't put himself beyond the reach of your bank account,' Panagoulos said. 'Don't worry about that.'

We had arrived back at the Bayswater Road flat and I waited in the car while he went inside to bring the other papyri. 'When do I see you?' I asked after we had stowed the valise safely in the car trunk.

'Tonight at your hotel. I'll try to have more on La Roche.'

The next question was a little harder to ask. 'George, about that girl this morning . . . We didn't talk much.'

'She's a little wiggy, but she makes her needs known.'

'You don't mind?'

'Doc, she's not my girl. I have other interests. Amalia just drops by sometimes.'

I laughed. 'I like your world, Panagoulos. I don't understand it. I suspect it appeals to the adolescent in me, or the middle-aged delinquent, but it has its charms.'

'Don't stop to analyze them. George Pan's prescription for happiness is Keep Moving. There may be others, but my span of attention is too short to find out.'

FIFTEEN

I drove fast from London to stay awake. There was little traffic at midday, and the Rover held the outer lane as if it were on tracks. It was one when I pulled into the parking area of the Rose and Thistle. Nicoletta had been sitting in the smokers' lounge and she ran into my arms as I entered the main hall. She was trembling, laughing on the edge of tears as she pressed her head against my chest and hugged with all her frail strength. I was glad she could not see the warm blush of guilt creep along my neck. Don't analyze it, Marcus. At forty, worry only diminishes a man. I kissed her and forgot the guilt. Judas.

'I was sure you'd fall asleep driving.' We walked into the lounge, arms still locked around each other. 'That was the longest night and morning I ever spent, Jay. Never again. How's Suriel?'

'No change. Which is good news under the circumstances.'

'Are you hungry?'

'Starved.'

'Shall we have lunch here?'

'As you like.'

She smiled. 'That sounds so veddy English. Are you aware you sound more English the longer we stay?'

'I'll take pains to correct it immediately.'

'See what I mean? George, on the other hand, could live here a hundred years and still sound American. It's not a criticism.'

'Of whom? Him or me?'

'Nobody, darling.'

We reached a table in the dining room and sat down under the frowning gaze of the manageress. Scampi cocktail, mutton chops with creamed potatoes, salad and sweet. My eyes were set in mucilage and I have only the faintest recollection of some leached-out peaches in a custard before I stumbled upstairs and collapsed on the bed.

At six Nicoletta gently prodded me awake with apologies, to remind me we had a dinner engagement with the Rosses that evening. Had I forgotten? Had I ever known? The Rose and Thistle shower was hopeless. I filled a tub, soaked awhile, dozed again, and finally emerged more or less fit to meet the world. Nicoletta was already dressed and curled on one corner of the bed, reading. She closed the book and swept the glasses from the end of her nose. She was wearing a tailored hound's-tooth suit, accented, as they say, by a weightless chiffon scarf of emerald green. Casual chic. 'We're going to be late, but I called to let them know.'

'Did you call the hospital?'

'He's still unconscious.'

'Panagoulos?'

'Coming by later.'

'I know.'

'So is your banker.'

'I didn't know.'

'I told him we wouldn't be back much before midnight, but he said that was quite all right. He is driving out and will wait here for your return. Are you overdrawn or something?'

'It's about arranging the money for Cheney.'

She drew a quick breath. 'Did you tell the police?'

'There's nothing to tell them yet. I think he's bluffing, but Panagoulos is sure he knows where the papyri are. So we are going through the motions.'

'What about Berman?'

'There's nothing he can do from Tel Aviv.'

'But he should know, Jay.'

'Maybe Cheney does have the rest of them stashed away somewhere. I don't know. He's obviously in on the thing with that sonofabitch La Roche, wherever he is. Maybe they'll gun him down on Piccadilly.'

'The English don't do things that way.'

'Just once, I wish they would.'

'Are you ready?'

'*Andiamo*, my sweet. I accept your word on everything, including our dinner date with the Rosses.'

In the car she told me about Mr. Emmons. 'He brought me two rubbings today. One from the tomb of a knight in Stokenchurch, and the other is . . . guess who?'

'Arnaud La Roche.'

'I'm serious. Margaret More, Sir Thomas's daughter.' She laughed gaily. 'He says it is a very popular item since women's liberation. He refused to take any money for them, though, so I'll have to find him a nice present before we leave.'

We were only half an hour late at the Rosses' and Natalie greeted us warmly at the door as the Yorkshires yapped about her heels. Sir William Ross surprised me. For some reason, perhaps the early photographs, I expected a lanky, dour kind of man. Instead my host was as plump as a dressed hen, with thick white hair and a pink, cherubic face. His eyes glinted with good humour as he bustled about, mixing drinks and telling us how delighted he was we had found time to join them that evening. There were two other guests, the physicist Kittering and his ethereal, pregnant wife, who sipped lemon squashes and smiled vacantly whenever anyone glanced in her direction. Sir William was as avid for information about what he called the 'Pontius Pilate Papers' as the most naïve newspaper reader. And that evening the newspapers were filled with the story.

Details of the previous night's shooting and the manhunt for La Roche dominated the front pages: he was reported seen in both Scotland and Ireland. A Reuters dispatch from Tel Aviv provided a recapitulation of the original museum theft and the Lanholtz murder, together with a fairly detailed account of the archbishop's arrest and the recovery of most of the 'mysterious parchments.' The museum collection was described as the most important find in archaeology since Troy, 'according to Dr. Aaron Marcus, President of the Board of Trustees of the Marcus Museum.' I laughed when Nicoletta read that part aloud, but then she said, 'Oh, my God! Listen to this. "Many of them are believed to be letters written by Pontius Pilate himself, although authorities at the Marcus Museum in Jerusalem have refused to confirm this." Can you just *see* Lev Vagan?'

'I believe you're mentioned in there somewhere too,' Sir William said to me. 'Toward the end.'

'Here it is,' Nicoletta said. ' "According to a museum

spokesman, millionaire American playboy Jay Marcus is personally directing the hunt for the Pontius Pilate Papers on three continents. Officials in charge of the upcoming Congress on Middle Eastern Archaeology at Oxford next week had no comment on the Pilate Papers, originally scheduled to be presented there publicly for the first time." What nonsense! And this: "Monsignor Gerald Dugan, S.J., spokesman for the Greater London Committee for the Defence of the Faith, said the existence of the Pontius Pilate Papers would not have any bearing on fundamental questions of Christian doctrine, although he acknowledged an interest in reading them if and when they became available." '

'It sounds like "The Curse of the Mummy's Tomb," ' I said as Natalie refilled my glass.

'You must admit,' she suggested, 'they don't get such a bloody good story every day.'

'The press never stopped calling my office today,' Ross said, 'but as you see, we gave them nothing to go on.'

'Unfortunately my uncle wasn't so discreet.'

'I suppose he had to say something,' Natalie said, 'or they would have invented worse.'

'What could be worse? At the moment, we're in the most delicate phase of negotiations for the remainder of the collection. Now that all this is out, the man we're dealing with is bound to break off contact.'

'He may not, Jay,' Nicoletta said hopefully.

'He's dim if he doesn't. He's sure to believe I'm setting him up. Even if the police haven't connected him with the theft, he doesn't know that. And furthermore, he wouldn't believe it now if I tried to tell him. No, two of the thieves are dead and the third will probably be caught shortly. That leaves our contact to look after himself.'

'How many of the scrolls have you recovered so far?' Ross asked.

'Two were left in a stolen van by the thieves. The Israeli police found sixteen more when they arrested that archbishop in Jerusalem, and I have three – no, four – in the car.'

'In *your* car?' Ross said incredulously.

'Jay, you're joking,' Nicoletta said.

'No, I'm not. Three were found in La Roche's hotel room

197

after the shootings last night. The fourth I got from the man who is selling them back to us.'

'You think that's quite the best place for them?' Kittering inquired mildly. Nicoletta gaped at me as if I had lost my mind.

'With everything that happened during the day, I simply forgot about putting them in a better place.'

'If you like, Doctor,' Kittering said slowly, 'you're welcome to leave them temporarily in my laboratory. I have a low-humidity vault where we often keep delicate things in storage.'

'That's very kind of you.'

'I suggest you do that,' Ross said, 'until you know where you are. Some of them were there before, if you recall.' Ross turned to Kittering. 'Clive did the carbon-14 dating on the papyri Lanholtz sent us last year.'

The physicist smiled shyly. 'Your things were simple enough. It's the older specimens that sometimes give us trouble.'

At dinner, Natalie cross-examined Nicoletta about her work with Lanholtz. The most prominent people in the field were regular guests of the Rosses when they visited Oxford, so Natalie was nearly as familiar with the digs in remote corners of the desert as she was with her own beloved garden. In addition, she had a graceful way of asking the pertinent question to elicit the illuminating answer. Nicoletta, normally a reluctant talker about her work, was soon chattering with the warm enthusiasm of a graduate student, while Kittering and Ross offered their own occasional comment. Only Kittering's wife seemed indifferent to the conversation.

Kittering, on the other hand, after an ample supply of claret, became almost expansive. He took delight in reminding us that it was the geologist, the meteorologist, the forestry engineer and, above all, the physicist who were responsible for showing the archaeologist that man was alive and well and hunting tigers in France thirty thousand years ago.

Nicoletta pursued Kittering's work with questions of her own, observing at one point, 'But you must find a way to date an artifact for us, Professor, without destroying it entirely.'

'A centimetre from one edge is all we need. Don't tell me that interferes with your work.'

'It's painful for an archaeologist just the same.'

'You're absolutely right, my dear,' Ross said. 'No deuced reason why they shouldn't be able to measure the radio-carbon content without having to sacrifice bits and pieces along the way. We find precious little as it is.'

As we left the table, Kittering's wife astounded me. Ross and Kittering had moved on ahead, sharing some further skirmish as they entered the big, low-ceilinged parlour of the cottage. Nicoletta mentioned we had best be thinking about returning to Abingdon because Panagoulos would be appearing shortly, and Mrs. Kittering said, 'Is that *George* Panagoulos?' It was the first question she had asked since our arrival. I said yes, of the health-farm Panagouloses.

'Is he a friend of yours?' For the first time during the evening she was alive, focused; waiting for confirmation. Nicoletta said he was a friend of ours.

'Would you give him a message from me?'

Somewhat uncomfortably, I agreed. The woman's sudden intensity was as unnerving as her previous indifference. I fumbled in my jacket pocket for pencil and paper.

'No,' she said, laying a hand on mine. 'Just tell him I'm not joking. I've had enough.'

Nicoletta said, 'Why not call him?'

'I will not do that,' Mrs. Kittering said emphatically, and walked on ahead to join the others.

Over a brandy before we left, I told Kittering I would bring the papyri by his laboratory in the morning for safekeeping. He gave me directions for finding the building and said he would be there from eight o'clock onward. Natalie kissed us both when we said good night and Ross walked with his hand on Nicoletta's arm as far as the car.

On the drive to the hotel, Nicoletta asked me what I made of Mrs. Kittering's desperate-sounding message.

'She's pregnant, that's all, and George is the father. You see what happens when town and gown don't keep their distance.'

'Don't joke.'

'It serves him right for bedding his betters.'

'*Really*. What could she have in mind?'

'Whatever it is, you can bet the great George Pan is up to

handling it without any help from us.' But Nicoletta was not satisfied.

At the hotel, I lugged the La Roche suitcase up to our room while she stopped at the desk for telephone messages. I also had the codex Cheney had given me tucked under one arm, anxious to read as much as I could before Panagoulos or the banker interrupted. It had been a while since I had heard from Gaius Longinus Procula.

'I don't know why you don't have a full-time travelling secretary,' Nicoletta said as she shed her gauzy green scarf.

'I have you.'

'Do you? Don't be all that sure about me. Now' – she frowned at the telephone messages – 'Mansour, your secretary, Berman, the Israeli embassy, George, Inspector Rowan, as well as Reuters, the *Daily Express*, the *Mirror* and CBS Television.'

'It's Aaron, that bastard. Promoting.'

'Don't be modest. It's your instant celebrity, darling. The millionaire playboy detective. After all, women find you irresistible, so why not journalists?'

'Certainly not Mrs. Kittering.'

'I was thinking of the one who scratched up your back.'

When I didn't answer, she turned away from me and said, 'Never mind. It's not my business. But don't be under any illusions. I was alone too long before you arrived. My values got a bit warped. Well, they're back in place again.'

We had, without intending it, laid the groundwork for our first quarrel. Except that I was determined not to participate. 'Look, Nicky . . .'

She breathed deeply and said, 'I should have known no one was quite as wonderful as I wanted you to be.' Her laugh was brittle. 'To think I *worried* about you when you were gone.' She looked at me and shook her head slowly. 'I'd like to put some scratches on you myself, *Doctor*, for different reasons.'

When I tried to put my arms around her, she pushed me away. Her mouth was rigid with the effort to keep from crying.

'I didn't mean to hurt you,' I said.

'You have nothing to say I want to hear on the subject.' She cleared her throat and went on calmly. 'I don't know yet what to do with that damned research paper.'

'I'll go along with whatever you want to do,' I told her, 'but I can't make your decision for you.'

'You can. What you mean is you won't.'

'Okay. I won't.'

'You're no help at all.'

'We can go back to Paris. You can plead illness.'

'After all the publicity? If Victor could give his life for these damned things, the least I can do is see it through.'

'Then see it through.'

'I'm frightened of all those archaeologists and even more terrified of the newspaper people. Victor would know how to handle it. He could be brilliant in an interview. I panic just thinking about it. I know I'll make a mess of things.'

'Whatever you want to do,' I said blandly.

'Oh, shit, Marcus! Stop trying to be so ... so damned fair.' She began to cry in a series of angry sniffs while I stood around like a great lump with my hands in my pockets, saying nothing, retreating from her sudden display of emotion. I was already rationalizing my own behaviour, but failed to realize the less I said at that moment, the better. My mother used to cry fairly often when I was young, and the reaction it provoked in me was not sympathetic. I felt that old cold indifference return as I calculated Nicoletta's menstrual cycle and arrived at what I considered a purely medical conclusion.

But she, the lovely witch, was ahead of me. 'If you think this has anything to do with you,' she sniffed, regaining her control, 'it doesn't. So don't go forming any hasty judgments. When I'm like this, it only means my period isn't far off.'

I said sententiously, 'I suggest a pyridoxine shot in the morning and then let's talk about it.'

'What's that?'

'Vitamin B^6.'

'You ass. I don't want Dr. Feelgood. I just want advice.'

'Come off it, Nicoletta. You're free to do as you wish.'

The tears had ceased and she was watching me with a kind of angry amazement. 'I'm glad you're not a gynaecologist,' she said. 'What you don't know would fill a whole university.'

I told her she was right.

'Oh! Your scrupulous objectivity!'

'It's your decision and I'm sorry I suggested it had anything to do with . . . well, with anything other than the situation.'

'I don't live in a vacuum, Mr. Jay Brian Marcus! At least not since I met you. I never would have gone this far if you hadn't encouraged me. It isn't that you don't want to make the decision. You've already made it in your mind, but like everything you do, you don't want the responsibility for it!'

'Then deliver the damned paper and that's that,' I replied, smarting under her attack.

'I'm not some chemical equation you can balance with a vitamin shot.' Her look was withering.

'I didn't say that.'

'Yes, you did.'

'Look . . .'

'Has it ever occurred to you that something else might be all that's needed at certain moments? Obviously it hasn't.'

'What?'

'Ever occurred to you.'

'A moment ago you told me not to touch you.'

'I didn't mean it the way it sounded.'

My impulse was to burst out laughing. Instead I drew her roughly to me. To my surprise, she became as soft and willing as a kitten, laying her head against my chest and locking her arms around my waist, moving her body with a gentle motion as I kissed her hair. 'I could kill you,' she whispered, 'now, now, now.' We sank to the bed, groping, fondling, as the telephone rang insistently. By the time it stopped, I was in her and we had come, quickly and fiercely. '*Mamma mia*,' she said, rolling away from me a few moments later, her brow dewy with perspiration.

Someone was knocking on the door.

'Night manager, sir.'

'Send him away,' she said. 'I haven't finished.'

'What do you want?'

'There's a gentleman in the lounge to see you.'

'Tell him I'll be down in a few minutes.' I heard the footsteps retreat along the corridor.

My back stung where she had raked it with her nails and I winced as I got off the bed. '*Vis medicatrix naturae*,' she said. 'It's a better fate than you deserve, you lout.'

In the hotel lounge the man from the bank awaited me.

We sat down at one of the writing tables and he withdrew a sheaf of papers from the wafer-thin attaché case he carried. 'There are several ways we can handle these payments, Doctor. I'll tell you what the bank advises first, and then give you the options if you like.'

'Would you like a drink?'

'I wouldn't mind, but I believe the bar's closed, isn't it?'

I called the undergraduate night manager over and asked him if he could find a bottle of Scotch with some ice and soda.

My banker friend was a handsome, white-haired man in his late fifties, immaculately dressed in dark suit, pearl-grey tie and pocket handkerchief, who spoke with a broad down-East accent, calling me 'Dahkta Mahkis.' Biddeford Pool by way of Harvard Business, Broad Street and the City. One glance at the memorandum he showed me and I saw he had it all wrong.

'It has to be a two- or even a three-step borrowing operation,' I said.

'I beg your pardon?'

'I know you didn't have much time to work this out, but look. My money cannot go directly to pay these people. I thought I made that clear on the telephone. If I do what you propose here, and secure the million with part of my own portfolio, then it's a one-step operation, a simple loan. I might deduct the interest from my taxes, but not the whole sum.'

'Yes, I see,' he said vaguely. 'But this plan was geared to provide the cash immediately.'

'If I must pay, then it has to be through the museum and the foundation. Otherwise I get bombed again by the Internal Revenue people.'

'I'm afraid we didn't have time to vet this with our tax department.'

'Or your trust department.'

'It's all in New York, as you know. We do our best here, but we don't have the staff.'

'Just see that museum funds are available to be deposited to those various accounts I gave you, upon my authorization.'

'But you have no authorization to spend museum funds,' he said.

'Then get it for me. It's only a formality. A few telephone calls, if necessary a trip to New York, and you should have it sorted out. But this way' – I pushed the memorandum back to him – 'what do I need your bank for, if you'll pardon my bluntness?'

'Yes, I see youah point,' he said, now very nervous, making the effort to recover his shredded banker's image. 'I'll get on it first thing in the morning, Dahkta Mahkis.'

I had not the slightest suspicion of him until the young man finally brought the whisky. When I poured a generous double, he refused the ice and soda, and knocked the Scotch back thirstily in one practised swallow.

'I'm also in need of some confidential information.'

He was delighted that I had changed the subject.

'I want to know in whose name or names those blind accounts are held at the Cayman Islands bank and the other banks.'

He looked up from his second straight Scotch. 'We'll certainly do everything possible,' he said uncertainly.

'That isn't all.'

He smiled again, waiting, nervous.

'There is a company incorporated in Nassau called Hi-Rise Investment. Offices in Miami. I want to know who is behind them. Offices, directors, main stockholders.'

Panagoulos appeared in the entrance, strode confidently across the room, ducking the beams, and introduced himself.

'The background on Cheney is coming in,' he said, 'when nobody needs it. Fat little facts.' He paused and grinned. (Look, Ma, no cavities!) 'Or would you rather have the bad news first?'

'Try me.'

'No sign of him at his office. His boyfriend cut out this afternoon with two suitcases and an airplane ticket to Paris.'

'So he's gone.'

'Only the boyfriend. Reservations booked by Cheney at an agency in Mayfair. Including Paris-Rome flight and a hotel at Capri.'

The banker was listening to all this in total bewilderment. I did not offer him another drink.

'Is that the good news or the bad news?' I asked Panagoulos, and he laughed.

'If we're in agreement, Dahkta Mahkis, I think I'll head

back. I have a busy night ahead.' The man shook hands, told Panagoulos he had enjoyed meeting him, recovered his topcoat and homburg from a nearby chair and went out the door.

'Not bad,' Panagoulos observed. 'You paying for the limo too?'

'Indirectly.'

'Good thing he has a driver.'

'Why?'

Panagoulos picked up the bottle of Johnnie Walker. 'He's pissed.'

'I had the impression he might be a drinker, but you saw him walk out. Straight and level.'

Panagoulos smiled. Not the advertising grin, but the one I liked, with the lips closed, his mind on his work and his eyes twinkling. 'Doc, you're such a baby. That walk took years to perfect and he can do it one minute before he passes out. I hope you didn't give him anything important to do.'

'Only the money arrangements.'

'Let me suggest you risk a duplication of effort with somebody else.' He poured himself a drink and looked toward the door. 'What do you suppose they pay a guy like that?'

'Plenty.'

Panagoulos shook his head sadly. 'Well, why not? Maybe once in his career he earned it.' He sipped slowly at his Scotch. 'Ever been in Damascus?'

'Not recently.'

'Well, Cheney was. By the wildest coincidence the dates coincide with La Roche's arrival there, which again by the strangest chance' – he was enjoying himself as he stretched it all out – 'happened to be only a few days after the great rip-off at the Marcus Museum.'

'Which tells us what?'

'It depends on how we read the spoor. But if you want an old cynic's educated guess, it ties these two together like asparagus. Obvious questions arise.'

'Such as whether Cheney hired La Roche and the others to steal the museum collection in the first place'.

'Or whether somebody else hired all of them.' Panagoulos swirled his Scotch around in the glass, sniffed at it suspiciously and drank it.

'Are you a gambler, Doc?'

'Sometimes.'

'You like long shots?'

'Not usually.'

'I'll put my hundred against your thousand that Cheney was financed by Hi-Rise Investment of Nassau.'

'With or without their knowledge?'

'I respect a careful gambler. Care tips the odds in your favour. Suppose Hi-Rise is a Mafia laundry. Miami, Nassau and the Caymans are full of them. A lot of the skim from Vegas is washed through those places. Cheney probably had connections from his jail days, so there you are.'

'Where am I?'

'With Hi-Rise backing the museum hit. The management would have had to know in general terms what he was up to or they never would have put a dime into his broken-down book-selling operation. And only one kind of management invests in a robbery.'

'So you think Cheney is the key.'

'Let's say I don't think we have to look much further, except to prove out the investment company. Like I said, I'll give you ten to one Cheney's the end of the road.'

'No deal.'

Panagoulos laughed his approval and nearly fractured my shoulder with one of his locker-room embraces.

After he had gone, it occurred to me that the day I had just put in was some kind of record. I make no pretension to the kind of nonstop stamina shown by Panagoulos, but I was discovering a new and interesting aspect to sex. Contrary to popular medical superstition, lack of sleep in no way reduced my appetite. Like many bachelors, I can go for long stretches, camel-fashion, without making love. But when at last I start in earnest, all the symptoms of incipient satyriasis immediately appear, and visions of uplifted skirts and softly spread thighs crowd all else from my otherwise tidy mind.

Nicoletta was in bed when I walked in, reading the Longinus codex retrieved from Cheney. She looked up immediately and said, 'What did he say when you told him?'

'What did who say?'

'About Mrs. Kittering.'

For a moment, I had to think.

'You did tell him, didn't you?'

'First he laughed. Then he said, "Good fences make good neighbours." It seems she was referring to Hermione's cows.'

'What on earth do you mean?'

'The Kittering property adjoins Les Sylphides. Hermione Panagoulos keeps dairy cattle, who eat Mrs. Kittering's delphiniums. She's going to court to force George to put up a fence.'

'The woman's mad.'

'That's what Panagoulos says, but he's going to put the fence up anyway. Titillating story, isn't it? Anybody call?'

She shook her head. I had my clothes off by then and was sliding into the bed beside her. 'Before you get too comfortable, there's something you should know.' She held the codex out to me with great care, resting it on a hotel towel so her fingers did not touch the pages. 'Did you read any of this?'

'A few lines.'

'Well, I've been at it now since you left.'

'You seem surprised.'

'I am. I worked on the entire collection with Victor almost from the start and I never saw this particular papyrus before tonight.'

SIXTEEN

XXX APRILIS ANNUM REGNUM TIB. CAES. XX

(The translation and paragraphing are mine. So are the modern place names.)

Fortress Antonia, Jerusalem

Greetings, Lucius, and may this letter find you in good health. I am well, having recovered from a bad molar drawn by my Greek surgeon, with much pus and bleeding. Our march from Caesarea was pleasant enough except for one nasty incident which left a worse taste in my mouth than that putrid tooth. On the third night some Sicarii crept into our bivouac at the Latrun oasis and slit the throats of twenty Judean pilgrims travelling to Jerusalem under our protection. Several were children and old people. When the bodies were found at dawn, still warm, I sent Annaeus Gallo's cavalry to cut off any escape to the south while my prefect Valerius and I led a hundred men in a pincers movement north of the village to root the terrorists out of the surrounding hills. We killed six and captured nine.

One of the prisoners, a tall, rugged savage with greasy beard and hair below his shoulders, made quite a speech, claiming their new king would be crowned at the Passover celebrations in Jerusalem, and that armies of angels would destroy our legions and depose Tiberius himself. Most of the men roared with laughter at this, although a few were so angered they were ready to cut him down on the spot. When Centurion Silius Rufus, who speaks Aramaic, asked him how he knew so much, he replied proudly that his brother was the king's closest confidant. Rufus tried to find out the man's name, but these fanatics don't give information easily, even those who talk a lot.

I ordered the prisoners executed and displayed. The idea is that it serves as a deterrent, which I doubt, even though I follow the form. My tooth was kicking up and I was anxious to be on the move, so we did not bother with the usual routine in matters of this kind. There was a grove of young pines near the road. The men cut nine of the smallest trees at shoulder height and impaled the prisoners on the sharpened stumps. Then I had Silius Rufus slit their throats. We did not reach Jerusalem until well after dark.

The next morning, before the men had time to clean the dust of the trip from their equipment, there was a near riot when one of our Greek sentries decided to amuse his friends by pissing from the fortress walls on a gathering of the faithful. The thing would have got completely out of hand if I had not had the offending soldier flogged to death in sight of the Jews. The Governor grumbled about this and asked why I did not send a force into the Temple court to put down the disturbance. My men are not short of courage, but most of them are veterans, and have not lived this long to die under the horny feet of a nationalist mob.

From the beginning, a stream of rumours found its way into the fortress, and gradually a pattern began to emerge which added grim significance to the claims of the Sicarius we had executed by the Latrun roadside. The hills around the city were filling with Zealot followers, all expecting to be on hand for the great coronation and the end of Roman rule. More importantly, most of them were armed to the teeth. One did not have to be a prophet to see what was in the making. The only question was when. Some said the coup was planned for the Jewish Sabbath at the end of their holy week, others for the week after.

The 'messiah,' or god-chosen liberator, would claim direct descent from their King David and be recognized immediately by the faithful because of certain signs, the most absurd of which was that he would enter the city astride a donkey.

I know this may sound quaint to you, so far away in Capri, but in this pesthole even the most fanciful rumour is easily reconciled to reality.

After we narrowed the list of possible candidates to a handful of known terrorists and rabble-rousers, our regular guards on the city gates were told to keep a sharp watch, but make no arrests. The odd thing was that in three days of surveillance, my men reported not one donkey-borne arrival. The word had spread among the Jews, apparently, that only the messiah would fulfil this bizarre prophecy, so even old men and pregnant women walked.

Money for bribes was plentiful, but it was not easy to find loose tongues among the lower-class pilgrims. The Jews are a puzzling people: the poorer they are, the more devout and less corruptible they seem to be.

The trick was to allow the conspiracy to mature and then lance it like a boil at a moment advantageous to us. But how far does one let a plot run before it is too late to check? I wanted the people to be convinced this man was the messiah they had promised themselves, that he was the anointed son of their exclusive god. Then, by striking *after* their belief was established, we could hope to discredit him and the prophets who had forecast his success.

As it turned out, there was no need for the guards to be on their toes. The leader's arrival was rumoured hours before he appeared outside the city, walking. Thousands went out with gifts of food and drink. Others, disfigured by cancers and crippled by all manner of wounds and paralysis, placed themselves in his path as he approached the gate, only to be shoved aside by the healthier Jews. Old crones followed the pathetic procession and young mothers held their children up to look.

The man had almost reached the gate when there was a great commotion and the crowd halted. The two thugs nearest him then entered the city while he waited. He was by no means as rugged as the others, but just as filthy. His hair and beard were matted and he wore a shabby robe like the rest. The men around him glanced at us and reported to him, but his dignity prevented him from raising his eyes in our direction.

After a few minutes, the two who had entered the city reappeared leading a donkey. A murmur of awe issued from five thousand throats as the man mounted and rode in through the gate at a brisk little trot, his followers fanning out ahead and behind.

Prefect Valerius said our worries were over if this was their king. But Gallo, who is more observant and serious-minded, called my attention to the size of the crowd. Later, when Rufus returned from mingling with them, I learned that the hard-core Sicarii who formed the bodyguard were heavily armed. He also brought news of more weapons stored in the hillside camps under guard, ready for distribution.

The Antonia Fortress was a hive of speculation. The man had spoken to a large crowd near the Temple, where Rufus heard him. He did not harangue, but talked compellingly about the kingdom he had come to claim. He said the Temple would be cleansed and those who profaned his holy city would be destroyed. He would lead them, the children of light, against us, the people of darkness. Rufus had not stayed for the whole speech, afraid someone might notice he was not one of them. I told him his smelly disguise was so effective, only his cock would have given him away.

While we were still discussing how far I should let things run, an aide brought news that there was rioting in the Temple court – a market area where pigeons and sheep are sold for sacrifice and where pilgrims change their money. The self-styled king had arrived, brandishing a whip, leading hundreds of his armed followers on a general rampage through the holy precincts.

We hurried to the walls, which afforded a good view.

Chaos. A sea of struggling people. Police visible around the edges but none making any effort to interfere. When the Governor himself appeared, in a great rage, I spent the next hour dissuading him from committing our men piecemeal.

The rioting ceased by nightfall, but isolated street-corner incidents kept our patrols busy. As the tension continued and our sentries watched the pilgrim campfires from atop the Antonia walls, part of the Siloam tower collapsed, killing the three guards posted there. Slaves worked through the night searching for others injured in the rubble. By dawn, three armed Jews had been extricated alive and eighteen other Jew bodies recovered. With them, beside their arms, were the picks and spades they had used to undermine the tower.

If another part of my programme had not paid off beyond my expectations, I would have had no alternative but to mount a reprisal against the pilgrim camps the following day. Luckily, one of the Greek spies under Centurion Rufus made contact with a disenchanted Sicarius in the Zealot camp, the brother, in fact, of the speechmaker I had executed on the Latrun road. The legionnaire learned that the messiah would be spending his nights in the nearby village of Bethany, where he was seldom accompanied by more than a few of his personal guard. The Greek arranged another meeting with the Sicarius for the following night, promising him a small purse if he could show us exactly where this would-be king was.

My immediate reaction was negative. After the Siloam tower treachery, it seemed no more than a clumsy attempt at drawing some of our men into a night ambush. I suggested that the Temple police go after this Zealot, rather than one of our patrols. My brother-in-law agreed we had nothing to lose by sending Jews to catch a Jew.

The next day, toward evening, word reached me that the Sicarius had collected his money, but claimed the man we wanted would be found in an olive grove across the Kidron Valley instead of at Bethany. I was sure then the whole thing was a ruse and I wondered what to propose as our next move – short of attacking the hillside camps – when Gallo looked in on me and said they had caught him.

I did not awaken the Governor, but sent Gallo for a full report. Word was also spread to the pilgrim camps that the

Jew king would be tried for treason by the Roman government at the Antonia Fortress in the morning. Outlying patrols were called in and our garrison guards tripled. Valerius had orders to admit at least three thousand spectators and not to molest them other than to search for weapons. An attentive Jewish public was, after all, the point of our exhibition. I wanted every Jew to tell his children this messiah was a fraud.

Gallo returned at dawn, tired and puzzled, to say he thought at first they had arrested the wrong man. But it was only a figure of speech, he assured me.

The Sicarius had been as good as his word, and after pocketing his money, led the police to Gethsemane, within sight of the city walls. The huge crowds apparently deserted their king by night, and he was accompanied by fewer than a dozen Sicarii toughs when the police found him. After a short struggle – one policeman lost an ear – they surrendered and were hustled back to the city.

Gallo's account cheered me. The man who two days earlier had been overturning stalls and breaking everything in sight now appeared to be the gentlest fellow alive. Gallo was careful to emphasize that this gentle quality in no way conveyed surrender. The weakness, it seemed, existed only among his followers. One of them, who practically wet himself every time Gallo glanced at him, astonished them all by denying he even knew his leader.

Without the keystone, the arch crashes. If they deserted at the first reversal of fortune, we could forget the 'hosts of avenging angels' he had threatened to call down upon our heads. As soon as word of his capture reached the others, we could conjure the messiah myth out of existence.

I proposed to try him with the three survivors of the tunnelling attempt on the Siloam tower. At midmorning we convened our theatre in the Praetorium with all the pomp and ceremony the Governor so dearly loves. His throne was established on a platform the height of a man, and above the paved marble court were silken awnings surrounded by our battle standards, with the imperial eagle dominating all. My officers turned out in dress armour and the solid ranks of my cohort stood at rest on all four sides of the fortress walls. The Jews found it awe-inspiring in spite of the heat.

The prisoners were led in as our war drums sounded a

dirge. Because of their injuries, the Zealots rescued from the rubble had trouble walking. Their leader, a huge, arrogant, red-headed fellow called Abbas, was brought forward first. He had to be supported by a slave because the bones of one leg stuck through the skin. The questioning was brief and he was given no opportunity to speak. After the charges had been read, he stepped back and the messiah was led to the foot of the platform where my brother-in-law sat. Under my orders, the guards had allowed the man no sleep, no water to wash and no food, so that his appearance was anything but kingly.

At first it all went well. The Temple priests were permitted to ask him some questions about the Jew prophecies and his role in fulfilling them. Apart from the Governor, who was slightly bored by this phase, there was a general atmosphere of mirth and ridicule, as the prisoner occasionally seemed bewildered by the questions, and uncertain what answers were expected of him.

Had he cured a Syrian girl of epilepsy?

No, he had only talked to the girl's mother. Loud laughter followed that. My brother-in-law was especially alert to this answer and greatly angered by the man's response.

Had he multiplied fish, bread and wine at various times to feed his impoverished followers?

God had done that at his request. Hooting and jeering until Prefect Valerius shouted down the crowd.

Had he spoken with god?

Often.

And god with him?

Yes.

Did he claim to be the son of god?

Yes, god was his father.

Then how could he also claim to be a descendant of the Jewish King David?

He hesitated before he answered. God tells me this.

More laughter.

Had he raised a man from the dead?

He drew a deep breath and seemed to ponder the question before he replied. God did that, he said finally.

But *he* had restored the sight of a blind man, had he not?

The blind man restored his own sight, he said, through his faith in me. There were angry cries from the

213

crowd and he hung his head as if he expected it to be stricken off at any moment.

Did he recognize the power of Rome over the world? The Governor waited impatiently as Rufus translated the question.

He recognized god, his father, over all men; and the Jews over all people. A hush fell upon the public. When this outrageous reply was translated, the Governor blinked in surprise and his eyes narrowed angrily, focusing on poor Silius Rufus.

Did he claim to be king of the Jews?

The man looked around him at the crowd and then at us on the platform. Yes, he said, my father sent me to lead my people.

As no one knows better than you, Lucius, kings are made only in Rome. This ignorant Jew could be the descendant of a hundred kings and the son of all the gods, as long as he did not claim a kingship for himself.

Did he predict the destruction of the Romans?

All will perish who do not follow me, said the man, Jews and Gentiles alike. The catcalls had ceased as the crowd reacted to the change in the air, nervous and expectant. I did not like it. It was our music, yet this egotistical beggar was making up his own steps.

It was then that the Governor left his throne and went halfway down the steps, hands on hips, breath coming in short, angry gasps. His polished breastplate rose and fell, a mirror in the warm sunlight.

Do you say the Divine Emperor himself must follow you to save his life? Is that what you say!

The man shook his head and spoke in a tone one might use with a slow-witted child. Anyone who believes in me shall not die, he said. This ultimate impertinence caused a murmur of awe among those who understood it.

I intervened then to suggest a short recess, and at my urging the Governor left the Praetorium. He berated me for having made a mess of things, but when he calmed down a bit I suggested now was the moment to do what we had talked about originally: flog and humiliate the man. Then commute his death sentence and toss him back discredited to his followers. This would consign the wretch's movement to obloquy while enhancing our own reputation for merciful

214

fair dealing. As for the other three terrorists, execution was a foregone conclusion. I failed to reckon with my brother-in-law's volatile temper, however, and his complete lack of noblesse oblige.

We had no sooner returned to the Praetorium, where the prisoners awaited sentencing, than I saw his anger build again at the sight of the so-called king of the Jews. His eyes moved from one to the other of the prisoners, in the midst of his speech on treason, an idea seemed to occur to him and the anger faded from his reddened eyes. He was describing the might and majesty of Rome and the power of mercy which was in his hands. The crowd was bored. Even I was lulled into the momentary illusion that all was going as I had supposed, when he astonished everyone by saying the terrorist Abbas was free to leave the city, but the false king would be crucified with the others.

Afterwards he was quite pleased with himself and invited Valerius, Gallo and me to lunch in his quarters. The condemned were already dying when Rufus reported that a rumour was spreading among the Zealots saying their martyred leader had prophesied his martyrdom. It was another proof, they claimed, of his divinity. He had foretold his arrest, his trial, his whipping and mock coronation by the legionnaires, even his crucifixion. What's more, he would rise from the tomb and return to destroy us.

I have spent much time since then trying to kill off this talk, but due to negligence on the part of the execution squad, the body was stolen, so you can imagine how that compounded my problem. But our official story is now gaining acceptance among the lower-class Jews. We made it known we would have cheerfully spared their hero, and in fact wished to do so, but their own priests demanded his death. If my brother-in-law can be restrained from persecuting them further, we may get some good results in time. If only to discourage other nationalist fanatics and assimilate the more sophisticated Jews peacefully into the Empire. Either that, or Pilate was right.

215

SEVENTEEN

Early in the morning, while Nicoletta slept, I stopped at the desk and asked the day manager not to put calls from the press through to the room.

'Ah, the press,' he sighed. 'We're not accustomed to it, you know.' There was a suggestion of reproof in his tone.

I slid fifty pounds across the desk and he pretended to ignore it. One may tip a hotel manager in England, but discreetly. 'Hire someone if necessary,' I said.

'It will come quite dear, sir,' he cautioned.

'No interviews, no comments and no photographs. I leave it entirely in your hands.' I laid another fifty on top of the first. A hundred pounds is no longer a tip; it is, as I suggested to the manager, merely an advance against small expenses that might come up.

At eight o'clock I parked the Rover in a reserved faculty space and walked across the Tom Quad to Kittering's laboratory at Christ Church. The autumn air was sharp and the bright morning sun not yet dimmed by the Oxford industrial smog. Leaves shone like gold pieces against the browning lawn as a pair of undergraduates zipped past me on bicycles, their gowns streaming black batwings. I found Kittering brewing tea in his crowded study, hedged in by books, charts and a blackboard covered with mathematical formulae. I handed him two scrolls and two codices, wrapped in hotel towels, and he asked me how much sugar I took.

He held up a small polished piece of wood. 'Bristlecone pine, the oldest living thing on earth, almost five thousand years. American forestry chaps have helped us correct our carbon dating with their tree-ring calibration work.'

'Proving what you said last night about the value of other disciplines to the archaeologist.'

Kittering beamed. 'As a medical doctor you probably understand better than most.' He unwrapped the Longinus codex and studied it intently without touching it. Then he took an archaeologist's tweezers from a nearby shelf and probed the cover.

When he looked up, I said, 'I would appreciate it if someone could copy it for me. It is the only piece in the collection that hasn't been photographed.'

'One of my assistants is first-class at that kind of thing. Absolutely first-class.'

He led me through a series of rooms in the ancient building, each one containing a bigger clutter than his study, crowded with books and dusty laboratory equipment. I was beginning to have my doubts about leaving our things in this man's hands, when we arrived at a metal door marked STAFF ONLY. Kittering let himself in with a key and beckoned me to follow. On the far side of the door was another world. Deep inside the labyrinth of rooms through which we now passed existed the most sparkling, modern, antiseptic-looking laboratory I had ever seen, staffed by a dozen busy people in white coats. A gaily coloured hand-lettered sign on the inside of the door read: ABANDON DOPE, ALL YE WHO ENTER HERE, and below it, another stuck up with Scotch tape: NUCLEAR POWER TO THE PEOPLE! THE ERG SHALL MAKE YOU FREE.

Kittering's climatic vault was a separate, dimly lit room off the laboratory, divided into a series of insulated airtight chambers. He explained that each had separate temperature and humidity controls, and suggested the papyri should be kept at less than ten percent humidity and fifty degrees Fahrenheit, the usual conditions they maintained for old books and documents. After signing a release absolving the university of any responsibility for the papyri while in the vault, I thanked him and left.

When I drove up to Les Sylphides, Panagoulos was standing on the lawn watching a grunting class of fatties run in place while Hermione walked among them beating her tom-tom. She smiled and waved.

We were on the M4, headed for London, when I said, 'I'm curious how George Pan manages to hold it all together. London, the health farm, a film career.'

'I do two hundred push-ups, press my weight on the barbells and never run less than two miles a day. I don't wear glasses, sniff glue or booze it. So what's the mystery?'

'Berman told me you worked for the CIA.'

'If he told you that much, he also told you why they canned me.'

'He did.'

'Bunch of boy scouts in spite of what you read,' he said. 'Greece is a poor country. If I had my relatives on the payroll, it was because they were the best I could find.'

'Like Mr. Emmons in Abingdon.'

'He may be blind, but I'd sooner trust him than that banker you trotted out last night.'

'I'll give you that.'

'Right,' Panagoulos said. 'So now would you like to hear about Deborah Jean Poor, society dropout?'

'Have we met?'

'The "gen," as Mr. Emmons would call it, gov'nor, is that Miss Poor – who is rich – married an El Al pilot about two years ago and left her father's estate in Berkshire to rough it in Israel. The pioneer life in Tel Aviv palled, as did the captain, and Miss Poor came back to daddy. Like the story?'

'Not so far.'

'She too is a pilot, which is how they met. But she's also a swinger and she made a few friends in Tel Aviv who were more interesting than her husband. Like Arnaud La Roche for one.'

'Now it grabs me.'

'I knew it would.'

'How did you find out about her?'

'It was Goff, as a matter of fact.'

'I don't understand.'

'I was on the telephone with him this morning.'

'Don't you ever sleep?'

'In between push-ups. Now pay attention. I located Deborah Jean through the Maidenhead Aeroclub, which is on our way. She keeps her own twin Cessna there and frequently makes trips to the Continent. Fun weekends, don't you know?'

'She sounds a bit out of La Roche's class.'

'Between the sheets you often find democracy in action. You should know that.'

'So La Roche knew her.'

'Carnally. One of her last junkets was to see him in Paris.'

'How in hell did Goff find all that out?'

'He didn't; I did. Goff only put me onto her.'

'You think he's with her now?'

'If you were running and had a girlfriend with an airplane, where would you be?'

'But she couldn't fly him out of the country. What about airport police checks?'

'She couldn't fly him far, but out of the U.K. is easy. She goes off for a joy ride without filing a flight plan, like hundreds of pilots every day. Only she nips across to France, staying well clear of the other low-level cross-channel traffic. Then up and away over Normandy, and she drops him at any one of a hundred country airstrips without anyone being the wiser. In three hours she's home again and Arnaud baby has faded into the woodwork.'

'That's what you think will happen?'

'That's what I think *already* happened. The best I hope for now is a lead from Debbie Jean on where she took our pal.'

'Wouldn't the police have a better chance of finding out?'

'Once the police know about Deborah Jean, nobody will find out.'

'Why do you say that?'

'You've read about the North Sea oil strikes?'

I nodded.

'That's daddy. Very heavy with the Labour government in spite of his capitalist image. Clout at the highest level. He might take a strap to his daughter, but Scotland Yard isn't going to bother her unless they have more than questions.'

'Why would she tell you anything?'

'I'm an old friend of La Roche's, remember? We were in jail together.'

'I believe you, but will she?'

'I'll ignore that witticism. If she doesn't believe me, daddy will, and she'll believe me when I tell her I'll tell daddy.'

'Suppose she didn't fly him to France?'

'What odds will you give me on that?'

'I'm serious.'

'Then I've wasted a couple of hours. It won't be the first time on this job.'

At the entrance to Croftwood Lodge, a mile from

Henley-on-Thames, seven miles from Maidenhead, is a metal sign that reads: 'A house has stood here for seven centuries. The present Lodge, a gift to Anne of Cleves by Henry VIII and later acquired by Lord Sandys, the king's Lord Chancellor, was architecturally enriched in Georgian times and completely restored in 1960 by Croftwood Lodge Trust Ltd., under the direction of Sir Humphrey Marsdown Poor OBE, Managing Director. Open to the Public by Appointment.'

Panagaoulos had made no appointment, but we drove up to the main entrance as if he had. The place was a massive brick and timber pile, with outbuildings of weathered stone, a huge gravel forecourt and acres of clipped yew trees and garden. Some yelping hounds immediately surrounded the car and a man in a wool cap appeared around one wing of the house, pushing a wheelbarrow. Panagoulos got out and said we were looking for Sir Humphrey Poor.

Small goiterous eyes appraised us sourly. 'He's not here.'

'And Miss Deborah?'

The man shook his head.

Panagoulos looked pained and said in his best affected City accent, 'Worse luck. It's about the aircraft insurance.' What followed, after he had complimented the man on the yew trees and patted all five dogs, was a lament about Miss Poor's policy expiring that very day if he did not have her father's signature or hers. But, he added, if she was not flying he guessed it would be all right. The man's reserve faded and he volunteered that Miss Poor could probably be found at the Aeroclub, where she went every morning when the weather favoured her.

'We'll try to catch her there, then,' Panagoulos said, scratching the ears of the most persistent hound. 'Lovely dog.'

'I'd drown the lot,' the man replied as Panagoulos returned to the car.

For the next half hour we drove up and down country lanes looking for the Maidenhead Aerodrome. When I found it finally, it was by following a low-flying sports trainer as it throttled back overhead for a landing. The little airport appeared suddenly as a surprise of lawn in the middle of nowhere.

I turned in through an open gate, drove slowly past some fuel pumps and parked behind a shabby, slab-sided one-storey barracks of the kind erected as temporary quarters for Spitfire crews during the Battle of Britain. Two tin-roofed hangars flanked the main building, facing the grass runways, and a dozen small aircraft occupied tie-down spaces. One of them was a twin-engine Cessna, and standing next to it, a pretty blond girl in blue jeans and black nylon windbreaker was talking earnestly with a man in coveralls.

Panagoulos said in his fake City accent, 'Nice bit of goods, our Deborah Jean. Why would a sweet thing like that get mixed up with the likes of Arnaud La Roche?' He clucked like a disapproving spinster as he stepped out of the car, straightened the immaculate knot in his tie and switched on his best George Pan smile. 'You don't mind waiting, do you, Doc?' He closed the door on my reply and was sauntering toward the girl with the supreme self-confidence of a man accustomed to having his way with women.

The mechanic had moved away from the aircraft when Panagoulos reached it, and the girl was squatting under one wing, examining the disc brake on a wheel. Panagoulos stood behind her, and when she stepped back and straightened up, she collided with him. He said something and the girl laughed. He spoke again and she shook her head, still smiling. They began to walk across the grass toward the Aeroclub headquarters. Her blond ponytail bobbed as she nodded with apparent pleasure, caught in some spell of charming nonsense by the great George Pan.

Kittering's tea had worked through my kidneys some time ago and I began to look around for a men's room. An old De Havilland Chipmunk skimmed in over the telephone wires with a whoosh as I left the car. It bounced two or three times on the grassy runway and with a roar of throttle took to the air again like a drunken bee. I walked around the front of the building. There was a bar and coffee shop inside, where the smiling Deborah Jean now sat at a table facing Panagoulos. The club mechanic informed me the facilities were at the opposite end of the building, clearly marked. I entered a hallway and saw the 'Gents' arrow over a display case of club emblems, dusty navigational aids, and pamphlets on instrumental flying. I

221

passed an office where a harried elderly man was pleading on the radio with the student pilot practising landings in the old Chipmunk. The ancient linoleum floor gave a little as I walked: it had not been designed for the ages. A huge map of southern England made from a series of pasted-up aviation charts covered one wall of the corridor. A piece of dirty string hung from a thumb-tack marking Maidenhead, and a line calibrated in miles intersected the thumb-tack beneath the hand-lettered message: 'Get Your Weather Before You Go!'

The men's room contained two sinks, two urinals and one enclosed stall. It was clean but the brown-stained porcelain and faded green walls betrayed its age. I was alone, facing the wall, in midstream, when someone entered. He came to the second urinal and we glanced at each other simultaneously. Our eyes held a fraction of a second, but as I looked away I knew I had seen him before, under quite different circumstances. Some deeper impulse cut my water and my pulse quickened. Fear? But of what? My urethra burned, but not another drop would pass. Hastily I stepped back without looking at the man again. I could feel his eyes on my back. My impulse was to walk directly out, but habit was stronger. At the sink I ran some water over my fingers and was holding a tin of abrasive soap powder in one hand, shaking a few grains into the other, when he said, 'Excuse me. Do you have a light?' As there was no mirror, he could not see my face, nor I his.

'I don't smoke,' I said without turning.

'You are Angleesh?' he said.

In that instant, I recognized the voice. The lack of a beard had thrown me off, but I remembered the unmistakable growl from the clinic in Neuilly. I don't recall by what process of thought – if any – I arrived at a decision.

I whirled, threw the soap powder in his face and drove my wet fist into his middle with such force he fell back across the room, striking the toilet stall with a resounding clang. He did not lose his footing, but I did, crashing into him as he rebounded off the stall. Though La Roche was no taller than I, he had the heavy shoulders and huge arms of a professional wrestler. I lashed out at him, partly to regain my balance, partly to hurt him before he caught his

222

wind or got the soap powder out of his eyes. But he swung too, in blind self-defence. The blow struck the side of my head like a stone, making my skull ring and sending a shock of pain to my spinal column. He clutched blindly at my jacket with his other hand. I heard the cloth rip but squirmed out of his reach before a second blow glanced off my shoulder. I was thinking if I could only make it out the door, Panagoulos could take the bastard.

Aiming a delaying punch, I miscalculated and he caught my wrist in one powerful hand. Before I could raise my left arm to protect my head, he hit me across the jaw. I tried to clinch, as boxers do, and free myself from his grasp, but he only pushed me back and struck again before bringing his knee up into my stomach with crushing force. When I went down, he let go and drove his foot into my face. On the floor, I managed to roll out of his way, tasting my own blood as it filled my mouth. I expected him to come for me again, or draw a gun and shoot, but he did neither. He reeled across the room like a drunk, clawing at his eyes with one hand while he groped for the door. Before I could stand, he had found the knob and was gone.

The look on Panagoulos's face when I staggered into the Aeroclub coffee shop told me all I needed to know about my own condition. La Roche was running, I said, seizing a handful of paper napkins to press against my bleeding mouth. Then I followed him out of the building, while the girl sat transfixed over her tea.

La Roche had not got far. He was a hundred yards from the building, by the open door of a yellow MG, daubing at his eyes with a cloth. Panagoulos started toward him at a run and had closed half the distance when the man saw him, sat down on the seat and raised his arm. I saw the little flash from the gun's muzzle at the same time Panagoulos went sprawling, and for a sickening second I thought he had been shot. But he had seen the pistol and deliberately hit the ground. Only I was standing still and upright as two more shots popped from the MG.

La Roche was in the car now. Dust and gravel flew as he spun the little roadster around in a tight circle and headed, not for the gate, as I would have expected, but across the greensward toward the far end of the airport. Panagaoulos was running toward the Rover.

I reached the car as he started the motor, and jumped in on the passenger side.

La Roche sideswiped the tail of a parked aircraft as he sped through the taxi area to the main runway, and the elderly man I had last seen talking on the radio was now standing outside the club building, shouting at us. Panagoulos gunned the Rover and skidded around the damaged airplane. Just in time he saw the deep drainage ditch that bordered the runway, and fishtailed as he turned onto the little dirt bridge used by the planes. Then he straightened out and pushed the accelerator to the floor. La Roche was nearly at the end of the runway, heading toward an old abandoned hangar. We were gaining, with every prospect of overtaking him, when I used up one life and began another.

Coming in to land on a collision course was the student pilot in the Chipmunk, blissfully unaware of us, hanging perhaps fifty feet off the grass, with power throttled back, flying right down our throats. Panagoulos saw him, but in the second or two left he could not avoid him.

The airplane's wheels touched the grass twenty yards in front of us. I glimpsed the amazed face of the young pilot as the landing gear sagged and the plane sprang back into the sky, kangarooing over us in what was, thank God, one of the worst landings ever made.

La Roche, nearing the hangar, braked but not in time to avoid the ditch at the runway's edge. The MG plunged into it, bounced in the air and miraculously remained upright as it ploughed into the uncut grass near the hangar and skidded to a stop. Panagoulos saw a dirt exit bridge and turned off the runway as a bullet thudded into the Rover's radiator. We pulled up to the hangar as La Roche ran inside.

'We're not going in there after him.'

'Damn right you're not,' Panagoulos said.

'Call the police.'

'By the time they get here, he'll be too old to prosecute.' More shots came from inside the hangar, one passing through the car door and into the fire wall. Panagoulos forced the car into gear, gunned the motor, and we skidded around to the rear of the hangar, where pieces of old airplanes rusted in the high brown grass.

'Stay here. He can't get out this way.' He jumped from the car and was gone before I could protest. It occurred to me after he had disappeared around the side of the hangar that if Arnaud La Roche decided to take another shot at me in the car, I was a conspicuous target. So I too got out and walked cautiously along the back of the hangar, keeping low and close to the rusty sheet-iron siding, stepping over discarded engine blocks and old wheel housings. All around me lay bent, twisted skeletons of wing and fuselage, shreds of rotting canvas still clinging to plywood and tube frames, like carrion on old bones.

My head throbbed, my jaw hurt, at least two teeth were loose and I had an overwhelming urge to urinate. I did, taking care to spray the stream into the grass and not make a noisy puddle.

There was a place to sit down against the hangar wall, where I presented as low a profile as possible. In the dirt I found a broken engine rod which made a handy weapon. It was not much use against a gun, but it gave me confidence. Five minutes had passed since Panagoulos had disappeared, and not a sound.

I crept along the back of the hangar to the side, the keys to the Rover safely in my pocket, the steel rod gripped like a war club in one hand. I had nothing in mind, certainly no plan to enter the hangar, until I saw the hole.

It was not much of a hole, but large enough to admit a man where the base of the sheet iron had rusted away from ground moisture. It was nearly hidden by the dead grass.

I knelt and listened. Nothing. I pulled up the weeds until I could slide through easily on my stomach. It was not Jay Brian Marcus, medical doctor, who crawled into the damp dark of that hangar, but a killer with no more on his mind than cracking another man's skull like an egg.

The only light came from an opening in the rusty doors at the front, where La Roche had entered, and from tiny pinpricks in the roof where the bolts had oxidized and fallen out. The floor was a concrete slab, soft with a patina of packed dirt and grease. Doves nested in the iron cross-beams above. The whole place – fifty feet long and eighty wide – was filled with airplanes, some dating back to the Second World War. Hulks without engines, wings without bodies, tail assemblies, instrument panels, bent propellers and rotting tyres; a mausoleum of mistakes, the last resting place of pilot error.

I lay quite still until my eyes became accustomed to the dimness. Within a moment or two I could see everything, ghostly and monochromatic, but clearly illuminated. Like a night animal, I crawled away from the small shaft of light that issued from the hole behind me.

La Roche was inside somewhere: a hundred things to hide behind. And Panagoulos? Certainly he was too clever to have entered the same way. If he had, there would have been more shooting. So he was still outside – waiting. La Roche could not stay where he was and he knew it. My eyes combed the shadowy shapes around me until I found what I was looking for: La Roche's reason for coming here. A 750 cc. Norton. Just inside the doorway someone was moving near it, partly hidden by the wings of a prehistoric Tiger Moth.

I crept closer. La Roche had his back to me and was pouring fuel from a plastic can into the motorcycle tank, watching the open hangar door, his pistol ready in his right hand. The voice of reason told me he would not get far on a motorcycle. Give it up, Marcus, crawl back to the Rover and go call the police. But I was experiencing another reaction as well, something close to elation. La Roche never once looked in my direction, or toward any of the other dim corners of the hangar. He was secure, satisfied no one could enter except through the gap in front. If I was quiet enough I could catch him from behind with my handy little steel bar. Or if Panagoulos attracted his attention . . .

La Roche fired and the shot reverberated inside the tin structure, deafening me.

I had been moving toward him, crouching low, from one piece of junk to the next, threading my way. Less than twenty feet separated us as he put down the fuel can and screwed the gas cap in place. He had fired the shot to scare Panagoulos. He was astride the bike now, twisting the handgrips, manipulating the choke. He might have one shot left, but if he was wasting them like that, he probably had reloaded the weapon.

I waited.

He suddenly jumped in the air and came down hard on the motorcycle starter. The machine kicked but did not turn over. Again. This time the movement was followed by an explosive roar as a cloud of blue smoke shot from the double chrome exhaust.

I was sprinting, my footsteps covered by the noise. As I reached La Roche, the motorcycle lurched forward and instead of the steel rod biting into his skull, as I intended, it glanced harmlessly off his back, hit the seat of the bike and flew from my hand. I collided with the side of the machine and fell, expecting a fusillade of bullets from the man on the motorcycle. Instead he veered sharply, crashed through some pieces of wreckage and was out the door.

Genius! I got to my feet and stumbled after him.

Out of the hangar into the bright, sudden autumn light. The motorcycle was fifty feet away, when a figure seemed to rise up from the grass as it passed. There was a loud explosion; the machine swerved, went out of control and disappeared, swallowed by the earth.

I ran across the runway toward the drainage ditch. The motorcycle was on its side, dying like a choked beast. La Roche was sprawled a few feet away, his trousers shredded, one leg a bloody pulp. Over him Panagoulos stood calmly, flipping the world's smallest shotgun in the palm of his hand, smiling for the cameras.

EIGHTEEN

'The system is not foolproof, you understand,' Mansour was saying, 'but the insurance companies like it. They wire all your doors and windows to the nearest gendarmerie post as well as to their own offices. If someone tries to cut a wire, the very act makes the alarm sound. Isn't that sublime?'

'That's what you've been calling to tell me?'

I had finally returned his calls after a gruelling afternoon with police and reporters.

'There was a rather bad photograph of you in *Figaro* this morning, by the way, and a story about the Pontius Pilate Papers. All the more reason to get an alarm system installed quickly. I don't think you're wise in seeking all this publicity, my dear.'

From where I stood in our room at the Rose and Thistle, I could see a clutch of reporters still stalking us from the lighted parking area near the hotel, waiting for Nicoletta or me to emerge.

'Anonymity is the only protection these days,' Mansour persisted. 'Fame is a drug, my dear, even though you find the taste sweet at the moment. The press has no mercy.'

'Look, Hippolyte –'

'You weren't injured, I hope, catching that murderer?'

'I didn't catch him. The detective did.'

'The press gives you the credit,' Mansour said, 'and we're proud of you, Coco and I. The newspapers say you are worth fifty million dollars. I told Coco they are mistaken because you are far richer, even though you like to play it down.'

'Hippolyte, you're still my main link with reality.'

'By the way, Coco located a mint edition of Vesalius's *Fabrica* the other day. The original 1543 with the Calcar illustrations. Do you want it?'

'You pick a hell of a time to sell me a book.'

'A steal, I assure you.' He chuckled.

'I'll think about it.'

'Of course, my dear. Love to Nicoletta and let the good times roll.' He hung up.

Nicoletta was in the bath. I poured myself a heavy Scotch and sat back on the bed, still unable to shake a curious sense of unease about the day. The capture of La Roche should have left me jubilant. The police were complimentary to Panagoulos for apprehending a man who had shot one of their uniformed constables, and except for Cheney's disappearance and the few papyri still missing, the case was as good as over.

Playing at the edges of my mind for nearly twenty-four hours had been Nicoletta's astonishing disclosure about the last Longinus codex. Why had Lanholtz never shown it to her? Why had he not even included it in the body of his paper on the Caesarea dig? If Gaius Longinus Procula was telling the truth – and I had no reason to doubt it – the traditional view of Pilate as a man who found nothing wrong with Jesus was historically inaccurate. He had found everything wrong with him, and went out of his way to crucify the man for treason.

I recalled what Lev Vagan had said on the night of my arrival with Aaron in Tel Aviv. Although he had not seen the codex, he certainly suspected its contents. And O'Hare? Had Lanholtz told him what it contained? Vagan was worried that the museum would be criticized by orthodox Christian theologians for premature publication of the scrolls. With good reason, it now seemed. The image of Jesus with a whip, at the head of a band of Jewish fanatics intent upon toppling the Roman government in Jerusalem, bore little resemblance to the gentle saviour of Christian tradition.

The fact that Christ was a Jew has long been a source of embarrassment to Christianity. He would have been better accepted had he been a Greek or a Roman, which, in a spiritual sense, is what Saint Paul tried to make of him.

Where the Jews went, Christianity went, carrying its Messianic message. As most Christians were Jews in the beginning, and the message now predicted the imminent return of the god-king who would take over the world, successive emperors quite naturally regarded it as subversive. Claudius briefly banned Jews from Rome. Caligula would have slaughtered them all if his own premature death had not overtaken him. Nero, whose evil reputation has survived nineteen centuries unblemished, murdered Jews wherever he found them, mainly because of their real or suspected Christian beliefs. It is not surprising that as the Christian movement was broadened by Paul to include the Gentiles, he and his followers had no scruples about revising history to divorce their Messiah from his nationalist revolutionary background. An obscure Judean freedom fighter could have no standing as a world saviour until his image had been cleaned up.

Had Lanholtz intended to make the crucifixion the subject of a separate report at a later date? It was my guess that that was what had been in mind: whet a few appetites with the first disclosures at the Oxford congress, then, six months or a year later, drop the big one without warning. Lanholtz had always insisted he would make a major discovery. Except that the shock value of the so-called Pontius Pilate Papers was more theological than archaeological. That, perhaps, was the final irony of the atheist scholar's lifelong search among the ruins.

Nicoletta emerged from the bath like Aphrodite, her lashes glistening from the steam, little locks of damp hair pasted against her thin neck.

'Would you like a drink?' I asked her.

'Do I have time to catch up?'

'We're not going anywhere.'

'Supper?'

'I ordered it served in the room. The management was delighted for the sake of the other guests.'

'But why?'

'Most of them are reporters.'

She was wearing a bath towel tied around her waist, man-style, and her nipples, invitingly, were hard. I caught her with one arm and drew her close as she passed and she pressed my face against her breasts, rubbing herself like a cat. Then, just as quickly, she slipped out of my grip and across the room, where she fluffed her hair and frowned at her face in the dressing table mirror.

On the bed beside me I had the little pile of papers that had arrived that day from Paris, the articles and notes belonging to Lanholtz which Professor Merle had sent. Nicoletta asked if I had found any answers from reading through it, and I shook my head.

She brushed her long, shining hair, sitting before the mirror, the white arch of her back toward me in the shadow, her face reflected in the glass. I poured us each another drink and kissed her lightly on the shoulder as I served it. By then she was intent on coating her lashes with a tiny mascara brush. 'You realize I can't assign the last codex an artifact number,' she said. 'I can't even prove it came from Caesarea except by association with the others. So what do I do?'

'The codices are all nearly alike in size and handwriting. The one in question and several others are even dated. You can presume the site location was the same.'

'Damn Victor anyway. If only he'd left something in writing, we wouldn't have to presume anything.' She turned away from the mirror in dismay. 'I sound like Ramsay O'Hare. By the way, he called again today. He's here.'

'In Abingdon?'

'London, but he's coming to Oxford tomorrow.'

'What the hell for?'

'To see us before the conference.'

'Why?'

'I suppose the publicity impressed him. He probably looks forward to being identified with the dig now that it's in all the newspapers. He asked us for lunch.'

'Sorry I won't be here.'

'Are you jealous?'

'Don't be ridiculous.'

She smiled. 'It was just your tone.'

There was a knock on the door and Nicoletta hastily drew on a dressing gown before the waiter entered with our supper: Colchester oysters, some poached turbot and an excellent bottle of Meursault. We ate, made love and finished a second bottle of wine. I was drifting off to sleep when Giles Morris called to confirm our luncheon for the following day and tell me he would have the information I had asked him for.

Rime coated the brown fields when Panagoulos and I drove to London early in the morning. Pigs scavenged among the rows of dead corn stalks that lined the motorway, and the breath of car exhaust hung in the chill air like tufts of dirty cotton. Trees that only days before had been a blaze of colour now stood etched like capillaries against the leaden sky.

Panagoulos looked very much the film star in cashmere turtle-neck, corduroys and suede boots. I had never seen him in better spirits, probably because Inspector Rowan had asked him by for lunch and a chat. 'In my business,' he told me, 'that's worth more than an invitation to Buckingham Palace.'

'Maybe La Roche has talked to them by now.'

'Why would he do that? If he shuts up, he's good for ten years in the nick, out in six on good behaviour. If he talks, the judge might knock a year or two off. But he still has Israeli extradition to face unless the British give him up on a murder charge.'

'Did he get a lawyer?'

'One who advised him to cooperate without incriminating himself. Which means shut up until we see how things are going to break.'

'How *are* things breaking?'

'He did a whole number about not understanding English, but I straightened Rowan out on that. They have his gun and the bullet that wounded the cop.'

'So the case is made.'

'I would think so. Enormous patience, the English.' Panagoulos wagged his head in admiration. 'They treated that bastard like a gentleman.'

'Nothing about Cheney?'

'La Roche never heard of him, naturally.'

'The girlfriend?'

'Out of it completely. The rumble on the runway frightened Debbie Jean. A little over her head and "teddibly grateful," don't you know. So I'll probably have to take her out one of these nights and talk about flying.'

'Did Scotland Yard notify Berman? I should have called him last night.'

'He wasn't available,' Panagoulos said.

'You'd think he would have let us know.'

'He's got other cases, Doc. And this one is probably wrapped up as far as he's concerned. The rest is just paper work. Speaking of paper work, when does Nicoletta deliver hers to the archaeologists? Tomorrow?'

'Day after.'

'That's the end of me too, then, unless you want me to hang around until you hear from Cheney.'

'You're the one who still thinks we will.'

I put the car in an underground garage near Trafalgar Square and we took separate taxis after arranging to keep in touch by telephone later in the day. It was ten when I arrived at the hospital.

The floor sister, a cheerful grey-haired Scotswoman, accompanied me down the corridor to Suriel's room, saying there was a ten-minute limit and to please remind the other gentleman visiting Mr. Sorrel as well.

The room was small and old, but glistened with a recent coat of ivory enamel. Suriel's bed had been cranked up to make him comfortable and a glucose drip hung nearby, running into his arm. He was nearly as pale as the punched-up pillows behind his head, but his eyes brightened a little when he saw me. Berman was sitting on the bed. He turned slightly, following Suriel's glance. There was no smile of welcome. When he shook hands, his face was as flat and expressionless as a monument. The London newspaper with the stories of La Roche's capture were spread over the foot of the bed.

Suriel smiled but a nasal infusion tube made speaking difficult. His pupils were dilated from sedation, so I guessed he was still in some pain. He congratulated me on La Roche and said he had been thinking a lot about the case while he was lying there in the hospital.

'I'll worry about the case,' Berman said irritably.

'Trying to help,' Suriel replied in a frail whisper.

'Dr. Marcus don't need your help,' Berman replied. 'He does everything by himself these days.'

I looked at Berman to see what that was all about. Suriel watched me, then let his gaze return to Berman.

'You're not supposed to talk,' Berman said, 'or you'll swallow that thing.'

Suriel shook his head, turning to me again. 'Gun running,' he said. 'The archbishop and La Roche.'

'Guns and plastic explosives coming in,' Berman said. 'Gold and foreign currency going out. Not to mention your things.'

'How did he get them out?'

'In his private limousine through the Golan Heights to Damascus. He had privileged status and nobody ever searched his car. Army intelligence was watching him, but needed an excuse to close in.'

'The batteries,' Suriel said. 'We never dusted the batteries from the flashlight.'

'Well, it don't matter now,' Berman said.

Suriel objected as the floor sister appeared, her fixed smile telling us time was up. I told Suriel I would try to visit him again tomorrow. Berman stayed a moment longer as I talked with the nurse in the corridor. Then he closed the door behind him and said he wanted a word with me.

When we reached the lounge, he steered my arm toward the main entrance and out on the steps of the hospital. There, in the gusty, cold morning, he stopped, pulled the collar of his cheap overcoat up around his ears and said, 'Lemme give you a scenario. You and I had a conversation a long time ago. I asked you not to deal with the people who robbed your museum without keeping me informed.

233

You said, Perish the thought, Inspector, we got too much principle to fuck around with crooks. But that's all you been doin' since you left Israel. I run up a telephone bill like the national debt trying to find out a few things and what do you tell me? As little as possible. Fuck off, Inspector. Talk to my secretary. Talk to my girlfriend. Make an appointment.'

'Now wait a minute!'

'Piss on your principles! I trusted you. You haven't played square with me, not one day since you started. You did just what you goddamned well pleased from the start. Get back your Pontius Pilate Papers and screw the police. You fuck up things in Vienna so I don't even have a live witness. I don't say anything, so you fuck things up again in Paris. All I get is an expense account from that *momzer* up there I can't explain to anybody in the government . . . while you're running newspaper ads. behind my back –'

'*You* recommended Goff. If anything in Vienna –'

'*Then* you fuck things up here so one of my best men gets shot! Let me tell you something else, mister! If that boy *had* died, I'd have come after you with my own bare hands. I *trusted* you! I *trusted* your uncle too! And I tell you I don't want to hear the name Marcus again. I've had all I want of your millionaire bullshit. From here on you and that old letch stay out of this case and out of my way or, so help me God, I'll . . .'

For a moment I thought he would seize me by the lapels. Instead he jammed his big fists in his overcoat pockets, and breathing hard, his eyes still flashing angrily, turned and hurried down the steps. At the kerb, he flagged a passing taxi and was gone.

My own heart pounded with anger and outraged dignity. Even if his attack had a just basis, I had not made that big a mess of things. If I had given in to the temptation to deal with the thieves, as he said, right from the start, that was partly Goff's fault. Some of my anger began to focus on the Austrian detective when I realized he must have told Berman. But accusing me of being responsible for Suriel's injuries was going too far. And Aaron? What in hell had he done to call down the wrath of Chief Inspector Shmuel Berman? The newspaper stories, probably, but for the life of me I could not imagine why they would have provoked anger.

At a call box near the hospital I tried to reach Panagoulos at New Scotland Yard, but a polite sergeant – Battle's replacement, no doubt – explained he was with Inspector Rowan and unavailable to come to the telephone. I took a taxi to the Savoy, where I established my identity with a Rothschild's card and asked for a telephone and a double Scotch to be brought to me in a far corner of the lounge.

It was too early to call the bank in New York and there was no point in bothering that poor alcoholic fool of a London manager. I tried Aaron in Jerusalem, but the overseas operator said it would be hours before she could get a line. Jeanette sounded her usual cheery self as I got through to the Paris apartment.

'He called,' she said.

'Do you know from where?'

'Not Paris. The local ring is slightly different from a direct-dial long-distance call. I told him you had decided the remaining papyri were not worth more than fifty thousand. He was furious, as you predicted.'

'But he agreed.'

'Immediately.'

'Where are they?'

'He's cagey, but he implied they are in England.'

'What about the jewellery?'

'He'll have it delivered here today. C.O.D.'

'Call Sterne. Hire him to watch the apartment.'

'Isn't there someone better?'

'He doesn't have to do anything except follow the person when you pay over the money. I've told the bank to give you whatever you need. If it's a delivery service, then the messenger will have to give the cash to someone. Sterne should find out who and where, then call you back.'

'Then what do I do?'

'Nothing. The money will be marked and you will both be witnesses. The police can move in later. How does Cheney want the payment made for the papyri?'

'He didn't have any clear idea, but I expect he will have when he calls back.'

'Tell him I'll meet him anywhere in England. If he's prepared to do that, we can arrange it in a few hours.'

'I got the impression he is in a hurry. Anything else?'

235

'Not a thing. I'll be talking to you.'

Across the lounge I saw the towering portly figure of Sir Giles Morris moving toward me. I hung up and rose to greet him.

'Jay, old boy, you *are* looking fit!' He shook my hand warmly, gazing about as if expecting to be mobbed any moment by an invisible crowd. 'No swooning women? No fawning autograph hunters?' Giles is a few years older than I, perhaps more, and he closely resembles the late Charles Laughton: long legs and arms connected to a rather roly-poly figure, large head hunched forward, big shoulders draped by Savile Row in banker's serge, broad sensuous lips and languid eyes smiling at some private amusement, skin as smooth and pale as a baby's under heavy white locks.

A steward hurried to us. 'Will you have drinks here, Sir Giles, or in the grill?'

'In the grill,' he boomed. Then, dropping his voice, 'If you're ready, Jay?'

I told him to lead the way. He is six feet four or five, and since Harrow, so he claims, has worn the same size-fourteen shoe. According to Aaron, Giles's Rolls was custom built to make room for his legs. He is rich, clever, cultivated and warm-hearted; a Labour party capitalist, a friend to presidents and prime ministers and an absolutely shameless, obsessive collector of rare books and manuscripts. It was on this common ground that we had become friends. Immediately upon arriving at his table, he proudly displayed a catalogue listing of his latest acquisition: *A Prooved Practice for all young chirurgians, concerning Burnings with Gunpowder and Wounds etc., 1588*, written by William Clowes.

'The first edition?' I asked him.

'Lamentably, the third,' Giles admitted. 'I suppose you own a copy of the first?'

I nodded and he sighed.

'All part of the great American conspiracy, as I've been saying for years. Our prime ministers worry about the brain drain and the balance of payments, but the rare-book drain, my boy, is a cultural haemorrhage. Oh, well. I can't buy them all, can I? Tell me, how have you been, apart from all these harum-scarum antics in the press?'

'Well, thanks, Giles. We missed you aboard the boat this summer.'

'Too busy shoring up the bloody economy. God knows, nobody else seems to give a damn about England anymore. Can you imagine that? Not giving a damn about England? I can't imagine it, which makes me redundant according to the new standard.'

'You *are* in a bleak mood.'

'If you read some of the profit-and-loss statements I do each week, you'd understand. As an ingrained optimist I only allow two hours a day for despair. Most of my colleagues require twenty-four.'

I laughed and the waiter came to take our order. Giles was a fussy eater but the Savoy staff suffered him with professional grace. We were half through our main-course entrecôte when he withdrew some notes from his coat pocket, put on heavy-rimmed glasses and glanced at them.

'Hi-Rise Investment shows an unhealthy profile all in all,' he said. 'Their most recent financial statement reveals an abnormally low earnings ratio for a Bahamian company of this size and type. I suspect they lost a bundle on currency speculation that doesn't show here. Do you want the figures?'

'No. Just the names. And anything about their purchase of Cunningham and Pine.'

'Ah, yes. No apparent reason *for* the purchase, you understand.' He turned over his notes. 'Cunningham and Pine were going under and there was not even any tax advantage for Hi-Rise. Odd, unless someone in the firm simply wanted to own an old London bookseller's. Furthermore, in the same period Hi-Rise sold off for quick cash two hotel properties, one casino licence in Jamaica, an auto rental company in Puerto Rico and a small shipyard in Brazil. Now, the company stock is held by ... there's quite a long list here – various trusts, holding companies and a few private individuals.'

'Who are the private stockholders?'

He read off about twenty names, none of them familiar. I don't know what I expected precisely, but I was disappointed. I asked Giles if I could keep the list of names, thinking one of them might be familiar to someone else who had known Victor Lanholtz.

'By all means, old chap. I brought it all for you to take. There's another thing which might interest you. You understand companies like Hi-Rise usually don't yield the kind of information you're after, which is basically who owns what. One must go a little deeper. I use a New York service – expensive as hell, I might add – which does the digging, then uses a computer to sort it all out.'

'I don't understand.'

'Very simple, really,' Giles said. 'One obtains the names of all trust officers, executors, directors and stockholders from the companies involved. For example, Hi-Rise is owned by nine trusts and a consortium of no less than seven companies. As you can see, the officers' and directors' lists could number hundreds; stockholders, thousands. But when the computer has all these lists, one just shoots in the Hi-Rise master list for a read-out on interlocking holdings or directorships. That's when the real owners turn up.'

'I had no idea.'

'You knew young Cheney is a drug addict, I suppose?'

'No.'

'That's not computer information,' Giles said, smiling, 'although the Americans will give us that too, if it's known to them.'

'Was that the reason for Cunningham and Pine's running into the red?'

Giles shook his head. 'His father and grandfather made a dreadful balls-up of things while the boy was growing up. Young Cheney simply came along in time to tip a tottering business into the street.'

'Could we get the computer read-out on Hi-Rise, Giles? How long would it take?'

'I have it here. The list is thin.' He peered through his reading glasses at the paper as he pushed aside the remains of his entrecôte. 'Let's see. Five names occur. Two are Italian, women with Las Vegas mailing addresses: Mrs. Gabriella Tozzi and Mrs. Laura Scarpitta. My guess is they do not work in the chorus line at The Sands but serve their husbands loyally in a variety of corporate ways.'

'And the others?'

'Carleton Resnik, attorney, of Miami ... and Oliver Browne-Milne of Nassau, Bahamas. It happens that I know

Mr. Browne-Milne, who is not brown at all, but black. Blacker, in fact, than the devil's arse, inside and out. A perfect discredit to his race, and the most powerful labour gangster in Nassau.'

'You said there were five?'

'I did indeed. The fifth, of course, is the clean-jawed American who fronts for the black gangster, the Mafia wives and the Jew lawyer. It's a classic read-out, you know. The perfect criminal cocktail through which America's ill-gotten gains are filtered into usually profitable Caribbean resort properties. Only in this case, they were going broke. Which one is the book freak, do you suppose?'

I gave him the name.

'Jay, there are times when you absolutely amaze an old friend. Indeed you do. Shall we have another bit of claret to toast Mr. O'Hare's future with Cunningham and Pine?'

NINETEEN

Nicoletta did not answer in our suite and the clerk at the Rose and Thistle said she had already left with a gentleman a few minutes earlier. An American gentleman: older, tall, somewhat distinguished. As the sense of alarm spread in me, making my palms sweat, I tried to second-guess Ramsay O'Hare. Should I call Inspector Rowan and have O'Hare arrested, dragged away from whatever luncheon table he was sitting at with Nicoletta? On what charge? I had no proof of his connection with La Roche that would easily satisfy a sceptical policeman. What was so chillingly obvious to me could appear weak and insubstantial to someone unacquainted with the facts of the case.

Panagoulos was nowhere to be found and I had no idea where to reach Berman, even if he would talk to me. I excused myself hastily, leaving poor Giles puzzled and just a little piqued. He had gone to a lot of trouble on my behalf and I had not even remembered to thank him.

Ten minutes from the Savoy to the underground garage by taxi, wondering the whole time what, if anything, O'Hare might do. He knew about La Roche from the newspapers and he probably knew by now that Nicoletta was planning to go before the congress with Victor Lanholtz's paper. Was he in touch with Cheney? I doubted it. Everything I learned pointed to a break between the two. Cheney seemed to be on an independent track at the moment, trying to get as much from me as he could before diving for cover. Probably frightened out of his wits that La Roche would talk and connect him to the murder.

The West End traffic was awful and it was half an hour before I turned onto the M4 and headed for Oxford. I had no plan, no clear idea of how to handle O'Hare. I was not even certain he had to be handled. The man's motive in the whole affair was still murky, yet as I carded through the facts on the long drive, it seemed that a million-dollar sale of the papyri was quite enough if he was in serious financial trouble. La Roche and the other killers had been hired for dirt. Cheney, acting as the broker, might have been in line for a substantial commission, like the Jerusalem archbishop. If O'Hare expected to realize six or eight hundred thousand tax-free dollars in cash, it was a good piece of business, even for a man who still claimed to be a millionaire.

Yet O'Hare was an unknown quantity. Except for his religious bias and his troubled business affairs, I knew little about the man. He used Mafia funds and wanted to restore the Latin mass in America. So what.

Why was he against publication of the paper? Or had it been a pose to remove himself even further from the light of suspicion? I tried to return to the beginning, to think what I would do if I planned to steal a priceless collection of antiquities and sell them back to their owners. Was murder part of the plan or merely a tragic consequence?

I covered the distance to Abingdon in fifty-one minutes and pulled into the Rose and Thistle parking space. The clerk informed me Nicoletta had not returned and a sick wave of panic was taking over when I caught sight of a familiar face ducking out of sight in the main lounge, trying to avoid me. Doubling back, I forced myself to smile as I confronted him in the lounge.

'Hello, Ted. How *are* you today?'

Ted Emmons grinned foolishly and stood where he was, twisting his cap desperately in his hands.

'How's your dad?' I asked, holding the smile, trying to reassure him. I knew since our first encounter he had been badly frightened.

'Foin . . .' The eyes darted right and left.

'I'd like to buy him a drink.'

He nodded, shifting his feet as he continued to twist the cap, biting his lower lip.

'I guess he's probably with the lady, is that it? I don't see him around here anywhere.'

Again the nod. I wanted to shake him. Instead I turned away, saying, 'If I could find him now, with the lady, I'd stand everyone to a glass of bitter.' I had nearly reached the door when he stammered, 'I know where th-th-they be . . .'

Ted Emmons drove the battered old Austin ahead while I followed slowly in the Rover. At a fork a few miles out on the road to Oxford, he pulled over in front of a small restaurant, surrounded by a brown lawn that sloped to the river. A sign announced boats for hire at the boathouse.

In the public bar, Mr. Emmons sat with the innkeeper, sipping a beer, his spaniel curled near his feet. I did not pause, although the owner was signalling me the place was closed. At first the dining room appeared empty.

Then I saw them. O'Hare was sitting with his back toward me, talking in a low voice to Nicoletta. I crossed the room to the table, my heart pounding. I had imagined everything in the previous two hours, including a Thames-side murder that could be made to look like an accident. I had not the vaguest idea of what to say, but when he turned around, it did not matter. The face belonged to Aaron.

'Jayzee, babes, how's the hero?' He threw his arms around me, planting a heavy kiss that exploded in my ear. 'Ain't he great?' he said to Nicoletta, holding me by the arm and standing back to beam in proprietary admiration. '*What* a promoter! What a genius! What a nephew!'

'How are you, Aaron?' The relief that flooded through me tied my tongue beyond that simple greeting.

'I told him he should have let us know,' Nicoletta said.

'Last-minute rush,' Aaron explained. 'One thing and another. You know how it is. Press conferences, TV interviews, tours of the museum. I love it!'

We returned to the Rose and Thistle after I settled the

241

cheque and made sure Mr. Emmons and his son had their drink. On the way, I began to tell Aaron and Nicoletta something of what I had discovered about Ramsay O'Hare.'

'Nothing you say surprises me,' Aaron responded, after I had described the purchase of Cunningham and Pine, and the computer investigation of the interlocking ownership. Nicoletta was harder to convince.

'Suppose it's just a terrible coincidence?'

'You can't mean that seriously?'

'But what can you prove?'

'That he knew Cheney.'

'That doesn't make him a guilty party.'

'Cheney knows La Roche.'

'So do you.'

'But we never worked together.'

I invited Aaron up to our suite while the conversation went on. There was a message that Panagoulos had called and would call again. Nicoletta said, 'What you are suggesting is that Ramsay O'Hare hired Cheney to rob Victor. And Cheney hired La Roche and the others. Is that it?'

'I'm only guessing at the order. Maybe La Roche was hired by O'Hare and put him in touch with Cheney, advising him to invest in Cunningham and Pine to make their job easier. All I know is that all of them were involved.'

But Nicoletta's doubt had now infected Aaron. 'I admit the coincidence is unlikely, Jay, but nothing you've found out connects O'Hare to the crime.'

I looked from him to Nicoletta, wondering if I understood. 'You don't believe it? Either of you?'

'I didn't say that,' Aaron protested immediately. 'He could be in it up to his neck. But speaking as an attorney, I say you haven't proved anything.'

'And you?'

Nicoletta pursed her lips doubtfully. 'You'd have to convince me more than you have, Jay.'

I exploded. 'What the hell do you want? The smoking gun? O'Hare is not such a fool as to be caught in the room with the body, but goddamn it, he isn't innocent! Suppose La Roche changes his mind and identifies O'Hare tomorrow? Will you accept that?'

'I'd settle for it,' Aaron said, 'but it still leaves holes.'

Nicoletta picked up one of the illustrated newspapers from a pile on the coffee table. A picture of La Roche was on the front page. 'If he's identified anyone, the police are being very quiet about it,' she said. 'You know he bothers me? I'd swear I'd seen him before somewhere.'

'Charles Manson without the beard?'

'The beard,' Nicoletta said. 'Of course.'

I rummaged through some of my papers until I found a copy of the Interpol circular Suriel had given me. Nicoletta only had to glance at it to be sure.

'But you've seen this before.'

'No,' she said, 'or I would have realized who he was.' She handed the photograph to Aaron, who compared it to the one in the newspaper.

'He even fooled Victor,' Nicoletta said. She sagged into a chair and put one hand to her cheek, shaking her head in disbelief. 'He was so nice, so helpful.'

I was unable to resist the easy shot. 'Maybe it was just a coincidence O'Hare happened to introduce him to Lanholtz.'

'I'm sorry,' Nicoletta said.

'Is that enough for you too, Mr. District Attorney?'

'The question is,' Aaron replied, 'what do we do? You know where O'Hare's staying, Nicoletta?'

'At Studley Priory. We're invited for drinks there before Sir William Ross's party.' She had turned quite pale as the possible consequences of her disclosure began to churn in her mind. 'If it's all true, and O'Hare discovers I am the only one who could connect him with La Roche, then . . .?'

'What we do,' I said, 'is call Inspector Rowan and have O'Hare arrested.'

'Slow down,' Aaron cautioned. 'Think. All Nicoletta can tell the police is that she was present when O'Hare introduced an alleged murderer to his victim. There's no law against that in any country I know of.'

'Then we've got to find Berman through the Israeli embassy. He must be able to get a warrant or an extradition request or whatever he needs.'

'We don't need Berman,' Aaron said brusquely. 'Anyway, he'd be up against the same problem. What's the charge?'

As he spoke, I was forced to concede that he was right. *We* knew O'Hare was deeply involved, but no detective could arrest him on the strength of our evidence. 'Do you mean he just walks away? No one can stop him?'

'Not unless they have a little more to base it on.'

'So we're back to square one.'

'Not quite,' Aaron said. 'What did you say a moment ago, my dear? You started to pose the question of what O'Hare might do if he knew you were the only one who could connect him with La Roche?'

Nicoletta nodded, her eyes still distant.

'What the hell are you suggesting, Aaron?'

'I'm thinking. If La Roche identifies him, he can always deny it. His word against a French ex-convict. But if La Roche identifies him *and* Nicoletta can connect them, then the cops would have reason to arrest him.'

'To assist in their inquiries,' Nicoletta said.

Aaron smiled. 'I love those English euphemisms.'

'How do we know La Roche hasn't already identified him?' Nicoletta asked. 'Can you find out, Jay?'

'I'll start trying right now.'

'Don't count on it,' Aaron said. 'My instinctive reaction to what I've heard is that La Roche is a punk who takes pride in keeping his mouth shut.'

'What options do we have' I asked myself aloud, 'if La Roche doesn't talk?'

'That's what occupies my thinking,' Aaron said slowly. 'Why don't you call the Scotland Yard inspector, Jay, and see where we stand?'

As I reached for the telephone, it rang. Jeanette came on the line, delighted to find me.

'At three, he called back,' she said, 'and this time the call came through the operator.'

'From?'

'London.'

'Go on.'

'The jewellery was exchanged for ten thousand pounds. I *hope* that money was marked, Jay.'

'Who collected it?'

'A very nervous young Englishman. A little swishy. He didn't even count it.'

'Cheney's boyfriend. Did Sterne follow him?'

'He called back an hour later to say the man had gone to a cheap hotel near Port Royal. Sterne is there and wants to know what he should do now.'

'Call the Sûreté. What about Cheney?'

She laughed. 'He wanted to be sure you had the cash with you. I said you did. He's going to start calling you at the hotel in half an hour to arrange a meeting tonight.'

As soon as Jeanette hung up, I asked the hotel operator to get me Inspector Rowan in London. There was a long wait before I was told the inspector would not be available until the following morning. I left my name, thinking I would try to reach Berman in spite of his rage. 'Aaron, what happened between you and Berman?'

'Berman? Nothing; why?' His expression told me a lot had happened, whether or not he wanted to admit it. I told him I had seen Berman that morning and I repeated what he had said.

'It's not me, it's Shana,' Aaron said.

'Shana?'

Aaron shifted in his chair like a dog with fleas. 'I was going to tell you, but I was waiting for the right time. Nicoletta agrees with me. That's what we were discussing at lunch when you surprised us.'

'What are you talking about?' I looked at Nicoletta for some explanation, but she simply looked at Aaron.

'Shana and I are going to be married,' Aaron announced.

'Shana who, for chrissake?'

'Shana Berman,' he said irritably.

I was numb as the whole picture flashed across my mind. 'No wonder Berman wants to lynch you, if you ran off with his wife!'

'His wife,' Aaron carefully pointed out, 'is fifty years old. Shana is Berman's daughter. You know her. You introduced us.'

'Don't drag me into this.'

Nicoletta was smiling, although at that moment I saw nothing at all amusing in the subject of Shana Berman, wife or daughter.

'At the airport. She runs the VIP lounge.'

'That girl can't be more than twenty.'

'She's older than she looks,' Aaron muttered.

'Is that right?'

'She's twenty-eight,' he said weakly. 'It's not so much of a difference.'

'No. What's fifty years between a man and a woman?'

'May and December,' Aaron said, smiling hopefully toward Nicoletta. 'It happens all the time. And the difference is not fifty years, it's only a little over forty.'

'Berman's right. You ought to be locked up. For your own protection.'

'What the hell do you know about it?' Aaron demanded, his embarrassment turning to indignation. 'I was married for years to people I didn't care about. Now I love this girl and she loves me and, goddamn it, our minds are made up. What left-over life I have I want to spend with her. I never thought you'd turn out to be a petty bourgeois like her old man. But I was wrong.' He started for the door. As he opened it, he turned to me again. 'I may be seventy-two years old,' he said with dignity, 'but if you were me, I'd have given *you* the benefit of the doubt.' Then he looked at Nicoletta. 'I take back what I said about him at lunch. He's not like my brother at all. Nate was never a prig.'

After he had gone, I paced angrily toward the window without looking at Nicoletta. When I moved back across the room to speak to her, she turned away from me.

'Well, Jesus . . .'

'Jay, you hurt him terribly.'

'Be sensible.'

'He was so sure that you, of all people, would approve.'

'Bullshit. He was trying to con you. How can he expect approval from anyone for a thing like that?'

'The entire Berman family approves except the inspector. After all, your uncle is a very engaging man in spite of his years.'

'My *great*-uncle. Of course, he's engaging. He could charm the ears off a snake. God knows what he told that poor innocent girl.'

'At twenty-eight, she's no longer a poor innocent girl. And he looks years younger than he is. Do you know he still plays tennis?'

'Doubles. Big deal.'

'Now *you're* being silly. If Shana Berman wants him, I think she's getting a bargain. Anyway, it's their business. If you love him, you should apologize and wish him all the happiness.'

'He'll marry her anyway, with or without my blessing. Nicoletta, the whole thing is ridiculous.'

'No, it isn't. I saw his eyes. He was so sure of you, Jay. Don't let him down. Go now.'

I went after a while and knocked lightly on his door. There was no answer and I tried the latch. It was unlocked. The Great Actor was sitting facing the window. He didn't look up when I walked in, but there is nothing wrong with his hearing, so I knew he was aware of my presence.

'Aaron, I owe you an apology,' I began, and to my surprise he cut me off.

'No, you don't.' His voice was flat, one-dimensional. 'You were right. I'm an old man who got carried away. It's not enough to have all your teeth and your hair and your appetites. Not enough even if you've never been sick in your life and don't feel a day over forty.'

'You're wrong. It is enough and I *was* being a prig. If Shana Berman loves you, then by all means marry her. Just don't forget to invite me to the wedding.'

'You mean that?' The life came back in his voice.

'If you didn't tell people, they wouldn't know you'd reached sixty.'

He was thoughtful for a moment before he said archly, 'I don't tell *too many* people, Jay, and I'd appreciate it if you'd shut up about it after we're married. In order not to embarrass Shana, you understand.'

'I understand, Aaron. Congratulations.'

He rose from the chair to shake my hand, the strength in his grip telling me he was no senile old fool. 'How about a drink?'

'I'll toast the bride and the groom.'

He poured two small tumblers of Scotch and we clinked glasses. 'Now, about Berman,' he began, putting one arm on my shoulder. 'I'd appreciate it, Jay, if you had a chat with him. You know, kind of talk him around? He likes you even if he was a little pissed off about the way things went with the Pontius Pilate Papers. I wouldn't emphasize the family money. He's proud and a little sensitive about that. But you know what to say, along the lines you were just talking to me about how young I really am and all that?' He paused and asked, 'What are you laughing at? Did I say something funny?'

TWENTY

The dinner planned for the delegates that night at Christ Church College would be hosted by Sir William Ross and Lady Ross, a black-tie affair scheduled for eight o'clock. Ramsay O'Hare's cocktail invitation at Studley Priory was for six and if we intended to go, there was twenty miles of driving to do as well.

'After everything we know,' Nicoletta said incredulously, 'you aren't thinking of *accepting*.'

'You already did, as I recall, after reneging on your luncheon date.'

'But you can't be serious, Jay.'

'He'll be at the reception anyway. Studying him *in situ* first may give me an idea. At this point, I could use one.'

'I'm no actress. I don't know if I could get through it alone.'

'You'll be with me. So get dressed or we'll be late.'

'What about Aaron?'

'He'll catch up at the dinner.'

Cheney's call cut our conversation short and Nicoletta disappeared into the bath.

'Marcus, no more games. The girl said you have the fifty thousand quid with you.'

'In tens and twenties, Cheney. But you get it only when I have the remaining papyri.'

'Any tricks and they'll be destroyed.'

'You got the ten thousand in Paris this afternoon, didn't you?'

'That was different. This is the last we'll be seeing of each other.'

'I certainly hope so. Now, where do you want to meet? I have to attend a dinner tonight in Oxford.'

'Be at the Slough exit of the M4 at eleven. Pull off the motorway and you will see a Fina petrol station. It will be closed at that hour. Leave your parking lights on and wait. What are you driving?'

I told him and added, 'Panagoulos or I will be there.'

'You,' Cheney insisted. 'And alone, or we call it off. If anyone follows you, I won't show.'

'Look, Cheney, all the hocus-pocus isn't necessary. I want the documents and I'm willing to pay your finder's fee. I've shown my good faith. I don't want police involved any more than you do because it makes problems getting the papyri out of England. Why don't we meet in a quiet pub somewhere around here?'

'Just follow instructions,' Cheney said curtly. 'You can drive there in forty minutes.'

'And if anything happens?'

'Just be there. How will you be carrying the money?'

'In a small brown valise. I'll make you a gift of that too, if you're careful with those papyri. The last one, by the way, was slightly damaged.'

'You get them as I receive them,' Cheney said irritably. 'I know how to treat old manuscripts. I've handled them all my life.'

'At eleven, then.'

I hurried Nicoletta from the bath, and was shaved and changed when Panagoulos called from his London flat.

'The main discussion around here is whether they try La Roche in England or let the Israelis have him.'

'No decision yet?'

'That will be made at a higher level.'

When I briefed him about O'Hare he whistled, and when I said we were going to see him for cocktails, he roared with laughter. 'This calls for a conference with Inspector Rowan.'

'He's unreachable,' I said. 'I already tried.'

'That's because he's with me,' Panagoulos said blithely. 'Has Cheney been in touch?'

I told him.

'No sweat. Just keep all your appointments and leave the rest to us. Hell, you don't need advice from me, Doc. You're shaping up like a real pro.'

'Did La Roche decide to talk today?'

'He won't even give his right name. But nobody needs it anymore, so screw him. Have a good time at your party.'

Studley Priory at Horton-cum-Studley is one of those eclectic architectural surprises one finds in the English countryside that, like English food, often turn out well in spite of unusual ingredients. Once a fourteenth-century Benedictine monastery with Jacobean stonework, mullioned windows and a magnificent park and gardens, it was converted into a modern hotel which is booked up most of the year. O'Hare had taken a large corner suite for the week of the archaeological congress. When we arrived shortly after six, we were his only guests.

He kissed Nicoletta warmly on the cheek and pumped my hand as if we were old friends. 'Scotch and soda, isn't it?' He made the drinks and sat opposite us. Through the window I could see the park beyond the priory, brown and dead in the autumn twilight. 'I called you several times from Miami, Marcus, but you never returned my calls.' He chuckled as if there was humour in the fact. 'Too busy running down crooks and recovering our property, so I guess I can't complain. A lot of trouble and expense, right?'

'Less than I expected. The thieves weren't very well organized.'

'That's one of the things I wanted to rap with you about. This La Roche character must have left a trail a mile wide.'

'No. We were tipped to him through one of the others in Vienna.'

'The one the police shot?'

'It's been a daisy chain from the beginning. And the archbishop was a big help.'

'Oh? In what way?'

'Very talkative. Feels the blame should be spread around, so he's been naming names.'

'Is that right. Arabs or Jews?'

'He didn't seem biased. He even had a French priest on the list.'

'They get desperate, I suppose. Accuse everyone in sight,' O'Hare said.

'You knew him, I believe. Isn't that right, Nicky? Didn't you say Ramsay knew the priest?'

O'Hare's eyes suddenly narrowed to small, wary slits.

'We all did,' she said brightly, responding to her cue with professional poise.

'Is that so?' O'Hare's tone dampened the question.

'Father Damien,' I said casually. 'The one from the Vatican Library.'

O'Hare forced a smile. 'Yes. He came to visit Victor last year when I was there.'

'I don't suppose you've seen him since?'

'I hardly knew him,' O'Hare said.

'I thought he was an old friend of yours.'

O'Hare said nothing.

Nicoletta sipped innocently at her drink. 'Jay probably has him mixed up with Mr. Cheney,' she said sweetly.

'You do know Cheney, of course?'

There was a long silence before O'Hare replied, 'No, I don't know anyone called Cheney.'

I rose from my chair. Things were moving faster now and I needed room, space to talk in, to manoeuvre. If I was going to provoke a reaction from Ramsay O'Hare, I had to keep the initiative. 'The head of Cunningham and Pine, Ramsay. You bought the company a few months ago. Certainly you remember Cheney?'

'I don't know what you're talking about.'

'Hi-Rise Investment? You and Carleton Resnik? If you don't remember Cheney, you must remember him.'

He sat like a stone figure in his chair, eyes fixed on mine. Nothing moved; no eyelid flicker, no muscle twitch – nothing. He was without reflexes at that moment, the coolest man I ever saw; or the craziest. I did not give him time to think. 'La Roche identified Cheney, of course,' I said. 'And the police discovered La Roche had been masquerading as Father Damien. These Scotland Yard people are amazing. Tying up all these odd little bits to make a case. But La Roche and Cheney are only hired hands. The police have the name of the man behind them, which was very fast work.'

I almost didn't hear him when he whispered hoarsely, 'Who?'

'I'll be frank, Ramsay. There was a while there when you were under suspicion yourself. But this thing always had a Mafia smell as far as the police were concerned, and it seems to be turning out that way.' I smiled at him and managed a wink. 'As one tax dodger to another, let me say you ought to be more careful of your business associates in the future. You were used, and it could have been damned embarrassing.'

'Resnik always set those things up,' O'Hare said quickly. 'I never asked where he found the capital.'

'It happens to all of us. Anyway, once we began recovering the papyri I was a lot more interested in you as a potential donor for our new building than anything else.' I smiled again, hard.

'You turned my offer down, Marcus.'

'I've had time to think it over. Nicoletta argued on your behalf, by the way. And your condition doesn't seem as unreasonable now as it did a month ago. After all, as you pointed out, Vagan did make rather a mess of things.'

He nodded but said nothing.

'So when his contract expires in January, it doesn't have to be renewed. Providing your offer still holds about setting up a trust for the Pontius Pilate Papers.'

'I'm not sure it does,' O'Hare said after a while.

'I beg your pardon?'

'Don't count on me for anything.'

'I don't understand. If I'm willing to meet that condition ... If you don't have the money, then naturally it's another matter.'

'Didn't she tell you?' O'Hare looked at Nicoletta. 'Never even a hint?' A twisted smile transformed his bland features.

It was my turn to be mystified.

Nicoletta leaned forward on her chair, exquisite in a buff chiffon evening dress, her expression as bewildered as my own.

'The Pontius Pilate Papers are a fake,' O'Hare said.

I stared at him.

'They're forgeries. Ask her. Lanholtz and this charming woman fooled us all.'

Nicoletta was on her feet. 'What are you saying!'

'Lanholtz betrayed me,' O'Hare continued grimly, 'leading me to believe they were something other than they were. Well, they're pure air from start to finish. He wrote them himself and planted them at the site.'

Nicoletta stood still, her fingers pressed white against her glass, eyes blazing. 'That's a vicious, ugly accusation, Ramsay. And a cheap way to get out of your offer.'

'It's true. Check it out.'

'The papyri were checked out ages ago,' I replied. 'Put

through carbon-14 dating here at Oxford and studied by experts. So I advise you not to start talking nonsense around people who know better. You'll only make an ass of yourself.'

'She will, if she reports on them at the congress tomorrow. She'll never get a job again. And your precious museum, Marcus, will be the joke of the year.'

'You picked a convenient time to tell us this.'

O'Hare tossed his head grandly, in complete control now. 'I wasn't going to. With Lanholtz dead, I was satisfied, willing to stay away from the whole mess and let you dig your grave. But you asked why my offer was withdrawn and I told you.'

'Strange you only decided they were forged *after* they were stolen,' Nicoletta said.

'Lanholtz misled me. I financed him because I thought he was with me and Holy Mother Church. But when he corrupted the Passion with a lot of lies, what did I owe him? Nothing.'

'How did you know he betrayed you, Ramsay?'

'I read the translation before he died, as she knows. I told him what I thought then.'

'But you were willing to go along with a forgery if it suited your own purposes, is that it?'

'He was an evil old man,' he said, breathing heavily, 'who fooled me for a while. Until he profaned our Blessed Saviour with his lies.'

'You're two thousand years too late, Ramsay.'

'No. *He* was.' His voice rose with emotion. 'He was going to write the Jews a new character reference at my expense. At the Church's expense! He said they didn't kill Our Lord, they suffered with him. Liar! To absolve them of the worst crime ever committed ...' His voice dropped to a whisper. 'He profaned the truth because *he* was guilty. That ... that Jew!'

Nicoletta gripped my arm. 'Jay, must we listen to any more of this?'

I turned her to the door and before I closed it behind us, I had a last glimpse of O'Hare, tall and mocking in his evening clothes, laughing at all of us: at Lanholtz, Berman, Suriel, Aaron, the lot.

The Senior Common Room at Christ Church, Oxford, is not the oldest or the largest or even the most attractive hall Sir William Ross could have selected in which to welcome the speakers and delegates to the Fourteenth International Congress of Middle Eastern Archaeology, but it has its place in the short history of the profession. It was there, in 1949, that Lord Cherwell related the first accounts of Libby's carbon-14 work in America to Crawford, the distinguished editor of *Antiquity*, and Sir Mortimer Wheeler, England's most exalted archaeologist. So it was fitting. As Nicoletta and I moved to our places, the air was heavy with talk of dendrochronological tables, charmstones, petroglyphs, mnemonic values and protoliterate tablets. As Aaron would say, I love it!

The dinner itself was surprisingly good for banquet fare, and the short welcoming speeches were for the most part witty and succinct in the English way. Nicoletta was a small magnet for a number of the Archaeologists, who circled around like fans after a movie star. Word of the Pontius Pilate Papers had by now been in the press for days, the first big popular story on archaeology since the Dead Sea Scrolls. I noticed with a certain amusement that those colleagues who were world-acknowledged experts on the Scrolls were not among the groupies. In fact, they avoided us with such obvious deliberation that Natalie Ross, who was attuned to the least change in academic frequencies, commented on it with delight.

'When the Charlemagne book came out, Jay, I attended a conference like this with Bill. I was the one person who knew the *whole* story. Two years divorced from Victor and eight months pregnant. Did you ever read the book?'

'No.'

'Victor, that right bastard, dedicated it to Bill, after having taken it over. Typical.'

'So I heard.'

'I'm sure,' she said casually. 'It was no secret. But the atmosphere of that meeting was incredible. Like a gangster's funeral. All of them came to Bill to offer condolences. It was a ritual. No one condemned what Victor had done. They all approved, in fact, but wanted Bill to know *they* knew he was responsible for most of the work. Of course, Victor had paid his own dues in his time.

That's the way they look at it. Some of them great men. But institutional frauds. Oh, well.'

Nicoletta was now besieged by a group of French archaeologists who had gone after her the moment we left the table. Familiar faces flecked the crowd. Aaron haranguing some American museum people. My friend Ari Ascher and his new wife, Lev Vagan lecturing poor puzzled Dr. Sherif over coffee.

A waiter brought us cognac. Natalie swirled it in her glass and sniffed. She still smiled with her eyes, but I sensed again the faint undercurrent of bitterness in her voice. She raised her glass and looked about the great hall. 'A hundred years ago, women weren't allowed in this dreary place. Now here we are. Is that progress?'

I shrugged and she said, 'Who is that dreadful American Kittering is talking with now?'

'Ramsay O'Hare.'

'A friend of yours?'

'No . . .'

'An enemy, then?'

I looked at her in surprise and she held my gaze. Finally she smiled and said, 'Oh, well. I'm being presumptuous. But you don't like him, do you?'

'No.'

'I don't like Kittering either, although God knows, I've tried. That pipe-smoking donnish look is a façade. I'm being a bitch, aren't I?'

'Since you ask, yes.'

'I love you, Jay, I really do. Don't look at your watch. It gives me a terrible complex.'

'I have to leave soon.'

'Will I never learn?'

'Don't be silly, Natalie.'

'My illusions often get in the way. If I were a man and you were a woman we could have a different kind of relationship.'

'I like the one we have.'

'I'll take that as a compliment, and go on being a bitch. I really enjoy it more anyway. How did you like Mrs. Kittering?'

I smiled.

'Exactly. She's fearless chasing foxes, but an absolute

slug socially. We're great friends since she stopped sleeping with my husband.'

The waiter passed with more brandy, which Natalie accepted happily. Her eyes were dewy as she said, 'I can't stand betrayal. And yet that's the story of life, isn't it? As children we're taught never, never to betray our friends, our lovers, our country. Yet that's how so many spend their time. Betraying. The Judas kiss was the original sin. We swear we'll never betray and we do, all of us. And as the saying goes, usually the thing we love most.'

'Do you want an argument?'

She shrugged indifferently. 'Look at it. The Germans betrayed Victor and made his early life a horror. So he became an American, and when it suited him, an Israeli. He betrayed the finest student he ever had when he published Bill's work under his name. But I betrayed Victor. And Bill's cheating on me, still. It is the game of life, don't you see?'

'Natalie, I think it's the brandy.'

'I even tried an affair with Kittering,' she said, as if she had not heard me. 'That self-serving little ass. And do you want to know something? I'm ashamed of it. Not the impulse, but choosing him. I could have had it off with the dustman and come out feeling cleaner.'

I started to get up.

'I'm sorry, Jay. I was being maudlin. But he is a little shit. Don't ever believe anything he says.'

It was nearly ten when I made my way to Nicoletta's side to tell her I was leaving. Aaron would take her home, and the Emmonses, père et fils, would probably camp outside the door of the Rose and Thistle. Bill Ross was chatting with Vagan and the Marcus Museum crowd when I made my manners and left. Everything under control except Natalie, but I chalked that up to a bad performance by the men in her life.

It was five of eleven when I turned off the exit for Slough and found the Fina station. I parked near the pumps, leaving my parking lights on. Half an hour passed before Cheney's Aston Martin purred up alongside the Rover. He got out – empty-handed, I noticed – and looked around at the damp, chill night. His breath hung in clouds as he slid into the front seat of the Rover next to me.

His eyes darted about warily and his delicate lips were taut with strain. I indicated the valise on the rear seat and he tumbled it into his lap, snapping it open greedily.

'Haven't you forgotten something?'

'While I count this,' he said without looking up, 'you can telephone your hotel from that call box.' He pointed to a public telephone booth a few feet away. 'If you don't have change, I do. You will find everything was delivered an hour ago.'

While he remained in the car, I made the call, and spoke with one of the detectives Rowan had sent to the hotel. 'They seem to be all here, sir,' the man said.

When I sat beside Cheney again, the windows were opaque with condensed moisture and the air inside the car was heavy with Cheney's cologne. 'All this was unnecessary, you know,' I told him.

'I'll be the judge of that. Had they arrived?'

'It seems so, but the hotel clerk is hardly qualified to make an appraisal.'

'They're all right.' He was flipping through the last packets of banded twenty-pound bank notes.

'They are old bills and nonsequential.'

He ignored me until he had satisfied himself. Then he stepped out of the car, taking the valise, looking around again and straightening the line of his belted jacket. 'Pleasure to do business with you, Doctor,' he said in his reedy voice. 'And in case you have any second thoughts about who this money belongs to, I refer you to our letter of agreement, duly signed, witnessed and legally binding. Cheerio.' He was in his car and off with a roar while I cleaned the Rover windshield with my handkerchief.

Panagoulos reported later that Cheney had squealed like a stuck shoat when they arrested him at the airport, but the drugs found in his luggage were more than enough to charge him. At the magistrate's session, when he saw Panagoulos and discovered the real reason behind his arrest, he shrieked, 'You cunt! You bloody great Greek cunt!' before his lawyer could calm him down.

'I don't know what else he expected,' Panagoulos said, delighted with the entire performance.

TWENTY-ONE

Nicoletta was up, having a nightcap with the bridegroom-to-be, when I returned. I poured one and joined them. Aaron said, 'Did Cheney finger O'Hare?'

'Not yet. But Panagoulos says he's angry enough to implicate the royal family.'

'They'll be able to hold him, won't they?' Aaron asked. 'You never know about English law.'

'Inspector Rowan seemed quite satisfied.'

'Berman ought to be grateful too, the way you've handed him everything.'

'He wasn't there.'

Aaron snorted with indignation. 'If he spent as much time doing his job as he does making trouble for his relatives, he'd be a cabinet minister by now.'

Nicoletta said she had told Aaron about Ramsay O'Hare's outburst at Studley Priory and the accusation concerning the papyri.

'Don't pay any attention,' Aaron said. 'He'll do anything to cover us with shit – Lanholtz, you, me, Nicky, the museum – *anything* to distract from his own involvement. He probably believes it because he's a classic paranoid. But we've got modern technology on our side and that's the best answer there is.'

'I'm not so sure.'

'That's a hell of a thing to say. You've seen the evidence.'

'Did Nicoletta bring you up to date on the last Longinus codex?' When she shook her head I started to explain, but he waved the words aside impatiently.

'So what else is new? We all know Lanholtz was an oddball. That's what bothered Vagan.'

'It's more than that, Aaron. This one turns a number of things around. It is, in fact, an eyewitness report on the trial and crucifixion which does not conform to any accepted account. Yet Lanholtz left no information about it, or if he did, it disappeared at the time of the robbery. So Nicky has to guess.'

'Guess? Doesn't it belong with the others?'

Nicoletta answered him, saying it was identical in every respect, except perhaps somewhat longer.

'Then you're nit-picking, Jay. Anyway, you can't have a carbon-14 series on every document. You wouldn't have anything left!'

'We don't need it,' I said. 'The practice of associative dating is a time-honoured one in archaeology.'

'Then what's the problem?'

'It's a bad time for someone to yell fake. The burden of proof is with us and although I'm worried about it, it *is* a burden at a time when we'll probably be under heavy fire from all sides.'

'I love it! This last one rewrites the crucifixion? We'll house it in a special room by itself. Did I tell you I hired a publicist for the Pontius Pilate Papers? He'll be in London tomorrow. I want you both to meet him.'

'You're not listening.'

'I heard you,' he insisted. 'You're worried about a few redneck Baptists and the Pope and all the Jesus freaks saying we're full of shit. That's Vagan's tune and he still sings it. But charges have to be proved before they can hurt. Otherwise they just keep us in the newspapers.'

'Just suppose,' I said, looking at Nicoletta, 'that O'Hare was right.'

'Are you crazy?'

She rose and refreshed her drink. 'No, but he's not sure, are you, Jay?'

'What the hell is all this?' Aaron demanded.

'O'Hare accused me of being in league with Victor to forge the scrolls and codices,' she said.

I raised one arm for silence before the discussion got out of hand. 'I didn't say I wasn't sure, Nicoletta. Damn it, don't put words in my mouth. I said, "Just suppose." You saw that last codex for the first time in your life this week. It's a theological H-bomb.' I turned to Aaron. 'I'm as sure as you are it wasn't forged, but Nicoletta cannot defend it. Don't you see what I'm saying? That's the one they'll attack if they attack any of them, and we better be one thousand percent certain we're talking from strength.'

'Okay, okay,' Aaron said. 'Where do you start?'

'It's up to Nicoletta.'

'The paper I'm going to read the day after tomorrow does not include this last papyrus. The question is why did Victor leave it out? Why did he hide it? Jay suggested he may have wanted to publish it separately.'

'Makes sense,' Aaron said.

'I'd feel better if we delayed things,' she suggested, 'until other scholars have had a chance to study them all together.'

Aaron groaned. 'You mean the whole works?'

She nodded.

'After all we've been through? I've got talk shows, magazine articles, even a children's book on Pontius Pilate ready to roll when you go public. You can't do this to me.'

'No one's doing anything to *you*, Aaron,' I said. 'I thought we were trying to reach a mutual decision.'

'You're both panicked. That Florida cupcake spooked you with the big lie. But you're forgetting the most important fact of all. Victor Lanholtz, one of the world's greatest scientists, would never in his life forge archae-ological evidence. It's that simple,' he said with absolute conviction. 'Now, if you want to invite in a bunch of second-rate trowel mechanics to check the most important find of the twentieth century, I can't stop you. But it's a disservice to the memory of a great man.'

The conversation more or less tapered off on that note, with Nicoletta agreeing to think on the matter before making her decision the following day. I collapsed into bed and was out before I hit the pillow.

At eight, I went to my round-table on Arab medicine completely unprepared. Luckily, the participants found their own material stimulating, so the first session turned out to be a fairly lively affair without any help from me. I lunched with the newly married Aschers and Lev Vagan at a small French restaurant on the High Street and we were all back at the conference hall by two to hear Sherif deliver a numbing report on the Gesher Tel excavations. After an hour I sneaked out while he was still droning on in the dark, clicking out-of-focus slides monotonously across the screen.

Bill Ross caught me as I was nearly out the door. 'I like Sherif's findings,' he said, 'but his presentation is not the standard we hoped for.'

'Amen.'

'Everyone's waiting for the Marcus Museum main entry tomorrow,' he said genially. 'I had a look myself at the papyri you left with Clive Kittering. Amazing. Did he reach you earlier, by the way?'

'No. About what?'

'Something to do with one of your codices. If you're not in a rush, I'm going past there now. Join me?'

'I was only in a rush to put myself beyond Menahem Sherif's reach.'

We crossed the Tom Quad to the Gothic building that housed Kittering's laboratories. Ross went ahead and called, 'Clive? You have important guests.'

Kittering was there, hidden behind the pile of books and papers, which seemed to have grown since my last visit. Natalie Ross's lover, I reminded myself, who let her down.

His gas ring was going and the tea-kettle boiled merrily. 'Rots your guts,' Ross said. 'Tans them actually. We've always been famous for guts, wot?'

Kittering forced a smile as he moved through his little tea ceremony by the kettle. 'I didn't expect you until later, Sir Will,' he said. 'How's the conference going? Off at a run, is it?'

'Hardly the Grand National,' Ross said.

Kittering handed me a chipped steaming cup and rummaged about among his papers to find a thick sheaf of photographs. 'Here are the copies you asked for, Doctor. No charge.' He blew on his tea and sipped. 'I tried to reach you this morning, but you'd left. Curious thing about that one codex. As you know, I did the carbon-14 sequences for Lanholtz last year.'

'I know.'

'There were eight separate specimens. We always take a great deal of care and all that. Don't want the blame if something goes wrong.' He looked at Ross, a little anxiously, I thought.

'Was this one of them?' I said hopefully.

'That's the curious thing. Yes and no.'

Ross chortled. 'I say, Clive, what kind of an answer is that?'

'Yes and no,' Kittering repeated. 'I was reading the original when I noticed the pages weren't all of equal size.'

'Nothing puzzling about that,' Ross said. 'The Bodleian's full of codices with pages of unequal size.'

'That's not what I mean,' Kittering said. 'When we did our original checks, several of the papyri we dated were blank sheets. Dr. Lanholtz sent those, as you recall, Sir Will, to risk as few of the *written* samples as possible.'

'Right. They'd been found together with the other material.'

'Exactly. Well, we measure everything to the millimetre before and after. I mean when we shave a sheet to burn for C-14, we're careful.'

'They even keep a scrap for their records in case any further examination is required later,' Ross added. 'Isn't that right, Clive?'

Kittering nodded, finished his tea and put the cup down on his messy desk. 'I remarked on the unequal size of the codex pages, and I measured them. The larger ones conformed to the dimensions of some of the blank pages we had examined. Look.' He opened a drawer in his desk and withdrew a file. 'Sir Will has seen all this before.' From the folder he took a tiny plastic envelope containing a small sliver of papyrus, about six inches long by a quarter inch wide. 'This was snipped from a blank sheet last year. The curious thing is that it fits perfectly one of the pages of this codex Dr. Marcus left with me.'

'Are you sure?' I asked him.

'No question of it. But last year it was blank, according to our records.'

'Perhaps one of your technicians made an error,' Ross said.

'That's not unheard of,' Kittering agreed. 'But in this case, there's no chance of it.'

'You're saying it is the same sheet of papyrus,' Ross said, his eyes on the ceiling. 'Is that what you're saying, Clive?'

'My laboratory assistant even compared the fibre ruptures on the sample with the codex page under the microscope. It is the same piece of material.'

'Is it at the beginning or the end of the codex?' I asked him.

'Smack in the middle,' was Kittering's reply.

After an embarrassingly long silence, Ross let his breath

out in a kind of soft whistle and turned to me. 'Do you accept this?'

'I'm forced to,' I said.

'I haven't read the codex,' he said. 'Is it a continuous piece?'

I nodded.

'The implications are clear, then,' Ross said. 'The great Victor Lanholtz. I can't believe it.'

'Nor can I.'

Kittering was both apologetic and sympathetic. But he stood by his analysis of that page of the codex. It was a fake, pure and simple, a modern forgery on a two-thousand-year-old papyrus, but a fake nevertheless. If one page in the middle of a continuous narrative was forged, well, then . . .

'Why?' I asked.

'How? Why? Who can quarrel with the results?' Ross said dejectedly.

'What about the others?' I said to Kittering, and the little physicist threw up his hands.

'We could check them too. But it takes time, as you know.'

Ross turned to me, his face a death mask. 'In view of this . . .' he began awkwardly.

'The museum will withdraw the Lanholtz paper,' I said. 'You can be sure of that.'

After a few more perfunctory questions, we left Kittering and walked across the quad. For a long time neither of us spoke. Then Ross said, 'Once he was a god. It took me twenty years to reach a state of equilibrium where we regarded each other simply as colleagues. An hour ago, I would have said I knew his mind, his tricks and his virtues as well as anyone on earth. Now I realize I didn't know him at all. Why? No reputation was more secure than his, no name more respected. It's worse than the Shapira scrolls.'

When I nodded, he continued, gazing around at the barren Oxford campus. 'At least *they* might have been legitimate. We'll never know. I did a book once on Clermont-Ganneau, the man who exposed Shapira. Oddly enough, his exposure failed to convince me.' He sighed. 'Not so with Kittering. He's a painstaking technician. If he says the fibres match, they do. That's a bitter cup, isn't it?'

'We don't know about the rest of them yet,' I said.

Ross shrugged. 'Does it matter? If one word is falsified, if one page is a hoax, then the man's whole life is tainted. The work is all suspect.'

We parted on the High Street and I got into the Rover to drive back to Abingdon. To describe my feelings accurately at that moment, I would say shock and sadness had taken over from the anger and frustration of the previous weeks. The worst of it was I thought I knew why Lanholtz might have done a thing like this. As Ari Ascher had once suggested, his battle against anti-Semitism had something to do with his death. Perhaps in some sad, warped way, he had forsaken a lifetime of scholarship for this last senseless effort. O'Hare said it: he was going to write the Jews a new character reference. They didn't kill Christ, the Romans did and then tried to fix the blame on the Jews. Gaius Longinus Procula ought to know, because he engineered both the execution and the frame-up, as carbon-14 dating had proved.

Then why did Lanholtz die? Or rather why did he die for that? I recalled the letter Lanholtz had written to Merle and never mailed. 'What an artist dies with me.' The precocious child from the big house on the Wannsee; anti-Nazi scholar, spy, army officer, teacher, husband, friend, genius. In the end, perhaps he saw himself as the instrument for redressing the balance. Had he determined then, in one final gesture of arrogant defiance, to undermine the ancient Christian rationale for persecuting Jews? He knew in his heart they were wrong, and he would use the only weapon he had to prove it.

In that moment I could not forgive him for what he had done, because he had failed.

There were too many questions for Nicoletta and not enough answers for Aaron, so I tried to avoid discussion as much as possible. We withdrew the paper from the conference and she seemed relieved. Aaron, predictably, was outraged, but found solace in his wedding plans the way Panagoulos took comfort from his astronomical bill.

The statements of Cheney and La Roche, with Nicoletta's deposition, gave Scotland Yard all they needed to take O'Hare off the National Airlines flight to Miami and bring him before a magistrate's court in West London. Extradition to Israel was only a matter of form.

After all possible tests had checked out the legitimacy of the remaining Pontius Pilate Papers, they were returned to the Marcus Museum. In January, persuaded finally by his daughters, Berman put in a grumpy appearance at Aaron's wedding, where we had a long chat.

The facts behind the robbery and Lanholtz's murder had turned out to be more or less what I expected – with a few refinements. O'Hare had lost a bundle of Hi-Rise Investment capital speculating in foreign currency. To make up the losses he had hired La Roche to steal the papyri, anticipating a million dollars or more from the Marcus Museum for their recovery. La Roche, who ingratiated himself with Lanholtz, using his phoney priest identity, had known Cheney and Gansfeld in prison; while Sussman, the Jerusalem archbishop and the Nablus Arabs had all been recruited locally. The purchase of Cunningham and Pine had been Cheney's idea, reluctantly accepted by O'Hare to provide a semblance of legitimacy for the eventual marketing of the Pontius Pilate Papers.

From the start, things had gone wrong. On the night of the robbery, Lanholtz returned unexpectedly, recognized La Roche, and the killing followed. The getaway was off schedule and the archbishop, alarmed by the newspaper publicity, refused to risk taking all the papyri out of Israel in one trip. Cheney, who had been waiting in Damascus for delivery, was forced to return to London with only a fraction of the total. According to him, the job on Nicoletta's apartment was done by Sussman to throw the police off.

It was all of a piece eventually, except for my incorrigible friend Mansour and his theories. One evening about four months later, after we had been discussing the case for the hundredth time, he said, 'Suppose Ross did it.'

'Did what?'

'Snipped a piece from that last codex you left with Kittering and then substituted it for one of the blanks examined the year before.'

'That's too absurd, Hippolyte.'

'Is it? I'd call it sublime. He had his reasons and there's really no way anyone could ever find out. You must admit, my dear, the probability is bound to intrigue the curious mind.'

Selected from the SPHERE fiction list

THE MITTENWALD SYNDICATE

Frederick Nolan

THE FACTS:

A fantastic fortune in gold and jewels lay buried in the mountains above the village of Mittenwald at the end of the Second World War. It comprised the last of the Reichsbank reserves, removed by the Nazis too late for shipment abroad. None of it has ever been recovered. And no one has ever been arrested for its theft.

THE NOVEL:

Frederick Nolan's brilliant thriller dares to speculate on what could easily have happened to the Nazi treasure. It explores a violent world of greed, intrigue, betrayal, killing and revenge – especially revenge. And, all the way, you will ask yourself where compelling fiction ends and terrifying fact takes over . . .

"A splendidly exciting novel"   *Daily Express*
"Genuine excitement"   *Sunday Times*

ADVENTURE/THRILLER FICTION
0 7221 6427 0   95p

It was the war to end all wars — and it seemed nothing could stop it!

THE CHINESE ULTIMATUM

Edward McGhee

and bestselling author of *The French Connection*

Robin Moore

COUNTDOWN TO ANNIHILATION . . .

It begins with a series of Sino—Soviet border skirmishes, small clashes between the troops of the two big Communist powers. But before long these "incidents" explode into monstrous proportions — *and Russia and China are at war!* When frantic negotiations fail, the Western powers are drawn into the maelstrom, and the entire world teeters on the brink of nuclear devastation. Only twenty men, in six nations, have the knowledge and power to avert a holocaust that could destroy civilisation.

The fate of the world is balancing on a desperate knife-edge!

"This novel is too incredibly real . . . and damnably possible!"

Anonymous US State Department Official

ADVENTURE/THRILLER FICTION
0 7221 5783 5

95p

SIR, YOU BASTARD

The bestselling novel of police brutality and
corruption by

G. F. Newman

To a copper like Sneed, ethics is a dirty word. . . .
Terry Sneed was ambitious. By the age of 26 he'd
already achieved plenty – seven years of
violence, deceit and corruption has taken him to
the rank of Detective Inspector in the CID. But
Sneed wanted more – much more. And he
played as dirty as he could to get it.

CRIME/MYSTERY FICTION 0 7221 6360 6 85p

Look out for further Terry Sneed books

YOU NICE BASTARD   95p
YOU FLASH BASTARD   85p

And don't miss these other G. F. Newman titles,
the Law and Order trilogy, now filmed as a TV
series by the BBC.

A PRISONER'S TALE   85p
A DETECTIVE'S TALE   85p
A VILLAIN'S TALE   85p

THE BLUE KNIGHT

Joseph Wambaugh

Bestselling author of *The Choirboys*

Bumper Morgan is a cop, a patrolman with twenty years' service under his belt and retirement looming ominously close. His outlook is old-fashioned; he believes in justice — even when it doesn't conform to the letter of the law. If a judicious bit of violence will give him what he needs to solve a crime, he'll use it. That's the way the game's played. And it usually works. Until the prospect of retirement clouds his judgement, and Bumper finds himself starting to make mistakes. The kind of mistakes that kill people . . .

"Abounds in vivid vignettes of police life and the Los Angeles streets . . . the portrait of Bumper has force and authenticity"

New York Times Book Review

CRIME/MYSTERY FICTION 0 7221 8894 3 95p

KRAMER'S WAR
Derek Robinson

When Lieutenant Earl Kramer crawled out of the sea and cut the throat of a German sentry one night in 1944, he made a big mistake. For Kramer, sole survivor of a ditched USAF bomber, was on the island of Jersey – and Jersey was under Nazi occupation! Trapped by the bloody conflicts of war, the islander's lives depended on a perilous balance of co-existence with their oppressors. They knew from bitter experience that any trouble would bring instant and savage reprisal.

But to Kramer, Jersey was an irresistible target. This stronghold of Hitler's armies was just asking to be blown apart and liberated, and it was a red-blooded American's duty to do it. So he embarked on a devastating one-man sabotage mission, aimed at wiping the Nazis from the face of the island.

Kramer's motives were sincere and patriotic. But to the survival of the islanders, he was as lethal as a flamethrower in a firework factory . . .

'An original and dazzlingly controlled novel'
Sunday Times
'Excellently plotted . . . the book moves along at a great lick to a splendid climax'
Guardian

WAR FICTION   0 7221 0439 1   £1.25

A selection of bestsellers from Sphere:

Fiction

THE WOMEN'S ROOM	Marilyn French	£1.50	☐
SINGLE	Harriet Frank	£1.10	☐
DEATH OF AN EXPERT WITNESS	P. D. James	95p	☐
THE VILLAGE: THE FIRST SUMMER			
	Mary Fraser	£1.00	☐
BLOOD OF THE BONDMASTER			
	Richard Tresillian	£1.25	☐
NOW AND FOREVER	Danielle Steel	£1.10	☐

Film and Television Tie-Ins

THE PASSAGE	Bruce Nicolaysen	95p	☐
INVASION OF THE BODY SNATCHERS			
	Jack Finney	85p	☐
THE EXPERIMENT	John Urling Clark	95p	☐
THE MUSIC MACHINE	Bill Stoddart	95p	☐
BUCK ROGERS IN THE 25TH CENTURY			
	Addison E. Steele	95p	☐
BUCK ROGERS 2: THAT MAN ON BETA			
	Addison E. Steele	95p	☐
DEATHSPORT	William Hughes	95p	☐

Non-Fiction

NINE AND A HALF WEEKS	Elizabeth McNeill	95p	☐
IN HIS IMAGE	David Rorvik	£1.00	☐
THE MUSICIANS OF AUSCHWITZ	Fania Fenelon	95p	☐
THE GREAT GAME	Leopold Trepper	£1.50	☐
THE SEXUAL CONNECTION	John Sparks	85p	☐

All Sphere books are available at your local bookshop or newsagent, or can be ordered direct from the publisher. Just tick the titles you want and fill in the form below.

Name ....

Address ....

....

Write to Sphere Books, Cash Sales Department, P.O. Box 11, Falmouth, Cornwall TR10 9EN

Please enclose cheque or postal order to the value of cover price plus:
UK: 22p for the first book plus 10p per copy for each additional book ordered to a maximum charge of 82p
OVERSEAS: 30p for the first book and 10p for each additional book
BFPO and EIRE: 22p for the first book plus 10p per copy for the next 6 books, thereafter 4p per book

Sphere Books reserve the rights to show new retail prices on covers which may differ from those previously advertised in the text or elsewhere, and to increase postal rates in accordance with the GPO.